"*The Bird's Child* is entirely orig... its ... y
set... ...gs set asparkle and rendered d... ...ke by ... ...igh
Price's lyrical and lovely writing. Th... ...s a magical ta... ...nat
penetrates to deep emotional truths"
Geraldine Brooks

"This debut novel brings 1920s Sydney to life through a
fairytale lens, highlighting the city's romance, its magic and
its mystery ... Price's dream-like portrayal of a bygone Sydney
– with its vaudeville shows and opium dens, lyrebirds and
swagmen – establishes a unique mood that transforms the local
into the exotic, making *The Bird's Child* a memorable tale"
Australian Book Review

"Gritty yet enchanting ... often deliciously sumptuous and
erotically charged ... unusual, imaginative"
Newtown Review of Books

"Skilfully written and richly imagined"
Sydney Morning Herald

The River Sings

SANDRA LEIGH PRICE

FOURTH ESTATE
An Imprint of HarperCollins*Publishers*

Fourth Estate

An imprint of HarperCollins*Publishers*

First published in Australia in 2017
by HarperCollins*Publishers* Australia Pty Limited
ABN 36 009 913 517
harpercollins.com.au

HarperCollins*Publishers*

Level 13, 201 Elizabeth Street, Sydney NSW 2000, Australia
Unit D1, 63 Apollo Drive, Rosedale, Auckland 0632, New Zealand
A 53, Sector 57, Noida, UP, India
1 London Bridge Street, London, SE1 9GF, United Kingdom
2 Bloor Street East, 20th floor, Toronto, Ontario M4W 1A8, Canada
195 Broadway, New York NY 10007, USA

National Library of Australia Cataloguing-in-Publication entry:

Price, Sandra Leigh, author.
The river sings / Sandra Leigh Price.
ISBN 978 1 4607 5001 8 (paperback)
ISBN 978 1 4607 0424 0 (ebook)
Thieves – New South Wales – Fiction.
Historical fiction.

Cover design by HarperCollins Design Studio
Cover image by Alexey Kuzma/stocksy.com/1114834; background images by shutterstock.com
Typeset in Bembo Std by Kirby Jones
Printed and bound in Australia by Griffin Press
The papers used by HarperCollins in the manufacture of this book are natural, recyclable products made from wood grown in sustainable plantation forests. The fibre source and manufacturing processes meet recognised international environmental standards, and carry certification.

To Little Jackie Winter
&
to my Noble & True.

Both
all that's bright in the world.

"Give the child into my hands, and I will do my best to bring you off. If you are saved, your child will be saved too; if you are lost, your child is still saved."

"It don't signify to you with your brilliant lookout, but as to myself, my guiding-star always is, 'Get hold of portable property'."

Charles Dickens, *Great Expectations*

ONE

Patrin, 1819

When my waters broke a whole river poured out of me and splashed into the dirt at the foot of the *vardo*. My mother let out a cry. Amberline rose to his feet, the horse brasses he'd been polishing fell to the ground. He stood palms outward, barehanded, his frightened face staring at me.

"Quick now," my mother said and took the short knife from her waistband and slit the knot that bound me to my apron.

"Quick, what?" Amberline said and I saw the panic in him, fumbling for his knife and unsure what to do with it. The sun hit it, slashing a blinding light across my eyes, and I felt the fist squeeze inside my womb, the fierce desire of my baby to be born.

"And you call yourself a Rom," my mother said to Amberline, disgusted. She tugged at the red satin ribbon that he had given me to hold back my hair and threw it at him. It fell to the ground at his feet. My hair closed around my face like a curtain.

My mother led me away from the camp just as my father rounded the rise of the nearest field. He carried a few rabbits by their swinging ears, snared for our dinner, and came running as he saw me in my mother's arms, though I was unclean.

Together they steered me towards the riverbank, the willow fronds rippling aside for the three of us, my father kissing me on the forehead before he left us, the leaves closing in behind him.

On my boots were the drops of water of my own making; I had leaked all the way to the river, my baby was turning the tide within me.

My mother lowered me to the ground and pulled the boots from my feet and the skirt from my waist, and I felt the cool air from the waterside brush up against my bare legs. The smell of the meadowsweet came from beneath me where I'd crushed it, the iron-flood of my blood wend out of me like a road for my child's tiny feet to follow.

The sun rose higher in the sky, gold striped with the willow's green. With each crest of pain my sight turned pale, the whole world drained of colour, my spirit coiling up inside me, trying to make the largest distance possible between the pain and itself; but I couldn't hide from it, it pulled at all my senses, demanded my attention, stole my breath, until I was the pain itself. My mother bent down between my legs and inspected me then cursed under her breath. How long had I been labouring? I was outside the limits of time, pain was my minutes and hours, my before, my after.

"Come, child, stand upright," she said, her hands clutching protectively beneath my arms as she lent me her strength, my legs no stronger than barley stalks. I saw the worry on her face, but she had no time to conceal it.

"Walk," she commanded, and the pain took me and turned the world to light, taking all my breath and strength. My mother held me and waited until the summit of the pain had passed. "Walk, Patrin, walk."

Walk? How could I walk? My feet had a memory of their own and made their own way, like a sleepwalker's, not quite believing in the solidity of the earth. My mother walked me towards the water, steering me past the nettles, slipping on the bankside silt, but still she held me up. When my feet hit the water I gasped at the coldness of it and the baby slid in my belly, as tricksy as a salmon avoiding the fisherman's worm, the water numbingly creeping up my knees, thighs, waist. Between my mother and the river, the water held me up.

With every pain that racked my body, my mother made me walk against the current, the cold splashing up into my face, my hands floating upward in the water like shells.

"Keep going, Patrin," my mother whispered in my ear and I kept moving, a living clock against the tide. Until my mother dipped her head beneath the surface, tiny fish, darting close to my bare legs beneath the clear water, scattering at her approach. The river shimmered with diamond light and from the willows' canopy came the *tchhh-tchhh* of magpies talking as my mother breached the water, telling me to push, before she dipped below the surface again. My body obeyed and all around me the water changed from gold to red as my blood bloomed upward.

And then there she was, held in my mother's arms, brought up out of the river, water pouring off her tiny limbs. The cord that bound her to me looped around her neck like a coral necklace, her head crowned in dark hair. My mother held her out towards me and I snatched her, her skin slippery in my hands, fearing the worst, her lips tinged blue. I peered into her scrunched face, waiting. Where was her first breath? Very carefully my mother unlooped the cord from around my baby's fragile neck, red sinew, coral banded with my own blood. I breathed in the scent of her damp dark head and I was frightened to love her. My mother tied a knot at my baby's navel and took her knife and hacked through the umbilical cord, knotted tight as a heart. She let it loose in the water and it slithered beneath the surface like an eel. Seized again by the squeezing of my womb, I felt the heat of my blood surge out into the river.

"'Tis just the afterbirth, baby has no need of it now," my mother said, and I watched it, seabloom of my love's making, disappear downstream. With a wild sadness I covered the baby's lips with my own and breathed, a kiss of air. I waited and tried again. Her little lungs rose and fell but once. I whispered her

3

secret name in her ear and her chest rose and fell again with her own breath.

We waded to the shore, my mother, my baby and I, blood running down my legs and into the mud. I held on tight to her and willed her to live. My mother took her from my arms and dried her with my old patched skirt and wrapped her tight in her shawl. Would she wear a swaddling cloth or a shroud? I didn't know. I sang to her, my lips pressed to her head that smelled of earth. I sang and I sang and I saw her little chest rise and fall again and I held my own breath, just to let her have the more. My mother gathered dry sticks from around us and set to striking her flint to make a fire and I saw my baby turn rosy like the dawn. Her eyes opened and she blinked and looked at me, her mouth opening and closing with a little yawn, a twitch of her nose no bigger than the nub of a mushroom. She yawned again then started burrowing into my chest, seeking the comfort of my nipple.

"Come along, girl, she's hungry," my mother said, pulling down the shoulders of my sodden blouse. My baby's mouth latched on and my whole body sang like the catgut string on a fiddle. As she fed she kneaded my breast with her tiny hand, her little nails surprisingly sharp. I watched her drink of me, marvelling. The magpies above us still chattered, observant, and I stood outside my own self, except for the pressure on my nipple. The ground felt warm beneath me and I was surprised to see I was sitting in a pool of my own blood. My mother bundled my old skirt and wedged it between my legs and told me to be still and that she would be back soon.

While I waited I ran the tip of my finger over every downy contour of my daughter's face and saw the blood caught in the folds of her neck and wondered if that was what had made her pause for breath.

I must have fallen asleep, my spine against the trunk of a willow, for when I woke there were women around me, pulling an oiled cloth over a branch and securing a tin pot over the flames, the smoke and smell of bitter herbs making my eyes water. The rags between my legs had been replaced and my baby slept against me, the skin on her hand almost as translucent as damsel flies' wings.

"Drink this, child," my mother said, holding a cup to my lips, and I drank the brew down, knowing that it would give me strength.

"She's bonny for being so early," my mother said, lifting the baby into her arms, and I saw how capable her hands were, how practised after the babies she had borne and now had grown, practised on me, her youngest and last.

"She has the gift for roving, a traveller's feet," she said, unfurling the shawl, and together we looked at her little naked form, all pink, perfect, each toe a bean. My mother took a bottle of oil from her pocket and dripped a few drops upon her palm, before rubbing her hands together to warm it and stroking it along the tenderness of new skin.

"But she's not been baptised yet," said one of the Lee women, standing outside the heated ring of the fire, a gathering of kindling in her arms. But my mother ignored her. We both knew she'd been born in the river, so she was as good as baptised already. A magpie hopped onto a lower branch to watch my baby's skin glow golden in the firelight and my mother swaddled her in fresh linen and handed her back to me, placing her in the basket made by my mother's hands. But the Lee woman wouldn't be put off by my mother's silence.

"It's bad luck," she said, her eyes observing the magpie closely; the magpie looked just as closely back before it set off on its chastisement, its mate flying closer down to the ground.

"Two for mirth," my mother said, ignoring her and stoking the fire with a branch so it roared.

* * *

The sky streaked violet. A kingfisher flashed across the surface of the river, a fish flip-flopping between its beak before disappearing down its throat. The baby was still sleeping, but the rising and falling of her chest was enough to satisfy me. To ignore the roar of hunger upon me I blew across her features and watched her tiny eyelashes flit at my breath. I didn't dare move the position of my arms that had made her perfect cradle. The magpies hadn't left my company, they took turns, wildly falling from the branches to scavenge the remains of my bread, their iridescent tail feathers all a rainbow caught in a pool of oil.

The squeak of Amberline's fine boots sent them back to the safety of the lower branches, their eyes in his direction and rightfully so. He was all sparkle, his fob chain a silver dangle, swinging backward and forward in the closing light, drawing their attention. My mother would have warned him to be quick about it, mindful of the *tsinivari*, spirits, that would follow on his heels at sunset, drawn by a new life. But beneath the oiled cloth, protected from the chill, with the river running alongside, I felt no harm would come to me while ever I held my charm of a girl in my arms.

"Patrin?" he called to me tentatively, unable to see us hidden by the canopy of willow and oilcloth.

"Here, we are here," I said and he ducked his head beneath the shivering leaves and stood still at the sight of her. He gathered his senses and crouched down beside me, dropping the sack of supplies close by. His eyes fixed on his sleeping daughter.

"Why are you left out here on your own, it's not right," he said, his finger reaching out to stroke her cheek, before awkwardly turning to embrace me. Above us the magpies started up their chatter and I pulled away. His touch foreign and strange, the river still rippled through my skin, she had made me her mother.

"May I hold her?" he said and I carefully lifted her into his awaiting arms, immediately feeling her absence in my own. "Eat something, gather your strength."

I undid the wrapped cloth my mother had sent down with him from the camp – cheese and rabbit still warm from the fire and a flask of milk. I pulled out the cork and drank it down, the cream of it, thick and sweet. The rabbit melted on my tongue. I threw a few crumbs for the magpies and they swept the ground with their fine tails just to gobble it down, hopping from one foot to the other for more.

Amberline took no notice, he took in every fresh feature of our daughter, as if he could stamp her on his mind's eye, a tremor in his hands.

"She's small, is she not?" he said, his voice very low.

"She's a little early is all," I said and he gestured with his chin for me to take her, which I willingly did. Out of his pocket Amberline pulled a little silver heart and gently wove the pin of it into the foot of her swaddling cloth, his thumb preventing the tip of it touching her.

"Made it myself. For our daughter," he said, the word large and new in his mouth. The silver heart had been cut from a coin, the king's head defaced and made blank, waiting for her name. I flipped the other side, marked with the date of her birth, twenty-fourth of May 1819. The last of the sunlight struck it gold and a magpie dropped to a lower branch to peer at it, his green-feathered tail nearly close enough for me to pluck a feather.

"It would be finer of course if we had been in London and I had my tools about me. Perhaps when we return," Amberline said emphatically, and I felt the breeze come off the water and I shivered and held our daughter closer. What would the likes of us have to do with London? It was only ever a place we skirted. We kept to the road and the common and the fields permitted to us.

"Does she have a name?" he said and the baby woke at the loudness in his voice and burrowed towards my chest. I rested her on my lap and pulled down my blouse for her to have the breast.

"She has only her secret name, hers for all her life but known only to me and her."

"And I her father, am I not to know it?"

I shook my head. "She'll get her name for the world at the baptism."

Amberline's eye was drawn to a splash in the water, but it was only the kingfisher again at his supper.

"Have you sent word to your mother? Perhaps she'd like to attend her naming?"

Amberline rubbed his hands across his face, the tips of his fine city fingers blackened by the work of camp life.

"I don't think it is possible," he said, the strain in his voice. I had almost asked just to hear him say it; I'd been asking about his parents since his arrival but he always found a way to slip between the questions. All I had ever gleaned was that his father was dead and his mother was somewhere in London.

"I look forward to having you back at the camp," he said then leaned towards me and kissed me softly on the lips before he bent his head and kissed our daughter. I should have pulled back, not let his lips touch mine, impure as I was until the baptism. "I don't know why you can't come back now. The baby is born, all is well," he said, his fingers lingering on the curve of her cheek. Our ways were as foreign to him as the moon.

I watched him walk back to the camp, knowing how hard it would be for him amongst the men who'd somehow keep the conversation to things Amberline would have no knowledge of just to see him slip, his words caught in their snare.

The stars pricked themselves out across the last of the blue until my eyelids grew heavy.

I was suddenly alert as if I'd never closed my eyes at all. I looked out into the downpour.

There was someone out there, their dark shadow cutting through the raindrops.

"Amberline?" I called, but no human sound replied, all I heard was the rushing of waters. I felt around in the darkness for the knife Amberline had brought with the bread and cheese. My fingers hit its handle, but the more I reached for it in the darkness, the further away it slipped from my grasp, until its tip pricked me.

"Who are you and what do you want?" I shouted, using the trunk of the willow to help me to my feet. But the figure remained where it was and I found my feet planted in the ground, unable to move even if I wanted to. The figure moved towards me and I held out the knife in front of me, but like a dowsing rod it pulled my grasp to the direction of the water. So I dropped the knife, the moonlight wavering on its blade in the mud.

"Speak!" Would someone hear me from the camp if I screamed? Suddenly my ears were crowded with the sound of gushing water, beyond sense. "I don't understand," I cried and the water turned to a low babble, the shapes of words bubbling out, popping in my ears, but I couldn't make them out. "In the name of Saint Sarah, show yourself," I said. The figure swelled towards me like a wave, then disappeared back into the water. The rain ceased, but all the world dripped around me. The basket was missing. My heart leapt in my chest and I ran down to the water's edge in the pre-dawn light. All along my path were spread the weeds of the river like flowers, an offering, my feet slipping on them. I heard her, her little voice concealed by the reeds; my blood surged as I waded into the water, the stones at the bottom slipping beneath my feet. I brushed the reeds away and their stalks scratched at my hands, my blood dissolving into the water, until I was surrounded by them. The sound of her coo turning to a cry drove me onward until my hands hit the wicker of her basket.

I started awake.

She was dry and warm, my little Moses in her coracle, her pink tongue darting like a minnow. She was unharmed but my heart skipped in its race, for upon her coverlet, next to Amberline's gift, was another, a perfectly river-smoothed white pebble. I rolled it in my palm, it was nearly as rare as a pearl, and tucked it into the pouch around my neck.

The sounds from the camp came down to me on the wind, the gathering of them, the kin arrived for the baptism, and I steeled myself. Together my child and I had formed a knot of our own making, her hand curled in mine; who knew where the thread of her started and the thread of me ended.

I struck the flint and kindled the fire and carefully lifted my baby to my breast, where she latched on and suckled, her eyes dark as the roiling sea.

* * *

Everyone walked down from the camp and the noise of them startled me, a wild chatter, for I was now used to the gentle sounds of the riverbank and preferred the conversation of the magpies who had nested in the boughs of the willow as my company.

Amberline walked amongst all the others but he looked apart in his neatly laundered clothes, his fairer hair filled with the sunshine. My father kept a cracking pace over the rise, itching to see his grandchild, to hold her in his arms. His face lit up at the sight of us and I lifted my hand to wave. Amberline came and stood in front of me stiffly and I saw the red thread wrapped around his wrist, his feet shifting uneasily on the ground. My mother stood beside him and encouraged him to step forward, all eyes watching him. Had my mother told him what was expected? He toyed with the red thread at his wrist, a fibrous constraint, and I wanted for him to meet my eye, his attention caught by all around us.

Reluctantly I placed our daughter on the ground before him and there she lay, obliviously asleep, waiting for her father to claim her as his own. Amberline looked at me as the magpies started up their scolding and he froze, the weight of expectation pushing like a tide behind him. I nodded at him and he reached down and picked her up, then she snuggled into his chest and he blinked at me, surprised, with a grin. Carefully he unlooped the red thread from his wrist and placed it over her head, where it sat above her swaddling cloth, red as a vein. Redder than the birthmark that linked around the folds of her neck. I had thought it was just my blood, but it had proved a red mark on her skin and I was afraid that she had already been claimed with her cord by the water. The river's own daughter.

Down to the water's edge Amberline carried her, the light turning the surface precious and shining. He scooped up a handful of water and let a tiny trickle fall across her brow.

"Let her be known as Eglantine," Amberline called out, his voice skimming across my ears. "My mother's name."

"Eglantine," he said again, the ownership in his voice making me squirm and reach for her, but Amberline was already in love, seeing his reflection mirrored in her tiny body, her fragile skin too tender for such a stamp. What was eglantine? The dog-rose, Christ's prickled crown, the false scent of apples.

I felt the heat surge from my breasts, up my throat and into my face. I had wanted to call her something altogether different: Darklis, Newsome, Defiance. Her name for the world. The name Eglantine was like thorns in my mouth, but I had given her yet another, a secret name. The sound the river made. *Riverling*.

Amberline placed her back in my arms and her dark eyes looked past me to the glare of the river. How could I call her Eglantine? I would call her Little Egg instead. My magpie-girl with an eye for the shine, just like her father.

Eglantine, 1825

Always the memory of water. When I closed my eyes I could hear the rushing of it sure and steady as my own heartbeat. I grew up hearing the other sounds of it – the shouts and calls of disembodied voices coming over the water, the seabirds, the clang of things being loaded and unloaded, the trills of whistles. But always the memory of water and I never knew why. I assumed it was because we lived by the river, but it always invaded my dreams; it was as vivid to me as my own breath and as constant, more vivid to me than the memory of my own mother. When I tried to recall her face it would never come; I scrunched my eyes tight, trying to remember, yet her face disappeared in the purl. When I tried to remember her voice, my ears roared with the current.

My earliest memory was wrapped up with Miss Poppet, my doll. I'd always seemed to have had her. She was made of wood and she was small, her little painted face as familiar to me as the lines of my hand. A little comb tucked in her painted hair. When I was at my saddest I would hold her in the space between my chin and my chest, then close my eyes and imagine my mother's love around me like a blanket. I willed my mother to me and she never came, but my father was always there. He was the only parent I ever knew. We lived together in a grand house on the bankside of the River Thames, with my stepmother whom I called aunt and the housekeeper, and no one ever came to call.

If my doll was the apple of my eye, I was the apple of my father's.

"Come here, apple of my eye, and give us a kiss," my father said and offered me his pocket to search through. Within its confines I found a marzipan apple that he wrapped not in the street seller's paper but in the folds of his monogrammed handkerchief that even then had the wrong initial upon it. When I questioned him, that he wasn't a *PF* as the copperplate embroidery indicated, he guffawed and flicked me with the handkerchief's fine tail until I took my first bite, and second, the bitter-sweetness of it too much. I would rather have had a real apple, the crisp bite, the fragrant juice run all down my chin, than an ill-gotten sweet, but I'd never have said so. To be in my father's company was enough.

My father encouraged me to search his other pocket.

"Don't let me feel your fingers even move," he said and I tried to make my fingers dart inside, but the sugar from the marzipan made them sticky.

"Try again," he said, and I licked my fingers and tried again; there was something slippery between the lining and the pocket, something hard and round. I gave it a quick tug, and my father smacked my hand, captured like a moth; I'd failed at the task, but he let me pull it regardless. Something altogether finer than a marzipan fruit. From inside his pocket out snaked pearl after pearl, a perfect strand.

"Papa!"

My father lifted my braids and clipped the clasp securely together. My fingers ran over the combination of nacre and skin, captivated.

"What do you think, Eglantine?" my father said. What did I think? I'd lost the capacity to think, just feeling the weight of them on my small chest, like silk across my collarbone. I longed for a mirror to see myself in, imagining myself a lady, so I made do with my fingers. Those pearls, wide as a smile.

"Now try again," he said as he plucked an elegant silken handkerchief out of his waistcoat pocket and wiped something from my face, before he concealed the handkerchief in his back pocket with a flourish. He pulled out another handkerchief from his coat sleeves and placed it in his coat pocket. Another he pulled from out of nowhere and stuffed into his trouser pocket. He jumped up and down then, the vibration on the floorboards sending a chill up my legs, a faint tinkling coming from within the confines of his clothes.

"Come and find them, my girl, and they aren't to make a sound." I hadn't seen any bells in the handkerchiefs and I said as much. My father smiled at me proudly. "First rule of the game is observation. You knew to use your eyes before your fingers. So if it's no bells, what jingles?"

"Things wrapped in the handkerchiefs of course."

"Observe. I'm a gentleman looking at the flower sellers, my nose is full of perfume, I lean down to select a posy. See what pocket is exposed, beware of your surroundings and who may be watching. Find your moment. Lean into the flowers yourself and use your spare hand. Conceal with your body. Let your fingers do all the work. Don't let the width of your hand get caught when he stands. Clutch the item you've found into your palm and lean into the smell of flowers again. Don't rush to get away. He doesn't know he's a few ounces lighter. Don't draw his attention. Don't smile or make eye contact any more than is necessary. Maybe ask the time if he looks at you too long, unless you have lifted his watch. Then make your way."

My father bent over and smelled his imaginary flowers like an act in a pantomime; I saw the opening of his coat pocket, hooked my finger in and looped his pocket watch, feeling the fob chain trail along in my fingers, still warm from his body, until it pooled in my hand. He grabbed my wrist and the fob chain clattered to the ground, the watch safe in the claw of my fingers.

"Try again." This time my father stood with his arms held high as if reading an imaginary broadsheet held aloft, his coat pocket flapping open. He smiled at me, it was all a game, we'd been playing this game all my life. I was in and out of his pocket without my fingers touching the lining, a silver embossed cigarillo case already concealed in my own pocket before he even noticed.

"You done yet, girl?" Without pause my fingers sought out the other pocket and evacuated a ring box which I had concealed under my armpit, before I overreached and got my fingers caught in his breast pocket. He smacked my fingers flat against the soft lining.

"Better, apple of my eye. Again," he commanded. It was the only time I ever recalled my father showing me how to do anything. His encouragement was something he'd saved up all until now and I felt the glow of it.

Makepeace the housekeeper passed in the hallway, we heard her footsteps. My father bid me stop and unlooped the pearls from my throat and poured them back into his pocket with a serpentine clink.

Makepeace entered the room, her dark skirt sweeping across the threshold and concealing the shine of her silver chatelaine. Her lace cap kept her hair tidy and neat and gave her face the look of a daisy closing its petals at sundown. She stared at my father and me and I saw that she knew what had been happening in the room only moments before, but she said nothing.

"Come along, child, kiss your father goodnight." And I did so obediently before she led me down to the kitchen, where a hipbath steamed. I watched as she rolled up her sleeves and put her apron on, before she took a scoop of water and spilled it on the floor purposefully.

"Why do you do that?" I said, my curiosity an itch.

Makepeace looked at me but just smiled as she did every time I asked the question that she never felt the need to answer. "Off with your clothes now, before the water cools."

I did as I was instructed and slipped my foot into the water, my toe breaking the surface until I stood like a crane with one foot in and one foot out, watching the rippling of my own reflection and seeing another face looking back at me. Makepeace unfurled the doll from my fingers, smoothed her wooden face with her thumbs and placed her on a chair within reach if I needed her, then she poured a ladle of water over my shoulders, warm as sleep, the smell of soap a dream. When the water started to cool, Makepeace helped me step out and folded me into a towel as I watched the water swoop into the space where I had been and the cold lapped around me. Goose flesh pricked at my shoulderblades, bone fins, until my nightgown was pulled down over my head. She roped my hair into a neat braid and smoothed the lick of hair that rebelled and fell over my face. My hair, dark like hers. Dark like my doll's.

"Come, your Aunt Ada wants to bid you goodnight," she said and I dutifully followed behind in my little slippers and walked up the stairs to Ada's room, every creak of the stairs ran up my legs, my doll's earrings tinkling in my hand.

Ada lay in her bed, all the pillows supporting her upright, her belly huge beneath the quilt. She was dozing while Makepeace gently ushered me inside and I waited patiently for her to wake up while running my finger over all the surfaces, silk coverlet, satin wood, silver jewellery box, tapestry, longing to turn the lamp up to see it all better.

"Eglantine?" Ada said, easing herself up onto her elbows. "Come closer, child."

I crept closer. Though I loved Ada's room, Ada's love confused me. She was all caresses, all longing, her touch made me feel she was trying to shape me into something else, something all her own.

"Yes, Aunt," I said and sat where she patted, my feet dangling, the cool air milling around my ankles; I wanted nothing more than to tuck my legs beneath her coverlet and soak in some of her warmth. She snatched my hand and laid it on the hill of her belly.

"Feel that?" she said and I felt the pulse of movement beneath the film of her nightgown, the tautness of her skin, and was sick with the vertigo of it – how had the baby got in there, how would it get out? I pulled my hand away then Ada caressed my hair and used the end of my braid to tickle my cheek. I feigned a smile.

"Put dolly here and get my jewellery box for me, there's a dear," she said, and reluctantly I placed my doll against her leg in the warm space I had carved from the bedclothes then lifted the silver box from her dresser. A thin white powdery line of dust traced the outline of where it had been, the ghost of the box, I felt compelled to blow it away. The box was as big as Makepeace's Bible and I heard the treasures clanking within it, minus her pearls: those were in the pink-shell lining of my father's coat pocket.

The surface of the box was bereft of anything except the swirl of an ornate letter A. With swollen fingers Ada lifted the lid and inside all her treasures shone against the red-heart interior of velvet.

"What would you like to try on this evening, *ma petite* Eglantine?" She smiled at me, her face pale. I ran my fingers over all the accumulated gems of her life – ruby earrings, a coral rattle, a pearl ring. She didn't notice that her strand of pearls was missing? Perhaps she kept them in one of the drawers of her dresser. Colour flooded my face with the shame of wearing them without her permission, when she was always so generous in all that she had, even to me, a small child.

"What about these?" she said, holding the earrings up to my face. "Petite Eglantine just like Miss Poppet." She screwed them onto my ears, the weight of them pulling at my lobes, and I looked in the mirror as she instructed. I didn't see any resemblance to Miss Poppet's red glass diamonds, but I saw the pull of my earlobes and thought they looked like something a fisherman might use to bait a hook rather than something on which to hang a jewel.

Makepeace breezed into the room and frowned at me with my earlobes dangling and I quickly tried to pull off the earrings, my earlobes pulsing through the small gap, drawing blood. Makepeace watched me as I placed them back in the jewellery box.

"Come now, Eglantine, time for bed," she said, not unkindly. "Say goodnight to your aunt." I obediently kissed her on her cheek, gathered up the remaining jewels and returned the box to the dresser, my doll beneath my arm. Ada was a series of white hills beneath the coverlet, her face smiling above. "Sleep well, little Eglantine."

I went up to the nursery, Makepeace's skirts a dark cloud along with my thoughts, the house whistling with draught. Why was Ada's baby going to have her as a mother, where was mine? As we climbed to the top of the house I heard the rain start to pound, hitting at the slate and rolling down the drain, louder and louder with each step. The river would be roiling brown with it.

Inside the nursery I stood on a chair near the window to peer at the river and see the boats rise and pitch, to watch the rain puncture the fog, but the night had closed in, all was darkness except for the lamps that winked in and out on the water. The fire glowed in the grate and Makepeace pulled back the bed for me, removing the warmer.

"Makepeace, where is my mama?" I said. The closeness of the night pressed in on me and I was glad to slip between the sheets of my bed, warm and crisp, but the coldness was in me, running like the river, longing for her but unable to even imagine her face, her voice. I ran my hands over my own face but found nothing familiar there.

"She's never far away, I'm sure," Makepeace said. Her voice was all control to cover the little crack in it. "Sleep well," she said and kissed me on my hair and closed the door. I listened to the hollow sound of her footsteps as she wound her way back down to the kitchen.

THREE

Eglantine, 1825

I lay in the darkness listening to the whole house settle. The rain began hitting the window in sheets and sent the fire spitting in the grate, sparks extinguished before they were sucked up the flue. I tossed off the bedclothes and stood on the chair again and watched the rain slice across the glass, each raindrop a precious stone, the lights on the water dancing now, all the vessels obscured by the fog, all the lights like fireflies. I grew sleepy, my breath becoming visible with my forehead against the glass. If Makepeace said my mother wasn't very far away, where was she? Why had I never seen her? Could she see me now? My eyes were growing heavy following the cloaking and revealing of the lights, the steady beat of the rain, when I heard a commotion on the stairs.

I crept, heavy limbed, to the door and creaked it open, the draught licking around my ankles like a cat. A loud cry burst through the house and raced up the stairs like a spirit; all the little hairs on my arms wavered. Ada's baby had come. I stood listening for its cry, feeling jealous that the baby would have a mother when I had none, until I pinched myself on my arm, sending the flesh between my fingers red. Ada had been nothing but kind to me, patient. She liked to brush my hair, loop it into strange styles, treating me like a living doll, and I let her though I hated it, resentful of her touch, prickly like my name, prickly by nature.

The front door opened and the roar of the rain came through the house, disguising a gentleman's voice as he announced who he was. He was ushered up the stairs, his shadow leading him, before Makepeace whisked open Ada's door and he disappeared. I took a few steps further out and peered down, but all that was left of the mysterious visitor were the dark stains of his wet footsteps. A cry came and I held my heart and prayed for Ada and her baby that they be safe.

The smell of tobacco wended its way up to me and I saw my father sitting on the stairs, his head in his hands, his pipe between his lips a little chimney trying to warm him. The rain pooled around him, but I'd neither heard nor seen him go in or out, my father part shadow. I stood where I was, afraid of the sounds that swirled up the staircase from Ada's room. Makepeace burst out of the door, her sleeves rolled up to her elbows, bloodied, the stairs rocked beneath my feet. My father looked up hopefully as she disappeared down to the kitchen and reappeared with a bucket of water, so full some slopped over the edge and onto the stairs, but she didn't falter. The room swallowed her and her bucket and let out Ada's scream into the hallway, my father's head sinking into his hands, a stifled sob.

I crept down the stairs and curled my arm around his, but it just made him sob all the more and he wrapped his arms around me, his tears salt on my lips. I must have fallen asleep, for next I knew my father stirred and leapt to his feet, rushing to the bedroom door and slamming it behind him, all rage. I strained to hear the sound of the baby's cry. The doctor saw himself out and Makepeace followed not long after, unaware of me watching. She stood at the door, took off her lace cap and cried silently into it until she saw me on the stairs and ushered me up to bed.

"I can't hear the baby," I said.

Makepeace shook her head. "Both baby and Ada have gone to God, Eglantine, gone to God," was all she said, her voice barely audible, before she tucked the blankets up around my neck and leaned down to kiss me. The weariness came off her in waves, it wouldn't have surprised me if she just lifted up her feet and lay beside me, but she pulled herself upright and disappeared out the door, the dawn a dull light through the window, the sun not having the strength to push through the rain. How could Ada and her baby be gone? I felt the shame of my repulsion of touching her moving belly, of my jealousy of the baby having a mother. Now neither of them would have anything except the grave.

* * *

The house was veiled in mourning and I was clearly instructed that Ada's room was no longer a room I was permitted to enter. The house was quiet without my aunt, her ringing of the bells in the kitchen and Makepeace's bustle to her post. When I tried to recall how long Ada had been bedridden, it felt that she'd always been in that silk-lined room, overheated and stuffy, queen of her mattress kingdom. My father was sombre; his mood took up the space of a guest, dark and brittle, something to be avoided, and Makepeace and I did our best. But all of our movements and sounds were irritations to him.

The night before the funeral I heard my father and Makepeace shouting in the kitchen, I listened from the top banister, their words rose and fell before they overlapped again.

Unable to make out the words, I made my way down the stairs to eavesdrop and noticed Ada's bedroom door was open. With trepidation I pushed the door wide and saw all Ada's clothes piled on the bed stripped of sheets. All her drawers emptied, her many pairs of slippers and shoes lined up on the floor. The window was wide open letting in a billowing gust; a pile of Ada's chemises had flitted off the bed and onto the floor, a bonnet spun at my feet, its ribbons tangling in my toes. All of Ada's things were cleared from the dresser, all her bottles of perfume and medicine had been smashed in the cold hearth, lending the ashes that swirled around the fireplace a sickly smell.

Something caught my eye amid the ashes, something silvery and bright and I reached my hand in and lay hold of the lid of Ada's jewellery box, ripped from its hinges. I spat on my finger and wiped the A of her name clear then set it down upon the floor. I thrust my hand back in the ashes and the broken glass and pulled out the husk of the box, all the lining tattered, holding on by threads. I set it on the ground too and sifted through the ashes, pulling a ruby that had hung in an earring. It rolled in my palm like a drop of blood. Why had all Ada's things been ruined? Had my father done it? I seized on something green, but it was just a shard of glass from a smashed bottle; it lay glittering in my palm, the sharp edges of it the brightest of all. I held it up to my eye and watched as the world turned to water, everything rippled and submerged. I held my own hand up to view it, green and swirling, my fingers surrounded by bubbles suspended in the water.

"What are you doing?" my father said. In my hurry to put the glass down I slashed the pad of my thumb, blood bubbled onto my nightgown. Makepeace appeared beside him.

"Eglantine!" she said and rushed forward, wrapping her apron around my wound.

"Why are all Ada's special things in the fireplace?" I said.

"You have no right to be in here, Eglantine," my father said, his face stern.

"Now she has gone, it's best we clear her room, so her spirit doesn't return," Makepeace said, quietly removing the items I'd saved from the ashes.

"You'll not fill her head with superstition," my father said, his anger rising in him. "Eglantine, these things were not of any value, they are worthless."

"But may I not keep them?" I asked, innocent as I was.

"No, you may not keep them," my father thundered. "And a girl soon to be a lady does not sit on the floor and paddle in the ashes of another's fire," he said, yanking me up by the elbow.

"Did you not listen? You were not to come in this room," he said and started pulling me down the stairs so that I began to cry. I tried to yank my arm away, but he held firm. I looked up at him and he was almost unrecognisable, his face transfigured by his anger. "What happens to little girls who don't listen, do you think?"

"Amberline," Makepeace said, but he ignored her and continued dragging me down the stairs.

"Stop, Father," I said. "I'm sorry, sorry." But he had no ears for me, he was deaf with his rage.

He led me through to the kitchen, my thumb leaving droplets of blood on the freshly scrubbed flags, and dragged me all the way to the cellar, the dark yawning up at me, my father's nails digging into my elbow. The smell was green, mildew and damp. He pushed me through the door and slammed the door behind me.

I screamed.

How long did I sit in the darkness? It rushed around me like I was at the bottom of the river, my own voice still lapping in my ears. Terror of the darkness engulfed me. What was this place, how long would they leave me here? Why had my father done this to me?

"Mama?" I called out in the darkness, unsure whether I was awake or asleep, sure that time had stopped and that I had dreamed everything. "Mama," I called out again, more urgently, waiting for the sound of her body rising from sleep, waiting for her feet to thud onto the floor, waiting for the swish of a curtain and the softness of my name on her lips, my face burrowing into her hair, the dream dispelled. But she didn't come. The silence wormed into my ears and I scratched at my palm with my nail just to make sure I was still here, that I hadn't disappeared.

All the darkness rushed up to me and I heard a dripping sound from down below. I knew the stairs were there, but I couldn't see them, I didn't dare move lest I fall down them. I'd never been in here before. I kept my hand on the door handle as if it was an anchor. A strip of light appeared beneath the door and I looked to it like a moth, my horizon. There was more shouting from within the house and I held my breath to hear what was said, but all I heard was the thumping in my ears, my heart as loud as an echo in a cavern. I ran my hand over the nearest wall and felt with my feet the first step, before I braved to take another, my eyes adjusting to the darkness, the spill of light from under the door allowing the next few steps to appear out of the dark.

Down I went, step by step by step, my hand on the wall running across moss that seemed to grow slightly raised from it, soft as velvet. The water dripped louder as I descended. Where was it coming from? It sounded like a song, a rhyme with which my breathing kept time.

> *What will I be?*
> *Lady, baby, gypsy, queen.*
> *What shall I wear?*
> *Silk, satin, velvet, lace.*
> *How shall I get it?*
> *Given, borrowed, bought, stolen.*
> *How shall I get to church?*
> *Coach, carriage, wheelbarrow, cart.*
> *Where shall I live?*
> *Big house, little house, pig-sty, barn.*

My foot slipped into water; the sharp chill of it bit through my ankles. Here at the bottom there seemed to be a pond, rippling with the arrival of my feet, a faint glow coming off the surface. But how had it got here? The water didn't come through the ceiling. It must have come up from the earth, a spring. I reached down and saw my own reflection looking up at me. How could I see in the dark? Had I an owl's eyes? *Weshimulmo*, the word whispered up to me in my mind.

Light flooded through the cellar as Makepeace opened the door, a lantern burning in her hand, sending her silhouette arching up the wall. I tried to vanish into myself, to make myself smaller, to turn to darkness.

"Eglantine," she called and I heard the panic in her voice. I should have answered her, but I didn't want to open my mouth, I wanted to slide into the water and be gone.

I heard her footsteps on the stairs, the dull tinkle of her chatelaine at her waist, the light flaring closer, until she faced me, caught in the ripple of the puddle.

"Eglantine," Makepeace said, "come out of there, you'll catch your death." At her words I shuddered and clutched my hands to my sides, thinking that death was some sort of ball that I might accidentally find in my hands.

Makepeace reached out her hand to me but I was full of my own anger, a whirlwind in the shape of a child. I struck the water with my hand and it arced all over her, sending her lantern hissing. I watched her face to see what she would do, expecting her to turn on her heel and leave me in the darkness again. She wiped the water from her face with her apron and stretched her hand to me again.

"Your father is not himself, Eglantine," she said, no rancour in her voice, not even a frown spreading across her features. The cold hummed up my legs, down my sleeves, the water wicked up my nightgown. It had been my anger that had kept me warm. I took her hand and she walked me up to the kitchen and wrapped me in a blanket by the fire, taking each of my feet that now felt like stone and rubbing them between her hands. The water from the cellar streaked all across the kitchen floor, like a line of footprints. She handed me my doll, Miss Poppet, lost from my pocket in the chaos, and I cradled her in my hands, seeking the familiar hewn markings on her body, my fingers running along them as if they were roads, until I fell asleep.

FOUR

Eglantine, 1825

In the morning my father came, all apology, and I looked in his face and believed what he said. That it wasn't my fault, that I didn't know, that he was overcome with sadness for losing his wife and his new baby and I was ashamed of myself for having touched Ada's things, for the size of his adult emotion, for having that flicker of jealousy as I had touched her belly. But I was wary of him, the scratches on my elbow still stung. I'd felt my whole world waver.

He decided that we should take the air and I clasped his hand; with my free hand I twirled my doll in my pocket, my compass and comfort. I peered up at him, tall and dark in his mourning clothes, my head close to his pocket, so close I heard the silken rush of the lining and the click-clacking of things within it.

The street was alive with its own commotion. A gentleman cantered past; the horse's hooves flicked up mud, which my father, by some sense, narrowly avoided. We walked towards the riverside, the seagulls flying low to the shore, watching. A chestnut boy was selling his wares over an old flame brazier; the smell would usually have made my mouth crave their soft flesh, but today they had no sway over me. A waterman's pole sliced through the water. The streets changed as we moved through them, but the river remained the same. The buildings became more decrepit, the people more ragged. My father paid them no attention, but I couldn't stop staring. "Don't hold my hand so tight," he chided and I tried to loosen my grip, but I felt buffeted by the growing traffic and was afraid.

We came to a shop, cast-iron tendrils swinging over the door, *Sweet's Emporium*, and my father dropped my hand.

I wanted to ask him what Emporium meant but when I glanced at his face I saw he was scowling. He pushed open the door and led me through. It took my eyes a little while to adjust to the gloom, before the light picked out the shape of a few things – a brass candlestick, a ticking clock in its wooden case like a coffin, an ornamental knife engraved with strange writing. I squeezed my doll tighter in my pocket, frightened of losing her here. From behind a curtain bustled Mr Sweet, pulling his rising waistcoat over his rotund belly.

"So good of you to come. How long has it been?"

"It's hardly as if we were invited now, is it, Mr Sweet?" my father replied. I could tell from his voice that he was irritated, that Sweet was distasteful to him. I stared at Sweet and saw on his lip a smear of grease, the glint in his eyeglass, the paw-like size of his hands, and I too was wary.

"How long has it been?" Sweet continued. "A year, three years, six years?"

"Since what?"

"Since you've gone and made yourself a gentleman, like a butterfly out of a cocoon of muck you are!"

My father pulled himself up taller; his hands gripped the counter, his fine suit brushing up against the dust. The sleeve of my father's jacket tightened as he flexed his arm and I watched the alarm spread across Sweet's face like a rash.

"Papa?" I said, but he bid me be quiet with a look.

My father pulled the pearls from his pocket and they fell from his hand onto the counter, thudding one after another, mermaid's dominoes.

Sweet picked up the pearls and ran them across his teeth, the sound of ivory on ivory.

"Careful now, Mr Sweet, don't want you to eat them before we have set a price."

Mr Sweet smiled and flipped his loupe to his eye. "I'm hardly Cleopatra now, am I? The only way to be sure they are real and not Venetian glass is to rub them across one's teeth. They may seem smooth but to the teeth they have roughness."

"Since when have I ever passed you anything less than quality? When have I passed you glass?"

He proffered them up to my father's lips, but my father closed his mouth in a grimace.

"Why not keep them for your girl, for when she is a full-grown lady?" Sweet said, weighing the pearls in his hand, and I remembered their weight on my chest, heavy as rope.

"You try, child." He smiled as he handed them to me and I was overcome with the impulse to run with them out the door just to feel them to be mine again. Instead I rubbed them across my own teeth, and found them exactly as Mr Sweet had said. Rough to the teeth though silken to the skin.

"An expert, your girl." The glare of his attention rested on me, my father's hand settled protectively on my shoulder. "Here, look at them through the loupe and tell me what you see?" He swung up the hinged portion of the counter and stepped out between my father and me. "Hold it just like this," he said. As he leaned down towards me his mustard-striped trousers let out a groan and my father smiled as if he were preparing for a tooth to be pulled. Sweet held the glass of the loupe up to my eye and put his hand over my other one and I saw the world made large. I wanted to step back. At first I was afraid of what I saw, the world was reduced and magnified like I was the eye of the Lord, seeing virtues few and faults many.

"Look closely," he said, his voice in my ear. If it wasn't for my father's reassuring feet, I would have elbowed him into his kingdom come. The pearls up close were like fish scales and I looked away, unable to believe my eyes, then squinted through the loupe again at the pearl in my palm, a tiny moon, smooth beneath my fingers.

"Now look at this," Sweet said as he eased off a diamond ring from his pinky finger and placed it warm and sweaty in my palm.

Beneath the loupe all I saw was colour, a rainbow captured in stone.

"How can it be?" My wonder grew as I turned the ring in my fingers, watching the colours flit through it, so I barely noticed the exchange – the pearls for money – between my father and Sweet. I was captivated by nature's telescope. The world only returned with the abrupt retrieval of the diamond and the loupe.

"Thank you, Mr Sweet," I said and I truly was grateful, for the earth seemed different now – the light shone through all the objects in Mr Sweet's shop, all the colours wedged in my eye. I blinked and still they would not clear, sparkling between the open and the closed. My father gave me a sharp glance.

"You wouldn't care to make a purchase?" Sweet said, stepping back and sweeping the dust off the top of the counter with the palm of his hand. "Anything in there to take your fancy?"

"We've done enough business with you for one day, Sweet," my father said, and made to take my hand to lead me out. But I saw something in the counter, it glowed with my name, *Eglantine*. I peered down at it and rubbed at my eyes, still seeing the light blading through my vision. Was I imagining things?

"Ah, she's the eyes of youth, she has," Sweet crowed and my father stopped and turned to see what it was I was looking at, having to crouch down to my level to see in.

I pointed at the small heart cut from a coin, tarnished silver, and my father beside me began to twitch. He was up on his feet and tapping the counter, his words fleeing his mouth, and

Sweet, smiling smugly, was only too happy to roll out a cloth and place the heart with my name on it on the counter for him. My father picked it up and turned it over in his hands, running his fingers around the edges of it.

"Where did you get this from, Sweet?" my father said, his voice low. Sweet held out his hand for it, but my father held it firm.

"Oh, I knew it would catch your fancy. How long has it been? It's been waiting for you all this time. Tempted to sell it for scrap, but I knew you'd be back at some point, whatever games you've been pursuing."

"What do you want for it?" My father's voice was firm, but I heard the little catch in it.

Sweet took a pencil from his waistcoat pocket and scribbled an amount on a piece of paper and slid it across to my father. My father read it and scoffed, flicking it to the floor.

"You must take me for an idiot, Sweet."

"No, not an idiot. That would be going too far. I'd say a sentimentalist, that is all."

My father took out two coins from his pocket and slid them across the counter, then took my hand and walked out of Sweet's Emporium, the bell pealing at our exit.

Outside, the colours lingered in my eyes and flashed when I looked up at the sky, a strange flare of lightning. On my own hand I saw colours splash there as if I had been staring at the sun. Had the light from the diamond infected me and given me a fever of the eyes? The low cloud bore down on me, but the colours whipped through them and distracted me, so I walked with my head down. Everything I passed glowed with a particular radiance – a raindrop on the low-hanging foliage of a tree, my own fingernail shone like a shell and I felt elated. A butcher's wagon rolled past leaving a trail of blood behind it on the road, perfect ruby droplets that held their shape before dissolving into the dust. I wanted to ask my father where we were going, but his silence pressed down on me and I knew better than to ask.

It was a lane he led me to, dirty and dank, the washing draped across it like a sad banner whipping against the wind. We passed a well in the middle of the street and I thought I heard the wind spiral down it to ruffle the water at the bottom. I dropped my father's hand and ran to the edge, feeling the need to peer in to see diamonds shining on the water, but my father pulled me back, his hand so firm on my arm that it made black spots dance on my eyes.

He led me to a door, so familiar as if I'd seen it in a dream, pulled a key out of his pocket and led me into the darkness.

My heart knock-knock-knocked against my ribs so loud I thought it would alert someone, but there was no one here. Out of the corner of my eye I saw something move, but it was merely my own reflection caught in an enormous cracked looking glass.

My father walked further in and kindled a light.

"I'm sorry for what I did, Eglantine, I was not in control of myself; I just wanted the whole business to be laid to rest," my father said, looking at me seriously. I nodded, unsure of exactly what he meant. "You are and always will be my daughter, Eglantine. All I have will one day be yours. You are the only one I can trust." His words lay heavy on me.

A large clock ticked at me, its pendulum a golden moon swinging back and forth; its ticking grew louder in my ears as I took courage and stepped further in. Tentatively I peered around the corner of a curtain: a small dead fire in the grate, a bed, the long blue shadows of the afternoon filling the room early. On the table were gouges in the wood, I ran my finger across them, roads of wood. On the floor had fallen a piece of card, I turned it upright and saw that it was a silhouette of a family of three. I heard a cry and it sent the hairs on my neck on end and made my heart pound. The sound had come out of my father. He held the little silver heart up to his lips.

"What is this place?" I said.

"It's where we lived, your mother and I and you."

The tears started to spill out of my eyes then, fractious little rainbows. I squeezed the doll in my pocket in a bid to stop them coming, I would not cry. How could I cry over what I didn't remember? But the tears came anyway. My father handed me the heart cut from a coin and turned to the fireplace, rain already pouring from the eaves outside, a torrent out of nowhere. A puddle swelled at the doorway, then started seeping beneath. He carefully removed his coat and hat and, after wiping the dust away, laid them on the table, before he piled whatever wood remained into the grate. When he found it not enough, he picked up a chair, held it above his head and smashed it on the ground, sending the legs spiralling into the air. The crack of it upon the wood frightened me, I felt the vibration of it run up my legs. He struck the floor again, until the chair was nothing but kindling. He gathered up the pieces and rammed them into the fireplace then pulled a tinderbox from the mantel and struck and struck and struck, but no flame would come to his bidding.

"Damned damp," he said and took a piece of paper out of his pocket, brought the flint to it and coaxed the tiniest of flames before the rest of the fire caught on wood, chair and all. The flames leapt upward like hair being pulled out by its roots.

My father went around finding whatever he could to stick in the fire: the only other chair, the silhouette, an old apron, a scarf, a petticoat, a pair of stockings. As the last of them was consumed by the flames I realised that they must have been my mother's things, whatever remained of hers disappearing from me a second time. Next came the bedding, the sheets, the pillows. He hauled the mattress off the bed and dragged it across the floor, mildew patterning the underside like a map. He took the knife concealed in his boot and slit open the mattress and out spilled amongst the horsehair all sorts of silver and gold pieces – brooches, earrings, a set of rosary beads, a hair comb, a watch. My father sifted through the rest of the horsehair, feeding some of it to the flames, but the acrid smell of it made us both cough. Once he'd made sure there was nothing of value left, he swung the door open and dumped the remains of the mattress in the street. From the doorway I watched him wrestle with it in the rain as if he was fighting a whale, before he came back in, his clothes patched with rain. The room grew hot and he left the door open and swept the remaining horsehair out into the street and I noticed with fascination as the puddle at the doorway remained unchanged, if anything it appeared to grow. My father's boots splashed right through it, oblivious. He stomped on the bed frame and split the slatted wood then piled it beside the fire to wait its turn, until nothing remained behind the curtain except an old blanket. My father plucked it up and dragged it towards the door, revealing what was left beneath it: one tiny leather baby shoe. I walked over and picked it up and held it in my hands.

"Father?" I said and he stopped to stare at me, before he saw the shoe. The blanket dropped to the floor in a pall of dust. He reached out his hand to the tiny shoe and traced the fine stitches in the leather, his eyes watering with the smell of the burning smoke, the dust. He took the shoe from my hand and shook it. Out onto the floor fell the spotted petals of a foxglove. He wept then, silent and angry, and threw the small elfin shoe into the fire. I cried out, but it was no use, the leather had already caught the flame and started to turn black before my eyes. My father had kept the past sealed up in these rooms and now he was trying to obliterate it, before I had a chance to learn anything.

"It was mine, wasn't it?" But he wouldn't answer me.

My father pulled out a small cast-iron pot and threw all the silver jewellery in it then held it over the flames with a clamp. I clutched the heart tightly in my palm, I'd not let him have it, he'd have to wrench it out of my hands. But my father seemed to have forgotten about it, absorbed in the slow dissolve of metal.

When we left I kept the heart in my palm, until I grew frightened I would drop it in the darkening streets, so I placed it in my mouth like a dead man, a coin for the ferryman, and prayed my father wouldn't ask me anything.

When we arrived home I noticed my father's hands were blackened with soot, his clothes dusty. Both of us dripped all over the floor. Makepeace took one glance at my father and said nothing. My father disappeared upstairs to his room. I made sure I heard the door click before I spat the heart into my palm, crest side up, the metallic flavour making my teeth vibrate in my head for using my mouth like a purse.

"What is that?" Makepeace said.

"Father found it at Sweet's." She glared at me then and I was made aware that I'd said something I shouldn't. She ran her hand over my hair. I had nothing more to add. I couldn't tell her about the place my father had taken me, the sound of the blade as it ripped through the mattress, the jewels that fell out of its stuffing. The last traces of my mother gone with the smoke.

Makepeace led me up to the nursery, muddy footsteps and all, and helped me remove my wet things, hanging them on the back of a chair, thick with water. Would I know my way back to the home I'd had with my mother? I ran my fingers through the thick wet plush of my coat, a track with my finger, a secret map through all the ocean of streets.

That night I stood at the window of the nursery and tried to catch sight of the way to the place where we had lived as a little family, but I could not see beyond the side of the house. The river was lit with strange lights in the distance and on the wind a voice called, but I neither heard what the words were nor who was speaking them. All I felt was a strange sensation in my chest, an unfurling, the sense of a seed that had been washed with rain pushing up through the darkness.

FIVE

Patrin, 1818

My father was lost in the stroke of his knife on the hazel branch as he removed the bark from a forked branch, Jupiter's head resting on his boot, the warmest place by the fire. My mother was asleep in the *vardo* and I was watching the fire from the top step. Our horse was tied to a tree at the edge of the camp, covered with a blanket; I heard him cropping the grass. This was all I knew, yet I craved something, although I couldn't exactly name what it was. I wanted to be other than a child, I wanted to find the shape of my own life.

When Amberline walked right into camp, his boots were so soundless and so fine that the firelight licked their polished surface. We didn't hear him because he didn't make a sound, no one challenged him, my father's dog, Jupiter, didn't even look up. Amberline's fancy boot heels made no strike upon the ground, no twig snapped beneath his step. His footsteps were silence, he walked like a thief.

But I saw him. I'd been watching from the shadow of the *vardo*, sitting on the step thinking I was dreaming. His pocket watch swung, a silver charm, to and fro, a will-o'-the-wisp, until he walked out of the darkness and into the circle of light.

My father leapt to his feet.

Jupiter bared his teeth at the stranger, knives of ivory.

"What do you want?" my father growled, his strong arms and chest as broad as an ale barrel, his knife resting in the palm of his hand.

"Please," the stranger said. Closer to the fire I saw he was from the city: his clothes, though splattered with mud at the trousers, were of a fine material and neatly cut; the lapel of his coat was velvet. The stranger held out his hands to my father to show him that he was unarmed and all I saw was the milk-white clean of his hands.

"Can I stay?" he asked. "Just for a few days, mind," he hurried on, confident in his request as if my father had already granted it.

"Why would we do that? We know not you nor your people." My father spat on the fire, the flames hissed. Jupiter was up on his feet by my father's side, his head lowered, his eyes tracking the stranger's movements, just waiting for the command, a long thin whine coming from his brindled snout.

"But you *are* my people," he said and he leaned closer to my father. Jupiter growled and my father's fingers spread across the hilt of his knife like a spider's legs, ready. "Please." Jupiter's barking echoed around the clearing and sent a bird complaining into the night. My mother woke and ducked her head out of the *vardo* doorway, brushing past me on the stairs.

"Hush now, Jupiter," my father said, his hand on Jupiter's collar.

"Say your piece, boy, and let it be done," my mother said.

The stranger lowered his voice, I tried to listen, but his words were lost to the crackle of the flames as they danced upwards, making their faces glow, and all watched in surprise as my father slapped the stranger into an embrace, a rough kiss on each cheek and the offer of a bed beneath the wagon. I heard his name for the first time. *Amberline*.

My mother bristled when she came back into the *vardo*. She rummaged in an old wooden chest and pulled out a horse blanket, ragged and rough. Why did she give him this one when we had others that were more fit for a guest, fit for kin? My mother only kept this blanket to jam beneath the door when the winter winds bit.

"Who is he?" I asked.

"Go inside, child," she said as she went back outside, but I didn't move. My father resumed his seat by the fire, the forked hazel branch back in his hands, the blade back to the whittling. Jupiter lay uneasy at his feet, ears already dowsing the direction of the stranger. My mother stood and handed Amberline the blanket until her instinct made her look up. I didn't need to be scolded like a child, I stood and went inside the *vardo*.

My ears were keen to every sound. I heard the stranger as he crawled under the *vardo* for the night, the thwack as he hit his head, a smothered curse. I heard him settle and stretch and yawn. But sleep evaded me knowing he slept beneath me.

* * *

In the early light I woke and leapt down from the *vardo*. And there he was, sitting by the coals of the dying fire, using a handkerchief to buff the toes of his boots. He looked up at me and I felt my whole skin turn red like a rabbit stripped to the sinew, but I kept walking to the river, bucket in my hand.

There was a mist rolling off the river and with each step that I took it rolled closer, making the grass but patches of green beneath my feet. A swan glided past, the colour of its orange beak cutting through the glare of the mist. I took my own ragged boots off and tied the laces together before slinging them around my neck: I didn't dare leave them on the riverbank in case the fog conceal them so well I never found them again. I hoisted up my skirt and petticoat and knotted them above my knees and slipped into the water; the trickle of it running across my bare feet made me gasp. The water rustled all around me as if it was speaking.

I looped the bucket handle over my wrist and let my hands dangle in the water as the sunlight struck the fog golden. Around me, disguised in the treetops, all the birds sang the sun brighter and light flickered across the surface. I leaned down and drank from the lip of the river, the end of my plait dragging in the water, and suddenly a face loomed into the water beside mine. I quickly stood up, blinking water from my eyes. Had I the gift?

I hurriedly skimmed the bucket across the surface of the water, flicking out a tadpole with my thumb, and strode out of the river.

And there as the fog lifted was Amberline walking towards me, a grin across his face as he took in the sight of my legs, my wet feet, my knotted skirt, my petticoat patched and patched again. Was it disdain I saw there? Him, in his fine clothes, every button on his coat matching, his trousers now sponged clean. A fine shadow of a beard grew across his face. How long had he been watching me?

"Good morning," he said with a smile so I thought he was mocking me. In a blind flash of anger, I emptied the contents of the bucket over his head. His blue eyes lit up with the shock of it. I saw his fingers clench and unclench as he stared at me. I turned and walked away, the sound of his laughter silencing the birds.

When I made it back to camp with my bucket refilled alone further downstream, he was bent over my mother's fire, the old horse blanket around his shoulders while his beautiful city clothes lay spread out over the bushes to dry.

"Daughter, do you know what happened to our guest here?" my father asked and I looked him straight in the eye.

"Must have been the slippery soles of those city boots," I said, pouring the water into the kettle and hanging it over the flames that quickly rushed towards its blackened bottom. The stranger's eyes followed me back to the *vardo*, my father's voice calling to me.

"Come, my daughter, and meet your kin." He was kin? How could he be? His hands were smooth, free of callouses. His boot soles were barely worn. What had the likes of him to do with us?

"Patrin, this is our kinsman, Amberline Stark, his family have long had ties with us Scamps. He will be staying with us for a while," my father said.

Why was he staying with us? I'd never even heard of him, I'd never heard of the Starks.

"Hello, Patrin," Amberline said, rising in his horse blanket, and I took satisfaction in his changed state. He bobbed his head to me, unable to offer his hand, but it was his knees I saw now.

"Patrin, is that a boy's name?" he said and if I'd had that bucket I would have swung it until the wooden side of it smacked his head.

"A fine name for a boy or a girl, Amberline, as it was my father's own." That made him pull his blanket tighter around him. "And a fine name for my firstborn daughter." My father ushered me closer towards Amberline. "Now, Patrin, say good morrow to our kinsman."

"Good morrow," I parroted, quick and short.

"Good morrow, Patrin," he said, his eyes smiling, blue as a magpie's egg and all delight. I couldn't look away. His hair started to dry in waves around his pale face that had been kept from the wind and rain. How was a gentleman our kin? My cheeks roared, self-conscious of my braid resting on my breast and leaving a damp mark where my heart beat wildly. I met his smile with my own.

Later, Mother and I went out to harvest the hedgerow that grew not far from our camp. We climbed a slight rise and the river ran like a silver ribbon, dazzling to the eye in the sunshine.

The sun grew hot on our backs as we bent to snick at the long tangle of hazel, ash, beech and dogwood, all while the sap was low, sending the creatures that called it home scratching deeper into the undergrowth. My mother was unusually silent, her hair pulled tight beneath her scarf, not even a hum at her lips, but all of me buzzed with questions. The knife slippery and my fingers fat as I worked alongside her. The smoke from our fire curled in the distance, my thoughts unable to leave off from our guest.

"So who are the Stark family, Mama?" I asked, unable to keep my questions from coming out of my mouth "And how come I've never heard of them?"

My mother stood straight, put her hand in the small of her back and stretched, leaning her face into the sunshine, in no rush to answer me. Slowly she wiped the perspiration from her face with her hand and took a long deep swig from the skin of water. I thought she hadn't heard me so I repeated my question and in doing so watched her twitch with irritation.

"I wish I could say the same thing," she said and adjusted her headscarf then bent again and set her back to the task. She cut another switch and said no more.

"What do you mean?" I said, knowing nothing more than I did before my frustration prickled.

"Least said best mended," she said, her hands not even pausing in their work.

"Mend what?" I was like a fly after the salt of her sweat, I wouldn't be waved off.

My mother stopped then, walked over to the bundle of twigs and bound them with a rag, before strapping them to her back. "Amberline Stark's father was a thief and his mother turned her back on our ways to live the life of a *gadji*," she said vehemently. "And let that be an end to it," she added before striding off down the hill.

I skipped to keep up with her. "So how is he kin?" I persisted.

"He's kin enough. But as soon as we meet the rest at the fair, he'll be finding other kin to belong to and we'll have no more to do with him," she said and spat on the ground.

My mother's version of events only made me more curious, but I knew better than to keep pushing at her.

By the time we arrived back at camp, Amberline was dressed, his fine clothes all dry, the horse blanket folded neatly on a log and my father by his side inspecting the contents of a handkerchief. My mother cast a cursory glance but I stopped to see. Amberline smiled up at me expectantly but I couldn't meet his eyes, the light hit them brightly but he didn't squint.

Inside his palm sat several little trinkets made of silver, each little hearts, their tips all touching like a flower.

"And you made these?" my father said, so delicate he only touched with his thumb.

"Yes, these and other things," Amberline said, "but they are in London."

"They are fine, are they not?" my father said and I nodded.

"That they are," I replied, feeling my mother's eyes on my back as she sat on the *vardo* step cutting the leaves off the branches, getting reading for weaving.

"Love tokens," Amberline said, "or witches' hearts, symbolising one's heart has been bewitched." I chanced to look at him and already found him staring into my face.

"They'll be worth a pretty penny at the fair, if you're willing to sell them," my father suggested. But Amberline shook his head and closed his fist around his handkerchief, all the bright hearts disappearing from the sunshine with an eclipse of his hand.

"With respect, sir, I'll not be selling them," Amberline said and my father stroked his beard and then regarded Amberline quizzically.

"Well, boy ..." my father began but my mother interrupted him.

"You'll have to earn your keep somehow. You can't eat silver unless you want to turn as blue as the river with the poison of it."

Amberline looked up at her, blinking as if he just woke up, the sunshine bathing his face.

"You better come and learn how to make baskets then to earn your keep."

* * *

All afternoon my mother, Amberline and I sat under a nearby yew and my mother and I watched as Amberline fumbled with the strands of dogweed and hazel, and though his frustrations mounted he kept them to himself and only released them with a muffled sigh. We didn't talk as my mother and I usually did, but kept to our own thoughts, having Amberline amongst us. My mother with quiet instruction made him undo any mistakes and he like an obedient student learned his lesson quickly, and soon a basket took shape beneath his fingers, his hand nicked and bloodied by the whipping of the dogwood. When he finally had finished one, each strand braided around the top, my mother and I had completed several baskets each, but my mother's instruction had softened as the day wore on. She took his finished basket in her hands and held it up to the light and, noticing the gaps between the weave, said nothing but pushed them down with her nail.

That night a light rain fell, the rhythmic pattering on the *vardo* roof sending both my parents to sleep quickly, but I lay awake listening to the sound of Amberline speaking in his dreams. I leaned closer to the floor to try to make out what he was saying, but the rain veiled his words. A drip started through the *vardo* roof, so I got up and placed the bowl we used to wash our utensils in beneath it and stood a moment and listened to each raindrop ring, a tiny bell. We had a bowl for everything – one for washing our faces, one for our meat, one for our towels, one for Jupiter, one for the washing of men's faces, one for the washing of ours. All the parts of our lives portioned into the size of a bowl, as constant as the curve of the stars above our heads. I lifted a finger and let a raindrop hit it, beading on the tip of it like a ball of mercury, precious as a pearl, before it dissolved and ran down my arm.

Amberline cried out and I froze. Jupiter whined beneath us, unhappily taking shelter from the rain with our guest. My father stirred and I leapt back into my bed and watched between lowered lids as he sat up and listened out through the rain but seemed to think nothing of it.

Before dawn we were up preparing to strike camp. The sky was as dark as the inside of a sleeper's eyelid, but I saw Amberline's fine boots just beneath the *vardo*, protected from the night-time rain. He lay quietly sleeping as we struck camp, our footsteps around him busy, Jupiter dancing around my father's feet as he secured the *vardo* to the horse, the horse whinnying in complaint. Amberline woke up.

"Come along, lad," my father said and offered his hand to help him out from beneath the *vardo*, dirt brushing the elbows of his coat jacket, Jupiter's hair clinging to his trousers. "It's time for us to be going."

My father stepped up to the *vardo* driver's seat and Jupiter ambled up behind him, ready for the fresh morning air to blow against his fur, his tongue dangling to taste the disappearing raindrops. Amberline rubbed his face, the sound his new beard made making him frown. He reached over and pulled on his immaculate boots, the one clean thing on him.

"We should have left you sleeping and driven right over you," my mother said, uncharacteristically sharp, "and you'd never have noticed, Amberline Stark." She turned to look at me, before saying to him: "And maybe that would have been a good thing, to leave you behind." She didn't spare him a second glance as she stepped up to the front of the *vardo*, taking her place beside my father and picking up the reins. She gestured for me to follow suit and I did, sitting beside her and feeling her frustration come off her in waves.

"My apologies, is there anything I can do?" Amberline said, stretching up to his full height, dusting off his trousers.

"No, you just take your time and make yourself presentable," she said and clicked her tongue, sending our horse stepping forward. The pots and pans, the horse brasses, my mother's earrings, all jangled and Amberline hurried forward, my father reaching out to him to hoist him up.

SIX

Patrin, 1818

When the sun rose it seemed that the rain had made the countryside a jewel box – all the greens of the fields were emerald, the horse's dappled back all tiger's eye and quartz, the sky turquoise. We stopped when the sun was at its highest and broke our fast, apples and bread and cheese, and water for the horse, before we travelled on, my father occasionally whistling or calling Jupiter, a black and white streak, back from bounding after a rabbit in the undergrowth. All the while the horse brasses jingled against each other and I felt Amberline's proximity and listened to the music of his voice as my father asked him of London, but Amberline was rather short on any answer that held much information.

We heard it before we reached it, the whistles and shouts, someone playing a fiddle, it rose up to our ears and my father didn't need to coax our horse to go faster, she'd already made up her own mind, knowing there was the promise of oats. Her feet struck out off the road and pulled the wagon faster than she had the whole journey, making my father laugh his deep bass.

From all across the country a hundred or so Rom had arrived with their horses, all groomed and hooves blacked. Their *vardos* dotted the field and several fires were already burning; the smell of meat cooking made Amberline's stomach growl and my mother raised her eyebrows, but said nothing.

"Father," a voice called and out strode my brother, a good ten years older than I, his hair pulled behind his head with a leather tie, a fine waistcoat embroidered all over by his wife's fine fingers. My other brother had been delayed, his wife approaching labour.

"Balthazar!" my father said, stepping over Amberline and handing him the reins, before he jumped down and embraced my brother. The reins sat like straps of liquorice in Amberline's hands and he stared at them, unsure what to do. My mother snatched them up and stepped over me, placing them in my hands, so that Amberline and I were left sitting on the bench together. He shuffled closer, I felt the heat coming from his leg, and he leaned towards me.

"What is this place?" he whispered, his eyes scanning the fair in front of him. I tried to see it through his outsider eyes and was surprised what chaos it appeared – all the saddleless riders racing down the stream, sending splashes every which way. A group of shoeless children kicking a ball made of bound rags. Old Grandma Lee, sitting on the step of her *vardo*, a hundred years in the shade, a corncob pipe between her teeth and surveying all her kin. Seeing things through his eyes, it all seemed strange. All of us were tatterdemalion compared to the likes of him.

"It's a horse fair is all," I said, my blood rising, stealing a glimpse at his face and expecting to find his smile pulled to a sneer, but he was just wide-eyed, curious. "Where Rom come to trade horses."

"But you've only one horse," he said and I couldn't suppress my laughter.

"We're not selling our horse, we just come to meet with family, for news, for trade. You say you are Rom, but you are not much of one."

"Oh, you are cruel, Patrin, cruel indeed," he said, smiling, and I took in his grinning face, his white teeth.

"You'll learn quick enough," I said, feeling my brother's eyes on me.

"Who is this you're talking to, Patrin?" my brother asked as I jumped down with Amberline following behind me. My father introduced them and my brother clasped his hand so hard that I saw the flicker of a wince on Amberline's face.

"Welcome, Cousin Stark," my brother said, then stood back and took in Amberline as we all had, frowning at his fine clothes and his city air and wondering how he fit in with us at all. Amberline looked at my brother, robust but not tall, like my father, but with a clean-shaven face, his wrists bound in leather cuffs, his waistcoat sewn with buttons made of coin, fine gold loops in his ears, his boots muddied up to his ankle. Amberline glanced down at his own boots, now blessed with mud also, and my brother and father led him off into the campground and I lost sight of them. My mother and I were left to strike camp by ourselves.

We spent the afternoon catching up on the news from the surrounding camp – a Heron girl had given birth to twins, a Boswell man had been arrested for horse theft, Old Grandma Lee had the ague but cured herself, for her knowledge of simples was unsurpassed by any of us – this we all learned, but all the women wanted to know was of Amberline, but Mother wouldn't answer their questions in front of me. She sent me down to the river with the bucket to gather water and I had no option than to dutifully do as I was asked, all their eyes stuck to my back like mayflies, waiting until I was out of earshot. The heat rose into my face, what was there to say that I wasn't allowed to hear? Why so secretive if he was allowed to sleep beneath our *vardo* a hand span and a few planks of wood between us each night, his breath co-mingling with ours?

The entire riverbank was muddied by the stamp of horses and had made the silt on the bottom rise, turning the water brown. My foot slipped and I almost landed on my rear, but I grabbed at the long grass and righted myself and made my way further downstream towards the willows. I was half tempted to circle around to the back of the camp to eavesdrop, but I knew it would be mostly speculation and gossip. I looked to the water and was startled by a pair of eyes watching me. A cloud passed over the sun, the water squelched through a hole in one of my boots as I stepped closer. It was an otter, his head above the water, and I laughed at my own fancies and he dipped his head below the surface, leaving the softest of ripples.

"I hope you are not laughing at me," a voice slurred from the curtain of willow branches and out stepped Amberline, his suit crumpled, his boots now as muddied as mine.

"I just saw an otter, that's all," I said and Amberline walked over to me, his breath smelling like a barrel of spilled ale. But the otter was long gone, only the V of his swim remained.

"I can't see it, but then I'm quite drunk as you can probably tell. Your father and brother filled my glass quicker than I was able to refuse them," he said and I knew that my brother would have wanted to test his mettle and to bring him down a notch. He stumbled trying to stand in one spot beside me.

"Come sit for a bit," I said. "Here, let me take your arm." And I curled my fingers around his arm and felt the solid warmth of him. I led him beneath the curtain of the willows and held his arm as he tripped on the roots and sat down, then a rich boom of laughter made the tree shed its birds. I ducked beneath the willow with my bucket and came back from the river with it full. Amberline's eyes were closed when I returned and he was beautiful. His lips were partly open, red as the berry from the yew. His eyes opened and took in the bucket.

"You're not going to tip that all over me again, are you?" he said and it was my turn to laugh. I scooped my hand into the bucket and held it to his lips and he drank and drank again, his lips remaining on my skin when the water had all gone. I did not want to pull my hand away.

He awkwardly took off his jacket and spread it beside him. "Come sit with me, Patrin, here, right here," he said, his hand outstretched, and I was self-conscious of my own dry and work-hardened hands next to his fine fingers.

"You are causing quite a stir, you know that?"

"How so?" he replied, his head lolling back against the trunk.

"No one can quite work out how you fit in, if you fit in at all."

He smiled. "Is that right?"

"That is right, so how about you tell me, since no one else will, I ..." But before I continued he pulled me to him and sealed up my mouth with his, engulfed in a kiss. The ground beneath me seemed to swirl. I pulled back and looked at him, wiping the kiss with the back of my hand.

"We are cousins," he said.

"How?" I said, startled, for I knew all my aunts and uncles and all my cousins, all my kin.

He looked at me, a soberness rising in him. "No one has told you?"

"Told me what?"

He took me in with those eyes that I couldn't recall anyone in our family having, blue as the summer sky reflected in a puddle, and he wavered, unsure of what to tell me. A strange feeling surged in my chest, it uncurled inside me like a green thing seeking the light, seeking his lips again on mine.

"Our mothers are sisters," he said and went to kiss me again, but I pulled away and scrutinised his face to catch him in the net of his lie, but there was no guile there, or if there was I didn't detect it.

I picked up the bucket and ducked my head beneath the willow's rippling branches and started to walk back to camp, my skirts kicking as wide as I could make them to create a distance between him and me, but he skipped to catch me up.

My cousin? Why would my parents conceal it? All my life

I'd not heard a word, and now my mother was set against him, treating him worse than a *gadjo*.

"How can I believe you? My mother has never mentioned her sister, never mentioned you. Why is that, do you think?" I said, my frustration rising as the water overlapped the rim of the bucket and hit my feet, the cold water seeping right through.

Amberline clutched my spare hand earnestly. "That, you'll have to ask her about, for it happened all before I was born."

All the way back to the camp I drew a map in my mind of all the things my mother had ever told me about our family, but I saw no path that led to a sister and her son.

The others had dispersed by the time I got back to our camp and my mother was at the fire, coaxing a flame, waiting for me. She looked at the half-full bucket and looked at me, but I wasn't going to tell her what had happened beneath a roof made of willow wands.

"So tell me about my aunt," I said matter-of-factly and put the bucket down on the ground, not caring if I was rough and more water splashed over the edge, I would be the one to go and fill it again anyway.

My mother blew at the embers and the fire leapt up and licked the kindling, sending a thin spiral of smoke wending up between us. "You know all your aunts, Patrin, spread across the country as they are, married into their husbands' families." She fed a few twigs onto the fire and, seeing the flames consume them, added the pieces of a branch.

"Even in London?"

She wiped her face with her hand and left a smudge.

"So you've spoken to my nephew, I see. What lies did he fill your head with?"

"No more than what your silence has," I said, and immediately regretted it for she began to cry, her tears hot and angry. The more she wiped them away the more smudge she made on her face. Her tears frightened me, I'd never seen her cry. I put my hand on her shoulder.

"I'm sorry, Mama," I said, "but he didn't tell me anything other than we were cousins and that his mother is your sister. The rest he knew nothing about." My mother spat on the ground then, all her tears drying up.

"If you believe that, then you are more a fool than I thought you were, Patrin."

"Well is it true?" I asked. I don't think I'd ever seen her so fierce.

"The day my sister left was the day she died for me. Let that be an end," my mother said.

"But Amberline …"

"He'll be finding other kin to stay with as soon as I can see fit," she said, and I felt Amberline's kiss flare on my lips and wondered if my mother could see it, for it had left its mark on me.

That night my father and Amberline didn't return until late. We heard them carousing like cockerels a few hours before dawn, their voices full of song. Jupiter was at their feet howling. My father stumbled up the *vardo* stairs and swore as he tripped in the darkness. I heard my mother sigh and roll over in her sleep and my father stumble in beside her, bringing with him the smell of spirits.

I listened as Amberline continued to sing, his voice as rich as honey. I heard him crawl beneath the *vardo*. I heard him hit his head, but he didn't curse, he just lay down and laughed.

In the morning Amberline was up before the rest of us, the water already boiling on the fire, waiting expectantly for us all. My mother said nothing but set to mixing the flour and water to make the bread that we ate, cooked in the coals.

"Good morning, thought you'd be in the land of nod from here until eternity," my father said to Amberline as Jupiter took leave of his place at the footstep of the *vardo* and danced around my father's feet.

"Thought that might be the case, so I tipped the ale out most of the time and filled with water," Amberline said, and my father paused before he roared with laughter.

"Aunt," Amberline said, and my mother's hands became stuck in the dough then she looked at him as if he was snow and her glare could melt him. "I have a gift for you."

My mother nodded and folded the dough into itself, pounded it with her fist, Amberline waited for her reply. She placed the bread in a tin and raked the coals with a shovel over it. Amberline took out the gift and held it out to her, her hands still covered in sticky flour, and she glanced at it and then glowered at him. My father sat down by the fire and filled his pipe, Jupiter's head resting on his thigh, his canine eyebrows almost human in their expressiveness as he watched my father's face and then my mother's. My mother tipped a little water from the bucket over her hands and dried them on her apron.

"I've no need of gifts from you," she said, filling the tin pot and hanging it over the fire. Amberline tried to catch my eye.

"It is in thanks for your hospitality," he said, and my father struck a match on his boot sole and lit his pipe.

"Sarah," my father said, and my mother stopped. Amberline stepped towards her and he placed the gift in her hands. It unwound as soon as she touched it, a woollen blue shawl with paisleys swimming around the border as plentiful as a school of fish. She fingered the fine weave and tried to disguise her admiration of it.

"Thank you, Amberline, but I can't accept such a fine gift," she said and folded it back up and handed it to him. He was crestfallen. He took the shawl and placed it on the *vardo* step.

"For you, Josiah, with my sincere thanks," Amberline said and he handed my father a knife, the blade engraved with swirls and curlicues. My father held it in his palm and let the light dance around the pattern.

"Thank you, Amberline," he said, standing up and slapping him in an embrace. He sat down and tested its blade on a branch, the bark separating like cream from butter.

"And for you, cousin," he said, stepping towards me and curling a pin into my hair, his fingers tangling as he tried to extract them. I found his fingers with my own and helped release them from the waves of my hair, and would not have let them go if not for my parents watching. I felt the top of the pin surrounded by a fanning crown of metal. I wanted to rush and look into the nearest shard of mirror to see my reflection, but I knew my mother wouldn't let me keep it.

"Thank you," I said, the colour flooding into my cheeks.

"Yes, very fine gifts, Amberline," my mother said. "One wonders how you found the money to pay for them."

Amberline's face went white and he turned to her. My father stood up and I was suddenly aware of the pin's point grazing against my scalp. I heard Amberline breathe.

"No money passed hands," he said.

"So you've a taste for your father's art then."

"Sarah," my father chided but she would have none of him.

"You're a thief," my mother said, goading him.

Amberline straightened his jacket collar and stood higher. "What my father did was no reflection on me," he said, "and I resent your implication."

"Implication?" my mother shouted back. "It's no implication, I called you a thief because I believe you to be one." The rest of the camp around us grew quiet, some peered out the nearby *vardo* windows to watch.

"Come now, Sarah," my father commanded, "let him explain. How did you come by such generous gifts, Amberline?"

"I traded the last of my handiwork, that is what I did. Though now I wonder whether that was wise," Amberline said quietly, looking steadily at my mother until she broke his gaze and stared at the shawl. Jupiter's nose was already at it, lifting the scent of it with his nostrils.

My father picked up the shawl and put it around my mother's shoulders, carefully smoothing out the creases with the palm of his hand. My mother kept her eyes lowered, her fingers brushing the soft fringe, and I knew that it was the finest shawl she would ever own.

"Well then, I give you my thanks," she said and I thought that was to be the end of it.

SEVEN

Patrin, 1818

As summer turned to autumn we travelled to the farm we worked on each year to harvest the hops alongside gypsies from across England. Still Amberline remained with us. Every time he looked at me I felt my lips burn, every time I saw my reflection I thought his kiss visible on my face, but there'd not been another. He kept a respectful distance, wanting to be accepted as one of us, as he learned how to be a good Rom.

The day after our arrival at the farm we rose at dawn and took a quick sup before we headed to the hops crib. Amberline looked up at the hops nodding on their bines, a moving cathedral of green blooms, and asked me where the ladders were to reach them in the heights above us. I laughed and pulled the wire that the bines had grown upon and showed Amberline how to pluck the hops' flowers, not their leaves, before letting them fall into the bin below. My mother and father worked alongside us as we cleared the avenue of hops, all hands to the task. Amberline's beautiful fingers grew stained, his clothes too, but he didn't care. He was all smiles and caught glances, his voice catching along with the picking songs *hop-o*.

The sun at the end of the day turned the whole world copper, even the water in the large buckets for washing was skimmed with lapping gold. Amberline waited his turn for the water, the sun burnishing him while my father washed first. I couldn't take my eyes off him, the outline of him gilded. The sun turned him into an idol. Jupiter's hairy feet danced in the splashes, the white hair on his underbelly turning dark with mud, sending a trail of mud up Amberline's trousers, but he didn't brush it away. His eyes were burning into mine. My mother was down at the river bathing and I was left to prepare a stew, slicing the rabbit meat from the sinew. Amberline stripped to the waist and dipped his whole head into the bucket. When he stood upright, a rainbow of droplets arced through the air, some hitting the flames and hissing, the water ran down his limbs, and I tried to avert my eyes. My father was towelling himself dry and shrugged on a clean shirt. Amberline flicked a palm full of water at me and I tried to conceal my smile as I bent my head to my task, the blade nicking my finger. I tossed a piece of rabbit into the pot and chanced to return his smile. My mother returned from the river, her skin all flushed, her newly washed hair covered with a damp scarf, Amberline's gift wrapped finely around her shoulders.

Amberline finished washing, the smell of soap filled the air. With the plentiful rivulets of mud, Jupiter rolled around, his feet in the air, his tongue lolling between his teeth, and we all laughed.

"Take that dog down to the river, Patrin, and give it a wash before you wash yourself, and before he turns the whole camp to muck," my mother said and I was glad to leave the rabbit to her hands.

I whistled and Jupiter came at my call. I gathered up my clean clothes and a piece of linen to dry myself, rescuing the soap from Jupiter's salivating tongue.

The sky had turned pink as blossom and the air still held its warmth as I walked down to the river, though I knew the water would make me gasp. The leaves of the poplars whispered, their undersides flicking silver and gold, a few trailing already on the ground as a *rooko-mengro* darted across my path. The squirrel was up and into the canopy of the nearest tree, the skittering of feet following close behind, the black and white blur of Jupiter at its heels. His bark echoed over the river and sent the ducks complaining into the reeds, though a heron wouldn't be moved, just stood on its yellow stalk legs and let the silver tail of a fish slide down its gullet.

"Down, boy," I commanded and Jupiter obliged, still looking at the tree and following all the whispering movements of the leaves with a ridiculous hope. He could catch a rat and a rabbit, but the squirrel was an animal beyond him. At catching a rat, he had no equal and neither did my father.

I removed my skirt and blouse and placed them on the top of the nearest bush, my clean blouse and linen to dry myself with also. My boots had grown so loose I just slipped my feet out.

In my shift I walked down to the shallowest part of the river and stepped in. I walked into the middle and sunk my head below the water and the cool seeped through my hair and into my scalp. Below the surface I saw the riverbed all made of smoothed pebbles, each as oval as an egg. I heard Jupiter's yap, but I ignored him, letting the water circle the space in my ears, enjoying the silence, until the pressure for another breath, but I was in no rush to leave the water. I rolled onto my back and let my hair open like a parasol around me in the water, my chemise following suit, and I felt as weightless as one of the silvery poplar leaves that crowded my vision. Jupiter barked again and I heard him splash into the shallows of the water.

"Stay, boy," I called out, not wanting to play, but that didn't silence him. "Jupiter," I scolded and then I heard the *chirr* of a magpie raising a complaint. I stood then and soaped myself, leaving my hair till last, and then I held my breath and dipped my head beneath the water several times until I saw that the foam of the soap no longer gathered on the surface. The river was like a cool dream. I would have spent the whole evening just floating, my muscles surrendered to the gentle current, the cool breeze skimming across the water. A dragonfly stopped the beating of its rainbowed wings and rested on my chest and I barely dared to breathe, its body as blue as the heart of flame.

Jupiter growled and I looked up and saw Amberline. He was standing a respectful distance from Jupiter's bared teeth.

"Patrin," he called out to me, the dragonfly abandoning its rest, and I was exposed and clutched my hands to my chest.

"What do you want?" I said, angry that he would take such a liberty with me.

He turned his back to me and called out over his shoulder, "I'm sorry, I'll let you finish and come back later. I just wanted to speak with you alone. I never get the chance with your mother and father watching my every movement."

"You'll be sorry if they catch you here," I said, striding out of the water and making for the piece of linen to dry myself hurriedly. I didn't want Amberline to see me looking like a drowned kitten, all matted hair, all pooling puddles. I pulled my skirt over my head and tied it around my waist, followed by my blouse that stuck to the damp of my arms; the stitching gave as I tugged at it.

"Patrin, are you still there?" he said, but didn't turn around and I could have picked up my boots and bolted like a deer back to camp before he even noticed, though I didn't.

"I'm here," I said, "you can turn around."

He stepped towards me and Jupiter started growling again. The magpie in the tree fell to the ground and started hopping territorially, a feathered adversary which only sent Jupiter into a frenzy.

"Jupiter," I commanded, "in the water." I didn't need to repeat it, he bounded into the depths, chasing the current and the eddy, his nose glistening.

Amberline laughed and it echoed all around us as he stepped closer towards me. "Patrin," he said, his voice choked in his throat, a redness coming into his cheeks, "I ..."

I stood and waited for him to speak, to clear the imaginary chicken bone from his throat, all the time my wet hair trickled all over me, rivulets down my back.

"Patrin," he tried again but grew exasperated with his words. He took the linen from my hands and I remembered his drunken kiss, but did he? Up close he smelled of sweat and sunshine; the heat came off him in waves as he turned me around and scooped up my hair with the cloth, carefully drying my hair for me in hanks, slowly pressing and squeezing until it released its water, his body pressed close to mine. This time it was my lips who sought his, his arms twining around me, we were pressed together like the leaves of a book.

Until Jupiter bounded out of the water and shook like the devil, sending hundreds of raindrops all over us and breaking whatever was gathering between us. I felt the laughter swell in me but Amberline's expression grew cold. Violently he kicked Jupiter in the ribs, the impact of his fine boot making a dull thud, leather on fur. With a high-pitched whine, Jupiter took to the undergrowth, a blur through the bracken. I stepped back, unsure of myself and of him. How did anyone change so quickly unless quicksilver ran in his veins instead of blood?

Amberline walked off to the camp ahead of me, gathering the kindling he had been sent to collect as he went. By the time I arrived back he was sitting next to my father, drinking from a mug of cider, his eyes to the flame, and Jupiter was nowhere to be seen. My father stood up and whistled for the dog, but he didn't come.

"Did he have his bath then, Patrin?" my father said and Amberline looked up at me.

"Yes, Father," I said, "but he seemed more intent on trying to catch a fish and roll around in the dirt than to come when I bid." As I said it, I was glad that the night sky was growing dark so only the evening star saw my shame burn from lying to my father. I put the soap back in the *vardo* and passed my mother lying down on the bed, her boots beside her, a cold cloth on her eyes, but I didn't want to disturb her and neither did she register my presence. The stew began to smell delicious, all the flavours merging together, but still she didn't move.

My father and Amberline helped themselves and I joined them, listening to the sound of the flames crackle. A cuckoo's two notes sounded from the nearest tree and my father's grey eyes raised up to look at it. Amberline continued eating undisturbed, his eyes seeking mine.

"Is Mother poorly?" I asked and my father nodded his head in the direction of the tree, the cuckoo sounding again.

"She's been lying down since that bird started singing, 'tis bad luck after midsummer," he said.

I put down my bowl, found the largest stone I could and pitched it into the nearby tree, all the leaves parting for it like a flaming comet across the night sky, until it hit the trunk. The bird shut up. I returned to my place by the fire, my father shaking his head at me and smiling.

"If only it was that easy," he said then wiped his mouth with the back of his hand and took a swig of ale. Amberline still sought my eye, but I wasn't going to willingly give it, not with my father present, not with Jupiter's whine still in my ears. We ate on in silence, but I felt the air growing colder, my hair still damp though Amberline had tried to dry it.

"Patrin," my father said, "Amberline has asked for your hand in marriage, would you accept him?" I dropped my eyes right to the heart of the flame, exposed. My mother's turn had more to do with this than a late-singing cuckoo.

Amberline stood, his shadow falling behind him. He reached his hand towards me and I knew what he had been trying to say back at the riverside, why his words had choked in his throat, his frustration at Jupiter.

"Patrin, I know I haven't much, not even a *vardo* or family to offer you, but we could start our own, if you consent to being my bride." In his palm I saw something shining, winking, silver as the moon. He unfurled it by the fire and I saw that it was a necklace of coins. My father blinked at Amberline, no doubt thinking the same thought as me, where had he got them from – but he said nothing, only uncorked a bottle of brandy and offered us each a swig. The liquor burned down my throat and made me want to retch, but Amberline drank his down as if it was water. This was my *pliasha*, my betrothal, the necklace of coins was to have been wrapped in a red silk handkerchief, brought by the groom's father, but Amberline's father was a mystery to me.

I lifted my still-damp hair and he placed the weight of the coin necklace on my chest. The necklace sat just below the *putsi*, the pouch that held the things that protected me, talismans of flower, rock, bone. The coins looked for all the world like something a queen should wear. Amberline offered me his hand and I took it.

"But Mother ..." I said.

"She'll come round," my father said.

Amberline closed my question with a kiss, his breath full of brandy fire.

* * *

The following morning the smell of bread woke me; my mother was at the fire blowing the cinders from the crust, the sky already a-blush.

"Mama?" I said and she turned around, her eyes full of tears.

"What does he have to offer you, Patrin? He has no family, no honour. His mother saw to that by marrying a *gadjo*. We took him in but at our peril." My mother wiped her tears away.

I stepped down from the *vardo*, the coins jingling on my chest, I was still not used to the weight of them. All night as I had turned trying to pursue sleep I had been woken by the tinkle of them. Some time in the early morning I had heard Amberline sigh loudly in his sleep and all I had thought of was that soon there would be no wooden floor between our bodies, there would be nothing between them but skin.

"Where is my father and Amberline, Mama?"

My mother stared towards the road leading from the hops farm. Over the rise of the road my father and Amberline came with the base of a wagon pulled between them, human drays. She set the bread down and grabbed my arms.

"Patrin, it's not too late to change your mind if it's something you don't want." Her thumb caressed my cheek. "There are other men who are a better match. Just say the word and we'll have an end to this."

Amberline's and my father's faces were red with exertion; a few of the other harvesters ran to help, the sound of their voices rising in the morning air towards us. Just seeing Amberline smile made me do the same, an invisible thread joining us together. He looked up at me and waved and I waved back, my mother watching all the while.

"Will you not give me your blessing, Mama?" I said and she stopped and put her hands on my shoulders and inspected my face, her eyes scrying every inch before she wrapped me in her arms and kissed my cheeks.

"Yes, my darling girl, if you will it." But her unease lingered with me.

EIGHT

Eglantine, 1833

When I was fourteen, my father made me his apprentice. The shine of his attention was on me and I felt myself grow like my name, becoming more briar than the rose.

After my lessons with Makepeace in the kitchen, my father led me out onto the street, my steps trying to keep up with his stride. I hurried, trying to avoid the horseshit and the spilled ale from a keg, the muddy streams, the grimy froth tipped from someone's washing, spoiled fruit, puddles and rough cobbles. All the while I glanced down at my own double reflection, the size of a teaspoon on the mirror surface of each leather shoe – free from ripple or blemish, two small faces. A pie man stood with his tray, whistled out his "Come all ye" and winked at me as I passed. We turned into the old lane, the well still standing amid the cobbles, to the door of our old home. The last time we had been here, my father had burned whatever remained before I could even touch it.

"Come, come," my father said, beckoning me through the door and into the room, but I hesitated, the room seeming so much smaller than I recalled, dark like a trap, but I did as I was told.

My father squeezed himself behind the table and flipped his coat-tails up as he sat down on a crate as if he were about to conjure music from the table's gouged surface, but he just rested his hands, his fingers splayed, his head lowered, composing himself. My heart was uneasy in his silence; I took surreptitious glances around the room. There was nothing from what was before except the crate and table, the chairs having been consigned to the flames. On top of the table was a small chest of drawers I'd never seen before, like the sort the apothecary kept. My gaze returned to my father, grey hair swirling down from his temple.

"Eglantine, my girl, my firstborn, this is your future, your inheritance, my little secret dolly house."

Dolly house? Was he making fun of me? In his face there wasn't a tinge of irony, all I saw was his pride. Dolly house? There were no dolls anywhere except the one in my pocket, no porcelain heads, no trays of arms and legs, no horsehair brushes and palettes of colour. No hanks of human hair or elfin-sized clothing. No wooden bodies. No pegs. The drawers were too small for all that, surely? My father was waiting for me to speak. The doll was in my hand at that moment. He cocked his head in my direction, eyebrows raised, but I brimmed with anger. What doll's house?

"Ain't no dolls here, Father," I said, the hairs on the back of my neck rising. My father laughed then, a great big bellow that incensed me. I slapped the table but this made him laugh all the more.

"And dolls ain't your inheritance, all you need is the velvet touch," he said and he peeled open my fist, examining the length of my fingers. "Your inheritance is in your hands, just like mine." My father dropped my hands and I watched in wonder as he proceeded to pull out and name jewels from my hair, my neck, my sleeve with his sleight of hand – diamond, ruby, sapphire, amethyst, tourmaline, pearl – their names incantations. I reached my hand in to touch one but my father brushed away my fingers.

"Who owns these jewels?" I said.

"People who didn't take care of them well enough. Pick one, whatever catches your fancy." My fingers hovered over the stones, the light sending a sparkle through their facets, coloured fire on my skin. I picked up the sunniest stone, a brooch like a sunflower, petals shaped in diamonds, and handed it to him.

"Yellow diamond, surrounded by white, marquise cut. Mounted in gold. That is what the constable's report will say." I pulled my fingers away as if the stones were ice. My father was a thief? All that we had was built on someone else's loss?

He pulled out a roll of tools, carefully selecting a pair of fine pliers. He peeled back the prongs and released a yellow diamond so it fell into his palm like an apricot stone. The other settings followed suit. The fire was burning in the grate but something about it filled me with unease. The smoke stung my eyes. He threw the gold setting bereft of stone into a little leaden pot sat on top of the flame, the gold setting like insect legs dissolving before my eyes, until all that remained was a small puddle of gold. My father strapped a leather glove onto his hand and gingerly poured the gold into a mould he had laid out, the heat from the burner rouging his cheeks, a moustache of perspiration beading on his upper lip. He doused the flame in a bucket of sand.

"What now?" I said, unsure what this display meant.

"This is our trade, my girl. We take what is stolen and turn it into something else and sell it back as supplies to the jewellers. The original is untraceable of course."

"But why?"

My father shucked off the glove, clutched my hands and spread my fingers to inspect them.

"You have the Stark hands, long fingers. If we were another family I would have thought you'd a talent for the piano."

I snatched my hands away and looked at them, imagining them upon ivory, but they weren't fine enough for that. I curled them into a fist. My father reached out, took my hands back into his and blew onto them as if they were merely daisy-clocks and he the wind, readying them for the opening.

"How?" I said.

"Don't you remember all those games we've played? Hiding and seeking with these fingers? You were born into it, my dear girl. You have that little doll still, the one you keep in your pocket?"

I nodded, exposed. The doll with her painted curls and pointed little face was my solace, the thing that belonged solely to me and me alone. I had to resist the urge to pat my pocket to see if she was still there, the panic spread through my body that my father had, with his flighty fingers, relieved her from my person.

"Your doll was your first theft, Eglantine, but you were too young to remember."

I was confused: all my memories began with the house we lived in. Of Ada in her room, her poor swollen belly and her jewellery box. Makepeace in the kitchen. My father's game of the handkerchiefs. If I tried to think beyond it, to the time when I was smaller, there was nothing but fog. My Miss Poppet was stolen? I'd stolen her? No memory of such an event offered itself to me. She had always been with me, as much part of my body as my fingers.

"Now you've grown, who knows what you'll be capable of." He kissed my fingers proudly and ran his thumb over the lines on my palm. "It wouldn't surprise me if you had the lightness of touch to steal the royal sceptre." I felt the colour rise into my face, the heat from the fire running down my arms and into my fingers. "Come, let's see what you can do." His voice encouraged me, but yet I doubted.

My father stood, his eyes closed, and I stood with my hands weighted by my sides, the room heavy with his expectation. I couldn't see what it was my father saw in them, their promise hidden from my eyes.

"Come, Eglantine, trust your fingers, let them be your divining rod, whatever is in my pockets is your water," he said, and my fingers sang. His pocket watch was in my fingers, but my father just stood there, his eyes closed.

"Come, my girl, at least try," he said.

"Father," I said.

"Eglantine, you must trust yourself," he said and I spun the watch in my hands, twirling it on its chain. The light caught it and sent shards dancing across his eyelids. "Eglantine?" He opened his eyes and blinked. And he smiled, seeing the watch already dangling from my fingers.

My father took me by the elbow and led me out onto the street. A woman walked past us from the well, a tattered apron tied around her waist. She stared, but my father ignored her; he was smiling down at me and I felt the full force of his love and attention.

"Did you see anything on that woman that would draw your eye? That is the first lesson. Let your eyes do the work," my father said.

The woman continued on down the lane, the contents of her bucket breaking the surface with each step, sending droplets of crystalline water into the air. If only I could catch those and fix them, they would contain more than just light, but silver, diamond, pearl. The woman turned and looked at me then spat on the ground. "Gypsy brat," I heard her say before disappearing around a corner. Her spit wobbled on the ground.

"Why did she say that? Who is she?" I said. The way she said the words burnt my cheeks.

My father continued his steady pace, patting my hand, but would not answer me. I kept hearing her words, *gypsy-brat, gypsy-brat, gypsy-brat* in each toe tap of his shoe. My father lifted my chin with his finger and saw me frowning. "Pay her no heed, Eglantine, it is jealousy that makes her say such things.

Look at us, what don't we have that we can't take for ourselves? The world is our oyster, my girl, and with our bare hands we will open it."

My father led me through the streets until I was disoriented and I held on to his elbow as if it were my anchor. He led me to a street that was lined with bookstalls; all the books and pamphlets were arranged on tables, and spread around them, like pigeons at crumbs, were city clerks, browsing pages. "Watch closely, Eglantine, look first, reach second, vanish third." I saw fob chains, the gaping lining of pockets, the silk thread trailing from a misplaced handkerchief; I was browsing people as they were browsing the pages of the books.

"Pick one," my father said, "and I'll wait for you here. Don't run, just walk. All will be well."

The books, the clerks, their pockets, made me dizzy. "Pick one?" I echoed, and my father's face clouded.

"Pick a pocket," he said, and I heard the shadow of disappointment in his voice.

I walked towards the young men in their suits and they took no notice of the likes of me, dark-haired in my plain clothes, following my father's footsteps, *gypsy-brat* still ringing in my ears. A young man with a pince-nez, his nose hidden in a book, was midway down the table, his hand on his hip, oblivious. I saw his pocket wide as a mouth, his handkerchief tip sticking out like a cat's tongue at the cream. I looked at my father. He'd picked up a book himself and appeared to be absorbed in the words, though I knew he was not a man for letters; he caught my eyes and nodded me onward. Quickly I lurched forward and plucked the tip of the handkerchief, but I was too fast, my movements too clumsy, I bumped into him enough to draw his attention from the book to me, to my hand on his handkerchief. His eyes appeared blue and huge in the reflection of the pince-nez and time was suspended. What did he see? A lady, baby, gypsy, queen? A girl, a thief, a gypsy brat?

"Sorry, sir, is this yours?" I said and hoped my voice didn't betray me as I held out to him his handkerchief as a peace offering. He took it from my hands and returned to his book. My hands were shaking. Where was the power of my fingers now? Where was their dexterity as my father had promised me? My father didn't meet my eyes but carefully put the book down and walked towards me, his face all frown, his disappointment bearing down on me. I couldn't breathe.

I felt the need to run, my feet called for it, to hit the road. How was this be my inheritance, how could he even ask me? His voice was in my ears, calling me, but I ran.

The whole of London spread before me like a body of water and I timid at its edge. At the end of the street the world roared up at me, a street seller's voice crying out above it all – "*Milko, Milko, Fish, Fisho, Dust, Dusto*" – my feet ran to the music of it. The sounds of commotion behind me were quickly replaced with the sound of my own heartbeat, the rolling drums of an execution. I ran through the swill and horseshit, puddles engulfing my boots, the liquid seeping in past my stockings, chilling my bones. The faces I passed were greasy streaks, their voices but a common roar. I ran until nothing seemed familiar, except the river, a constant.

Sunlight split through the clouds and something twined around my chest, a memory, the calling of the water, the call of my mother's voice. My face was a furnace, all I wanted was to be cool.

I slipped my shoes off and rolled off my stockings, the cold rushed around my legs, the pebbles and dirt clinging to the soles of my feet. The first step into the water made me gasp, the current caressing my skin, making me want to walk in until only my neck remained above the water. I held it in my hand and the water trickled through, clear fingers to my flesh ones. The water came up to my thighs and ballooned my skirts around me. I went deeper still, and then taking a big gulp of air, I dipped my head below the surface and looked through the gloom at the light as it sliced through the surface, hitting the orange paddle of a swan's foot.

The bird was upon me, her wings summoning the air, whipping the water, her long neck snaking forward hissing at my face. I tried to back away but the swan lunged again, its wings high and holy like an angel's, brushing at my face. The beak and wings buffeted me between feather and water. The swan clacked its beak close to my ear, enclosing me in its wings, until I heard a voice in my ears: *Be still*. That is all the swan wanted, my stillness, and that I could give. The swan's beak snapped at my hair, which seemed to tangle with each clack, and I watched it beneath my eyelashes, frightened to look it in the eye. Once it had finished grooming my hair, it rested its head on my shoulder, damp down soft on my chin, its breast feathers warm against my own chest as the current swayed around us. I heard the swan breathing, the river breathing, my own heartbeat stilled by the waters enclosing around me, when I heard a voice coming from no direction in particular: *My Riverling. Riverling, Riverling*, until I doubted myself as to whether someone spoke at all or if it was just the sounds the water made as it swirled around me.

My father called me and I felt the whip of feathers and the whoosh in my ears as the swan flew away, the whistle of the pebble my father had thrown splashing and rippling in the water.

* * *

The house was silent except for the constant time-keeping of a clock. I put my hand on the banister and took the first step, the floor rushed up to me, the house rang like a bell in my ears, tick-heartbeat, tick-heartbeat, but I forced my feet onwards, hanging on to the banister, my lifeline. I was drenched through, wet and cold. The whole house was dark. I heard the words in my head, a voice running through the soles of my feet, words that I did not know but somehow understood: *patinor* – leave, *hoffeno* – liar, *Puvvo* – earth. My father barely met my eye, as if he was frightened of something strange looking back at him through me. My feet hummed with words.

Makepeace appeared out of nowhere and helped me shed my wet clothes and change into a dry shift. She brushed my hair back from my forehead before she exhaled, a burdened breath, and I braced myself, seeing myself in the pair of milky glasses perched on her nose like a cat's eyes glinting in the dark. The pad of her fingers ran themselves over the strange knotty lines around my throat, my birthmark angry from the water, and down my arms. I pulled away, not wanting her disapproving touch on my skin.

My doll fell out of my pocket and onto the floor, leaving her own damp stain. Makepeace's eyes followed her fall. I quickly retrieved Miss Poppet. I knew it was time to put childish things behind me, but Miss Poppet was the only possession I had from my time with my mother.

Makepeace pulled back the bed and bid me get in it, before she turned to close the sash window, stopping a gust of air slicing through the heat of the room. She tormented the fire with the poker.

I was restless to be up, to be out, to catch the world from the window, to see the comfort of the river. Returning to the dolly house again had unnerved me. It had never occurred to me how my father made his way in the world; he came and went with his own business and Makepeace and I remained at home. I looked at my own hands, the wrinkles of the water still pruned my fingertips. My father expected so much from them.

Makepeace pulled a needle from her chatelaine, plied the blunt end beneath my nails and cleared the silt from there, her touch as familiar as a mother's, but it lent no reassurance. Was she as much my father's tool as he expected my hands to be?

Makepeace never gave anything away. Did she know how my father provided for her keep and mine?

Her touch was gentle as she methodically swiped the needle beneath my nails, her eyes large behind her glasses. The dirt she harvested fell into her apron; when she had collected it all and my nails were as shells, she tossed the dirt into the flames, whispering something beneath her breath. She was as familiar to me as my own shadow, always nearby, so close and constant that I'd never stopped to see her as someone apart from me or my father. Yet here she was. It was Makepeace who had shepherded me in the days after Ada's death, shielding me from my father's grief. It was Makepeace who had taught me my letters and comforted me in the night when I called for my own mother, though I had no memory of her face. It was Makepeace who had tried to fill her absence.

"What happened to you, child? Always a magnet for the water you are," she said and the fireplace hissed as raindrops scattered down the chimney.

I should have said the water was a magnet for me. I heard the voice in my head again, the one I heard in the river, soft as a whisper. *Prey o pani*, it said. The river.

"*Prey o pani*," I said.

Makepeace turned to stare at me.

"What did you say?"

"*Prey o pani*," I said, growing in confidence, the words pulsing beneath my skin with their own heat.

"What do you recall of your mother?" Makepeace said abruptly, her fingers tangling themselves in her chatelaine, all of it jangling. I turned over to face the wall and let my back speak to her. My memories were my own. I'd not give them up to her because she asked me, they were fragile, thin as gossamer. I myself only looked at them slantwise, as if to reach and touch them front on would make them disappear.

"She was a gypsy," Makepeace said, "those are Rom words." All my skin prickled.

"What do you mean?" I said, not wanting to turn over, not wanting to look at her.

"She was a traveller, a Rom," Makepeace said.

All of me was hot. All of me was angry. "Am I Rom?"

"In blood only," she said.

My body emptied and filled with water, like a shell on the edge of the sand at the turning tide. I eased myself up in the bed, eager to know more, to be up, but she wouldn't let me free myself from the covers, her familiar hand steadying my legs.

"Not yet, Eglantine, it's time to rest," she said.

"Tell me about my mother," I demanded and watched her face colour; the heat rushed to my own face, my question a ripple of discomfort between us. I scratched at the birthmark around my neck and it began to sting.

She rubbed her face, wiping the tiredness from her eyes, and I watched her sift through her thoughts. She picked up a glass of water and held it up to my lips and bade me drink, but it wouldn't extinguish my question.

"Her name was Patrin," she said, lowering her voice, glancing to the door.

"What does that mean?" I said and Makepeace took a jar of salve and lifted the cork from its top, the smell of it filling the room.

"It means leaf," she said, scooping the salve from the jar and warming it between her fingers.

"Leaf?" She put her hands on my skin and began to rub the salve in, cold as river mud across the raised and angry marks on my throat. I caught my breath at the relief of the salve and of hearing my mother's name.

"Leaf. But it means more. A patrin is a special sign for the Romany people, a signpost. Sometimes a bunch of twigs tied to a tree, sometimes a mark etched in bark. A way for us to communicate, a map, a message, a story," she said, not meeting my eye.

She said so many things I didn't understand. "Romany?"

"Gypsy. Travellers. Those who prefer to live the life of the road."

"Are you Romany?" I said. She wiped her hands on her apron and nodded.

"Once," she said.

"And Father too?"

"I suppose so, yes." Her voice grew quieter.

"But we live in a house?" I said, more confused than ever. "How so, if we belong on the road?"

"Those times are long gone, Eglantine."

"But I want to know more," I said.

Makepeace poured some liquid into a spoon, bid me open my mouth and I swallowed down its bitterness.

"What is there to tell you? What need do you have to know of the life on the road when you live in a house? The seasons no longer dictate, the weather no longer speaks, I've nothing to tell you, except that you are better off here," Makepeace said.

"But my mother never lived in this house, did she?" I asked, struggling to imagine the time before, but nothing came. From somewhere within the house a door slammed.

"Your father has bid me not to speak of her," she whispered. "I've said enough for the time being. Rest now, Eglantine." Makepeace kissed me on the forehead. Why would he not have anyone speak of her? All of me yearned to know more.

Makepeace found my doll in the bedclothes and brought her up to my arms. It was a familiar exchange, the clockwork of our arms, as Miss Poppet went from Makepeace's hands to mine, though I was probably too old for such things.

The rain started up again outside and it beat hard on the roof. *Pat-rin, Pat-rin.* Patrin, my mother's name. A million little round silverdrops, were they signposts for me?

My fingers kept time with the rain on the counterpane. How small they were compared to my father's expectations of them.

NINE

Patrin, 1818

The last day of harvest was the day of our wedding. Inside our *vardo* my mother strung a string with acorns over my head and unloosed my hair, before she crowned me with a wreath of iris. She anointed my wrists, neck and throat with attar of rose and led the way out of the *vardo*. Each of her gestures was slow and deliberate; I couldn't tell if it was because she was trying to delay me, or her actions held more meaning than I understood. She brushed my cheek with the back of her hand.

I took one last look at everything familiar – the old Persian rugs that decked the floor; our bedding that was rolled away; the pictures of the Virgin, Saint Sarah and Saint George that my mother kept dust-free even in the driest of summers; the hanging herbs of rosemary, yarrow, foxglove and rosehip all strung up to dry.

Outside on the fire a pig was on the spit, its flesh crackling to the flame; a barrel of scrumpy was open and ready to spill into the cup; and Amberline stood in the distance scuffing his boots and I knew he was nervous.

The other Rom from the camp came and gathered around then someone plucked a few notes on their fiddle and the notes spun around me. I felt disoriented, not being able to see Amberline amongst the throng that parted and clapped as I passed. The blood surged to my face, and I was grateful for the bluish twilight concealing my blush.

In a clear spot my father and Amberline waited and I moved towards the chairs meant for us. My father tore two pieces of bread and placed one on my knee and one on Amberline's and then drew his knife. Amberline looked at me and my father guffawed, before he took my finger and then Amberline's to be pierced by the tip of his knife so that a bead of blood ripened, a perfect drop, to be sopped by the bread.

"Now eat," my father commanded and I bent to Amberline's knee and ate the bread and he did the same with mine, I felt his face tickle my knee through the weave of my skirt. My father bid us rise then, the necklace of coins jingling, and he tied a scarf over my hair, a *diklo*, the badge of all married women.

"Welcome, Patrin and Amberline Stark," my father cried, crushed us in his arms and all around us the other Rom let out a cheer. The firelight struck the world golden – Amberline's face shining most of all. Someone threw salt over us and it caught in my lip just as Amberline kissed me so it was like swallowing the sea.

Around us the dancing started. We were swept up into it and I danced in and out of so many arms, my face growing hot, until I landed back in Amberline's arms. As soon as we were near the outskirts of the fire, he pulled my arm and we were off over the fields, our feet hitting puddles and disturbing the songbirds in the hedgerow, skidding in the mud and laughing, but not falling. The sound of the river was like a voice calling and I stopped in my tracks and Amberline followed suit.

"Second thoughts or second sight?" he said and the scrumpy roiled in my stomach, but still I felt the voice of the river in my ears and I tried to quell my dizziness.

"Neither," I lied, for the river was calling to me, speaking, but I did not understand the language of water. My breath was lost. Amberline clutched me under the arms, then took me towards the water and sat me down on the damp grass. He took the scarf from my hair, dragged it through the water and placed it on my eyes yet I heard the voice louder than before in my own ears, all vowels, before I vomited on the grass.

When I woke, Amberline was resting by my side, one of his arms beneath my head as a pillow, the other thrown over me, his jacket covering us. I sat up, but we were no longer so close by the river and the voice had vanished.

Amberline sat up beside me and his hands moved through his jacket before he extracted something. Light flared in the darkness; he had a candle and it lit up the green of the tree branches we sheltered under. We sat on a blanket, but beneath that we were cushioned by moss, and he held a skin of water to my lips and I drank deep.

"That scrumpy is rough," he said and I laughed.

"I'd be glad never to taste it again," I said and drank once more.

"Come, give us a kiss," he said and suddenly I was exposed, shy, all the darkness watching. His fingers beneath my chin drew my lips to his and then his hands were on my blouse lifting it over my arms, my head. The cold tip of his finger outlined my breast and I slid his shirt off his shoulders. Gently he pushed me backward and rucked my skirt to my knees. The warmth and sweetness of his skin pressing on mine, all our breath together. Amberline's hands twined around my back and drew me towards him; my blood hummed like spring sap as the leaves brushed over our faces like fingertips, the *putsi* around my neck squashed between our chests, a third heart beating between us. "What is this thing you wear?" Amberline said, slight irritation in his voice.

I sat up. "Why are you frightened of a pouch?" I smiled, but he didn't smile back. "It's a *putsi*, to keep herbs and charms in, it can only do good," I said.

"Why, my love, I'll be your luck now," he said as he went to lift the *putsi* over my head, but I stayed his hand.

* * *

We remained in our green canopy until the morning came and pushed at our eyelids and then we straggled back to camp, not knowing if Amberline would come inside my parents' *vardo* or if I was expected now to sleep under it. The *vardo* wagon my father had secured had no roof nor bed yet, it was just bare wood, as unseasoned as I was to life as a married woman.

As we entered camp I saw Jupiter had returned, Amberline's eyes flicking warily between the dog and my father who had his back to us, the strike of his axe echoing out around us, a sickening thud. Jupiter was drowsing across the threshold of my parents' *vardo*, barring the step to anyone who'd dare enter. All his fur was matted and covered with burs and grass, his paws coated in mud. As soon as he saw Amberline he lifted his head, alert, his eyes following Amberline's every move.

My father strode towards us, his arms outstretched, when I saw it. Beside my parents' *vardo* was hitched another with a white horse tied by a rough rope. My father grinned at me and Amberline and I saw all the love in his face and realised that this was a gift for us, my *darro*, a home for Amberline and me, the wagon base now transformed.

"What do you think?" he said. I threw my arms around his neck and he lifted me off the ground with his strong arms and twirled me as if I was nothing more than a wee girl.

"Thank you, Papa," I said, all my feelings welling to the surface, an anxiety falling over me so that I didn't want to let him go.

Amberline's face was blank, I couldn't read him. "Thank you, Josiah," he said, parrot fashion, shaking my father's hand.

"You'll see it's all new. I hope it is to your liking?" my father said, but Amberline just nodded. My mother saw what I saw, but I would not keep her gaze. I stepped up into the *vardo* and saw how much my father had invested in us, beds and cupboards fixed to the walls, with new fine china just waiting to be used. The little windows had curtains made of calico and there was a small woodstove with cast-iron rail. Amberline followed up behind me and kissed my cheek.

"It is modest," he said. I looked at him in disbelief at his ingratitude, his hands reaching up to touch the ceiling, stretching out to touch each of the walls, filling all the space with his dissatisfaction.

* * *

And so it was that Amberline and I began our married life, wrapped in each other's arms in our *vardo* as we travelled across the country with the rest, from farm to farm, bringing the harvest in, Amberline's body growing more muscular, beneath my touch. After the hops were in it was harvesting time for onions, and come November it was time to bring in the potatoes. When winter came we'd make do with whatever work to be had. For my father, it was rat-season.

My father, Josiah Scamp, came from a long line of royal ratcatchers. It was a title he had bestowed upon himself and no one complained, for it was a job that no one else cared to do. Jupiter sniffed them out or caught them by the tail or throat if the opportunity arose and my father would thwack the rodent across the back of the head with a small club. His father before him used to lay them out one by one, whiskery corpses all in a row upon the fine Turkey carpet, to the horror of the head housekeeper, who would pay him double to remove them quickly; my father didn't follow his father's example, however. Instead he placed the dead animals reverentially inside an old hemp sack and sold them to the neighbouring households who kept hounds for the hunt, the rats used as dog feed. Some ratcatchers preferred just to stun the rats and be left with a writhing sack to use for sport – dog versus rat – but at least with my father's method the rats were out of their misery before the dogs pierced their flesh. He was in demand at all the big houses.

We set off, the horse's reins in my hands, Amberline's leg pressing into mine, my mother walking behind to pick meadow herbs to sell as posies, gathering them up in her skirt so as to not damage the petals. Amberline grew bolder when he thought my mother was obscured by the *vardo* and leaned over and tried to steal a kiss; even though we were husband and wife, I was conscious of my mother being nearby. I turned my head and let him kiss the whip and rein of my hair.

My father had already set off while it was still dark. It was an honour to go to the big houses and my father liked to arrive as soon as the house awoke to take advantage of the last of the lingering darkness to set Jupiter amongst the hallways, the dog's finely tuned nose on the scent of the rats.

My father had left a patrin on the side of the road, a low-lying branch tied with a red thread, a sign that we were on the outskirts of royal lands and had free passage through the fields. Mother caught up with us and sat inside and tied her simples in ribbon. With a click of my tongue I directed the horse off the track, the low-lying branch tangling satisfyingly in Amberline's hair.

"What are you doing?" he said, flicking leaves from his hair, the horse easily pulling the *vardo* through the mud.

"Didn't you see my father's signs? His patrin?" I replied as we pushed forward through the woodland, a short cut to the big house where we'd been given permission to camp. Not all were so accommodating to our ways.

"Patrin," Amberline said, "it's your name."

Had his mother taught him nothing of our ways?

"It's more than that. It means leaf but is also the word for signs, for messages, for our people to communicate the way of the path ahead – my father's branch tied with string means to turn here, a branch broken in two, notched bark, a rag tied to a stick – all are patrin."

The horse's hooves kept a steady strike and I heard my mother whistling behind me. Somewhere in the treetops above me a cuckoo called, a fraudulent orphan for its devoted mother.

Amberline swept my hair off my face and I was compelled to look at him, those eyes that were promises. He cupped my face in his hands and breathed me in with his kiss. My breasts ached beneath my shift with each jolt of the wagon.

"You are my sign, my own patrin," he whispered, and the sunlight seemed to agree with him for the light burst through the leaf cover, sending tiny diamonds of light dancing across my face and hands.

On seeing my parents' *vardo*, we pulled into the field on the other side of the woods and watered the horse, before leading him up to the big house, his brasses polished bright and chiming together, his teeth ready to crop the royal clover. We walked up through the fields, passing a windbreak of elm trees; the house seemed to hide behind them like a blushing lady behind her fan. It was the largest house I'd ever seen. Father usually went up to the big house without us, while we waited out of sight in the woodland and made camp. But the last time we were at this house the maids had begged him to bring Mother, someone who saw a sweetheart's name written in the tea leaves, a fortune found in a palm, the face of a lost one gesturing in the surface of a mirror. My mother was only too glad to oblige, any extra money to get us through the winter was a blessing. Not that she didn't have the gift. She was able to read the signs of the faces of the clouds, the flight of birds, the broken stalks of a wheat field, but what was an art and what was a gift? She'd twine the two skills together. But what had she seen with Amberline? She would never tell me.

The building loomed ahead, solitary as an island. As we neared a low fog concealed our footsteps and rolled thick on the ground but didn't even touch the first floor of windows. We walked through the silhouetted trees and closer to the building but could not tell which was the front or which was the back, the whole facade grey. My neck strained to see where the building ended and the sky began. The house was leviathan. Our horse paused to snap a dandelion with his teeth before stepping onward. The morning light slashed across the windows of the building, hitting a sea of glass, each window as bright as a jewel, and I heard Amberline count quietly beneath his breath. My mother raised her eyes at me.

"I hope you are not counting how many silver spoons you can cram into your jacket pockets and how many ways you can run," she said. That stopped Amberline's counting.

"I'd never do such a thing, I'd never bring shame on your family after all the hospitality you've afforded me," he said, earnestly. But it was our family, he still held himself at one remove, and I saw my mother's expression: she was already tallying his would-be misdemeanours in her mind.

"Well, what you be counting for?" my mother asked suspiciously, sensing something of the lie in his voice.

"I'm counting windows, Aunt, I've never seen so many. They are made of sand and fire, to think of it, and here they all are clearer than a mirror. The marvel of it," Amberline said, his face lit with the morning sun as if the Lord had special favour for him.

My mother rolled her eyes for my benefit. "*Dinneleskoe* or *diviou*." Foolish or mad. Amberline avoided her eye, he knew a Romany insult when he heard one.

As we walked around the outskirts of the rest of the building I caught a face looking back at us from the prison of glass. Was it a *bavol-engro*, a wind fellow, a ghost? A slim hand shielding her eyes against the piercing light proved her human after all. The horse's ears swivelled and the face disappeared back behind the golden surface.

Father was at the entrance on the other side of the house, retrieving a stunned rat from the confines of Jupiter's jaw, the white hair around the dog's mouth starting to stain. My father

wrung the rat's neck and tossed it into the sack. Already two full
sacks had been knotted and leaned head to head in condolence.
My father gave Jupiter a joyful rub of the ears and wiped his
hands upon his apron, before greeting us, his hands covered in
fine red-thread scratches. The smell of the rats made my stomach
roll and I willed myself not to be sick.

"Come now, Amberline, time to roll up your sleeves." My
father slapped him across the back and Amberline laughed,
thinking he had made a joke, but I knew my father. He stood
patiently waiting until Amberline's expression changed from
one of humour to one of disgust. Eventually Amberline carefully
rolled up his fine shirtsleeves as high as they would go, and I
feared Father would find him an unworthy accomplice.

"Patrin, lead your mother around to the door near the kitchen
garden, but tie the horse up first, we don't want him eating his
fill of their patch," my father said and walked off, Amberline
following unhappily behind.

I tied the horse with a double knot to a gate and he was happy
enough with the plush clover at his hooves, then Mother and I
made our way to the kitchen door to find the cook red-faced and
hot with a bunch of thyme in her hand.

"Come along, ladies," she said, standing back to let us
through. She smelled of onions and butter, as did the whole
kitchen – a whole tribe of women in starched aprons stirring,
serving, frying, slicing, more food than I'd seen in a lifetime. She
led us through the servants' dining room where another group
of women sat, elbows on tables, hurriedly eating their dinner
in a forced silence. All their eyes turned towards Mother and
me, and I felt our strangeness in our long red skirts and jackets,
our pierced ears, the mud on our boots. I touched my *putsi*
instinctively before I noticed the dirt beneath my fingernails. I
hid my hands in my skirts.

A chair was found for Mother and she sat down upon it,
her skirts falling over her mud-caked boots. I stood patiently

behind her as each servant waited to see who would be the first to thrust a coin in her hand and give their open palm. The herbs of her favours sat upon the table next to a posy grown in a hothouse, the smell of dog-rose scent twining into the air. But before Mother started, all the servants rose up in their chairs at the entrance of the head housekeeper, Mrs Davey, her skirt alive with keys.

"Would the young one please come with me," she said bluntly and I felt my blood run faster. What did she want with the likes of me? Mother gave her a piercing stare and nodded. I went with the head housekeeper, half expecting her to escort me by the elbow back outside or ask for me to empty my pockets, but she said nothing. And I followed.

The keys about her person jingled like a bit between a horse's teeth and she kept a steady pace, leading me through a door into a staircase that climbed upwards so that if she were to leave me there I'd have no idea of my way back to the kitchen. Questions flung around my mind but I knew better than to ask.

She led me through a door into a large draughty room, not at all what I imagined a room in a house like this would be like; it looked forgotten, abandoned. An old gilt mirror held the whole room in its reflection; in it I saw the face of the lady in the window. She was lying back against the sofa, her poor swollen feet pushing against the confines of her stockinged toes, stretching towards the small fire, the chimney barely able to suck. The housekeeper coughed and the lady's eyes snapped open – disoriented, half in the room, half in a dream, the sewing in her lap falling to the floor. The housekeeper had already turned on her heel and tinkled away, leaving us alone.

The lady rubbed her face with her hands, the dark curls gathered at her temples falling over her pale face like a bunch of grapes. She struggled to retrieve her sewing, her cheeks flushed from sitting too close to the fire, but I swooped in and gathered it up for her – a fine little red velvet gown, a pattern of stars picked out in golden thread at the hem. The touch of the fabric beneath my fingers was a revelation – softer than down, the colour richer than wine. Instinctively I touched it to my cheek, forgetting myself and where I was. The lady's outstretched hand waited patiently for me to return it.

"*Wilkommen*," she said and gestured for me to sit upon the stool in front of her. As I sat I saw the cause of her immobility: a baby in her belly, pushing against the fabric of her dress. Propped beside her a small doll, the glimmer of her black hair rippling with the firelight, little feet pointed towards the hearth.

The lady held out her palm to me and it hung in the air heavy between us. I was startled by the fineness of her skin, the diamonds upon her finger, the imploring expression upon her face. With great effort she reached further, and I leaned closer, taking her gentle hand in my calloused one, and touched all the roads, pathways and holloways of a life. I may not have had my mother's surety but I saw in her face as much as her palm what she wanted to hear.

"You will give birth to a bonny baby," I said quietly.

"*Kind*," she said and nodded. I lay my hands on her belly and felt the smooth tautness, the balloon of flesh and the life it held. Without warning, the unborn baby's hand struck out at my own and I drew my hand away faster than was polite, afraid, a cold thread of recognition twisting in me. The lady laughed and reached for my hand again and I submitted to the pressure of her soft hand guiding mine. Then I was struck with an image in the corner of my eye – the luminous glow of a golden ring, a crown, burning.

"Madam," I said hesitantly, "I think your baby will be a queen."

The lady peered earnestly into my face and, seeing no insincerity there, smiled.

"*Königin*," she said quietly to her belly. "My *kind*, my *schoen*." The way she patted her belly, the soft caress of her voice, made me uncomfortable, as though interrupting the enclosed circle of mother and child. The doll and myself were outside of it and together we stared into the distance, the poorer for it. Beside the lady's sewing was a tiny matching velvet gown the perfect size for the doll's little wooden limbs. With great effort the lady rose from her chair, taking my proffered hand for support.

"*Für gluck*," she said, folding a coin and a small piece of fabric into my hand. Could she tell? Did a life leap inside me like a salmon against the current?

The housekeeper quickly reappeared; perhaps she had been eavesdropping. I left the confines of that once grand chamber and followed the housekeeper down the maze of stairs, touching the softness of the nap of velvet all the way to the bottom where I concealed both coin and cloth in my *putsi*.

* * *

When my father had finished his work we walked back to the *vardos*, carrying the sacks slung over our shoulders, the sharp smell of them filling my nostrils and making my stomach whirl. Jupiter ran between my legs and barked, excited by the scent. I'd carried such sacks before and never felt such revulsion churn through my stomach. Amberline's footsteps fell in with mine as my mother and father walked on ahead, eager to get the camp struck before nightfall, the fire laid and roaring.

"Did you see it, Patrin?" he said reverentially.

"See what?" I looked over my shoulder at the night falling, the sky flushed as a baby's cheek, the first star sweet as a dimple.

"That house, that palace. The rooms, the damask, the silk, the silver plate, the carpets, the marble, the grandeur," he said breathlessly.

What could I say? All I'd seen was the rabbit warren of the staircase and the shabby interior of a once grand apartment that let in more of a draught than our humble *vardo*. I rubbed at the piece of rich velvet that the German duchess had given me, afraid.

TEN

Patrin, 1818

The following morning when I woke, weak light trickled in the window. I was alone in our *vardo*. Amberline's bedding was cold to the touch; the bile rose in my throat.

I slipped out of the *vardo*; my parents still hadn't stirred from theirs, though a scribble of smoke began to leak out of their flue. Our horse tossed his head at me and I followed the lead of his nose down towards the water.

And there Amberline was, by the stream, his shirt in one hand, a sliver of tallow in the other as he attended to the collar with a dip and a scrub, not surrendering his finely woven shirt to a threshing upon the river stones, not trusting me with his fine clothes.

I watched him from behind the willow, the fronds obscuring me like a waterfall. Dip and scrub, dip and scrub, muttering under his breath all the while, the sound of his words carried away on the water. His coat already lay across the thorny side of a bush, waiting for the morning rays, sending the steam skywards. His boots sat beside him, a scrap of newspaper tucked inside ready for the buff of print.

"You know I can see you skulking there," he said without looking up. "I've the fox's sight."

I felt his voice on my skin as he caught me out, but I didn't move, only stepped closer to the heart of the tree to watch him as he laid his newly washed shirt on the grass. He stood bare-chested before he broke through the green curtains of the willow and wound me into his arms, his lips seeking mine as much as mine sought his. He smelled like the earth, but I pushed him backwards, the blood rushing into my face.

"I thought you'd gone," I said and he looked at me and laughed.

"Patrin, Patrin," he said, unwinding my hair from its braid so that it rippled with the willow leaves.

"Is the *vardo* not good enough for you?" I asked, regretting it immediately the words left my mouth, suddenly ashamed. My father had spent a fortune on our *vardo*, for Amberline and me. I didn't tell him the bride usually moves in with the husband's family, for all Amberline had brought with him were the clothes on his back.

He grabbed my hand and I wanted to extract it, but he held me firm.

"Patrin, listen to me. We could move to London," he said loudly, the boom of his voice echoing around the canopy, frightening the chorus from the birds. His admiration for the grand house and all its finery had made him covetous.

"Why would I go to London?" I answered. "There's nowhere to camp, the water comes from a pump and they throw their waste from the windows – it's hardly an enticing place."

"There's that to be sure, but there is also so much more, Patrin. The world doesn't end at the edge of your camp," he said and his chiding sent an angry rash of goose flesh across my arms. It was *our* camp now, my father had extended our hospitality, admitted him into our family and provided us with a home.

"London is the capital of the world, Patrin. If something you are looking for is not in London then it's nowhere. Why, just imagine if you will the Pleasure Gardens, the trees all lit up, music wafting out across the lawn, the ladies dressed in more silk than a mulberry forest can contain, shimmering like butterflies in and out of the shadows. Then there's the markets, Patrin; whatever you want you can buy. Imagine it, no more skinned rabbits tossed in stew, no wild onions and fallen fruit, the market makes an emperor of the common man. For a price you can buy anything from a basket of oranges to a pet peacock to enough velvet to make a gown three times over."

Instinctively I clutched at my *putsi* and tried to ignore the sparrow that chirped above us in alarm. His little voice resonated in my chest, *be-ware*, *be-ware*, but I closed my eyes and just let Amberline's words paint pictures behind my eyelids.

"And the jewels in the shop windows – why, the tears of angels are not more beautiful set in clusters of gold. I would set such clusters in your hair, Patrin, a crown of them, but they'd be nothing compared to your eyes."

He kissed me tenderly on the eyelids and that little voice in my head silenced. Whatever signs presented themselves to me, I was blind to reading them. Even my own body spoke to me in a language I didn't understand. My breasts ached. Everything smelled rotten. Everything I tasted was ash. I was unable to read my namesake patrin, the leaves, sticks and stones that directed my own life. Even a duchess had more insight into the workings of my own womb than I did.

* * *

As my belly grew Amberline became more erratic and critical of all the things my father had provided for us. It was not uncommon for me to wake in the night and find him not there. I'd lie awake listening for his return, marked by Jupiter's low growl followed by a swift whine as Amberline's boot made its mark in his ribs. He'd enter the *vardo* and drop down beside me in his clothes and fall fast asleep. Sometimes he smelled of smoke or wine, other times of grass or manure. But in the morning he'd scrubbed his suit clean. Then things started appearing in the *vardo* unexpectedly, the cupboard filling with china, a ring of gold around the rim, a fine coverlet for the baby to come made with down, and a fine bridle for our horse.

He spent his days over the fire with a bellows, coaxing the flame to grow hotter while he melted down whatever metal he lay his hands on, the coins from my necklace growing fewer as my belly grew. Inside an old iron pan he made the metal surrender to its liquid state and it lapped thin as a puddle from the moon before he poured it into a mould he had made.

"Stand back, Patrin," he ordered and he didn't have to ask twice as the heat from the fire roared on my cheeks and made the baby squirm against the confines of my belly as if she too were made of something shiny, something liquid, and was waiting to wrest into her final form.

Once the metal had cooled, Amberline would tap out whatever it was he had made, often a ring or a charm, and toss it into a bucket of river water, a hiss of hot complaint before it was back in his palm. From his pocket he unrolled a cloth where all his fine tools were kept, then gouged the tool's ready tip into the newly formed metal, and I shivered at the marks he made on the pure surface, scrolls and curlicues and leaves all at his command. Spirals of silver dropped like seed into his cloth and Amberline carefully scooped up the shavings and put them in a small jar, to return to liquid later.

"Where did you learn such things?" I said as a magpie flew close to us with his chittering. Amberline kicked a stone in its direction, so that I didn't even have time to say, "Good morning, Mr Magpie, and good morning to your family," for luck.

"Where do you think, Patrin?" he snapped and began the whole process over again, the flames rising at the snap and suck of the bellows. Every question I seemed to ask him had the answer of London. My father was splitting a log nearby with deft heavy strokes.

"Let the man work, Patrin, and come with me up to the field, the farmer's expecting me," my father said as he laid down his axe and Jupiter leapt up from his place in the sunlight at my father's first footsteps. Mother was off selling pegs she'd whittled. I was glad to be clear of Amberline's mood which grew more mercurial.

My father walked slower than his usual stride, allowing me to keep up, but try as I might I still puffed away like a faulty bellows, my father lending me his arm on the steeper parts of ground. I pulled my shawl closer around me, the wind had the touch of ice.

The farmer was waiting for us in the field, the smoke from his pipe billowing towards us, the smell of the tobacco making me feel as if I would throw up. The field itself was lying fallow, the clods of earth dry and harrowed, thick with clay. He leaned on his shovel and watched us approach. Jupiter roared ahead, his feet kicking up dirt, and the farmer laughed.

"Good lad," he said and patted Jupiter's shaggy coat. "You wouldn't think of selling him to me, would you, Scamp? He'd make a good sheepdog yet," the farmer said.

"Not on the soul of the Baptist, Richards. If he wasn't a dog I'd have him baptised and given the family name, I'll not part with him," my father said and shook the farmer's hand. "You remember my daughter Patrin?"

Richards took my hand and shook it gently, his eyes on my belly. "Good day to you, miss," he said. "You brought your rod?" he directed to my father and my father took out the dowsing rod from inside his waistcoat, the wood stripped of all bark, and it sat lightly in his hands. "Well let's to it," said Richards and my father stood steady with his eyes closed until he jerked forward and we all followed the arrow of wood.

"When are you due, missy?" he asked me, and I knew though this baby was due in the summer she'd be early.

"End of June," I replied.

"Hard to believe it, I remember your mother carrying you across her front. Time is a fickle mistress." Jupiter reached up and licked the farmer's hand before he disappeared off into the hedgerow, his nose sensitive to the scent of a hare or hedgehog. "If he catches anything, we'll share it," Richards said. "And let's hope your father is quick." He surveyed his fields, the gathering clouds, all swollen with rain.

I think we walked all around the farm for the whole morning, the only water to be found was a light drizzle that barely did anything but net our hair. The farmer's wells had gone dry and the harvest had not been as plentiful as he'd hoped. To water the animals he'd taken to getting his boy to drive an hour to the river to bring back a barrel full, but that would hardly do once the snows set in.

The rod moved only very slightly in my father's hands, as if it was straining to hear a piece of far distant music, but try as my father might, he only led us in circles. "Lost the touch, Scamp?" Richards mocked. Jupiter came bounding back, his fur matted with leaves, but he'd found nothing either.

"You try, Patrin," my father said. The farmer raised his eyebrows at me and I resented it, superstitious and fearful, reminding me we were Rom and we were outsiders.

My father handed me the rod. The tip of the Y poked my belly and the farmer laughed and my father encouraged me with a nod. "I'll be up at the house, come get me if you find anything," Richards said with little faith, before giving Jupiter a scratch behind the ears. I watched him walk away towards the buildings in the distance. A cow lowed at us before returning to her grazing; Jupiter started towards her but my father brought him to heel.

"Now, Patrin, hold the wand out from your body a little, just let it sit in your hands. Let it lead you." I did as he said and took a tentative step, my breath like a wave in my head. My mind's eye went blank and I felt the nausea rise but bid it be. The wand started to move in my hand, jerking me forwards, like a rein does its mistress.

"Don't hold so tight," my father coaxed and I opened my eyes, but I was unable to loosen my grip, it was the only thing that stopped me from falling, this little fork of a branch, whittled by my father's hand. Jupiter bounded around my feet, excited by the sudden movement, and his bark echoed repetitively across the fields, sending a pair of jackdaws skyward.

"Patrin, slow down for goodness sake," my father said, trotting beside me to keep up, but I couldn't speak nor slow down. The wand hummed in my hand. I tripped over clods of earth, a stone, an old tree root, but the wand held me up, I was but a leaf on the wind. I don't know how long I was pulled along with the promise of water, a thin line of sweat breaking out on my father's lip and he a strong man. And all I craved was a drink of water from my father's skin but couldn't break my pace to drink from it.

"*Rockra, rockra*, speak, speak," my father began to shout, but I had no breath left for speaking. He tried to grab my elbow, but I was slippery as if my elbow was made of scales. I heard the water before I saw it and I wanted nothing more than to throw myself into it like into a lover's arms and feel myself quenched, borne up, made new. The river sang my name. A rushing sound filling all my senses, just as my father snatched the divining rod from my hand. He snapped it over his knee and then snapped it again and again until there was nothing but tiny kindling and I stopped walking, the hum gone from my palms. "*Prikasa*," he said underneath his breath and I stood blinking, the light suddenly too bright. Jupiter headed for the water but my father called him off, his face ashen.

"What was that, Father?" I said and he shook his head, not wanting to repeat it, but I suddenly heard it again in my head, *prikasa*, an omen.

"What do you mean, Father?" I looked around me and saw how close to the river we had come: the river was an hour away from Richards's farm but hadn't it only been moments that I held the wand in my hand?

"Come along now, my darling," he said and brought his arm around my shoulders. Yet as we walked away, the river still called my name, though I said nothing.

By the time we got back to camp the rain had already set in, but Amberline was still at his makeshift forge, cursing the rain and the clouds.

ELEVEN

Patrin, 1819

That winter was a wet one and the snow often turned to a grey slush, wedging the wheels of our *vardo* into muddy ruts. Father and Amberline had to put their shoulders to the back and push as Mother called the horse to pull. I was left in the unmanned *vardo* to wait, my hands resting on my growing belly. Sometimes a farmer would let us camp in a copse on his property and sometimes we kept to the back roads and wilder places and hoped that no one would come and move us on. Mother went from door to door selling besom brooms and pegs and baskets and telling a fortune or two for an extra coin. We spent more time inside the *vardo* with winter upon us, Amberline's hands always moving – polishing whatever he had made, rings or horse brasses, earrings or charms, the supply of his metal I never questioned. When I asked what they were for, he'd bristle, "I'll not be beholden to your father for much longer."

"How so?" I asked and he stopped moving and laid all he had made on the table. "Once I sell these and make more, I'll have enough," he said emphatically. But enough of what he wouldn't say.

Once the first daffodils pushed through the sodden loam, yellow promises of better weather, he began roaming at night again, his pockets jingling with coin as he stepped up into our *vardo*.

"Amberline?" I said, feeling sleep pull at my limbs.

"Hush," he said and kissed my forehead, the smell of ale on his lips. I heard him pour the money into a jar, hide it beneath the bed and I resolved that I should trust him, that he was somehow selling at the closest inns the things he made, saving to repay my father, saving for our child to be.

And come May she was born, spinning through my body like the pin in a compass, my little brightness, my little magpie, her eyes following all that shone, the sound of the river in our ears. When I first held her I was frightened, how could I love her, the risk of it, but then the love came crashing down on me, violent as a wave.

Eglantine. Little Egg. Mine.

Amberline made her a silver heart, my father made her a pair of tiny soft-soled boots and my mother made her a soft flannel gown embroidered with flowers, and she lit up our worlds.

* * *

Little Egg was only a few months old when the *shanglo*, the constables, came for my father. He was cradling her in his arms and singing to her soft and low by the fire, her fingers tangling in the bobbing of his beard, her big fire-lit eyes following the shape of his mouth. Amberline was at the axe, cutting wood, and Mother was stitching the holes in my father's linen. I was stirring the pot, the potatoes almost soft. They walked quietly into camp, Jupiter's low whine drawing our eyes to them before they saw us. Little Egg turned her little eyes to the gleam of their brass buttons.

My father stood up, Little Egg still in his arms, his shadow stretching out behind him, strong as a tree.

"Josiah Scamp?" the older constable asked, stepping closer, noting Amberline's hand on the axe, my hand near a knife and my mother's scissors for mending as if he were expecting us to use them against him. The younger constable put his hand on his truncheon.

"I am. State your name and business and be gone with you. This is common land, we have rights to camp here, but be assured we'll be gone in the morning."

"You are to come with us, Josiah Scamp."

"On what grounds?" my father said, standing taller, Little Egg starting to grow restless in his arms, yanking at his beard like a rope.

"For theft, you bleeding gypsy, now give the baby back to its mother and come along with us," the constable said. My father didn't move.

"Josiah?" my mother said, the sewing abandoned on the ground.

"On what proof?" Amberline stepped forward, the axe handle still gripped in his hand, but the constable still wouldn't be intimidated.

"On the proof we shall find soon enough," he said and set off towards our *vardo*, his muddy boots leaving marks all over the inside. I rushed over but Amberline stopped me, he was going to find what he was going to find. My parents shared a glance, all our drawers were opened, their contents shed, but nothing was found. My mother watched as the constable did the same in their *vardo*, but still the constable found nothing.

"Search under them," the older constable said and the younger did as he was bid, feeling under the frames of the *vardo*, again finding nothing.

Amberline stood beside me, his fingers closing and unclosing on the handle of the axe, and I willed him to put it down. Just as the constable was about to finish his search our horse began to grow skittish with the visitors, his feet sidestepping over the dirt; it was nothing, but it was enough to draw the constable's attention. Jupiter started barking the same three barks over and over and Little Egg began to cry. The constable walked towards the baskets between the *vardos* and toppled them over with his foot, finding what he sought. Bright gold watch cases falling to the ground, their fob chains clanking tails behind. Smugly he gathered them up and waved them in front of my father's face.

"They are not mine," my father said, his big arms around Little Egg as if they contained all the world.

"Do you recall how these came to be in your possession? Or do you need to read lines on the palm of your hand to recall?" The constable laughed, putting the watches in his pocket.

My father looked at all our faces, searchingly.

"Josiah?" my mother said again. She knew as well as I did that the likelihood of my father having stolen the pocket watches was as likely as the sun eclipsing the moon at that very moment.

His eyes stopped at Amberline and he spat on the ground; he knew as well as I did who had taken the watches. But then my father looked at me and then at Little Egg, gathering her features to his memory, embracing the steady little weight of her before he handed her into my safekeeping.

"If I'm not back in the morning, come and find me," my father said, before walking towards the constables, wedging himself between them like a fugitive, and off they walked together, concealed by the darkness.

* * *

We were up before dawn, my mother and I not speaking, but I knew what my mother wanted to say. All her questions she saved for Amberline but to no avail. He'd gone to ground as soon as the constables left, laying down the axe and disappearing into the woods without turning back. Not a word to me nor a glance at Little Egg. Part of me hoped that he'd already gone to right whatever wrong he had done, not thinking how.

Mother and I made our way to the lockup, Little Egg sleeping strapped on my chest, oblivious to the hand that fate had thrown us. Mother was allowed in first, fresh bread and some meat from the night before wrapped up in a cloth that she was made to break open first to prove there was nothing concealed in there, and I was made to wait outside, watching my own breath and Little Egg's cloud out of our mouths.

Mother was down there for some time. When she walked straight out of there ignoring me, I didn't know what I should do, run and keep up with her or stay until she returned. Would I be able to see my father?

I watched my mother's fierce walk and let her be before I knocked on the door and found myself admitted to the lockup.

The cell my father was in was damp, the very walls seemed to be weeping, stone covered in the velvet of moss. My father was standing, his head in his hands. The only light came from between the bars, the shape of unlit candles on the floor.

"I won't have my mind changed, so there's no point in arguing." He looked up at me and I saw his face contort with emotion upon seeing me.

"Papa?" I said, and Little Egg yawned on my chest, the sound of it so gentle and out of place.

"You shouldn't bring the little one here, 'tis no place for her."

"What do you mean, you'll not change your mind?" I said.

My father reached out a finger through the bars to stroke Little Egg's downy head, but he wouldn't be drawn into an answer.

"Trust in me, my darling girl, and take care of your mother," he said before ushering me away with his hand, "and take care of our dear little girl," his voice stark and bare. I took his hand and held it. I was as powerless as a child.

* * *

I walked back to camp, hearing shouting before I saw them. I clutched onto Little Egg and ran. Amberline was back and my mother had unleashed herself on him. Jupiter's bark grew louder and louder, a rabid frothing at his mouth.

"You let him be arrested, Amberline Stark. After everything he's done for you. It was against my better judgment that we gave you shelter. And I certainly was against your match to our daughter. Once the baby was born I thought that would be the tie that binds, but no, nothing is sacred to you." She swung back her hand and slapped him across the mouth. Amberline's hand flew to his face and between his fingers was blood.

Everything up to that moment had felt like I was asleep, but the sound of that slap woke me up. My days and nights had been parcelled up by Little Egg's needs, divided between her feeding and sleeping, so that my own thoughts had become narrowed, starting and ending with the opening and closing of her eyes. Amberline had stolen the watches, for the metal for the things he was making. But why had he let them take my father away?

"Amberline," I cried, the weight of what was about to unfold pressing down on me. "Amberline, you must say something."

My mother spat on the ground. "He'll not put out his own neck, Patrin, he'd rather your father's be broken for his crime than his own." She fell down sobbing in the grass, her skirt soaking up the dew as her blouse did her tears. Would it come to that? I wrapped my arms around Little Egg. Would it be either she lose a father or I?

"Amberline?" I said. "Can't you do something?"

His eyes were stone. "What can I do? If I say I did it, I'll hang. He's not been tried yet. His best hope is that the witness will not recognise him. But they'd recognise me all right. All I can do for your father is to give this place as much distance as I can. It will be worse for us all if they identify me, he'll be made my accomplice." Amberline stepped up into the *vardo* and shrugged on his coat, stuffing apples into his pockets, a knife into his belt.

"Believe me, Patrin, it's the only way," he said and jumped down from the *vardo*, kissing Little Egg on the head before squeezing my hand. My mother's lips moved quietly, deftly, and I knew it was no prayer on her lips but a curse, true and strong.

And like a tree split by lightning I was divided in two between the family that I was raised in and the family I had created, pulled apart by the strike of my husband. Whatever side I took, I would lose.

* * *

While my father remained locked up, awaiting his sentence, Amberline remained in hiding in the woods, the trees his bars, becoming more ragged by the day. When I went to collect water or kindling, he would appear, stepping out of the shadows of the trees like a *mulo*, a spirit of the dead, making me spill or drop whatever I held, grateful for the weave of fabric that kept Little Egg secure to my chest.

"My, she grows," he said one day, lifting Little Egg out of the shawl and cradling her, her soft little hand tangling in the beginnings of his straggly beard. He folded me into his body with his spare arm, not wanting to let either of us go.

"Amberline, you must do something," I said, pulling away. I could feel my desperation seeping out of me. Little Egg cried and my breasts leaked milk onto my blouse, two damp stains, but Amberline wouldn't return my daughter to my arms. The heat rose in me.

"What would you have me do, Patrin? Surrender myself? Then what? I'd never know my daughter," he said, his voice choked in his throat. He put his cheek against hers and she blinked back at me, her blue eyes the same as his.

"And you'd deprive a daughter of her father," I said emphatically, reaching out my arms for Little Egg to ease the flow of my milk. Amberline stood and stared at me, his eyes gripping mine, before he gently kissed Little Egg's lips and handed her to me. My nipple went into her mouth and she gave a contented snuffle.

"Which daughter, which father? It is the same weighted dice whichever way you throw it." And I knew he was right. It was either my father or Little Egg's father, but it wasn't a choice at all.

"Write a letter, confess your crime and flee, Amberline," I said. "They'll release him then."

"Flee to where? Where in this land doesn't the law stretch, Patrin? Tell me that," he said bitterly, and it struck me that when he arrived at our camp he'd probably already been on the run from the law.

"Why did you take the watches, Amberline? For what purpose? My father has provided everything we need."

"Was I never to strike out and become my own man, provide for my own family? I want more, Patrin, for all of us."

"Does he have to give his life for your crime, Amberline? Does he have to give you that? Will that satisfy you?"

"Would you rather us both dead?" His words hung in the air. He was right. There was no justice for the Rom. My father's silence kept us safe.

Little Egg kept suckling, my nipple cracked and aching, but I let her be.

TWELVE

Eglantine, 1833

My brush with the swan made my father wary of taking me out into the miasma of the streets, but it didn't stop my lessons, instead they doubled. I was his glittering thing, his jewel, his prize; being his apprentice had made me shine in a different light for him.

He decided that whatever woman I should become it would be at his hands, shaped for the world as he saw it. We were self-reliant, we would prevail. My father taught me the value of keeping a clean ledger, percentages, the principles of metal, the value of gold and silver. I learned the finger in the pocket, the lightness of the lift, the sign of a perfect mark. My fingers learned to be like small birds, in and out of his pocket with a bright catch between them. I was as clever a thief as I could be within the confines of our house, but I was yet untested.

Each night before I fell asleep, after I ran my fingers across my throat, the raised flesh of my birthmark, knotty like a scar, I twirled the doll in my hands and looked at the world through her ruby-glass earrings, as if through the petals of a rose. How did I steal Miss Poppet? She'd be like stealing a breath. Was my father right? Was this the destiny of my hands? To take what wasn't mine for us to live by? It had been my father's speed and wit that had housed me and clothed me and it was expected that I'd contribute and help pay my way. But what of those stolen from? Were they in turn supposed to steal to keep themselves in bread and shelter? Would not my hands have a more prudent use than to be the net of plenty my father imagined?

In the morning, while Makepeace stirred the porridge over the fire, my father had me practise my fingers dancing through his pockets, his face shaded by the growth of his beard, his eyes darkly watching each pass of my fingers, swatting them to his chest. Makepeace served up the porridge, her wooden spoon wiping the contents of her pot into our bowls. A large thick lump overreached my father's bowl and spilled onto his clothes. Disgusted, he stood up and the porridge rolled to the floor, Makepeace's eyes following it, before he left the kitchen, the telltale stamp of footsteps running up the stairs. My father's moods were as changeable as the light from across the river. I hurriedly ate a few spoons of porridge, listening to his movements through the house before my father called for me. Makepeace leaned down and wiped up the spilled porridge with a cloth. I swallowed my tea. My father was waiting for me.

Out on the street it was raining, but my father was undeterred, he walked on regardless with me at his side, his strides so long I had to double my step to keep up, leaping the worst of the puddles, but still I felt the water seep up through the stitching in the soles of my shoes, wicked into my stockings.

"Where are we going, Father?" I asked, raindrops falling into my mouth, but he wouldn't answer. I thought we were walking in the direction of the dollyshop and Old Sweet. The streets were changing around us, the river had turned to a blur of grey, the rain and cloud obscuring the horizon so that I didn't know where the sky ended and the land began, and when we stopped and I looked around I was disoriented. My father had led me to a high street; light from the shop windows glowed on the road as golden glitter. Noise roared from the public house as the door opened and dispersed as the door closed. Huddled in the doorway, sheltering from the rain, was an older woman in a red skirt, her shawl wrapped around a young boy. My eyes were drawn to his feet, the strange shape of his boots, until I realised that what I was looking at were his poor blackened feet and ankles. On seeing the woman and boy my father grabbed hard at my arm so that I felt his fingers squeeze through my clothing, clutching me to the very bone.

"Look away, Eglantine, avert your eyes," he said sternly, but I stared. I knew what they were, he didn't need to tell me, they were what my mother was. They were gypsy. My father pulled at my arm so hard I thought I'd cry out.

"Do you remember all I taught you, Eglantine?" he said, so that my mind whirred with all the lessons wrapped up in games, my hands the hunter, people's pockets my quarry, but I still couldn't keep my eyes from the gypsies, the Rom. The part of me that was my mother sung out to them, drew my eyes towards them.

The woman was neatly dressed in her red skirts and coat, a pair of silver earrings threaded through her ears. Her hair was tied up beneath a simple straw bonnet, knotted under her chin with a black velvet ribbon. The boy, too, wore a coat, with short trousers, though tattered at the hem. The woman's eyes burned into my father with curiosity, every inch of him she examined and assessed. My father walked towards them, the grip on my arm tight, until we were right beside them. My father's hand on the doorknob.

"Move," he said, but the woman held her head up, her spine straight.

"*Drabaneysapa!*" She spat at his shoes so that the phlegm sat there, a dull jewel. My father looked at it disgusted and shook it off into the rain and reached for the door to the public house so that the woman and boy were forced to step out into the rain. Even inside I felt the burn of their eyes on our backs.

"What did she say, Father? What was that word?" But he either wouldn't answer me or couldn't hear me in the roar of voices.

He found us a table, ordered a chop and ale and we sat in our own silence as we watched the hub around us.

"This is a regular stopping point for travellers on the coach, Eglantine. Everyone is just passing through." He was right, all the clusters of people were wedged in with their luggage like bookends holding them up on their tired journey, everyone except us. A man in a leather apron came and placed our food in front of us, the ale slopping onto the table, which he hurriedly wiped away with the flat of his palm onto the sticky floor. My father paid him and the man went back through the mess of people.

"Look at their faces, Eglantine," my father said. "All they are interested in is getting refreshments and meeting the next coach to get them to their destination. They are not keeping watch of their possessions, their portable property. They are too busy being portable property themselves." My father drank his ale slowly and carefully ate his chop so as to not get grease on his clothes. For food or portable property I had no appetite, all I thought of was that gypsy woman and boy in the doorway.

"Father, that woman, what did she say? She was gypsy, wasn't she?" My father now wiped his hands vigorously on his handkerchief and drained his ale.

"Maybe she was, but she's nothing to do with the likes of us, Eglantine, nothing at all."

"But my mother, she was gypsy, she was Rom," I said, the noise bubbling around me.

He'd not be able to ignore my question now. He kept wiping his hands though the grease was long gone from his fingers.

"I've not forgotten her," I said.

My father looked at me then and ran the back of his hand gently across my cheek with such surprising tenderness I felt tears spring to my eyes. I banished them with a blink. My father stood up and walked through the crowded inn, eel-slippery; as he passed between the travellers I barely saw his hands, nor the expression on his face. He made it to the bar and back again, taking his seat beside me, nodding at me to look at his hands beneath the table. In one hand he held a locket, in the other a small purse. He pulled up his trouser leg and deposited his haul into the confines of his sock.

No one noticed anything. No one called *Thief!*, all continued as before.

"Your turn, Eglantine," he said and smiled at me. I felt all the love he had for me push me on. I stood, uneasy on my own feet, and wove myself through the tangle of people. No one paid attention to me – what was I but a slip of a girl with her father for all anyone cared to see, absent of luggage, ready to easily lighten anyone of theirs. My eye was full of the shine, all I saw were the things I could take – a reticule; a watch chain; a pocket opening, the inside lined with coins like a nest with eggs. They were in my hands without thinking, the owner of them none the wiser. I walked back to my father, the smile on his face a beacon. My father's pride in me glowed in my chest as we left. The gypsy and the boy, long gone.

My father clasped my shoulder, with a quickness in his step. Around the corner he retrieved the locket and inspected it, finding a blonde curl of hair, which he promptly flicked into the oncoming path of a chandler's wagon. The hair disappeared into the tread of dirt and dust until it was gone and it made me uneasy. A baby's first curl. My father led me to Sweet's and pawned the locket, not of pure enough silver for him to bother melting it down; his pockets jangled with coin, an invisible tambourine for us to walk the beat to.

"What shall you have, Eglantine? What would you like for yourself? Name it and I'll get it for you. A reward for your first success," my father said, his voice full of brightness. But what I wanted was the truth about my mother but I knew he wouldn't give it to me if I asked.

"I'd like a new pair of boots," I said and my father grinned at me.

He walked me back to the house and left me to let myself in. I stood in the doorway as he walked down the street, the rain having lifted, turning the world to pearl.

Makepeace was waiting for me so I gave her the money Sweet had given us and she carefully placed it in her chatelaine. I set to waiting to see what my father would bring, but he didn't return.

At supper Makepeace and I ate very quietly in the kitchen, waiting for him, but he didn't come.

"What did your father say again?" Makepeace said, trying to hide the quaver in her voice; her fork waltzed around the plate, a solo dancer.

"He said he was off to buy some boots," I said and looked at the clock, hoping it had answers.

Come bedtime, my father still had not arrived home. I threw the covers off and made for the window to keep watch, the river dark with secrets. Not even a waterman crossed its surface or a barge, no lights shone except for the moon. The raised rope of my skin began to itch and burn and I couldn't resist the scratch.

When the morning came my neck was raw and my father still had not returned.

"Go to the dolly house and see if he's there," Makepeace said in the kitchen, the fire not lit in the grate during her all-night vigil.

"How do you know about it?" I said, feeling the cold seep through my clothes, making me feel exposed; my father's secret had now become mine and I felt the weight of it.

"How do you think, child? Your step-mother Ada's family owned this grand house and that sad one as well. There is nothing that goes on that I don't know about. Quick now, make yourself scarce," she said. The emotion in her voice alarmed me.

I walked the streets, scouring every man's face, shaded by a hat or not, but none was my father. The wind skipped across the river, sending spray into my face like a handful of stones.

It was at the dolly house door that I realised my father had the key. The lone window was dark with a curtain. I listened at the door before I knocked, but there was no reply. The burn around my neck hummed with its own heat and I was overcome with thirst. I walked the few steps to the well and bent over it, feeling the cool of the water calm my panic, but before I could drink I watched the ripple that I thought had been my own reflection transform into another's. I turned to look around, thinking someone stood behind me, but no one was there.

* * *

My father didn't appear that day or the next. Makepeace and I rattled around the house, alert to all perceptible sounds. On the third evening a mad knocking came at the front door and Makepeace swooped for the handle, her chair tipping over with a slap. I was at her side in an instant.

A small ragged boy stood on the doorstep with a piece of tattered paper in his hand. Behind him all the sounds of the river billowed while he stood waiting as Makepeace read, before she took a coin from the purse in her chatelaine and pressed it into his hand. The boy was gone from the doorstep and into the fog with barely an outline of him remaining.

Makepeace told me to get my coat on and I did as I was told. Father had been arrested and was being held at Newgate.

THIRTEEN

Patrin, 1819

The trial came and my father remained resolute: he would not implicate Amberline, and neither would Amberline confess his role in the theft. When the judge passed sentence my mother howled beside me. I felt myself disappear and grow transparent, faint as water. Her hand gripped my back. It was all that held me up.

The news of my father's sentence was a patrin of its own. Overnight, Rom came from far and wide to plead for his clemency, faces I hadn't seen as a child, all moths around his light, all hoping. Both my brothers and their families appeared but they were as powerless as we were. A list of my father's good deeds, his royal connections, his standing in our community, all fell on deaf ears. We were Rom, without land or house, tolerated but not accepted. Good enough to harvest crops and catch your rats, but not good enough for justice.

They led him out at daybreak and he stepped out of the lockup blinking, his head bowed until he was clear of the lintel and then he stood tall. My mother ran and threw her arms around him, her face buried in his neck, and he tried to caress her hair though his hands were manacled as if he were a danger to the world. My father. My mother was removed by one of the constables and I trailed beside him and reached for his hands, just wanting to feel them, his strong fingers dwarfing mine as they had when I was small, his touch telling me all was right in the world. He reached and kissed me on the head and then Little Egg and I felt the earth turn beneath my feet as the scaffold came into view.

My father mounted the steps with dignity, his feet leading him on, his eyes kept on us and not the gibbet that awaited. There were a dozen people waiting and I felt sick to the core. From behind me I felt Amberline's arm wrap around my shoulders, his arm as leaden as a yoke; he'd left the cover of the woods for this, the danger now over for him. My mother stood with my brothers. She looked and saw Amberline and spat on the ground.

The hangman held the length of rope in his hand and was ready to loop it over my father's head, when my father quietly spoke. The hangman released him from the manacle and someone below reached up towards my father and handed him his own rope. My father took it, thick and twisted, a rope made strong by a Rom's hands. The ground beneath my feet roiled. My father, steady of hand, tied the knot that would kill him. He pulled the rope straight of any kink and tested it with a final tug, before he placed the noose around his own neck, a savage garland. My father looked up, squinting into the sun, until he found our faces.

"You see what you've brought me to," he said, and I shivered before I realised he wasn't addressing me at all. "Live soberly and take care of your wife and family." His meaning was only too clear, his message for Amberline. I felt him stiffen beside me.

My father gave the signal. The hangman, his job diminished by my father's own assistance, quickly dropped the trapdoor. I closed my eyes. There was a loud snap, the creak of the rope and the sound of the gathering wind. I couldn't breathe, the inside of my eyelids held a darkness I thought I'd never wake from. I heard my mother's gasp and cry and wanted to go to her. Amberline pulled me away.

That afternoon my father's body was claimed and made ready for burial. My mother wouldn't let anyone else prepare him. It was she who cleaned his body, washing his face and tying a clean *diklo* around his poor broken neck in a fragile knot, not daring to tie it close to his poor bruised and broken flesh. She polished his boots and buckles and placed a coin in each of his hands and all I could do was stand behind her and watch, for she'd not let me help, she'd not spoken a word to me, nor caught my eye. When Little Egg cried she looked up only briefly, blinking as if surfacing from a dream, startled by her surroundings, her face softening, before the reality of what occurred scattered her expression and she resumed the mask she needed to get her through.

My brothers had dug the grave and all the men carried my father's body in its coffin to its resting place. Amberline offered to help, but they ignored him, spurned his offer to assist as if he was nothing at all. Little Egg reached out her hand towards the wood as it passed, but I scooped up her hand and tucked it away.

With my father lowered into his grave, we each took a handful of good dark earth and it hit the coffin like thrown cake, until my brothers snatched up the shovels and filled the grave. Their arms and backs in steady motion didn't cease in their action until the surface was near smooth. My mother carefully bent and scooped out a hole; I thought she was digging down again, until I saw the branch of thorn by her side; it would grow, sustained by the earth and my father's goodness. My mother's expression was stone. We would come each year on this date to tie red thread and ribbon in his remembrance.

We made our way back to camp, all the other *vardos* and wagons making ready for the night, set up further away from my parents' *vardo*, keeping their distance for the spark that would come. My mother took no rest nor water; she gathered the few possessions that were her own in a small pile on the grass – her clothes, her herbs, a bundle containing her needles and thread, a Bible. I went to help her but she waved me away. My brothers led the horse away and nodded to me, but ignored Amberline. How much did they know of Amberline's role in my father's death? If they had known the whole of it, they'd have plunged a knife into his heart, just as they were about to do to the horse.

My mother smashed all their fine china onto the floor, the clatter of it ringing through the night disturbing a pigeon who'd already set for the roost. She'd be forced to live with one of my brothers and his wife now.

"What is she doing that for?" Amberline said, confused at the storm growing around us, his hand curling protectively around my shoulder. But what could I tell him? These were our ways. All that had belonged to the living must be destroyed; his act had led to not only the death of my father but the destruction of my mother's home and all their worldly possessions. My mother threw out the silver teapot and tray, sugar bowl and spoons and they landed at our feet. Amberline stepped back. My mother came out of the *vardo* with a shovel and started dashing them into the ground. Little Egg began to cry at the sharp sounds. Amberline took her into his arms, unrolled her small angry fist and blew a puff of air into her palm. At this, she hushed and he held her close to his chest. My mother smashed with her shovel and the side of the teapot split, collapsed like an overripe fruit. My mother looked up at Amberline.

"Want these too, do you?" she said bitterly, still striking down with the shovel. She drew my father's knife from her belt, the one that Amberline had given him, and submitted it to the same attack, watching the pattern on the blade disappear, mangled to ribbon. When she had finished I went to gather them into a sack for her, but she held her hand up against me, she would not have my help. She tied a rope around the sack again and again, as if it were rats inside and not silver, the sickening tie of the knot made me lose my footing, though I stood on solid ground, Amberline's hand steadying my elbow.

My mother turned in disgust and went to the wood pile, gathered all the wood she could and took it inside the *vardo*. I heard the strike of her flint, I knew it would have shaken in her hands. She struck again, the flame must have caught. A curl of smoke followed her out over the threshold as she stepped down and stood apart from us, watching. All the camp was silent.

"Is she deranged, Patrin? Should we try and stop her?" I shook my head and took Little Egg back in my arms.

The fire had caught and the whole interior glowed, the flames licking at the roof, the floor. The wooden beams started to crack and spit as the heat released the oils from the wood. The fire hit my father's bottle of brandy and it exploded and encouraged the flames to go higher, popping out the wooden shutters of the window, using the curtains as a bellows – in and out they were sucked until the flames devoured them completely. From the doorframe the fire started to venture, sending its fingers curling around the frame until the fire ran all across the exterior. With a *whomph* all the air was sucked out of the *vardo*; the roof danced with spitting flames, the smoke stung my eyes and made me cough. I pulled my shawl over Little Egg's head to shield her from the ashes that had started to fall, a bitter snow, but my mother would not step back. She shrugged off my touch, her skin hot from the fire; her dark hair grew grey from the falling ash, her face was lit with the fire, her eyes feverish with grief. The walls of the *vardo* collapsed in on themselves as we heard the horse scream, the blade ending its life, and for a moment the walls of the *vardo* remained, painted in blinding light, then were gone, the remains of my family's life a heap of burning wood.

Jupiter howled and started running around the burning *vardo* looking for my father, poor animal, so I took him and tied him to a tree, lest he injure himself. His whimpers stung my ears as much as the smoke did my eyes.

I went back to my mother but she was already walking off in the direction of the river to throw the bag of smashed silver in the waters, so I had to chase her.

"Mother?" I called but she was silent. "Mother, speak to me," I tried again.

She turned on her foot then, the flames painting her face red. "You choose, Patrin, you choose. It's either him or us, there is not room in our family for both," and with that she struck off for the river, leaving me with ash burning my eyes.

FOURTEEN

Patrin, 1819

Later that night, as the others slept in the camp, Amberline clapped his hand over my mouth in the darkness and I woke fighting for breath until I realised who it was. Once he had my silence he lifted Little Egg into my shaking arms and I carefully strapped her to me, all my fingers thumbs. Her little head lolled against my chest and I hoped the smell of me wouldn't wake her. He bid me follow and I hesitated. Where were we going? He led me out of the *vardo* and I waited for Jupiter's loyal bark, half hoping it would ring out across the camp to rouse my mother, but the dog just lay there in the embers of the fire, prone and still, his tongue unrolled, a spool of unmoving red ribbon, puddled in blood.

We walked in the veil of darkness, Amberline's feet stepping gingerly over the fallen branches, heading Lord knew where, until we were out of earshot from anyone in the camp.

"Where are we going?" I asked.

Amberline put his finger gently to my lip. "What chance have we here? I can't change what happened, but we can start anew, Patrin, our little family, you, me and Eglantine," he said, his arms reaching round both of us, Eglantine a little human wedge made of our love, our skin. He was right, how could I spend another minute in this camp? My mother would only try to drive Amberline out, unable to endure my father's sacrifice.

None of us could live here without his calm presence. If I didn't go with Amberline, my father's sacrifice would be for nothing, the sacrifice he made not just for Amberline but for me and my daughter also. The only chance we had was if we broke ties with the old ways of the camp and tried to forge a new life.

We hurried at such speed in the dark without lantern or caution, further than I'd been from the camp before, our belongings jangling on Amberline's back. The image of my father's beloved dog cut through the fog of my mind, to wake me up from this walking nightmare.

"But Jupiter?" I said, imagining the swivel of his loyal ears.

"It was a mercy, poor beast," Amberline said and he was right. What life would Jupiter have without my father? He'd be always on the lookout for him, waiting to catch the scent of his pipe, bounding to his side at a whistle. His suffering was over.

The morning bled over the horizon and my feet felt they had become a part of the ground we staggered on. We trespassed through the fields and meadows until the road offered itself up to us, a rope to the drowning, pulling us all the way to the beast of London.

* * *

The roar rose up towards us as we entered the city. I'd never heard such a clamour, where did it all come from? The higgledy-piggledy houses crammed together, the effluent running past our feet in the gutter; hooves and wheels pounded on the road, a bigger caravan of wagons I'd never seen. The brackish air almost unbreathable.

Amberline darted through the streets, a fish in his own river, while I floundered, my senses overwhelmed by all I saw, heard, smelled. If Amberline let go of my hand, I would be lost in the tide of people, wagons, buildings, so I held on tighter and tried to take note of my surrounds. But every corner appeared to have the sign of a public house, the painted signs hanging low, but as soon as I recalled one, I forgot another – the Red Lion, The Lion and the Unicorn, The Unicorn and Lion – all the buildings bleeding into each other, varying only in size and squalor. The streets were pulsing with wheels – carts, wagons, hansom cabs, jigs. Amberline led me all through this until we left the thoroughfare into a maze of small lanes and he instructed me to stay put beside a well. He kissed me and put his coat around us to keep us warm while we waited, before he disappeared. My heart lurched. What if he never came back? All I had was Little Egg and the clothes on my back. I leaned against the well and listened to the water speaking and I felt my legs sway. How far had we come? I closed my eyes and when I opened them again, Amberline was walking towards me, a grin on his face, a key in his hand. He led me further down the lane and stopped at a small door.

This was to be our home.

He opened the door and I stepped inside the darkness, my eyes adjusting. One large room divided by a torn, stained curtain, a small grubby pane of glass letting in light like fog. I looked behind the curtain and saw an old mattress on the dirt floor, and a spidery web of mould running across the walls and up the ceiling.

The fireplace was a black gaping mouth in the wall, the hearth stone never having seen the bristle side of a brush. Our *vardo* may have been small, the contents patched and worn, but there was never any filth, it was clean and neat, my mother as house proud as the King's housekeeper, even if it was no house we lived in. I felt the damp of that squalid room close around me and squeeze at my lungs and I wondered how would we live in this place. The only walls I knew were of the *vardo* and the hedgerow. The only ceiling I knew was the vault of the sky. My floor had extended across field and moor, woodland and fen, but now it was circumscribed, fenced in by the walls of Amberline's choosing.

"I know it isn't much, but with a bit of a clean and tidy I'm sure we will make the best of it," he said and, seeing my expression, cupped my face in his hands. "Just until I get back on my feet," he said.

What of my mother? My old life? The words bubbled in me. I heard Little Egg open her eyes with a little click like the cogs of a tiny clockwork. Amberline reached down and brushed his eyelashes across her cheek just to see the dimples of her new smile. I looked at them both, they were all I had in the world now, I'd have to make this place a home, for all our sakes, for our new life.

* * *

The first morning Amberline rose before dawn. Little Egg was at my breast having woken to the noise of the city, sucking the last of the free-roaming milk that I had. Her little hand went for the jangle of the coin necklace that was my dowry, as was her wont, but it was no longer there. Amberline had used the last of the coins on our journey and had melted down the chain. Now, he went out to enquire about work and I set to making this place our new home.

My heart was heavy as I stepped outside, looking at the jostle of buildings, the fog, the dawn not even a patch of sky. All the houses looked nearer to falling down than to standing, and I felt them press against me, the soot shadowing the edges of them. Only a few had windows; ours having a small pane of glass was, I now saw, a luxury, for most had plain shutters or were bare, some with tattered curtains only or a cupboard pushed up against the frame to stop the elements. I walked towards the well, bucket in hand, and felt eyes upon me. I stopped and looked up, but nothing stirred, no face looked back at me. I heard shouting from one of the buildings and I hurried to the well, Little Egg bobbing on my chest, her eyes watching me, her mouth opening and closing; she'd cry soon with hunger. The stones grew slippery beneath my feet and I felt the seep of damp go through my shoes and stockings to my skin. The smell of the water rose up to me, so sour I wanted to cry. The stones around the well were slippery with moss; the water pooled in a fetid puddle on the ground.

I lowered the bucket into the well, the rope slick and damp like a water spirit's braid unravelling in my hands. The wood hit the water and threw a few droplets into the air as the bucket filled. When I went to wind it up, the bucket stuck. I peered over the edge and carefully looked in, but all that revealed itself to me was a dark shape. Little Egg began to babble. I looked at her face, her eyes clouded by the shadow. I pulled at the bucket and felt the rope strain. Little Egg kept up her chatter, but it grew louder, bouncing off the walls. I kissed her head to quiet her, but she continued. I pulled angrily at the rope and the bucket came up, released from whatever it was caught on, and tipped over the edge, drenching my feet for my efforts.

I swore under my breath and tried again, watching the bucket lower towards the water. When I saw the circle of its rim dip into the water a face slowly rose up out of the deep to look at me. I clutched Little Egg closer to me in dread of the spirit that shimmered for a moment, seeing a face, but as the water stilled I saw it was just my reflection looking up at me from the depths. I pulled up the bucket, slower this time, careful not to spill a drop, and decanted it into our own bucket, glad the ordeal of water was over. A pigeon flapped down and drank at the spill, his iridescent feathers covered in soot.

When I turned to walk back I saw a man watching me from the doorway of his house, a pipe between his teeth, his eyes looking at my red skirts, the brightest thing in the crooked lane. The *putsi* around my neck drew his gaze so I carefully tucked it beneath my shawl and kept my eyes directed at my feet. A woman sloshed the night waste out of her bucket and into the gutter and I stepped backwards. A cart turned into the lane, wheels striking cobble. All of me felt a stranger. I counted the steps to the door and made sure it was securely latched behind me. I placed the bucket next to the fireplace and set to making the fire roar. The water in the bucket was dark and still, but it would need boiling twice over. I laid the twigs and sticks and struck the tinderbox, grateful for a small stack of wood left by the fire by previous occupants, for where would you find enough wood for the fire in this treeless place? The flames were reluctant to take suck, the chimney no doubt caked in soot and ash; as if on cue a pile of soot started sifting down the chimney and a fine coat sprinkled over Little Egg's face. I dipped my shawl in the bucket and wiped her face clean, before I put her to the breast, willing the fire to take.

Slowly the flames grew and I stood up with Little Egg in the crook of my arm and reached for the split wood, but as I pulled it out I saw something had been buried beneath: a cloth, a sack? Whatever it was, I pulled at it, hidden as it was, and I felt sick with the discovery. Amberline had taken the sack my mother had thrown in the river, the sack filled with the smashed silver teapot and sugar bowl, the silver spoons, the knife. He was blinded by silver. I carefully poked the sack back in where I'd found it, pushing it deep down into the cavity, and piled up the wood over it, hoping that whatever Amberline would melt it down into would be enough to let my father's spirit take its rest. I told myself he took it just to put food in our mouths until he found work for a jeweller. Little Egg cried out, the fire had made the room smoky and I was glad of the sting, for at least she wouldn't see my own eyes, spilling with tears. When I stopped crying I set Little Egg down on my shawl on the mattress, rolled my sleeves up and set to cleaning.

That night Little Egg cried out for me from her cradle, an emptied drawer I had lined with all the soft things I had brought with me, her mattress a sheepskin my father had skinned from a lamb bought from a farmer. My fingers struck the softness of it as I lifted her to me and I felt my sorrow eddy around me. How was it that my father was on this earth no longer? The heat inside pressed down on us as Amberline stoked on the other side of the curtain. The shadow of the flames flickered over the ceiling; I gave Little Egg my breast and watched the flames dance, my eyes growing heavy, the air bitter with the smell of Amberline submitting metal to his pot. I would not look.

FIFTEEN

Eglantine, 1833

The night was like a hood pulled down over London; the river churned as we passed and it eerily threw up its own light towards us, a world of drowned stars. Was my mother's starry face amongst them? All was darkness except for the dogged determination on Makepeace's face as we made our way to see my father.

Newgate Prison's cold metal-studded doors were bolted against us, but Makepeace rapped hard enough to wake the dead, until the door opened and she pushed a coin in someone's hand and one by one the bolts were unlocked to admit us.

We walked down into the holding cells, the echo of the key in the lock, the jarring of the bars, the sickening stench that rose up to our nostrils with each step. The turnkey to the cells where the men were held put out his hand and Makepeace shed yet another coin. I felt the damp wick up my skirt; a rat's furred shape crossed our path and I heard Makepeace swear under her breath. We were led through the dim light and the dank walls that trickled with rivulets to a shadowy cell where the turnkey halted. I peered in, only to see a cluster of poor grubby souls crammed together, resting however they were able, tossed about like shipwrecked survivors, abandoned and exhausted though the ship was still to sail. The cold bars bit at my cheek, but look as I might, I couldn't see my father anywhere. The men grew aware of our presence at the door, poised and alert as if we had the means to let them out. Oh, I would have if I could have, every last one of them. The despair of them.

"He's not here," Makepeace whispered close to my face.

"Father?" I shouted. "Father?" My voice echoed and if any men had been asleep they weren't now.

"Eglantine?" My father moved from the back of the cell, made from shadows until he stood before us. Makepeace stepped back and looked at him. If not for the fine cut of his coat, I doubt she would have recognised him. His face was grimy and crowned with a black eye.

I looked at his hand that reached towards us and saw then how my father stood apart from his cellmates, in his clothes, his manner, his demeanour. I took his hand, my arm pressed by the damp bars on either side, my cheek scratched by metal, lime rust scraping against my skin, just to get closer.

"Father," I said, wanting reassurance. I looked at the lock and back to the turnkey who held a ring of keys, like a giant's chatelaine, wondering which key would open it, rusted as it was.

"I'm sorry, Eglantine, I didn't get you your boots," my father said and attempted a smile. Someone laughed behind him. I looked down at his hands, his fingernails silted up with grime. Makepeace frowned at him, at his attempt to make light.

"Amberline," she said, her hand reaching through the bars for his other hand, holding it to her. My father kissed both our hands, before he reached through the bar to wrap around me, in an awkward embrace, my father, Makepeace, the bars and I.

"What happened, Amberline?" Makepeace asked. "What went wrong?"

My father hesitated. His eyes fell to his hands, looking at them in disbelief, his faith in them shaken. "I thought I saw her," he said very quietly.

"Who?" I said. To see my father transformed from a gentleman to a prisoner unnerved me.

"I was in a crowded street, beside me was a woman with a child in her arms, wrapped in a fine blanket. In the child's drowsy fist was a coral-handled silver rattle close to dropping. It was the sort of rattle you should have had, Eglantine, wrought so finely. The mother was distracted by a street singer, as were those around us. No one paid attention to my fingers as I caught the rattle in my grasp and concealed it without a sound. But as soon as I placed it in my pocket, my whole pocket mysteriously filled with water and started to drip, splashing my trousers, my shoes, the road. The singer stopped singing and the baby cried. Then the mother turned to look at me and I saw her face, Patrin's face looking back at me. I was apprehended and charged and brought here." My father put his hands away under his armpits and I felt water run down the back of my own neck, the cells dripping with their own rain.

"Eglantine, listen now and listen closely. It's up to you now, you'll provide for us," he said, close to my ear. I smelled the sourness of his breath. "You've learned all I could teach you, it's up to you to keep yourself and Makepeace safe."

"But we could sell the house, Father, let Makepeace go. Let me come with you," I said. Makepeace stiffened beside me.

"No, the house is our one non-portable asset, Eglantine. We'll not sell it, I've worked too hard to keep it, I'd not have a misstep make us lose it. We'll not return to the old ways." The turnkey appeared and I felt the cold seep up from the floor. "And I'd not have you leave Makepeace or England and follow me to God knows where. Makepeace will be your guardian and you be a good girl. Remember what I taught you," my father said. We were escorted out then, Makepeace's coin having run out.

* * *

Makepeace and I awaited the day of the trial, and like an out-of-control wheel it came too soon. The court was a hive of

127

noise – weeping, shouting, screaming, howling – until the judges walked in. Their grey wigs fell down the sides of their faces like aging cocker spaniels' ears. The stalls were quiet until the judges sat and then there was a burst of noise. The awesome might of the Empire was in the scrawl of their hands as they sat above, looking down on us all.

For the next few hours we sat perched listening to a world of inventory – a stolen pocket handkerchief, a filched loaf of bread, a length of satin ribbon, a fork, a thimble, a plank of wood, a bushel of tea, a bristle brush, a dozen iron nails, a pamphlet, a pair of stockings, a funnel, a cooling pie, a lace parasol, a gentleman's tie, a bobbin of thread, a pat of butter, a vial of laudanum, a shawl, a pair of sturdy hobnailed boots, a skein of rope, a saucepan, a ladle, a pair of woollen mittens, a pair of kid gloves, a posy of violets, a cake of soap, a bottle of castor oil. Imprisonment, banishment or death dependent on the value of the goods. Above a shilling, most received His Majesty's one-way ticket, but some were unlucky to get the rope. When those unfortunates heard the news most of them crumbled and pleaded for clemency, mercy, that they were a mother or a father, as if their parenthood would save them. In some instances the judges commuted their sentence, but others were left with it, the thought of it already crushing their throats.

When they led my father out from the cells to the dock, my heart tiptoed in my chest. My father looked around, confused at the sea of faces. He stood straighter when he looked up and recognised us, his hand floated up from his shackles. I cried out for him, but Makepeace tugged on my arm to silence me. My father tripped as he took the stand and the crowd tittered until he righted himself and stood straight again, running his hands through his greasy hair.

The charge was read out and he was asked his plea. "Not guilty." His voice filled the court and someone upon hearing him for the first time would feel obliged to believe him. His voice was honey.

"But you were caught red-handed," a judge said, frowning, and looked at his papers then looked my father up and down. The most senior-looking judge cleared his throat and spoke and my ears filled with the roar of my own blood.

"The prisoner is guilty. He is sentenced to fourteen years. In the Colony of New South Wales."

My father turned to us, his eyes wild, gulping air, showing his bound wrists to us but we had no way to throw him a rescuing line. Makepeace raised her hand out to him, but his time upon the stand was up and he was being led by the court officer to the cells below. The next to be banished was already being led to the stand to await the judgment of the law. A judge stifled a yawn with the back of his hand.

* * *

Makepeace and I returned to the house and I saw it with different eyes. Before it had been the only home I recalled, never seeing it as anything more than the place where I lived. But as Makepeace and I walked along the river, the current running alongside us like a silent companion, the silence brewed between us. Our lives had been emptied of my father's life in a word – guilty – and Makepeace and I would be alone in the house, rattling around like my doll did in my pocket.

As we walked up the step together and entered the house, I realised what a big house it was for the three of us, let alone two. Makepeace put her key in the lock and opened the door, and the whole house seemed to whisper my father's absence.

Makepeace went down to her room that was next to the kitchen and I wandered like a will-o'-the-wisp through the rooms of the house. Nothing appeared to be the same; it felt as if the whole house had been submerged and dragged up again, things distorted and dripped. How was it that we had this house after all? How shabby and old it seemed now Makepeace

and I were alone in it; without my father the very walls turned
into a different kind of cage. How was it that we had all these
rooms, when all those in that cell had hardly enough room
to stretch their arms? The sitting room as I walked into it felt
overstuffed, the damask creeping off the walls and onto the
furniture. I looked up at the ornate moulded ceiling, the glass
in the window, that wavered, the bubbles trapped in the glass.
Airless and crowded, though I was alone in the room. I pushed
at the sash of the window and found the damp had wedged it
shut, so I hit it again and again with the heel of my hand, until
the wood gave way. In blew the breeze from the river, bringing
with it many sounds; a seagull hovered just outside the frame
of the window and was gone; the curtains disappeared out the
window with a suck, but still I couldn't breathe.

I raced up the stairs, the balustrade as cold as water beneath
my palm, to where Ada's room had been and was left bare, and
I pushed the window open and let in the air. It whipped in and
filled the room, finding the walls and space to its liking, like a
cat spiralling on a lap.

Up the stairs to the nursery, the wind cooled the damp sweat
on my back. It was filled with all the things of childhoods before
me, things I had played with but which had never been mine.
All the fancies a childish heart dreamt of: rocking horse, dolls,
shelves of books with coloured spines. A doll's house replica of
the house stood pride of place on an elegant pair of wooden
legs. I stepped closer and put my eye to the window. I was
grown a giantess to spy on the little inhabitants: a little cook
in the kitchen, her arms up to her elbows lost in a bowl; a little
family sitting around a dining table, plates as big as buttons; a
maid laying a fire in the sitting room; a grandmother sleeping in
her bed, her gold-rimmed glasses on the tip of her nose; up the
staircase the same paintings hung; a gentleman sat at his desk
in a book-lined library, his quill feathered as if with eyelashes.
And in the nursery a governess in her serge uniform rocked a

tiny baby in a cradle beside a miniature doll's house as tall as a match.

Were we prisoners now in this house just as the doll's house kept the dolls prisoner? My father had been imprisoned. Was this our fate too? All I could hear was the roar of water, the room slipping beneath the surface. The little doll flipped in my pocket like a landed fish and spurred me to action. The wind was already rattling the sash waiting for me; the nursery windows rose at my touch, pushing my hair across my face and chasing the wind through the doll's house, the tiny curtains whisked out the tiny windows.

Only my father's rooms remained.

Walking down the stairs I smelled the brine of the river fill my lungs; the breezes made my skirt billow around my legs like a sail. The wind had already pushed open the door to my father's study and made the pages on his desk flutter and spill to the floor. The window wouldn't give, no matter how I shoved at it. The sash had been nailed shut, but the wind still came through; I wedged open the door to allow it admittance.

I stood outside my father's bedroom door, my hand on the wood, and listened, half expecting to hear sounds of my father bustling around inside, but all that I heard was the wind already pushing beneath the door crack. Who was I to let it wait?

Inside the room it was as my father had left it. All was neat. All was quiet. His bed was made, his drawers all closed. A pair of cufflinks lay on top of his dresser; the wind pushed one to the floor with a clink. I opened his windows and let the air come swirling in. Cautiously I opened the drawers, feeling them glide – every item was perfectly folded, drawer after drawer of handkerchiefs with his own monogram. Why so many handkerchiefs? I ran my hand under the rim of the drawers, seeking a secret spring. Nothing. I pulled open another drawer; his shirts all ordered. On his dresser were bottles of powder and lavender water and his long razor that he would shave with every day, the pulse of his neck so close to the blade, his Adam's apple bobbing close with a swallow. With a quick tug I pulled the drawer free and shook all those handkerchiefs on the bed and with them fell all that my father had hidden – gold coins fell out and I felt hot as if the devil's own breath were warm upon my face. I stripped my father's pillow of its case and rushed to fill it, stealing from the master thief. Just as I had finished I saw something remaining in the drawer and I felt time spin.

It was a little leather pouch, the cord around it tied with a knot, though the cord had been cut. Gingerly I plucked it from the drawer, a splinter of wood keeping the cord from coming free, and then there it was, a familiar reassuring little measure in my hand. I held it to my nose and breathed deeply, and with my eyes closed for the briefest of moments I felt her with me, it was something of my mother's. I stood frozen with the wind coming at me from all directions; a spit of rain came through the window, a sun shower, a fox's wedding. All the doors slammed with the gust throughout the house, one after the other like a series of fireworks, waking me to myself. What would happen to us if these things of my father's were found here, what fate would befall us? Part of me wanted to hurl the pillowcase and its contents out into the street, but I realised this was what paid for our clothes, our comforts, our bread, and we might yet have need of my father's provisions. The walls wavered in front of my eyes; this house might just as well be made of water.

I curled the leather pouch in my fist, took the pillowcase with me to the nursery and threw it beneath my bed for a temporary home. I'd bury it somewhere, until it was needed. What world had my father brought me into, what world would it become? My father had instructed me to be his hands, to continue his bitter trade. Why couldn't I determine my own fate, put my hands to a better use? But what use would that be? My father had trained my fingers from the earliest, his ten white servants, and they knew nothing else. Other girls my age would know how to sew and mend and make. But all my father had me truly learn was how to steal, how to take, without regard for the consequences. Where was my father now? Was he already on board the ship that would transport him, or was he still waiting in the cells? Would we even know if he survived the voyage? If I continued as my father wanted me to, what would prevent me falling the same way, bound for Botany Bay, my own life dropped like a stone to the bottom of a well?

I lay on the bed, not caring that my boots hit the coverlet. I took the pouch from my fist and placed it on my forehead as though it was a poultice, then reached for my doll in my pocket, my fingers travelling the worn grooves scratched in her back. I closed my eyes, surrendering to whatever wind would blow, feeling myself adrift as if the house was already a part of the river, already gone with the tide.

SIXTEEN

Patrin, 1819

The little room divided with a curtain became more like a *vardo*, but devoid of wheels and horse. The fire didn't thrive as it did in a circle of stones but struggled in the hearth, which I had scrubbed trying to expel the grime. Every morning Amberline left to try to increase our fortunes and every day he returned with his feet soiled from the street, his footprints making a mockery of my cleanliness as he bustled in, always animated with the plans and schemes that were more alive in his head than they were in practicality. No matter how I cleaned the window it was covered in a film of soot that renewed itself every day.

The rhythms of the day were my reason, the things I held on to, to stop the world from slipping. Without my father, the world that I had known had ceased. My grief was mine alone, for Amberline bid me look forward and not behind. But how could I? Every time I picked up Little Egg and held her in my arms I remembered her in his arms, strong as branches, her feet clothed in the little loving shoes of his own making. I saved my tears for when Amberline was sleeping and Little Egg was at my breast, her head becoming damp from them.

My namesake signs were unreadable. I was lost. My father would have known the right thing to do, the right way to go. I willed his voice to my ears, to speak to me, to guide me, but all

I could hear was the sickening crack of his poor neck. In the city nothing made sense; sounds seemed closer but they were an echo from far away; there were no trees or plants in our lane that turned with the seasons, just a woodland made of brick, stone and wood. But for Little Egg and Amberline I was rootless. My father had tried to teach me the ways to divine water, to feel the way in my hands, but without him I was made a husk by my grief.

One morning I woke with the boom of silence in my ears, the quiet slamming my face. Did I dream the door closing? Disoriented, I sat up in the bed, my breasts stinging hot with milk, already dampening my shift. I reached for Little Egg but her truckle was empty, the bedding cold. Frantically I tripped out of the bed and stumbled past the curtained division – my daughter was not nestled in her father's arms. The hearth billowed cold ash onto the floor and dirtied my feet. I tiptoed up to the window and willed them to appear but all the glass would show me was the curtain of soot that the city had woven.

I opened the door, my shift flapping around my legs, the sound of the lane rushing up to me – the waterfall of a bucket being emptied into the gutter, a door being slammed, a cart turning on the road, a stick flickering in the wheels – but no sign of Amberline and Little Egg.

My feet turned as cold as the stone I stood on in the threshold, unable to move. How had my world shrunk to several square feet? My past world had been the earth wide, the heavens long; the hedgerows and woodlands, the rivers and waterways had been my boundaries, as familiar to me as the lines on my palms, but now I lived in a prison of walls.

I stood there for an hour, my neighbours walking past, all but ignoring me as I became made of shade, when around the corner a gentleman walked with a child in his arms, a fine blanket wrapped around her delicate limbs, and I wondered what gentleman would be seen walking down this dark corner of earth with his precious child. He wore a felted beaver fur topper and finely pressed trousers, a stripe running through them, a neat coat buttoned over his chest. When I heard his voice float up to me my horizon wavered, my impulse to run vanished – the voice was unmistakably Amberline's. When he looked at me in my shift, hair wild, my toes turning blue, his face darkened.

"Give her to me, Amberline." I shook, apoplectic with anger. But Amberline just continued walking, his pace unhurried, knowing that daily the walls of my entire world had shrunk to the confines of this room, chained as I was by invisible ties to the circumference around the hearth.

As soon as he was in reach I snatched her from his arms. My daughter looked up at me contentedly and I felt that soft blanket between my thumb and forefinger, soft lamb's wool finely knitted.

"Why did you take her? Where have you been?" I said, clutching her to my chest and not wanting to let her go ever again.

Amberline deliberately closed the door, the ominous click of the latch. All the time on the doorstep I had thought that once I got my daughter back in my arms I would pack all I had into a bundle, strap Little Egg to my chest and seek out my mother and beg her forgiveness.

"I've been for a walk with my daughter," Amberline said glibly and I felt blood race into my face.

"In those clothes? I've never seen them folded in our chest of drawers."

"Well one can hardly expect you to be taking her for air. Look at you, Patrin, you look like a madwoman. Get dressed, brush your hair. Make yourself presentable." I saw myself through his eyes then and I was frightened – would he seek to have me committed? Or worse, take my daughter away?

"Surely I've a right to know if you are taking her anywhere," I said, trying to calm myself, feeling Little Egg reach for my breast, between my shift, her mouth opening and closing for it on the surface of the fabric.

Amberline tossed his hat onto the table and shrugged his coat off his shoulders, carefully placing it on the back of a chair. Upon our daughter's little head was a new bonnet, edged with a little strip of lace like hawthorn blossom around her face.

"My mother has a right to see her grandchild," Amberline said matter-of-factly.

His mother.

His mother, my aunt, our daughter's namesake. She remained in London yet Amberline had said nothing. What else had he kept from me? Had he told her about the sacrifice of my father for him, for us? I felt I'd be sick and moved to the table to feel something solid beneath my hand.

Amberline emptied his pockets onto the table – a silken handkerchief, a reticule, a watch chain – all clattered and spun. Little Egg moved her head in the direction of the sound and smiled as I pulled my shift down, relieved to have her skin on mine, the quiet snuffle and suck, but it didn't extinguish the anger in me.

"Was my father's sacrifice not enough for you?"

Amberline looked coldly at me. "What would you have me do, Patrin? Hang with him?"

"But for everything he did for you – he took you in, he let you court me, everything against my mother's better judgment. Did you even thank him?" I felt my blood get hot, Little Egg's cheek burned against my breast. I longed for air, cool, wide open gusts of it.

"*I chatski tsinuda de tehara, vai de haino, khal tut*," I said beneath my breath. The true nettle stings from the beginning. I clutched the *putsi* around my throat.

"Are you cursing me now too, just like your mother? I'm stealing to give us a life, Patrin. A chance in the city. There is no future in the Romanyjib and Romany ways."

"Well they were good enough when you needed them," I said and spat at his feet.

Amberline prickled with a silent rage and snapped the *putsi* cord from around my throat. I grabbed at his wrist, Little Egg still at my breast, but he was too tall for me. He held it between us, that little chamois pouch that my mother had given me, and let it dangle in the air – my neck burned from the cord being tugged.

"Amberline," I said. "Please?" I put out my hand. "I'm sorry."

But his eyes darkened as he looked into the fireplace and I thought he'd burn all I had brought from the camp, turning it to ash. Amberline hesitated, then tipped all the contents onto the floor – strands of hair, my mother's and mine twisted together; angelica leaves, rosemary and acorn, the little piece of fraying velvet the German duchess had given me, the river's perfect stone – all trampled beneath his foot. He weighed the leather pouch in his hand with contempt before he tossed it on the ground, storming out the door. I bent down and gathered up each precious thing and looped the *putsi* back around my neck, tucking it deep into the folds of my clothes, away from Amberline's fingers. Little Egg's lips fell from my nipple, a dribble of milk pooling in the birthmark around her neck, turning the red strands of it white.

That night I slept lightly, keeping my senses tuned to Amberline's movements, the trust between us as tenuous as a spider web. Unlike the bond between Little Egg and me, a bond that stretched stronger than skin, an umbilical cord of the spirit. When I woke in the night disturbed by my dreams, Eglantine stirred, her eyes blinking at me in the darkness; I could hear the kitten-shaped yawn of her thirsty mouth as I too yawned. I was afraid to return her to the makeshift cradle lest Amberline take her without my knowing, so I kept her close, in my arms.

SEVENTEEN

Eglantine, 1833

I woke when my bedroom window was pulled closed, Makepeace having gone and closed each and every one. Sleep had taken me and washed me up on the shore, disoriented as to what the time was: all the light was wrong. I snatched the pouch into my fist for safekeeping, before Makepeace saw it.

She came and sat beside me, put her hand to my forehead, a forked line of worry running across her own, but I had no fever, all I had was the cold truth brushing up against me and I wondered if I'd be strong enough to withstand it.

"Your father was born in a storm, did you know that?" she said. I shook my head. I knew nothing of my father's life outside of this house, outside of the dolly house.

"The men had gone *bokra-choring*, sheep stealing, his father lost his life for it at the end of a farmer's gun." The Romany words flushed into me with familiarity but their meaning disappeared like smoke in the daylight.

"All my husband's belongings were put to the flame, lest the spirit remain and weigh heavy on the living. I was to move into his parents' caravan with the baby. But I'd had enough of the road and the country life, the selling of baskets and pegs, the silver across my palm for a fortune told. I wanted to strike out and find my own fortune, not have it dictated to me by my in-laws. I wanted more. In the dead of night I took our horse and all I owned tied into a shawl strapped to my back, and with another shawl strapped the baby to my front. I sold the horse to the first person who offered me money for it on the outskirts of the city, on Makepeace Lane, and I changed my name accordingly. At night we slept under the twisted canopies of hedgerows, hedgehogs rootling for night crawlers around us, waking to hayricks alive with sparrows."

Why was she telling me this? All the hairs on my arms stood on end, the shiver running feverishly across them as the thought formed in my head. That baby was my father. Makepeace was my grandmother. Makepeace nodded her head, reading the doubt in my frown. "Yes, child. This is the truth. Amberline never wanted me to tell you, but I can tell you now he's gone." She looked away then, but I could see the pain in her face, the mastery of her tears.

"I walked into the heart of the city and picked another street, all the colourful painted doors and beautiful whitewashed steps, polished door knockers like horse brasses on fair day. I knocked proudly on each and asked for work and was turned away from every one. My baby strapped to my chest was a repellent to employment, but I would not surrender him as a foundling or return him to the life I was so desperate to leave behind. He cried for the breast and I took him down to the riverside, settling beneath a willow, watching the hair-like leaves waft in the water and the gaping mouths of the little fishes dart, listening to the happy suck, wondering what I would do next, when a young lady approached me, her miniature image dozing beneath a silk coverlet in her arms. She was dressed in a long muslin gown, her hem tainted green, stained by the grass. A snug little red velvet jacket cloaked her, damp at the breast where her milk sprang. The lady took me on as a wet nurse for her baby in exchange for a room and meals. She was Mrs Fitzroy. She'd lost her husband in the wars and was glad of company for herself and her baby daughter, Ada. She employed me as her wet nurse first. Later I became her housekeeper."

"Why are you telling me this?" I said, unable to keep the bitterness from my voice. How could she have kept me at a distance for so long?

Makepeace's eyes clouded over. "We're all the family left that each of us has got, Eglantine." She took my hand in hers. I wanted to pull away. This was my grandmother, the only family I had left in all the world, and she was holding my hand. My emotions shot through me with as much force and colour as looking at the diamond through Old Sweet's loupe, all of them overlapping and vivid. All her little tendernesses added up. Housekeepers didn't tend to the children of the house as she did. But she was my father's mother, her bedroom was the tiny room off the kitchen, bereft of light.

"You have lived like a servant."

"It was your father's idea, Eglantine. I'd kept this house for years already by the time it came into his possession," she said.

"And how did he come to own this house?" I said, the truth hovering somewhere between us, but I was unsure if she would pin it down, for once and for all.

Makepeace sighed and looked out the window. "Amberline and Ada grew up side by side, he was the shadow to her light. Their games and laughter filled the house. But when Ada came of age, Mrs Fitzroy decided it was no longer appropriate for her to be so close with a servant's boy. Amberline was old enough to earn his keep. But this sent him into a temper. His taste of fine things only made him want more. He found a job at a stable, but he felt it was beneath him, shovelling shit and hay. He became wilful, uncontrollable. He'd steal to buy Ada gifts and fancies. It was when Mrs Fitzroy discovered his gifts to Ada that she sent him away."

She released my hand to smooth the chatelaine chains along her skirt. "He made this for me, did you know?" she asked, trying to divert my attention. Her chatelaine was more lock than key. It was a weight that had anchored her to my father, to his house.

"You haven't answered my question," I said. I would not let her distract me.

Makepeace sighed. "I didn't see him for some time, though I ached to hear of him. And then, one day he reappeared, with his fine clothes and money in his pocket. He didn't tell me where he'd been or where the money had come from and I knew better than to ask. And in his arms he held you. He left you in my care while he paid his respects to Mrs Fitzroy. I knew he was keen to see her face at his change in fortune. And I was amazed and relieved, for I not only had my son back, but I had a new grand-daughter, named for me. I kept you quiet in the kitchen. But not long after Amberline returned, Mrs Fitzroy died. Amberline only had to ask for Ada's hand and she gave it. Your father passed you off as a foundling and Ada, soft-hearted creature she was, took you in. When he married her, the house – and all her wealth – became his. I stayed on as housekeeper. He wanted it so."

The walls seemed to press in on us; this house had been the centre of my father's empire? I looked at the ceiling and the floor. The house was just an illusion. It wasn't made of four safe walls and a sheltering roof, it wasn't a place of safety and refuge, it was my father's masterstroke, his biggest theft yet.

"You must believe me," Makepeace said, "too long I've kept it to myself. The weight of it."

Our home was something my father had taken by stealth. All of me was incendiary. I wanted to see the house burn. The last of my father's litany of thefts gone in smoke. But the place was so damp, I doubted a flame would bother to take.

"What about my mother?" I said and saw Makepeace flinch, not realising how much she had given away, forgetting how the silences usually fuelled my questions about my mother. "When did I come to live here without her?" Makepeace looked at me. All the pieces shone dangerously and I struggled against putting them together, not wanting to see the blade that they had become. "He was married to them at the same time?" Makepeace went pale with the truth of what I had gleaned.

"He's my son, Eglantine. What was I to do? Even as a boy he was full of his own thoughts and ideas. When I tried to teach him his letters, they wouldn't stick, he was all for playing tricks with his hands, unable to sit still. I came and saw you and your mother every chance I could."

"What sort of excuse is that?" I prickled.

"The Rom in him loved your mother, but he craved being a gentleman and marrying Ada gave him that. He was his own man, Eglantine, I'd no more influence over him as a grown man."

Outside a cat wailed and sent my heart racing, for my ears perceived it as a child's cry first before I made sense of the sound. Makepeace, too, sat a little higher, stiller, until we both breathed again. She squeezed my hand gently in hers and I felt the papery dry skin of her hand. I wept. Angry tears. My own doll held tight in my fist, my first theft, I was a thief's daughter, whatever way I looked at it. He'd stolen this house, and all the contents of it. I was just another spoil. And somehow, still yet unbeknownst to me, he'd stolen my mother from me. I'd no proof, but I felt it in my marrow.

At the first opportunity I got, I took the pillowcase of money and my doll and consigned them to the darkness at the bottom of the cellar. I'd not be his walking legacy, the keeper of his flame. I'd not be the strength of his hands.

EIGHTEEN

Patrin, 1819

As the season turned, wind gusted under our door and through the cracks in the walls that I had stuffed with rags to try to stem the cold. Rain fell intermittently and slipped through a hole in the ceiling, a bucket beneath to catch it. I lifted Little Egg to my breast and felt the dry radiant heat of her cheek on my breast.

"Amberline," I called, but he was not here; his absence was growing more familiar than he was. I let my daughter drink, hoping my milk would cool her, before I carried her to the fire, the flames throwing their light across her small body, the telltale spots, the painted rouge of illness on her cheeks. The scarlatina. Quickly I stripped her of her swaddling cloth and gown and saw the rash lick down her arms. Eerily she didn't cry out, just lay on my lap with her tongue, speckled like a strawberry, resting in her mouth. The red lines on her throat looked caked with blood, like twisted rope. I ran a damp cloth down her face and limbs hoping to cool her. I rocked her in my arms, all the while a prayer on my lips, one hand on my daughter, one hand on my *putsi*, willing her well with whatever power could hold true. Saint Sarah of the Sea deliver us.

Amberline came in from the darkness, the rain dripping from his hat, elbows, shoulders; like the face of a mountain he had his own waterfalls. His face just as impassive.

"What on earth are you doing? She'll catch a chill," he scolded, wanting to scoop my daughter from my arms, but I moved away from him, so all he gathered was air.

"She has the fever, the scarlatina." The words bobbed in my throat, yet my mind still clung to the prayer. "We have to draw the fever away," I said, trickling a little water into her mouth. "This is your doing, Amberline, taking her out to see your mother, wherever she lives, without my knowing."

Amberline peered into her face and I looked away, not wanting to see his fear, my own was too large, it prickled around me and I held her tighter.

"I'll go to the apothecary," Amberline said, his hand on the door, not waiting for me to respond. He hurried out, leaving behind him a pool of water that snaked towards us. Should I take her out in the rain? Would that even cool her? My mother would have known how to bring the fever down and I at once felt the burden of leaving her behind, how little thought I'd given to anything at all, intoxicated by a kiss and the promise of a new start.

Amberline returned with a dirty-looking bottle stoppered with cork and some scribbled instructions that the rain had run to babble. His hand shook as he tried to pour the required amount into a spoon, some escaping its lip and down onto the floor, the smell of alcohol strong and sharp in my nostrils. It trickled into Little Egg's mouth and for a moment her face contorted red before she vomited it out. Her little tongue grew more swollen, a slug in her mouth.

The fever burned us together. All the love we had, united against the illness, a presence inside the room, making the three of us four.

By the second night her breathing grew ragged and Amberline thought we should have her baptised in a church and a blessing from the Holy Spirit. It was the only thing we hadn't tried. We owed her that, he implored. We looked at each other, the fear unsaid between us. That the debt of my father's life was yet to be paid.

Out in the rain, Amberline pulled his coat over us to try to keep us dry, but the rain would not be deterred. We staggered through the streets, knocking on every church door we passed. Most of them were locked against the poor, frightened that their silver plate be the stuff for the dollyshop. If anyone came to answer we were met with expressions of disgust; few would even exchange a word with us before the door closed between us. All Amberline's fine clothes were worthless now, the rain had reduced us to the damp origins of what we were – gypsies – and that was all anyone saw: the despised, the vagrant, the poor. Our one true joy was strapped to my chest and I willed my heart to pick up the slack beat of hers.

The next church door we arrived at, Amberline's foot was wedged in the doorway before the churchman forced it closed. A coin allowed us in, but he wouldn't baptise our daughter until we were married in the eyes of his Lord, our Romany union had no place here. I thought of my father's happiness at our union, my mother's distrust; how I longed for them both now, my father's strength, my mother's knowledge, together we'd scatter this fever to the winds. Amberline gave him another coin.

The churchman waited scowling and I wanted to tell him that Little Egg had already been baptised by a river, but what good would that serve? Our wet clothes dripped onto the floor and the churchman's eyes looked at the puddles of us and no doubt wished us gone. Would Amberline dig into his pockets again? Would I have to shake him to make the pennies rain down onto the floor? Why did he hesitate? He disappeared outside through the doorway into the rain and left me with the glowering parson. I saw myself through his eyes – nothing more than a beggar with a soul not worthy of his breath and my baby's worth even less. He saw me not as a person but as an inconvenience. Amberline stepped back through the doorway, his face impervious.

"We shall wait a little longer, dear sir," he said, placing another coin in the parson's palm, dripping water onto the lines in which my mother would have forecast a fortune for her grand-daughter's life. How did Amberline's pockets overflow with silver, his clothing so fine, when we lived as we did? How much money would he pay to save our daughter?

The church was all stone and cold. Would God hear a prayer from in here? In response the wind crept beneath the door and howled through the room and into the rest of the church.

We must have waited an uncomfortable half an hour with the churchman drinking from a flask he had hidden about himself and dozing in a pew, the only thing that held him the promise of more coin, like Judas's secret bargain, when a pounding came at the door. Amberline swift upon his feet opened it to admit the soaked visitors – an older woman and a tattered child who disappeared from the doorway as soon as Amberline bestowed a shilling, a child made of raindrops, then darkness, then gone.

The older lady stepped forward and threw her shawl from her head, a soft lace cap stuck around her face, a silver chatelaine glinting at her waist, vanishing into her voluminous skirts.

"Give me the child," she said urgently, reaching her hands towards my chest. I resisted. Who was she and what did she want with my child? Amberline nodded to me to do as I was directed and carefully I unstrapped Little Egg from my chest, her lace-worked bonnet matching the trim on the older woman's cap. Hawk-eyed I watched her, lest she try to remove her from the church. Amberline stamped his foot and the churchman bumbled up to the altar and said the most perfunctory of vows which we agreed to, short one witness so the churchman signed the register. I wrote my name as best I was able and Amberline made an X, while the older lady waited, her pale blue eyes not daring to meet mine. He handed her the pen and she took it slowly and applied it to the writing of her name. First an E then a Stark. She was Amberline's mother. My aunt, the first Eglantine Stark.

Mrs Stark handed the baby to the churchman reluctantly, undoing the little ribbons under Egg's chin gently, before he tilted her backwards and let the holy water trickle over her fontanelle, the cool water making her blink, but she did not cry out. Where was the singing, where was the beauty of the river running free over her limbs, where was all the welcoming joy? This was a baptism of tears.

Mrs Stark took Little Egg back into her arms before unwrapping her swaddling cloth, her little chest peeking from the woollen shawl also a rouge-pot red. Her fingers gently ran themselves over the corded red marks around her neck, enflamed with the scarlatina. Gently Mrs Stark wrapped her back up again and looked into my baby's mouth. The parson stood, about to speak, to encourage us to leave, but Mrs Stark silenced him with a glance and handed my daughter back to me.

From within the cavernous folds of her skirts, Mrs Stark drew out a small bottle and dipped the tip of her finger in before offering it to Egg to suck. I fought back my aversion for another woman's claim to closeness with my child, for I knew she was only trying to help. There was something about her, the surety of her hands, the ease around Egg, the net of her love thrown wide around her.

"It is foxglove. It will take her fever down," Mrs Stark said as Egg sucked upon her finger and winced. Mrs Stark dipped her finger in the font and dripped some holy water into Egg's mouth.

The churchman mumbled under his breath but we ignored him. Carefully Mrs Stark untied Egg's little shoes and I felt my breath strain in my throat, the little shoes my father had made for her on her first baptism day. She carefully blew into each little piece of stitched kid and the shoe inflated like a drinking bladder does with water. She reached into her pockets and sprinkled the crushed bloom of the foxglove at the toe of each shoe, before she carefully dipped Egg's feet back into her slippers.

NINETEEN

Patrin, 1819

Little Egg recovered from her bout of scarlatina; Mrs Stark's medicine had worked better than the apothecary's bitter brew. The only remnant of it was the red flush that had seeped into her cheeks. The lines around her throat faded but their presence ate at me, the thought of that rope going over my father's head, my mother's curse, the fear that they had somehow mingled together on my baby's flesh. I bathed her skin in chamomile, but the herb was old and withered. How long ago had it been picked? Desiccated as ash.

I was bathing Egg's tender skin when there was a knock at the door and I stood, my hand suspended between bowl and skin, unsure what the sound was for a moment, when the knock came again. No one had knocked on our door before. I wrapped Egg back up and carefully opened the door, my foot wedged against it, expecting someone to push it in. But when I opened it there was Amberline's mother, her lace cap pushed up by the wind.

"Patrin," she said, "let me in." And I hesitated. In the daylight, looking at her, I saw my mother's features, the shape of her face, her frame, her forthright stare. All I wanted was to be back with her, not having the stink of the street come up to us every time the door opened, the neighbours' effluent on our threshold.

I opened the door and she stepped in, kissing me chastely on the cheek, her eyes on Little Egg, her grand-daughter, her namesake. In her arms she carried a basket filled with food. A bottle of milk stoppered up with a clean rag, apples, a loaf of bread. She cast her eye quickly around the decrepit room but said nothing about it.

"How is she then?" Amberline's mother asked and I was struck with not knowing what to call her – Mother, Eglantine, Aunt.

"She is well, thanks to you," I said and her face coloured with pride. She leaned down and ran a cool finger across the redness in Egg's cheeks, her touch resting on the red lines around her throat. I knew she wanted to hold her, but I held firm. For all the blood we shared she was still the stranger.

"She's had them since she was born," I said, looking at the chain-like wrinkle of skin. Amberline's mother looked at me.

"I'm sure they'll fade with time, maybe just a little rash is all. I'll bring some ointment next time I come."

I nodded, wondering if she was telling the truth; the lines around Egg's neck seemed angry, permanent.

"May I hold her?" she asked and reluctantly I handed her over, placing myself between the door and their embrace, frightened that she would try to take her back to whatever place she had come from. Her clothes were modest and simple, yes, but the weave fine, not a thread loose. Her boots were of fine leather and peeked from beneath the hem of her skirt. Her lace cap, like her blouse, was moon-white; how she got her clothes so clean without soot or dirt, I didn't dare ask.

"I was very sorry to hear about your father," she said. "He was the finest of men." My stomach clenched and I thought I'd be sick on the floor. "He saved my son," she continued. "I'll never forget it."

"But still he continues. Stealing things. For someone who wants to avoid the noose, he is doing all he can to court it," I said, bitterness swirling in my words and in my voice.

She looked at me blankly, as though not sure what to say. "He is his own man, for good or ill. I've hopes he'll find his way yet," she said, "but it weighs heavy on me the loss to your mother and yourself for his sake." Her words were kindness, but they were empty to me. Amberline was a slippery knot between us, I could not make the shape of it or find where the ends were to unravel it.

Little Egg's hands shot up to her grandmother's face and Mrs Stark laughed, her laugh so similar to my mother's it squeezed at the core of me. Her little fingers caught on something and from beneath the fabric folds of her blouse a small pouch dangled in the air between them, Little Egg's hands batting it, all a game. So Amberline was wrong, the old ways were not all gone from London.

"Amberline has forbidden me from speaking our tongue," I said without thinking, but she didn't look up from her grand-daughter's face.

"I wish that surprised me. It is partially my fault, I'm afraid. I've raised him without a father, outside of what even I knew myself, so forgive him if he tends to strike strong opinions."

I stood straighter, the anger rising.

"He's like an airborne seed. Look up at the top of the buildings and you'll see them, trees taken root in the crevices and corners of the tallest of buildings, their roots clinging in shallow dirt and muck, still reaching towards the fresher air, the brighter light. Reaching. Determined. That's Amberline." She handed Little Egg back to me and I could smell in the folds of her swaddling cloth and her cheek the fragrance of Mrs Stark's perfume, lavender, and for a moment I was jealous that she smelled of her grandmother and not of me.

"Perhaps it is just a bit of milk rash around Little Eglantine's neck. Let the air get to it and it should clear up."

"And where am I supposed to find that here?" The bitterness was in my voice again. Her fingers toyed with the chain of her chatelaine.

I pined for the signs of living green things, for the sound of freely running water rather than the dirty splash of the well and the stink of the chamber-pot.

"Down by the river, it's only a few streets from here." She bent down and kissed Little Egg on the cheek before she wrapped her arms around me in an embrace that made me stiffen, fighting my tears.

"I'll come again," she said and I was unsure whether to believe her or not.

* * *

That night Amberline asked me to pick the monograms from the pocket handkerchiefs he had stolen and to launder them of whatever pestilence he'd brought in. And I resentfully did as he requested. As I put the needle to the first initial he stoked the fire, a fresh batch of silver falling from his pockets, readying to run as molten as mercury, the air turning sour and coating our nostrils. If ever we had need of air it was now.

In the morning I waited for Amberline to leave before strapping Egg to my chest, I didn't want to ask his permission to go out in case he denied it. I wasn't a prisoner, though all the buildings of the city made me feel caged. I walked out the door and stood in the lane – no bells clanged my doom, no one cast a sideways glance. How quickly my world had been curtailed, how quickly the end of the lane rushed towards me and I walked out into the wider street. Egg's little eyes watched me, a yawn twisting her little features and then the inquisitive little blink. I took heart in her tiny face and I stuck to the side of the street where the weak sunshine fell and lifted my face to it as a sunflower does. I would have followed it anywhere, a golden sign in the sky. I followed the direction that Mrs Stark had given me, for a good half an hour, until I heard the sounds of the river rush up to me – the waterman's call, the wash of water upon pebbles, the tern's cry. I ran and felt the wind blow my scarf from my head.

We came to a bridge and I leaned over. The water danced with light. Little Egg's eyes tried to follow each glittering shard of it, her hand reaching out to them as if light was something to catch and keep and kindle in the palm of your hand. One foot carefully after the other, I walked down the small stone steps to the pebble-lined shore of the river, the smell of the city still filling my nostrils, but with the running water and the light and the wind, it felt like a broom sweeping all the crowded and confined oppressions from my heart and mind. All this time I had been carrying a stone in my chest, how little I had breathed, as if it was I who had been laid in the earth bereft of air and light. This was my grief. Little Egg's fine lace bonnet flittered in my fingers as I walked down to the water's edge. I bent down and let the water rush across my fingers and I whispered her secret name into the fragile whelk-shell of her ear. If she could survive this life, so could I. We would endure. The bargeman's singing, clipped notes, sliced across the waters and filled me with longing to see my mother, though now we'd be *marime*, outcast. Surely she'd forgive and embrace us and call us her own? Amberline's affections had burned bright for but a season, half in love with the idea of his past than the reality of us, with the law full of the scent of him.

Down on the shoreline things dazzled at the corner of my eye, shining wet, demanding my attention, a patrin of a different kind, the patrin of the lost and torn away. I squinted against the sunlight and kicked at the pebbles. Little Egg's head lolled onto my chest asleep, her eyelashes moving like moths. What do babes dream of? The river had left its own messages amongst the clumps of water weed and pebbles – an old blue apothecary bottle, a button, a shoe with no sole – all had the otherworldly gloss from the glistening water yet to dry. In the distance I saw a figure bent, scouring the lip of the shoreline, plucking up whatever thing their foot turned up, a human waterfowl.

At my foot I turned over a glossy moss-veined stone, thinking it would be a pretty enough thing to keep on our windowsill. But there beneath something winked, caked with muck, something golden. I picked it up and rolled it in my palm, blowing off the grit, spitting on it to reclaim it from the river's silt, to return it to its shine. Egg stirred awake. Holding it to my eye, I surveyed the whole river through the circle of beaten gold, the whole world roaring around Little Egg and me like an ocean, but in that circled view all was quiet. I held the ring up to her little eye and peeked through at her and a smile ran fleetingly across her dimpled cheeks at my game. It was cold when I placed it on my finger, and I spun it round, large as it was, a gold flashing wheel fit for a fairy's wagon.

I wanted to wear it on my finger – the bride of the river – but I knew better; things bauble-bright would disappear as they appeared, submitted to the flame, changed form, turned to liquid, made new. Amberline was a thief, things danced through his hands, would he dance us through them with just as much lightness, with just as little thought? I opened my *putsi*, the leather squeaked as I tucked the ring deep inside, feeling the other things brush against my fingers.

From across the stones the mudlarks approached. Had the glint of the gold caught their eyes, a lure as for a fish? As they neared I saw they were only children. One was half my height and tipped his cap at me with a "Morning missus", while his companion in a coat fit for a scarecrow, beyond mending, pulled the holey fabric tighter around himself and stood tall, chin a-jut at me.

"What did you find, missus? You know right well this is our patch and whatever you find belongs more to us than to you," he said, running his hands through his lank hair, the sparse growth of first whiskers atop his lip.

I admired his pluck, but I'd not have a child bully me. "Where is it writ?" I said. "Be off with you and find your own," and I stepped forward, not intimidated.

"We'll make you give us what you found," he said and I felt the iron run in my blood.

"Will you now?" I said. "Then I'll raise the spirits to curse you, I will, for I am gypsy by birth and I'll make sure they harm you until you plead for your death." The words ran out of me, and Little Egg, who had remained concealed beneath my shawl, began to cry like a curlew, thin and high, caught on the wind.

But it was enough, the two boys thought my baby's cry was the beginning of my curse and ran, losing their balance on the stony shore.

"Be off with you," I cried and threw a stone wide, not wanting to hit them, but enough to give them the gift of speed. Little Egg bawled then and I lowered my breast into her mouth as I resolved to stand my ground, to find the mettle in me.

* * *

Amberline was waiting for us when we returned and he was livid, his eyes burning at me as soon as I entered, an interrogation flying off his lips. But my confrontation with the mudlarks had given me a new boldness, the secreted ring concealed around my neck fortified me.

"Am I your prisoner now?" I said, my voice low as Egg snuggled up to my breast, asleep, her snuffles warm on my skin. Amberline's face went white and he stepped backwards as if my words were a blow. The fire of Little Egg's fever had burned off all illusions. Is this what I wanted for my child? A squalid room, impossible to keep clean in the middle of a city? A city that would strip you naked to sell your rags if it could? Yet Amberline and his mother always seemed well kept, a steady stream of silver ran through his hands, but none stopped with us. Amberline had dazzled me with his fine clean hands and his fair skin, his clothes from a tailor's workshop, but he was no gentleman. He slapped me then. The back of his hand rang across my face. The blow turned my world black and white. I staggered backward, trying to protect Little Egg with one hand, trying to steady myself with the other. He had struck me with no thought for her.

I drew myself up high and felt the words course through me. "Damn you straight to hell, Amberline Stark."

He pulled me away from the door by my hair and I felt I was drowning in mid-air trying to keep my arms as a shield around our daughter, more fearful for her safety than my own. With an agonising tear, a clump of my hair came away in his hand. In disgust he threw the dark threads of it to the floor and left us, the door shuddering in its frame. I sat upright and looked at that patch of hair and skin and blood which had most recently been fixed to my own head and recalled my father attaching a piece of meat to a string and twirling it round and round his head to tempt the trout before skimming it across the water, the lips of the fish reaching towards the surface.

Amberline could twirl my hair and skin, my very breath, and I'd come when called, but I'd be biding my time. Little Egg whimpered in my arms, my mind was already running. Better a bride of the river than his. The patrin in my mind's eye marked the way, the secret route to escape.

* * *

When Amberline returned he was all remorse, all repentance, his hand gently brushing where before it had pulled, though I flinched. From his pocket he produced a red ribbon for my hair and I thanked him for it and tucked it down the front of my bodice. It would be the ribbon I'd tie on the thornbush of my father's grave. Amberline kept a close eye upon Little Egg and me, as if we were the jewels that he would not be parted from, jewels to be used bright as lures, tangled in his schemes. And I submitted, knowing it would lull him into trust.

He bid me walk with him, Little Egg strapped to my chest, a little play all mapped out on the streets fanning around us. Little Egg's boot was loose enough to fall on cue just as a mark passed by, the delicate pink squirm of her foot, her toes the worm. The retrieval of her boot was bait, providing enough distraction for Amberline to get closer, his fingers hovering like mayflies before they danced through the Samaritan's pockets, while I looked at the handiwork of my father offered back to me in a stranger's palm, thanks spilling out of my mouth. How did it come to this? How had Egg and I become Amberline's feeble instruments? My father had sacrificed his life to give us a chance, but Amberline appeared unable to grasp what that chance was. My father had made these little shoes for Little Egg's feet, all his love for her fixed with each stitch. The leather warm. I had to pretend to be grateful to the stranger, all the while bristling with the charade, knowing full well that Amberline's trick would be enough to have us all transported if caught.

TWENTY

Patrin, 1821

When Little Egg's baby shoes no longer fit her feet, I put them away, the little stitches and knots of my father's making still held true. In the darkness while Amberline slept I ran my fingers over that stitching, round and around, a little amulet. I felt my father's skill with the needle, the reinforcement of the leather at heel and toe. The leather had taken on the wear of Egg's small foot and given the shoe the ghost shape of it – heel, arch, toes. I didn't know whether it cradled my hand or my hand it. Little Egg was growing faster than my eye could track her. She'd already pulled herself up by the leg of the table and had taken her first tentative steps, her hands outstretched for balance as if she was floating in air. As soon as she walked she ran. Out to the well she'd run around the puddles, her feet hitting them, sending the water skyward.

But Amberline had grand plans.

One day towards Egg's second birthday, Amberline came in the door holding a large box, looped with a string, a fine stamp upon it. He placed it down on the rickety table and Egg climbed up onto a chair, the feet of which wobbled. Amberline reached out his hand to steady her. She looked at the box as if it was a thing in itself, her finger reaching towards the lid, and I felt a dread come over me as to what was inside. Amberline slid off the string and she helped him lift the lid, a tumble of bright

158

satin spilling over the edge. The chortle of her voice. Her little hand reached for it but the slipperiness of the fabric evaded her fingers. She laughed, reached again and pulled out a white satin dress; the glare of it in the gloom made it look like silver. Around the waist was a dark blue velvet sash. Beneath it in the box was a small dress in the reverse: a blue velvet dress and a white satin sash. Amberline held it out towards me, the plush of it, soft to the touch. I held it to my cheek and closed my eyes, seduced by the nap of it. Amberline kissed me on the mouth unawares and I was startled, I'd forgotten the sweetness of his lips. How much had these dresses cost? How many weeks' rent would they have provided? If he could afford dresses like these, could we afford a better place to live? Better food to eat? A better life for all of us? They were too fine, too delicate.

"Come, try them on," Amberline smiled and though I was wary I remembered that face when I first saw it, the glitter of those eyes, that smile that reeled me in. Amberline waited on the other side of the curtain as we dressed and as soon as I slipped the dress over my head I felt transformed, the fabric cool as water. Little Egg fidgeted as I fastened the buttons and tied her sash, eager to see her father's smile. With a lock of her dark hair, I tried to tempt a curl around her face. She was so excited and wriggling that she spun off my fingers, enjoying the feel of the silken fabric on her legs. Amberline's gifts were extravagant, blinding. With a flourish of the curtain, we stepped out into Amberline's smile, all light, all brightness.

From under the table he pulled out two identical hatboxes and plucked out a pair of bonnets then helped Egg tie the big blue ribbons beneath her chin, his tickling fingers making her laugh.

"And lastly," Amberline said, lifting Little Egg onto the chair, her little feet swinging in the air, "take a look in my pockets." She looked at him and looked at his pockets, her hand reaching in and pulling out a small boot from one and its pair from the other. Amberline kneeled down, fed her foot to the boot and tied the laces, the leather white kid. Once the laces were firmly tied, she leapt down and grinned at me as the sole made a resounding *thwack*.

"Are you ready?" he said.

"Ready for what?" I asked, but he wouldn't answer me, he just smiled and opened the door.

* * *

Amberline led us down to the river which crawled with people, all waiting for the royal ship upon the water. The wind whipped at our skirts, a spray of water crested our heads and sprayed the canopy of stallholders selling chestnuts, ale, silhouettes for half a crown. The fresh air was tonic. Amberline wove us through the crowds and ushered us into a tent and the portraitist rubbed his hands together at our entrance, bidding us take our seats behind the screen, a candle flickering from the draught distorting our shadow, so that sometimes I was small and Egg was large and Amberline's hat arched over us, a dark sky.

Behind the curtain the silhouettist's scissors snipped through the black card with a crunch and a snick and within three minutes the portrait was done, the wasted cardboard unwound like orange peel on the floor. He handed the silhouette to Amberline like a prize and I saw our bodies shrunk to shadows, the three of us, and I shivered, though I saw no fault in it.

Amberline disappeared in a wave of people and returned minutes after. I knew he'd been unable to resist the opportunity, the parade of people running past his fingers like a shoal. I knew his pockets would be lined with precious metals, his fingers miners, but he returned to us with warm chestnuts or to twirl Little Egg by the side of a brass band or to watch Punch and Judy's loud complaints.

We threw crumbs at the seagulls and laughed at their squabbles over penny cakes. A lady, a widow she told us, was wound in by the sound of Egg's chirp and came up and asked me questions about her sleeping and teething, happy for a reprieve from her loneliness. She jingled her golden chatelaine, with a thimble turned bell on it, waiting for a smile, her dark cuffed wrist resting on Egg's leg. The tenderness of that touch made me long for my mother, abandoned by her daughter, denied her grand-daughter, made widow by her son-in-law. Little Egg's face shone with the happiness of the sound, the bunting above her head like a row of colourful birds bobbing in the breeze.

The widow passed Amberline as she drifted off into the crowd and I was wary. Amberline was too bright, his movements too large and animated, drunk on the sound of all the coins in everyone's pockets.

"Would you like to see something wonderful?" he said and Little Egg began to skip in anticipation. "Hurry along now." What could Amberline have to surprise us with next? His surprises were like cold water. Amberline led us a roundabout way home. His steps became more excited. He began to rush as he led us onward.

Street by street the houses began to change, growing neater, whiter, finer. Little gardens, flower boxes, blooms. Horses on the road had high-stepping gaits. The ladies we passed on the footpath wore lace collars and sleeves, their slippers made of satin, tiny pearls around their throats. Their hands concealed in gloves, their fingers and wrists encased in a second skin. I carefully concealed my hand around Little Egg's and the other in my skirts, hoping they wouldn't see the wear in mine.

Amberline led us into a singular street, the afternoon sunlight striking all the street-fronted windows golden. We were probably less than a mile from where we lived and here even the sunlight was brighter, the street facing the riverfront.

"Here we are," he said, straightened his spine and held himself aloft.

"But what are we looking at?" I asked, watching him dissemble and transform, turn gentleman before me. He dropped my hand and offered me his elbow and we walked down the street slowly at a measured pace as if we belonged there.

"What are we looking at? Can't you see it? Look at that glass, is it not fine? How much light it lets in. Not a speck on that doorstep. The proportion of the windows."

I looked at the house and all he pointed at, but I saw only another pillar of stones, glass and wood. What value did it have to me? All the windows were just eyes that watched the world go by. The house was no better than a cage for wild things.

Amberline, frustrated by my lack of excitement, crouched down close to Egg and hoisted her up into his arms.

"What can you see, Eglantine?"

Her face looked earnestly from me to him; I saw that she didn't want to displease him, that the question confused her.

"House," she said tentatively.

Amberline waited for her to say more, to say what she saw, and my breath caught in my chest. He peered into her face and the new dress he'd bought me felt constrictive, suffocating. If I could have torn it off right there in the street I would have. Across my skin, a crawling sensation of ants on the march, and I felt the panic get beneath my skin. Is this where he took her to see his mother? Did he hope to install our daughter there without me? Why would he show it to her, unless to introduce it as her new home? My child was my whole world. The earth I walked on, the heavens I slept under. What need did I have of such a fancy house and fine manners? Or for a *vardo* and the Romanyjib? If I had my daughter, I had my everything. But Amberline was all silver, all mercury, all hot and cold. I had no way of reading him.

Amberline looked away, distracted by the sound of horses.

A fine landau approached the house, and the driver sat dressed in smart livery, whip poised in the air like a question mark, before he brought the horse to a sharp stop. A cloud of spit formed at the horse's mouth. How hard had he ridden it? A young woman, her maid beside her, sat in the landau, their faces obscured by their bonnets. The driver jumped down and offered the young woman his hand, and I watched as her blonde ringlets bobbed around her face, her kid slipper hit the path, and the pearls around her throat, white as the tip of a fox's tail. I was overcome with the whiteness of her. I stared at Amberline. Had we been made puppets again so he could quarry his mark? But his face was turned away from me, looking directly at her, the shadow of his hat obscuring his face, his shoulder turned as they trailed up the stairs. The maid carried the purchases wrapped in brown paper and string and opened the door. The young woman had her fingers on the doorframe, ready to close the door and dismiss the street. But something on the street drew her eye and she looked towards us, then Amberline stepped forward, relegating us to the shadow.

Her face lit up in recognition of him and he smiled back at her, a smile that I'd never seen, a smile that he had kept in reserve, just for her. And just as it came it vanished as her name was called through the house and echoed down to us on the footpath, thrown like a vandal's stone. Ada. She turned and disappeared into the house. Who was she and how did Amberline know a woman like that? Amberline would not meet my eye, dissembler.

The darkening sky ran like a river above us, streaked with catkins of clouds, as we continued our walk home. I had tried to keep it bright and clean, being as house proud as any Rom, but now it seemed seedy and dark and small. And we were to be trapped in it with our fine clothes, fireflies in a jar.

All of me burned with the shame of being paraded like his actress. From beneath the hem of my new dress, my old battered boots still peeped, scuffed and worn. They stuck out, false notes in Amberline's song. Our dresses were nothing but costumes in his great play. But what were our parts? How were we to behave? We were mere figments of his imagination, characters of his invention rather than living flesh.

Amberline's feet dragged as we turned into our enclosed lane, the displeasure coming off him in waves as he closed the door to the world. I watched his face, but he gave nothing away, yet I felt it as surely as a twisted branch or twig pierced through a leaf. Amberline pulled the silhouette out of his pocket and placed it on the mantelpiece upside down. He fumbled inside the rest of his pockets and pulled out all the things he'd stolen. Just as I'd suspected, the widow's chatelaine the last thing to fall, all its chains tangled, so that it looked like a golden beetle trapped in his hand.

I took off our dresses, folded them back into the box and returned our limbs to our old clothes. Carefully I eased off Little Egg's boots, two matching blisters red as yew berries on the back of each of her heels.

Amberline spun the chatelaine in his hands and the sound of the thimble striking the other chains made Egg grin so he did it again.

"'Tis so fine a piece," he said and I knew what he meant – each chain held something delicate: a tiny pair of scissors, the point shaped to a beak; a case for needles; a piece of ivory slid between two ornately carved gold pieces; a clock as big as my fingernail.

"I hope it didn't hurt her to take it," I said but he ignored me.

"It would be a shame to melt it down, the workmanship is quite something. It's too distinctive to pawn."

With his pliers he carefully undid the link that held each piece, until the chatelaine was dismantled, the pieces of gold from the aide-mémoire like plucked butterfly wings.

Amberline kindled the fire and the flames gathered at his touch, the room growing hot and stuffy. He fed the fire wood, sticks and twigs until all our faces glowed with the heat of it. The metallic smell made our eyes water. I sprinkled flour on the table and Little Egg climbed up on the chair, ready to continue her letters, learning the letters of her name in a sprinkle of flour upon the table, just as I had learned mine with a stick in the dirt, though she was probably too young to remember them. On my lap she grew restless, the letters powdering together, but I persevered. She was more interested in making clouds by smacking her palms together or blowing a trail with her lips, but I took her finger and started again each time. A woman in charge of her letters could rule her own world, I thought. All I could write was my own name.

The smelting billowed black smoke into the air and it made both our noses run. Piece by piece Amberline fed the chatelaine into the fire, holding a pestle over the flames in the fireplace with a pair of iron grips.

"Amberline," I said, but he ignored me, the metal dissolving in front of his eyes more captivating than we were. All that shone he felt he was king of. Silver was his religion, gold his god.

"Amberline," I said again, louder. He turned in his blacksmith's glove and apron and, though he looked at me, it was as if his thoughts were elsewhere. He steadied his wrist to pour the liquid metal into a mould. But Egg in frustration rammed the table. The wood shuddered violently at her push at her twisted letters and Amberline lost his grip.

Everything moved slowly. The liquid gold spooled through the air, serpent like and glowing as I shoved my little girl away, and she with unsteady feet wobbled on the chair and I stepped in front of her. The gold slithered onto my skin, feeling wet, but then the skin of my arm began to burn with it as the metal pierced deep. The smell of my own flesh cooking. The pain made me pant. Amberline lifted the bucket of water and tipped it over me, my poor skin hissing, an insult of steam, but the bucket had only a dribble. My knees weakened, Amberline at my side, supporting my weight. Egg's voice came from far away, calling me. The world drained from my eyes.

* * *

When I woke my arms were bandaged by my side and Little Egg was asleep beside me. How long had she been waiting for my eyes to open? I felt her breath on my legs through the thin blanket and hear the steady rhythm of her sleep. She'd climbed gingerly up onto the bed and snuggled around my legs, keeping clear of the stiff branches of my arms in case she hurt me more. All I wanted to do was take her in my arms and run my hands through her lovely flyaway dark hair. On the chest of drawers sat a clean roll of bandages and a brown jar of ointment. The burn on my arms turned to a low throb, sleep tugging at my eyelids.

When I woke again I heard voices from the other room, whispers thinly coming from behind the curtain. One was Egg's chirrup but the other was a woman's. Panicked, I sat up in the bed and swung my feet over the edge, feeling the pulse of the burn spread across my arms, up into my neck, down my fingers. From the gap in the curtain I saw Amberline's mother sitting with Little Egg as she quietly twiddled with all the little silver pieces hanging off her chatelaine, listening. I strained to hear and when I did I felt the ache for my own parents surge up through the ground and into my feet, the earth calling to me.

"Let me tell you of Dark Sarah," Mrs Stark said, her hand on Egg's hair. "Black Sarah, Sarah of the Sea."

"Who is she?" Egg said, her voice rushing up to me. How was it that I hadn't told her? How had I let the city take over our stories? I'd told her nothing of her other grandparents. I'd tell her of them, her grandfather who made a rat dance into his sack, her grandmother who helped her come into the world.

"Sarah was dark and she was comely and like her people before her she wore travellers' shoes. She knew the road and the road knew her. One day she had a dream that the Virgin and her maids – all three Marys – were banished from a faraway kingdom, lost upon the sea. And it was Black Sarah who saw to their rescue.

"She read the signs. She raced down to the shore and saw their vessel tossed upon the waves. She threw her cloak out across the water, where it turned into a boat for them to step safely upon, Black Sarah at the helm, guiding them to shore.

"And now on the twenty-fourth of every May, the Romany people descend on the Saintes-Maries-de-la-Mer in France. They take the statue of Black Sarah and dress her like a doll, before they walk with her upon their shoulders into the ocean to recreate the journey she made and to bring a good year. Your birthday, Eglantine."

Amberline's mother looked up then, her attention drawn by the movement of the curtain.

"Mama," Egg cried and ran to me, embracing me around the middle. Even her hair as it brushed my bandages made my skin scream. Amberline's mother's cap lay upturned on the table, inside it a little twist of sweets.

"Patrin, you should be resting," she said, getting to her feet and guiding me back to the bed, her steady hand in the small of my back. Egg's aniseed breath filled my nostrils.

"How long have I been asleep for," I said; the shadows on the wall were longer than I imagined, stretching all around us like a canopy.

"As long as you needed," she said. "How is the pain?" I watched Little Egg's face looking up at me, frowning with concern. The pain was like a new skin, a web pulling tight, needle sharp.

"Where is Amberline?" I looked at the black sooty marks on the table; the gold that had spilled had been gouged out, had the same happened to my skin? Had he peeled the gold off the surface of my skin like candle wax?

Amberline's mother produced a little wooden spinning top from her cavernous pockets and presented it to Little Egg in her palm.

"Child, try spinning this," she said and Egg's face lit up at the wonder, the thank you slipping out of her lips as she crouched on the floor for its mad spin.

"Look the little hare, he runs as it spins," she said delightedly. Egg was absorbed.

"Where is Amberline?" I asked again.

Amberline's mother lowered her voice. "I don't know." The sound of the spinning top's base bashing over the grooves between the floorboards boomed loudly.

My mind was spinning, spinning, spinning. How many days had she been here, how many days had Amberline been gone? How much time did I have remaining to me?

I reached for the jar I kept beneath the bed, a few pennies was all that was in it. My arms sang with burn, as did my anger. I'd been a lovelorn foolish girl, seduced by a pair of leather boots and a man's city ways. And now here was the chance I'd been waiting for. I'd given it all up – my family, my traditions, my place in the world – for a kiss and a honeyed word from a so-called kinsman. I was greener than a spring bud when Amberline plucked me and now my life felt more like stunted wood. Surely the sap still ran, green to my green heart.

The top stopped spinning and Egg held it still before setting it spinning again, the hare running for its life across the city, hoping to reach the hare's corner, the little edge of field the farmer left for its protection from the harvester's hand.

Amberline's mother undid my bandages and I winced at her touch. The gold had left nasty scarlet scalds running across my arms, roads not travelled glaring up at me, my constant reminder. I prayed to Black Sarah as I had as a child for our deliverance, for my arms to heal well enough to carry Little Egg, for I had no horse or *vardo*, all I had were my arms, burned and afflicted as they were. Carefully she rewrapped them and left the ointment and clean bandages. She looked into my face and I wondered if she saw that green leap through me. All of me was sprung to the task of it.

TWENTY-ONE

Eglantine, 1833

Without my father's constant income we'd soon be without funds. My father had left a trail of bills that we had to pay unless the house was to be taken from us. Each day brought a new bill – the coalman, his tailor, the butcher, the baker. Makepeace and I learned to beg for extensions, but they would still have to be paid. The money that we raised was no match for the march of living.

I did what was necessary then and went to my father's room and stripped anything of value from it – a pair of cufflinks, a diamond tie pin, a drawer full of linen shirts hardly worn, a beaver top hat in a lush blue silken case; all my father's portable property would keep us afloat yet. I took what I had to the pawnbrokers my father had taken me to as a child, and it was there that I'd go to see if I could wring a little pity from my father's associate. Makepeace watched as I left, knowing what cargo I carried, but she nodded her consent. She knew as well as I that my father's return was something we never dared hope for.

I wore the worst of my clothes, the skirts faded from washing, but as I made my way through the streets to where I recalled the shop, I saw that Makepeace and I were queens in a kingdom compared to the rest of our neighbours who survived like rats only blocks away. What did they do if their menfolk were gone across the seas?

Sweet's Emporium had changed in the intervening years. The sign hung precariously from a rusted hinge and my heart sank: if the shop wasn't doing well, what hope did I have of getting a good price for my father's things?

I pushed open the door, the bell a dull thud against the glass as if it couldn't be bothered. Old Sweet was at the counter, sitting like a toad in the circle of light his lamp made, but he didn't look up, too busy counting his money. As I made my approach he gently drifted the broadsheet of a newspaper atop the surface rather than have me play at guessing his accounts.

"Yes?" he said and squinted through his pince-nez at me, the light striking the lenses gold so that, disconcertingly, I was unable to see his eyes.

"How much for these?" I asked, lifting the hatbox onto the countertop and hearing the collapse of his coins beneath the broadsheet. He peered over the pince-nez at me, his eyes poring over me. I flipped the lid of the box and he pawed through it, looking over the make of the shirts and the wear in the hat band before he flipped out the loupe and examined the gold in the cufflinks, the diamond in the tie pin. He held this item particularly close to his field of vision, tilting it to the light.

"They ain't worth much, that 'diamond' is paste for one thing," he said, lowering his loupe, looking at me again.

"Are you quite sure?" I said, pulling myself upright and haughty, hoping that he'd respond to the force of my will, my tone, my superior manner. But it just made him look at me more.

"Do I know you?" he said, his eyes greasily following the outline of my body, and I shivered with revulsion, glad for the barrier of the counter between us.

"You know my father, Amberline Stark," I said and watched his response with a sense of satisfaction. He recoiled and I relished that his pince-nez fell from the bridge of his nose.

"Know him? I was glad to see the back of him, bound for Botany Bay and not too soon," he said.

I felt blood whoosh in my ears as steadily as holding a seashell there; the rest of the world turned quiet.

"Don't think I don't know your kind, Mr Sweet. You'll pay me a fair sum for the items or you may just find yourself on a prison hulk begging for Botany Bay."

He stood there and looked at me and I felt my skin hum and burn.

"You are a piece of work, Miss Stark, a piece of work, just like your bastard father and your whore gypsy mother," he said and I saw he was just waiting for me to crumble, to cry, to wilt like some poor flower picked and not put in water. He didn't know that I was like a willow, my roots ran deep and unseen, interlacing against whatever fate would hurl at me; I'd seek out the water regardless.

I pushed my father's hatbox to the ground on the other side of the counter and with it the veil of the broadsheet, enjoying the sound of the coins falling onto the counter, the pound notes falling like ash all around. Sweet had no time to speak. He was too shocked. At first he stood with his mouth open, trying to shape an expletive, but then his moneylender's conscience got the better of him, his instinct to retrieve his money and the goods, and when he bent I lightly swept all the coins he had been carefully counting, disappearing with a clink into my pocket before he even had a chance to look up.

The doorbell didn't make a sound when I opened it and I left it open as I went, Old Sweet cursing at the top of his lungs, down on his knees gathering his precious notes.

My fingers danced through the coins in my pocket and I felt all that my father had taught me: the lightness of my fingers, the delicate lift, the thrill of the theft – the only thing I had skills in but was unproved on my own, until now.

When I returned, two men were carrying out all the items from the study in wooden crates. Makepeace held the door open for them, the books as heavy as carrying a tree between them. With great effort they loaded them onto a cart, the horse sidestepping beneath the weight. I hoped that Makepeace had flicked through the pages before she allowed them to be packed, never knowing what things my father might have cached.

"What did you get from Sweet?" she asked, frowning as I cupped the stolen coins in my hand.

"He was feeling generous," I said before sweeping in the door, tingling with equal parts shame and thrill at what I had done.

"It's a start," Makepeace said. I knew she was talking about repairs and living expenses, but she was more right than she knew, for what had my father really trained me in, what other skill did I have except for the lightness of my fingers and the secrecy of my touch?

Everything extraneous was sold – Ada's old things from the nursery: the doll's house, the rocking horse, the nursing chair, the cradle, until all that remained was the chest of drawers, a mirror and my narrow bed. My father's room the same. In the dining room Makepeace carefully dusted and packed ornaments and candlesticks in straw-lined cases and took whatever she could get for them. Yet the money we raised was not enough: the roof needed repair, the chimneys had to be swept, the house was in constant complaint.

In the morning, a poor boy, soot black, came with his rods and brushes, carefully removed his two mismatched and ruined shoes and placed them on the canvas cloth Makepeace had laid out to protect the floor, then he crawled up through the hearth in bare feet, all the better to grip the blackened stone. I looked at those two sad little shoes and listened to him scuttle upwards, his bristling brush being pushed into the spaces where he no longer fitted. Soot rained down until the cold hearth was covered in black ash. Fireplace after fireplace he climbed up, his face growing blacker as he went, and still his little shoes remained. In my father's room an old bird's nest came down, blackened twigs and feathered down, a dead baby bird's bones white as teeth. How easily that boy could have been me, how easily I could have been him.

Makepeace dismissed him with a few coins and a slice of bread which he fell upon, his mouth as wide as a cat's before it was gone. When Makepeace disappeared into the kitchen, I saw to it that he was paid a little extra and told him to keep some aside from his master. The copper pennies in his hand had all the brightness of the sun compared to the soot that encased him; why, even the lines of his palm had been erased as if he had no past and no future. He was about to leave when I bid him wait a moment and I returned with a pair of old shoes I'd found at the bottom of my father's wardrobe, old and worn, not like the neat shoes he always wore.

"What are you doing?" Makepeace said, coming back from the kitchen with a glass of milk for the chimney boy.

He looked stricken at the items and dropped them on the floor, the lines around his eyes crinkling with apology.

"Miss?" he said imploringly.

"Better he have them than they moulder," I said and picked them up, but Makepeace stepped forward and snatched the shoes away, the milk spilling from the cup in her hand.

The poor sweep looked as if he would cry, a single tear tracking through the soot. I took the milk and gave it to him and he drained the cup, a white tideline above his lip, a dark shadow of soot left on the cup. I eased the shoes out of Makepeace's hands and gave them back to the boy. She just let him have them. Her own tears fell. Makepeace took the cup in her hand, a foreign thing, and came to herself. The shoes were too large by half. Makepeace disappeared and returned with rags. Together we bundled them into the toes of the shoes until the boy's feet fit, the laces tight.

"Thank you," he said, his tongue sticking to the top of his mouth.

Makepeace picked up the old shoes gingerly by the heel and went to bid the boy good day.

"May I have my shoes back, ma'am?" the sweep asked. "I'll give them to me brother, for he has none."

Makepeace gave them back to him and we watched him go down the stairs, his brushes over his shoulder, his old shoes in his hand, whistling.

"The boy is in want of a bath," Makepeace said and she was right, if a wind blew it would turn the street to a storm of black dust. He was in want of more than that. He was in want of his own mother. I looked at Makepeace, a mother in want of her own wayward son. But what of my mother?

* * *

We needn't have worried about having the chimneys swept, for soon we didn't have any coal to coax a fire, inviting the damp to spread. It crept up the walls from the cellar and spread into the kitchen; it turned the potatoes a sharp green and Makepeace had no choice but to throw them away. When it rained, the water found a way to slip beneath the slates and slowly pool somewhere in the cavity of the roof, making a puddle of a stain appear on the ceiling of the nursery. The wallpaper in the drawing room grew speckled with mildew. It felt as if the house had gone out in sympathy with the boat that transported my father, mimicking the sensation of the waves. Money danced through our hands so we had hardly any to live on.

A loaf of bread sat on the table, untouched. Neither of us willing to take the first slice. It sat, a white accusation on the breadboard, for how long would it last once we started eating it? But Makepeace knew how I felt, she didn't urge me out onto the street, to send my hands, butterflies at her bidding, through the pockets of strangers. She didn't say a word. Our utter dependence on my father became more obvious with each day that passed, with each bill that we paid. All I craved was an orange, or a glass of milk, so knowing that the money sat in the cellar became a torment, until I could stand it no longer.

Waiting until Makepeace's soft snores cut through the cold air, I coaxed a wick to the fire and waited for it to kindle, before I opened the cellar door. The damp rushed up to meet me and I struggled to protect the candle from a gust. I breathed and waited, thinking Makepeace had heard me, but she slept on. The only sound the echo of a drip.

Each stair seemed more slippery than the one before, the candle sending a golden ripple across the wet wall. How did we continue to live in it? It was a house built on water. The pillowcase was where I had left it and my pride made me reluctant to pick it up again, but I thought of the warmth the coal would bring, the luxury of butter on our bread, a new pair of thick stockings for Makepeace and me, and it propelled me. The candle sputtered when I put it on the stair, the air so damp I feared it would extinguish the flame, so I hurriedly lifted the pillowcase into my hands and let the knot untwirl; with each spin it felt lighter than I remembered. Inside, all that remained was my poor Miss Poppet, her familiar smooth head cupped in my hand. The idea of warmth and butter and stockings receded and hot tears cut through the cold of my skin. Where was the last of my father's money? I clutched Miss Poppet to my chest and felt like a child again, tiny and insignificant.

"Eglantine?" Makepeace's voice came from the top of the stairs and I quickly stuffed my poor Miss Poppet back in her cocoon of cloth and let her be. Childish props would not hold me up. The candle sputtered with a black hiss, forcing me to walk by Makepeace's light. I took each step with my hand running along the wall until it was wet and I walked into the kitchen, where it was not much warmer than the cellar.

"'Tis spent," Makepeace said as she closed the cellar latch, but it was no repellent to the damp air which seeped up beneath the crack and swirled around our ankles. "I'm sorry. I had no choice. Your father …"

Hearing his name pained me; I missed him. Any mention of him invoked his absence, made my thoughts linger, made the question scratch at me, the question that might never be answered now – what had become of my mother? My thoughts would circle around, a maze without entrance or exit.

Makepeace looked at my hands, green with moss or mould, and picked up the bucket of water, sprinkling drops on the ground before she poured some water into a bowl.

"Why do you do that?" I said, having seen her do it many times before, my voice all frustration.

Makepeace didn't look up. "It's for the spirit in the water, to say thank you," she said, taking my hands in hers and plunging them into the bucket, applying the last of the soap to the grime.

"Is there nothing in those lines of my hands? Is nothing written? You were raised a gypsy, surely you can see something there?"

Makepeace shook her head.

I took the soap from her and dug it into the lines of my hands. I was no longer a child, I scrubbed at every inch of them until the skin of them was red, trying to dissolve all the lines of my past and future until the soap disappeared. Makepeace pulled my hands out of the water, kissed my palms and folded them in hers.

"I'm sorry, Eglantine, it was your other grandmother, Sarah, who had the gift for reading palms, not I."

My other grandmother. My mother's mother. She had the gift for reading palms and I'd never even known her name, nor been allowed to give her even a shape in my mind. All I'd been permitted was half of a family and even that I'd been only allowed to view through the shadow and fog of my father's lies.

Makepeace held my gaze. She may not have been able to read my palm but she read my mind. In that moment we both knew that it was inevitable: for us to survive, I needed to put my hands to better use.

* * *

Out on the street without the shadow of my father I had felt all his lessons course through my hands, the street a pocket. I kept telling myself that this was just a game, knowing that it was the furthest thing from it. Makepeace and I both depended on what lessons my father had taught me, but it sat uneasy on me, the pressure upon me to be more than the apple of his eye.

The street was full of reminders of my father. A costermonger's tanned face had his smile as he pulled the silver change out of his pocket; the cut of a minister's black spotless clothes; a lady bending down and giving her child a piece of orange, the perfume of it following me down the street. How could I choose which pocket to take from, knowing there would be no gentle bells ringing if I got caught nor affectionate press of my hand against his jacket. There would be no praise.

I watched a servant girl with her pressed apron and cap go up to the costermonger, his sing-song call ending as she arrived to peruse the fruit, saving his banter for her. And I watched her face colour with each of his compliments, each cheek turning ripe as a plum. When he turned to serve another customer, I plucked her pocket of a small purse, and was gone.

TWENTY-TWO

Patrin, 1821

Amberline had still not returned and I made up my mind. I gathered whatever was of value and bundled it into a carpet bag and with Little Egg at my feet, her warm hand in mine like a seed, went down to the pawnbrokers, ignoring the constant hum of my skin.

We walked into the shop, so full of stock that daylight barely penetrated the insides. A greasy lamp on the counter threw a pool of light over the claws of a stuffed bear, a silver teapot and a rack of plates, porcelain moons. Mr Sweet sat behind the counter. He watched me walk towards him, his feathered eyebrows raised above his pince-nez, like an owl upon spying a mouse. At the counter I spread out the things that had been in our home; he hardly suppressed a scoff as he'd seen them all before, having passed through his shop already. How easily I had been seduced by the idea of the home Amberline had promised for the three of us. The *vardo* I'd been raised in was a palace compared to it, for it moved with the seasons. We followed the sun, the seasons, the work. Peg-making, berry-picking, basket-making.

Old Sweet turned a small cup in his hands and fingered the fringe of our frayed tablecloth until he ferreted to the middle of the pile and pulled out the silver heart that Amberline had made for Egg. He rolled it in his palm. Little Egg watched from my skirts, her eyes wide. I'd kept it from her, saving it for this very day, to pay for whatever she needed.

"Stark won't be happy," Old Sweet said. His incisors were made of gold. Amberline's happiness held no sway with me.

"What will you give me for it?" I asked, wanting to be gone from the shop, more like a tomb, all the discarded objects squeezing out the air, exhaling dust.

Sweet's teeth gleamed in a grin as he handed me a few coins. "I'll hang on to this one," he said. "I'll charge Stark double to have it back."

"And the rest?" I said, needing to feel the road moving beneath my feet.

"That's for the lot. Now be off with you and your gypsy brat."

I cursed him under my breath but was glad to go.

* * *

The wind ruffled our bonnets and teased the hem of our coats and I felt the wind propel each footstep we took and the chance of undoing all the tangle of our lives. The burn throbbed in my arms, but I ignored it, though at times it pulsed so much that it was like a blinding light caught in the corner of my eye that I could not blink away.

"Mama?" Little Egg said, her little legs skipping to keep up. I hadn't realised I had been striding so fast, the wind at my back, a human sail. I pulled her up into my arms.

"We are going to the country," I said. But was I doing the right thing tearing her away from the only life she'd known and her precious father? But it was he who had abandoned us, not leaving word or hope of his return, treating the truth like silvered baubles to be melted down with brass and called gold. Fool's gold. And I had been the fool.

"Papa?"

"He's had to go away for a little while," I said and felt the creep of guilt – for I knew he loved her, but I knew also that we'd always come second to the sight of a more glittering prize. Amberline was all magpie, all bravado. His eye was always on the shine. The quick grab and theft of it. His kingdom made of glitter, facet, carat, coin. My kingdom I ached to return to – green canopy, red wagon, leaves and water. At the heart of it I wanted to place my daughter, to keep her safe, that would be my blessing, that I owed her. To see her thrive, beyond the soot, the smutty fog and the never-ending hoarfrost of grime.

The city receded as I pushed forward; a skylark wheeled above our heads in the blue, transfixing Little Egg's eye. The only birds she'd ever seen were the gulls and the crows that scavenged in the dust heaps and the shoreline of the Thames. The traffic reduced to the odd farmer's wagon, their horse bits singing past us, my heart singing along with it, music to my ears.

I lifted Egg onto my back, all the skin on my arms screaming, and walked with her strapped there with my shawl. When night fell we camped beneath a hayrick, wrapped close together in my woollen cloak. At first light I hoisted my still-sleeping girl onto my back, the shawl keeping her close. The last of the evening stars were extinguished one by one with my footsteps.

I walked like that for three days, keeping to the quiet paths, the ones that ran like a snail's trail, silvery through the long grass and overgrown, my eyes to the tops of the branches, the arrangement of stones, the twisted knots of grass, the signs that would lead me home.

But I saw nothing, no patrin to guide me. There was nothing but myself. All the pain in my arms, all the burn, like a rope pulling me forward.

It was Little Egg who saw them first, the painted *vardo* tucked out of the way beneath an oak, a horse grazing on the acorns that scattered the ground.

Her feet knew the way, the speed of her, her scrawny attempt at a braid flying made my heart cinch tight as I ran to keep up, but my legs had grown weak from walking, their strength had diminished confined by city ways.

I grabbed Egg's hand just as a dog snarled at us from the borders of the camp, the Rom sitting around a newly lit fire all staring at us and I saw ourselves through their eyes, just as I had seen Amberline that first time, dressed in his fine clothes – outsider, stranger, trespasser.

A woman stood, her dark patched skirt edged in ribbon, a coin necklace jangling at her chest.

"No fortunes today," she said and gestured for me to go. I felt heartsick. The smell of the wood burning, the smoke stung my eyes. The woman turned away.

"I'm no *gadji*, I'm Rom," I cried.

The two men at the fire looked at me then. One was very old, his beard grizzled to the point of a lightning rod. The other I assumed was his son.

"Where are your people?" asked the younger one.

"I am Rom, daughter of Josiah Scamp," I said defiantly, my heels pressing into the dirt.

They all shared a glance, the circle of which I could not decipher until their eyes fell on Little Egg. She was oblivious of course, distracted by the horse brasses shining, the gleam spreading across her face. I held her hand tightly, feeling the fear of their displeasure run up my legs, the impulse to run.

"Are you now?" the patriarch said and returned to his mug of tea, wrapping his hands around it for warmth.

"Do you know where my mother is camped?" I said, feeling the need to be gone while the day was still on my side, the daylight enough to guide me.

"Maybe," the patriarch said, keeping his eyes to the contents of his mug, not meeting my eye.

"Then please tell me," I pleaded against my better judgment.

"Mama?" Egg said, her arm reaching, keen to touch the horse's velvet muzzle. I looked down at her bright eyes. What did she know of our ways and traditions? Why would I tell her? We were *marime* now, tainted. How could a little girl be impure? The ridiculousness of the law struck me and I wanted to strike it back.

"If you'll tell me where she is, we'll be gone," I said, summoning my will to do the thing which I knew would anger them. I twitched my skirt with my spare hand as a warning. I might be an impure outcast, but I knew their ways, though I'd forsaken them. Still they remained silent; with a flick of my wrist I made to pull up my hem, to do so is seen as a curse.

"Try west," the woman said, "and take this for the little one and be gone." She threw a windblown apple in the air but I didn't try to catch it, I let it fall to the ground with a thud and watched it split. A grub squirmed at its heart. I had no need of her charity. Not yet.

The old man spat his tobacco on the ground. "She is dead, girl, dead this last six months. Her heart gone and broke after what your husband did. Ungrateful daughter."

Dead? Why say west if she was dead? When a tree falls they say it screams, and that before it dies one must cover one's ears. But I pulled the scarf from my head and listened for the tell of his lie until I walked off in a daze. Wouldn't I have felt her soul depart this earth, wouldn't I have felt something? I didn't believe them.

With night falling we walked into the woods, intertwined branches turning shadows to black lace on the ground. The remaining daylight was fast diminishing, patches of violet peeking through the canopy. Rain was on its way, I smelled it. The bandages on my arms itched and burned, an occasional glare of heat running all the way up to my neck.

"Mama," Egg whispered, and as she yanked down on my arm I felt a black wave wash over me. "Look."

In the lower branches of an oak tree's spotted leaves a barn owl, a ghost of a bird, peered at us, impervious.

"It's a *weshimulo*, an owl," I said to her and she tried the word out in her own mouth, the gush and flight of it.

The owl bobbed his head up and down, talons clutching and reclutching the branch, and Little Egg clapped, the dull percussion of it damped down by the thickness of leaf fall. The sound startled the owl and he took his leave of us, ready for the night hunt.

I made a small fire, gathered up the leaf litter, banked it up close to the roots of an alder and wrapped Egg in my shawl. From my bag I pulled out some bread and cheese and gave Egg a long swig of water from the skin.

She looked up at the tree at the shivering foxtails of the catkins, her little hand reaching.

"They are the tree's flowers, my love," and I listened to the happy sound of her eating while I poked the surrounding twigs into the small flames, willing it to pulse out heat. The owl hunting out in the darkness let out a warrior's screech, talons full of vole or mouse.

Egg nestled into her burrow beside the fire and I scooped my body around hers, watching the smoke wend its way up towards the canopy, as it knotted itself and twisted into shapes and vanished as if it were to signal which direction we should head in. A fox observed us opposite, Egg's eyes wide in the firelight.

"We call them *weshen-juggal*, dogs of the wood." As I spoke my ears were filled with my parents' voices, the remembrance of them speaking in the Romany tongue as I fell asleep inside the wagon. That wagon would be but ash now, both their bodies in the ground. No Romany would leave any possessions behind lest the spirit take home in it. How would anyone have got word to me, swallowed up by Amberline's words and the swell of the city? *Ungrateful daughter*, the patriarch's words were true. I'd never even said goodbye.

Sleep overtook Egg, and I slowly undid the bandage and looked at the burns on my arms. The smell of them met me before the sight of my skin did, the sour fester caught my breath. The flame showed me what I feared: the yellow crust of infection. A catkin fell into my lap and I rolled the green serpentine shape filled with tiny petals across my palm and felt the delicate tickle of it like Little Egg's eyelashes against my face and the memory came sharp as a stitch.

Jupiter had been a new pup, my father had picked him, the runt from the farmer's litter, chosen for his nose, the twitchiest of them all. My father thought he'd be the perfect Romany dog, sure-footed and quick to pick a rabbit's scent, and he was right. But while Jupiter was learning to become my father's shadow, he had to learn to compensate for those large dog paws. He pulled the drying washing from the bush, scrambled up the *vardo* steps and muddied the bedding. My father bundled him and his huge paws out the door, dropping him onto the ground, those large paws holding him in good stead, landing him upright and ready to go again. My mother latched the door against the loving slobber of his tongue and the happy pant in our ears.

But the fire was to be Jupiter's defeat. In his youth, the smell of my mother's rabbit stew atop the fire sent Jupiter dancing, trying to reason a way to access the contents. He leapt at the pot and knocked it to the ground, standing on the coals with the tender pads of his feet burning. The sickening sound of his yelp had us running.

With curses under her breath, my mother stripped the nearest alder of its bark, her knife snicking through to the whitest part, and set to boiling it in a small amount of water. I cradled Jupiter's head in my lap, a high whine puncturing the air, his pink pads blistering black; what was burn and what was soot? When the water had boiled my mother plunged the pot into a bucket, the hiss and spit of it as it cooled suddenly joining the pitch of Jupiter's cry. Very carefully Mother took each of

Jupiter's paws and soaked them in the lukewarm tincture while I held tight to his neck, his breath turning to a pant.

Father arrived just as we were binding Jupiter's feet in rags, and my father who like all Roms thought dogs unclean, lifted him into his arms and let him rest inside the *vardo* that night and my mother permitted it, seeing my father's concern and knowing Jupiter with his feet bound would be unable to stamp his muddy footprints across our floor, nor his teeth shred our bedding. My father was a soft-hearted soul. He was too kind, too generous. My mother was as strong as the tree I leaned on. How could she be gone too? Amberline's crime had extinguished all of my family, one by one, yet my skin burned still. I had not enough energy left to cry.

With the catkin in my lap, I carefully eased out of my spot so as to avoid waking Egg. I tried to peel off some of the bark with my own knife, blunt as it was; slivers of it fell into my palm but what had I to boil it in? My makeshift camp was hastily constructed – a flint, a cloak, a skin of water, bread and cheese and a little bit of money that I had to eke out. We had no caravan except my arms and even they were scalded and put us both in danger. If the infection set in and fever struck, who would help us? Would I be able to make it back to the city? The rashness of my decision slapped me afresh with each throb of the infection, little flecks of gold embedded in my skin like fireflies in the night.

* * *

Little Egg woke me, her breath hot on my face, her hand whisking the hair from my ear, her words a loving whoosh, although I hardly made them out.

"Mama," she said and I listened, only hearing my thumping heart at being woken so suddenly. But then there on the wind I heard it, the faint sound of bells.

She clapped her hands and I pressed my finger to my lips, trying to determine what the sound was, fearful it was the bridle of an estate manager or farmer drawn by the fading curlicues of smoke coming from their woods. Without a moment to lose, I threw a handful of dust and dirt over the smouldering fire, threw everything back into the sack and scooped Egg into my arms. We slid through the trees like hunting owls, between the falling slants of downward light that barred our path, the morning song of dawn rising behind us as we fled.

The bells came louder, clearer. A little will-o'-the-wisp of light danced on Little Egg's face and she tried to catch it but it eluded her and flicked onto the back of her hand. Above our heads were tiny bells strung to a tree, not a bridle at all. I leaned down and breathed in the sweetness that seemed to pool between her neck and her ear with relief.

The lower branches flickered with ribbons, pieces of paper and prayers, a curl of hair, a baby's shoe. A prayer tree. A clootie well.

I put Little Egg down on the ground and she ran around the tree, the light chasing behind her. I followed. There, surrounded by the mossy roots, was a little blue pool that reflected back the dewy morning. Little Egg leaned at the edge of it, watching her own expressions. "Careful now, don't lean too close," I said and hurried to her side to stop her falling in, feeling the pull of the scab on my arms and catching my breath. In the reflection of the water I saw our faces knit together, mother and daughter made of water.

Little Egg skittered out of my arms and ran her hands over pennies studded into the bark, bronze and silver as the light struck. They'd grown into the skin of the tree as the flecks of gold had become stuck in my arm, unexpelled from my body, becoming part of it, becoming part of me. Was this mix of scar and burn and gold to be a blessing too? Now I'd become a glittering thing, would Amberline love me more? Had I done the right thing? Doubt flooded me. With his absence I felt the harshness of my judgment – hadn't he provided for us, didn't he care for his child, hadn't he shown nothing but love for me? Maybe I'd been named Patrin for all the signs I'd never read. Here I was standing beneath a canopy of directions, hope's signs, but could I read one of them? A sparrow dipped into the pool for his morning bath and at Little Egg's laughter indignantly fluffed his feathers and flew away.

I took the knife from my sack and bid Egg present herself to me. She looked up at me so trustingly as I sliced a tiny lick of her hair before doing so with my own, two dark paintbrush tips in my palm before I knotted them together, a double twist of darkness.

"Come, Egg," I said and I took her cool little hand in mine and warmed it as we stepped towards the pool and saw our own pale faces rise in it like moons.

"We give a little something for the *Wodna zena*, the spirit in the water," I said and curled Egg into my arms. The weight of her small body pressing in to mine was my tether to this world. Amberline and I had made her, together; the home we had in London was all the home we had left to us in this world. I would twist myself like one of the ribbons to the tree and hope it was enough. I scooped a little water and offered it to the ground before cupping the water to Egg's lips and mine.

"Make a wish," I said and watched with a painful delight as she screwed up her face, her eyelashes pinched tight. My heart squeezed with love for her.

"I wish …" she whispered.

"It has to be silent, my darling little *kakkaratchi*, my little magpie."

She mouthed words hard to decipher. My wish was all for her. To be safe, to be loved, to have all she needed. We dropped our twined hair into the pool. We peered at the reflection of the ribboned branches, the flickering paper and our hair on the surface of the water floating, before it disappeared suddenly below. And I hoped that Saint Sarah would give me the strength to get us home.

My arms hummed with the burn and the weight of her. London felt so far away. I willed myself to walk: Egg was the last of my family, I'd do everything to protect her. She was all I had.

TWENTY-THREE

Eglantine, 1838

I provided. My fingers were what kept the food on our table. As the years passed, I became more like a shadow that brushed against people without their knowing, as I skimmed from whatever pocket I found. My father's faith in me was well founded. Money was my chief desire, for it was the thing in itself, it didn't need to be filtered through a pawnbroker or melted down. I'd not risk myself like my father, I'd not be reckless. I only took what we needed and never too much. If I found a chain or match case, I'd barter it directly with someone at the market for food. My fingers may have had their skill from my father, but I kept my own conscience. I did not want to find my fate at the end of a rope or with a sentence for life. With each theft, my birthmark began to itch. But no matter what I stole, it never seemed enough. The house seemed to long to return to the river.

After the roof was fixed, the floors in the kitchen began to rot, the damp soaking and swelling the boards, the cost to replace more than possible to gather. It was then that Makepeace proposed her plan to accept lodgers for a fee. As reluctant as I was, I saw the sense in Makepeace's plan. Together we cleaned the house from hearth to hearth – my father's room, Ada's room – all were transformed to plain bedrooms for lodgers. The thought of strangers in our home turned my stomach, the staircase and halls would become as ill trod as the open streets, but we both knew without a word passing between us that we had no choice, unless I took the same risks my father had.

Makepeace put an advertisement in the newspaper and waited for our potential house guests to come and fill the rooms, but hardly any did. Those that did come took one look at the damp creeping through the whitewash and pleaded rheumatism, dropsy and the gout, and I was secretly pleased for their rejection of the house and the damp river-laden air the rooms contained. Only one enquirer was undeterred.

I watched him come up the stairs and hesitate at the front door, checking the print of the newspaper, held close to his nose. He stepped back down the stairs and looked up at the house and I stepped back from the window, not wanting to be seen. He was not much older than myself, dressed neatly in the clothes of a countryman, his brown hair curled beneath his cap, and beneath his arm he held a leather case close to his chest, the most valuable of his possessions; across his back was slung a calico bag. I watched him step back into the road to get a better view of the building and felt a sick twist in my stomach as he almost clipped a carriage belting down the street. But he was as nimble on his feet as a pugilist, sidestepped out of the way and looked up at the house once again. The rain began to fall then, silver strands running down over him. When he leapt across the first puddle barring his way, I was already waiting for him as he bounded up the stairs, so that he almost toppled inside as his hand met the knocker.

He brought the rain in with him as he stepped over the threshold, so close I saw it dripping off his eyelashes, running down the flush of his face.

"Morning, miss, it's a gypsy's wedding all right." He looked up at me with smiling eyes and I felt the raw skin around my neck prickle.

"Gypsy wedding?" I repeated, feeling exposed and mocked before I realised he meant the rain.

His boots squeaked as he took another step inside so that I had to stand back, the rain from his clothes dripping onto the floor, dripping onto my skirts and joining us together with a ring of water, the blessing of a puddle like an island.

"I've come about the lodgings." He held the damp newspaper out to me with Makepeace's advertisement and the words *affordable* and *comfortable* before the print had turned to black tears. He clutched his leather case close to his chest.

"What's in your bag?" I asked, unable to resist speaking my thoughts, realising how rude I was, not letting him further into the house nor exchanging names.

The young man patted the bag affectionately and brushed the remaining raindrops from it so that they turned the leather a darker shade. "This here is my fortune, Miss ..." he said and extended his hand towards mine so that I was obliged to take it.

"Stark," I said. "And yours?"

"Fookes, Francis Fookes," he said and smiled, his teeth revealed in a broad grin.

Makepeace came up from the kitchen, pulling the apron from around her waist and adjusting her lace cap, her chatelaine all a-jingle at the thought of a lodger, the natural order of the house returning.

"Let the poor fellow in, Eglantine, and close the door, for goodness sake, look at the floor," she said and I did as I was instructed. I hadn't noticed while standing with Fookes how much water we'd let in. "Would you care for some tea, Mr Fookes?"

"I'd be much obliged, if it is not too much trouble. I've walked a long way."

"No problem at all, show him to the drawing room, Eglantine," Makepeace said and disappeared down to the kitchen. I showed Mr Fookes to the drawing room, a somewhat closer resemblance to a Quaker's meeting room than a cosy sitting room; only the damask on the walls and sofa lent it any warmth. The grate was cold. I left Mr Fookes and attended to the water on the floor in the entrance way, soaking the puddle up with a rag before I returned to the sitting room, where Mr Fookes still stood, shivering in his wet clothes.

I pulled out the tinderbox and tried to coax a flame from the damp flint, but it wouldn't kindle to my touch.

"Don't worry on account of me, Miss Stark," he said, a suppressed chatter through his teeth. I ignored him and continued with a persistent strike, but no flame would play my servant.

"May I?" Fookes offered, and I reluctantly passed him the tinder. He struck the flint decisively and fed the spark a curl of sawdust before he surrendered it to the waiting wood. The flue sucked at the fire like a baby at the breast.

Makepeace came in, looked from me to Fookes and said nothing, settling the tray down on the table between the sofa and the chairs.

"I've come about the room, Mrs Stark?"

"Makepeace," she said, her lace cap neatly arranged around her face.

"Mrs Makepeace, I've come about the room. I plan to stay in London for a time before my ship is due to leave and take me with it," he said proudly, "for I'm going to try my luck in New South Wales."

Makepeace's face went grey. I picked up the teapot, poured the tea then handed her a cup; she barely kept the saucer from striking the base, all nerves.

"But why have you need of New South Wales if you are a man that has a fortune?" I asked, gesturing to the leather case that he'd placed closer to the fire to dry, the steam a small fog in the room.

He bent down over the case and opened it, unfolding the sides filled with small tools – pincer, awl, hammers large and small, a pair of compasses, rasps, kit files, nippers, shoe nails, leather laces sitting in a cloth pocket – to reveal a compartment beneath. Carefully he pulled out handfuls of tiny shoes, each finer than the next, and laid them in our hands.

"A doll's shoemaker," I said, marvelling at them, the tiny stitches, the softness of the leather.

Mr Fookes stood up and laughed. "No, they are samples of my craft is all."

"They are very fine, Mr Fookes," Makepeace said. "Too fine for the likes of those in the Colony."

Fookes collected his precious samples from our hands and placed them back in the confines of his case. "There you are wrong, Mrs Makepeace. Why, a shoemaker is exactly what is needed, all those feet coming off the boats, shoes ruined by sea water. Then there is the need for workmen to have sturdier shoes and boots in the clearing of the land. The need for someone who can also make a saddle if need be, or nail in the iron to the hoof, if he's comfortable with horses. Why, there's work for the taking." Mr Fookes looked from Makepeace to me and I was impressed by his confidence. How did Makepeace and I look to him? All we both thought of when he spoke of New South Wales was my father, his absence coloured everything. Mr Fookes swilled his tea down and resumed his seat.

"Believe me, what I tell you is true, there are more opportunities for those willing to work than here."

Makepeace nodded, a slight shake to her hand as she stood and smoothed her skirts. "Eglantine will show you the rooms available. Breakfast is at seven in the kitchen. Rent needs to be paid a month in advance. Good day, Mr Fookes," she said and hurried out of the sitting room, leaving Mr Fookes and myself standing opposite each other in her wake.

"Did I offend?" he said, looking at me, his face earnest. "I didn't mean to offend." He waited for me to answer and I looked back at him, the colour flooded into my face; I'd never spoken to a young man before by myself, a young man with ambition.

194

"We lost someone close to us to the Colony is all," I said. "Come, gather your treasure and I'll show you the rooms." I watched as he picked up his case and his calico sack, noticing the strength of his arms press at his jacket sleeve. Could he really be a shoemaker? I'd learned to trust no one.

Mr Fookes followed me up the stairs and I showed him the newly transformed rooms, Ada's room, my father's – and he stopped at each and looked out each of their windows, though the view was swirling in rain. I watched from the thresholds as he looked at the old pitcher and jug on each chest of drawers, the linen newly washed and darned and hidden beneath the best of the counterpanes. Mr Fookes ran a hand along the barley twists of my father's chest of drawers, admiring their craftsmanship. I held my breath, hoping he'd not ask me who had last slept in this room, concerned my father's taint would reach us still. I buried my hands in my pockets, banishing the thought that my hands were just my father's creatures.

"How long have yourself and Mrs Makepeace run your establishment?" he asked, placing his leather case on the bed.

"You'll be our first guest," I said. "Do you need any more assistance? If not, I'll leave you to get yourself settled." My fingers in my pocket toyed with an errant string, curling it and uncurling it with one finger. I missed the comfort of my doll, but I'd not retrieve her, my stolen goods, my first theft as my father said.

"Thank you, Miss Stark, or shall I call you Eglantine?"

"Makes no difference to me, sir," I said, sweeping up the stairs to my own room. Beneath me I listened to the sound of the drawers open and close as he filled them with his possessions, his footsteps shuffling along the floor, the sigh and release of the springs of the bed. I tiptoed over to the window, not wanting him to hear my own footsteps, and looked out the window at the river, a dark line beneath the incoming fog.

TWENTY-FOUR

Patrin, 1821

As we neared the grounds I heard a dog bark and I immediately whistled, expecting Jupiter to come to my heel, my father's tread behind me, the bridle of the horse keeping time like a tambourine. The smell of my mother's herbs came rushing up to me on the wind. I closed my eyes and willed them back. But all that came to me was the pulse of my own fever making the fields glow greener, the trees wave higher, the sky leached of all colour around the sun.

As we approached I wiped Little Egg's face and mine with a corner of my cloak and took a deep breath. We passed through fields, the sheep never turning their eyes to us as they harvested the sweet grass. Egg plucked off tufts of wool from the odd nettle and set them free to the breeze, tumbling curls of wool. We passed beneath the windbreak, interlaced trees bordering the edge of the palace grounds, the dew soaking our skirts, a dark tideline. All the palace windows seemed dark, the windows that Amberline had counted as if they were silver pieces for his pocket. I had planned to walk up to the palace and ask after the housekeeper, hoping she would remember me and give us shelter for the night in a stable or barn, maybe some food. Would she remember the fortunes my mother had given and the rats that my father had cleared the house of? The young German duchess with her swollen ankles, had she delivered a healthy child? On cue a rat crossed our path before bolting to the undergrowth. Little Egg let out a squeal, but when I turned to look at her, it wasn't the rat that had caught her attention – it was a squeal of pleasure.

On the grass ahead of us was a tiny carriage, a dappled pony still in its miniature harness, its tail sweeping the air contentedly while a little girl by the pony's side played in the long grass. She was as fair as Little Egg was dark and of a similar age and height, but there the similarities ended. The little girl was oblivious to us, plucking dandelions from the grass and offering them upon leaves to her tiny dolls propped up against each other, their wooden heads looking like toadstools in a circle. She looked up at Egg and her whole face burst into a rapturous smile, a playmate built from her wishes.

"Come," she called and Egg ran at the summons, her whole face fixated by the sight of the little fair girl in her grass-stained muslin, a little red jacket also abandoned to the damp grass.

The little girl offered Egg an array of dandelion petals on a leaf and Egg carefully put out her palm to receive it. I held back, not wanting to disturb their little game. The maid was lying further off, cap over her eyes, fast asleep; could this be the little girl grown from the duchess's belly? The child that I had predicted would be queen? And here she was queen of her grassy patch, her dolls the subjects of her kingdom. It felt so long ago and now she was as bright as an angel, in piping conversation with my girl, her equal. The little dolls sat silent and watched the living, one wore a little red velvet gown, the same as the one the duchess had been sewing, the bodice sewn with gold thread. I fondled the *putsi* around my neck and rubbed until I felt the velvet beneath the leather.

Little Egg plucked her own dandelion harvest and sprinkled the soft confetti all over the golden girl's pale eyelashes. Their laughter was like a crystal glass singing with a wet finger, a bright circle enclosing them, the life and light of them. I felt lucky just to witness it, to be near its glow. I leaned near against a tree and felt the sun's warmth seep up my back, the bark rough, reassuring, and I closed my eyes, feeling my own blood run like sap, the pounding ache swell over me, the sun leaching into my bones.

"Alexandrina!" A voice shouted and I started, not sure where I was or what was happening – the sun was still in its same position in the sky. How long had I slept? Hurrying, I rose to my feet. Little Egg and the fair girl stood arrested by the sound of the screeching voice tearing across their imaginary world like a thrown stone.

"Alexandrina, what are you doing?"

The maid who had been asleep scrambled to her feet, her knees catching in her skirts and sending her sprawling.

"Playing, Madame Lehzen," the little golden girl replied, sprinkling more petals from her upturned skirt like a farmer's wife sows seeds.

"Come this instant," the governess said before flipping the child's skirt down. The spilled petals made her frown, the swell of a tantrum souring her features.

"I shan't," the little girl said and proceeded to lean down and start her harvesting again.

Egg was all eyes, watching the scene unfold, stepping back towards me. The governess clutched the child by the wrist and the girl screamed. Egg reached for me. The pony's ears swivelled with only slight irritation, undeterred from his green breakfast.

The governess raised her voice. "And you, who are you to be trespassing? Off with you!"

"The housekeeper, Mrs Davey, knows me," I said, seeing my chance slip from my grasp.

"Does she now?" the governess replied, pulling at the child's arm, but the little girl had mettle and would not budge. "She won't be much help to you where she is now. She moved east to be closer to her family." And with a final yank she pulled the child up towards the palace, the heels of her satin slippers kicking the sod. The threats grew fainter as they walked off, the maid nearly running to keep up with them.

The pony remained attached to the carriage and Little Egg took her opportunity to sit upon the seat and feel the weight of the reins in her hands and I bid her be quick about it, not wanting another lash of the governess's tongue.

From the direction of the palace came a stableboy racing across the grass towards us so Egg jumped off the soft plump cushion and sought my hand. He tugged his cap when he saw us and blushed before taking the pony by the bit and walking the ornate little carriage back to the stables.

Egg watched as the pony vanished from her sight. I took her hand and we walked back through the windbreak where I stopped and ran my hand over the trunk of a poplar, the white bark as supple as a page. My father had left a mark here once, a patrin for us to find our way, but it was long gone. I checked all the other trunks, but time and the seasons had done to the mark as it would do to us all.

As I walked my eyes kept flicking to the branches, hoping to find a thread caught there, or a nick in a tree trunk, a stick stuck through a leaf, something to show me they had been here, that I was still here, that I was heading the right way. I stumbled with Little Egg in my arms, the horizon tilting, but I didn't fall. Little Egg craned her neck as we walked around the lake and long water, her eyes taking in the sight of the palace, the sunlight turning all the windows to quicksilver, until we found our own way back to the river to use as our guide.

We heard it before we saw it, the babble of the waters obscured by the brambles rich in blackberries hanging over the banks. The air blew across our faces, cool. A moment's relief. Little Egg's body was damp through with the sweat from my body. I let her down to the ground gently when I noticed I was wet through. I hitched our skirts to our knees, tying the excess into a knot, then reached for the nearest blackberries. I fed them to Egg, one by one, her whole face animated with the sensation of the blackberry releasing its juice into her mouth, dribbling down her chin, staining her clothes. The world came to me in waves, all the colours growing brighter. Egg smeared another berry into her mouth, her lips and cheeks stained purple. My limbs were slow, heavy, turning to tree trunk, tree root, branch. Soon I'd be nothing but a leaf. Egg was beside me then suddenly far away, hungry for fruit. The sun lit them, berries like jewels. I watched her move away, but I was slower than slow. Her little hand reached through the overhanging foliage. Her frustration at getting tangled in the bramble, the thorns nicking her fingers. She inched closer to the riper fruit, closer to the edge. I called for her to come, my feet slowly obeying me. I reached her just as the dirt rolled down the riverbank, when she fell into the water without a sound. Her little body disturbed the froth of frog spawn before the water closed over her head as if it was receiving a gift.

I shouted out her name but my voice was like a bird cry in my ear. The river rose to meet me as I scrabbled down the riverbank, screaming for my Little Egg, my Eglantine. The fruit she had picked began to disappear beneath the water, fish mouths puckering against the surface.

I willed her presence back to me, holding the pouch around my throat, and prayed for all I was worth for my daughter to be returned to me. I prayed to Dark Sarah, to Jesus the Lord, I prayed to the water itself as I waded into it. The cold entered me, the current hungry to sweep me off my feet. Duckweed stuck to my fingers and I tried to scry the surface of the river to see below, but only the hurrying clouds reflected from above.

I plunged my face into the water but drew my head quickly back, my breath knocked out of me, the water freezing. The current made my skirts billow up, fabric seaweed, a fish nibbled at my leg and my whole heart screamed for my daughter. My feet slipped on the slime of the riverbed; I plunged again beneath the river's surface, against my will.

Below the line of the water I could barely see a thing. My own reaching, searching hands were lost to me, until a ray of sunlight sliced through the silt and mud and I could make out the pebbly bottom of the riverbed.

Please, I thought, *give her back to me*. I pushed against the current and reached out my arms into the shadows, clutching at what I thought to be my Little Egg's hair, but found only a clump of wild orris root in my hand. I released it and it bobbed past me in the water. Ahead I saw a flash of silver, the promise of her hand, and I struggled against the current to reach it. But it was no hand, they were minnows flickering through my fingers, and I gulped a lungful of water in despair.

Then I saw her, wrapped in a tangle of weeds, her eyes staring at me like periwinkles, bubbles forming on her fingertips. I reached for her hand and found it cold, heavy, reluctant to be pulled upwards towards the surface, the weeds fixed, firm as a fist. I ran my hand down her legs, her old shoe trapped in a tangle of roots from the willow. I tugged at it and felt her release. She was in my embrace and I dragged her upward, her lips blue. We were near the surface when a root untangled from the undercroft of the bankside and reached for my daughter, clutching at her wrist, but I pulled onwards. Light danced on the surface above us, the promise of air. I tugged harder. But the roots pricked deeper into her skin, a spawn of blood clouding the water. She was my daughter, my love, I'd be damned if I'd let the river have her.

Before we broke the surface, I saw an eye, older than life, unfurl from the darkness, milky as the interior of an oyster shell, and I pushed against the current even harder until I broke the mirrored surface and placed my Little Egg, fragile and floppy, on the riverbank, her heels still puddling in the water. I pulled down her chin and greenish water trickled out. I squeezed her stomach, leaned her on her side, slapped her on the back and willed her to breathe. But she just lay there, muddy dress, weeds for hair. The river had made her its creature and I fell into the mud and scooped her up in my arms. "Please," I cried, "please, please, please."

I placed my lips over hers and breathed into her and she stirred, retching out all the water she had swallowed, a tadpole wriggling in her bile.

She looked at me and cried until all the river had been expelled by her tears. She looked down at her hands, two sodden blackberries bled into her palms. I scooped them out of her hands and flung them into the water, where they disappeared beneath the surface without a word. They reminded me too much of the Romany tradition of laying acorns in lost children's palms, to bury them by the side of the road, so that they could be found again.

With each step I took with my daughter back to the city I saw that eye. The spirit of the water or a fevered delusion? Every time I closed my eyes it opened: old, ancient, familiar. The water was with us still; it squeaked in my boots and dripped from Little Egg's hair; it was wet between our clothes so that it felt as if we were joined together, skin to skin. Had the river wanted to claim her? Was it only the pity of Old Father Thames that had released her into my keeping? The little red linked lines around Little Egg's throat glistened like coral knotted on a string. My daughter had been born in the river, her name given in the water, the river had given her gifts.

"Did you see anything in the water?" I asked Little Egg, but she had fallen asleep on my shoulder, her dribble falling in the crease of my neck. The river had a strong current, yet she had remained where she'd fallen in, the waters closing over her, the roots of the willow tangling her in their grasp with all the grip of a parent's arms. Perhaps the river had kept her safe, saving her from the rush of the current, knowing I would come. Perhaps I owed the river my thanks. The water seeped down between my bandages and my wounds, and as they dried I felt them contract and squeeze in waves. My arm was throbbing with its own tidal force, the fever washing over me, propelling me.

I was filled with the rush of the current, I had got us safely back to London.

* * *

"Papa," Little Egg called, sing-song. "Papa?"

How much time had passed? Quickly I pulled off my muddy boots and I slung the sack I had beneath the table. Had he returned? Would he be able to see my betrayal by the things I had used for escape?

She looked at me with her father's bright blue eyes, clear and unclouded. "Where's Papa?"

My attention was drawn to the fireplace – was the wood freshly laid? Did I fill that bucket of water on the floor? A loaf of bread remained untouched on the table. I put my hand against it. Was it still warm? Could Amberline be back? His coat wasn't behind the door, nor his hat. I wiped the road from both our faces and hands and I set to kindling the fire to life. Little Egg broke into song behind the curtain and I thought nothing of it, coaxing the flame, blowing on it, willing it into being, hoping for it to climb up the chimney and resemble a fire that had never been cold. My arms sang with their own flames and I carefully unbound the bandages; the smell that rose from them made my breath catch. I had turned to the muck of the tide, my own skin rancid. The bandage was filled with dirt and broken filaments of leaves. I tossed the tattered cloth into the flames but it only smouldered, still damp from the river. A vile smell filled the room before the fire consumed the bandage, took its essence and burned brighter. On my knees I prayed to Dark Sarah to keep us safe, Little Egg and I, while Little Egg played behind the curtain, a little imaginary conversation going on, as reassuring as birdsong, as breath, as the stars in their heavens.

TWENTY-FIVE

Eglantine, 1838

The house felt different. Makepeace and I had grown accustomed to being two, but now we were three again and it felt like we were tilting all at one end of a boat, the damp overleaping the bounds to tip us in the deep. For the first night Fookes was with us all I did was listen to the sounds of his movements. The pound of his step. The pour of the pitcher and the replacement of the jug on the stand. I heard the long stream of his piss in the chamber-pot and I fumed. My father had never made those sorts of sounds, he was all stealth, I hardly ever heard him come or go.

I lay awake for hours. I got up and dressed and lay back down, knowing the house was dark and quiet, as I liked it. In my hands I weighed the pouch I'd found in my father's drawer and ran my thumb over the leather, over and over, closing my eyes and imagining it to be my mother's skin. I put it to my lips, and kissed it, hoping a picture of her would come at my call, the image of her face, the sound of her voice, but nothing came. My memories of her only came with the sound of water. I got up and opened the window to let in the sounds of the river, a substitute for her voice. I was listless, neither able to sleep nor rouse myself to go downstairs and warm my hands around the kettle waiting for it to boil. I rolled the pouch in my hands, tempted to open it, yet frightened that if I did, whatever remnant of her remained would be but a breath out the window. Makepeace had made sure all of Ada's things had been burned and broken when she died so that her spirit would be free. But had my father in keeping this kept a little of my mother's spirit for me?

I heard Fookes get up and begin the whole splashing, pissing, stamping routine. For a shoemaker, he had the footsteps of a horse, all clip and clop, his shoes striking like flint on the floors. I listened as he neatly skipped down the stairs and then silence at the bottom.

"Good morning, Mrs Makepeace," he chortled, his voice threading up the stairs to me. Makepeace bid him good morning in reply and I heard him follow her down to the kitchen; the dining room was never used now. The cloths and silver had all gone to the likes of Old Sweet at a trifle of their worth.

I tucked the pouch into my pocket and followed down the stairs. I heard Fookes's voice alive with the morning, all confidence to Makepeace's quiet questions, and I felt resentment rise in me as I walked into the kitchen.

Fookes stood up and his napkin fell to the ground as I entered; he quickly swooped it up and nodded at me.

"Morning, Miss Eglantine," he said and I was embarrassed by his manners. Makepeace was bent over the stove, sausages spitting fat in the pan.

"Good morning," I said quietly and took my seat, poured tea into my cup, and wished for the usual balance of quiet that Makepeace and I thrived upon. Fookes was unaware; he crowded the kitchen with his company.

"Did you sleep well?" he said, all brightness, and I wanted to tell him that he was as noisy as the newly planned railway trapped in a wooden box. If only I had all his little hammers and nails I'd shut him up.

"Well," I said, hoping he'd leave me to my breakfast, but he would not be stopped, he was all rolling stone and I was moss.

"The river is mighty noisy, isn't it?" he said by way of making conversation.

Makepeace walked over with the pan and slid the sausages onto his plate. "You'll grow used to it, Mr Fookes," she said.

"I'm sure I will," he said amiably, sticking his knife into a sausage and spearing it with his fork, before it disappeared into his mouth and he was blessedly silent for a moment.

I drank my tea and felt my appetite disappear with the longing for quiet, to hear my own thoughts, my fingers pressing the roundness of the pouch as if it was a fruit I was checking for ripeness, trying to feel what it contained, its skin taut as rosehip. The bell rang at the door and Makepeace stood and went to answer it, her chatelaine its own little echo, leaving me alone with the sound of Mr Fookes, his cheery nature shining out of him so that I averted my eyes to avoid his smile.

"How long have you lived here, Miss Eglantine?" he said, and I was forced to look up at him, unused to the dance of polite conversation.

"Most of my life," I replied. "This house is my father's house." I smelled the start of something burning.

His eyes followed me as I took a cloth, opened the stove and rescued Makepeace's loaf that had started to turn from gold to brown. I tipped it out onto a board, the steam from it swelling the kitchen with the sweetness of yeast.

"Your father, is he ..." Fookes began.

I placed the bread on the table, shaking so much that a knife fell into the butter, sending a golden smear onto the cloth.

"He's not dead," I said. "Not that we know of." My voice quavered and I grew angry with myself. Makepeace and I had tied the ends of our lives together and remade the knot, and here was Fookes snapping at it with his questions like a loose thread. "He was transported to your beloved Colony," I said and watched Fookes's face lose all its curious, kind shine. I felt a gust of air come down the stairs as Makepeace closed the front door, I breathed it in, lightened by saying it, the words free.

Makepeace came back down into the kitchen, tucking a piece of paper into her apron, and I looked at her stricken face, worried she'd overheard me. Fookes would be leaving us sooner than we thought after my outburst, he'd not want to lodge with us now.

"Tell us of your people, Mr Fookes," Makepeace said, falling into the nearest chair, her hands in her pocket.

Fookes told us of his mother and father and his six brothers and sisters on the small farm holding. How his oldest brother would take over the farm, how he'd gone and got him apprenticed to the shoemaker in the nearest village. A kindly man who'd offered him a share of his business on completion of his apprenticeship, but Fookes didn't want to be tied to the village, not when he'd heard that there were fortunes to be made in the Colony.

He looked at me then and smiled, but at what? Was he gloating? I looked over at Makepeace, she was a million miles away.

"Fortunes?" Makepeace echoed. She picked up the teapot and poured, a spill into her saucer.

"Yes, Mrs Makepeace, fortunes. If it's not the wool and the sheep there for the grazing, it's for supplying all the things that money can buy. I plan to set myself up a shop in Richmond, along the Hawkesbury River, the ripest of places, to make the finest footwear that money can buy, the best crafted shoes that the Colony has seen." He was all hope and optimism. They were strange things to find in our house, as if a celandine had taken root in the kitchen damp and had unfurled its double crown of yellow petals and drawn my eyes against my will. We had become seasonless with my father gone. Spring came as a surprise and Fookes's brightness made me angry that he was here and my father was not, sitting in his chair full of his grand plans. He'd made Makepeace and me living ghosts haunting the house of his making. And here was Fookes, oblivious, drunk on his dreams and his chances; he'd make his fortune if he couldn't find one. My only skill was to take another's fortune. My jealousy turned in me like a curling snake.

I stood to leave and wished Mr Fookes good day. Makepeace poured the tea from her saucer into her cup and banished it in a sip. I turned to leave.

"Miss Eglantine?" Fookes said, and I looked at him. "Is your shoe giving you trouble? I can fix it later if you like."

I looked down at my shoe, my stockinged heel peeking out like a shy foreigner.

"Thank you," Makepeace said on my behalf when I wasn't forthcoming with a response.

* * *

I leapt the stairs to the nursery and slammed the door when I got there, delighting in the echo of it across the house, the reply of the glass rattling in the windows. What was I doing in this house? All my father's ideas for me had come to fruition, I was merely his instrument with only one purpose.

I took the pouch from my pocket and rolled it in my palm. What would my mother have wanted for me? Surely she wouldn't have wanted me to live as a thief, trapped by my father's expectations, without the chance to become the woman I was meant to be.

Very carefully I undid the leather tie around the neck of the pouch, vigilantly avoiding the knot that had been left tied in the cord that would have hung around her throat. At first the leather wouldn't give way, it had grown as old and hard as shoelace; I plucked at it gently, persistently with my nail until it gave a little space for me to be able to untwine it, dirt sprinkling in my hand. With the lace free, the pouch still remained closed; it sat like a bulb in my hand ready for the earth. I listened to the house, but all was quiet. I got up and superstitiously closed the window; whatever remnant of my mother had remained in this small leather pouch small as a hare's heart, I wanted it to remain with me.

The leather had fused at the top of the pouch, the sides of it dried together like a healed wound. One part at a time I pulled it open until the contents were revealed to me in a circle of leather.

My hands shook. My heartbeat kept time with hers, it had measured my life from its earliest beginnings. Only now I sensed how the absence of her had marked my life apart.

Here were her precious little things. Four seeds, a tarnished threepence from the year of my birth. A thin gold wedding band. A baby's tooth, an iron needle, a lock of my dark hair tied with a delicate thread. The confetti of dried flowers, some crumbled, some petrified, some folded back into themselves as if returning to the bud. A tiny branch of coral. A patch of ragged red velvet. A smooth white stone. Each thing I picked up and held in my palm I marvelled at – these things my mother had kept so close to her, lining them up in size from largest to smallest, wondering at each of them, letting them roll in my palm, feeling my mother's presence in every one.

I hardly heard Makepeace come in.

"She's in the room with us, you know, she always has been," Makepeace whispered as she cautiously stepped over the threshold and I felt the hairs on the back of my neck rise. "It is the tradition to destroy all of the dead's possessions, home, horse, clothes, so the spirit does not linger. Your father knew that, but still he kept that *putsi*." Around the house floorboards creaked slowly one after another, though no feet stirred.

"What was she like?" I asked. The more I thought of her face the more it receded from my memory.

Makepeace sat beside me on the quilt; the seeds rolled towards her, disappearing beneath her seat, and she carefully plucked them out.

"She was young, too young to die. And she loved you fiercely."

I swept the tears from my eyes. "What are they?" I had no idea what those seeds were for.

Makepeace rolled them around her palm. "These are beans, dried beans. They are to cast a fortune," Makepeace continued. "Four in a row means someone is coming, two grouped to the left mean a man, two to the right mean a woman."

"You can't really suggest that they can predict a fortune?" I asked incredulously, gathering up all the other little contents and tucking them back in the pouch.

"I don't know," Makepeace said, weighing them in her hand.

"Cast them for me," I said bluntly and Makepeace looked up from the beans. A wind whipped up outside and sent a gust of air down the chimney and around our legs like a homeless cat.

"It's been a long time. It is something we would do in the camp in lean times in winter, when no one wanted our hand-made bone buttons or wicker baskets or their pots and pans mended. We'd knock on the doors of the big houses and cast fortunes for scullery maids and valets and occasionally the lady of the house if the master was out. I just read the beans as I saw them."

"Cast them," I repeated and the wind pitched itself against the window and shook in its pane, startling us.

Makepeace closed her eyes and ran her fingers over the beans, her face creased in concentration, her lips moving silently, before she shook them in her fist in each direction and dropped them palm down, fingers outstretched, and together we watched as they fell, weightless as snow. I looked at their resting place and saw no discernible pattern. Makepeace looked at them ashen-faced, but they communicated to her and to her alone. Four little beans that had survived all this time, polished as pearls and buffed by the nap interior of the leather pouch.

"What does it say?" I prodded, the silence growing, muffling my ears.

"Nothing," she said with finality and swept the beans into her palm.

I grabbed her wrist. "Tell me," I demanded.

She looked at me, her cheeks growing red, a thin line of perspiration atop her lips, so I squeezed her wrist harder, feeling the frailty of her bones as she flexed her hand beneath my grasp. I released her, ashamed of myself.

"A journey is what they said, a journey beyond all you know, a crossing, a departure of no return," she said very quietly.

My sorrow swelled up within and crashed down upon me. Makepeace poured the beans back into the pouch carefully, tenderly patting them back into the safety of their skin, and I flinched, expecting the righteous deserts of a slap.

"But not alone, Eglantine, not alone," she hummed and patted my hair. "Far from alone. Beans are but seeds after all."

Eglantine, 1838

Until Fookes mended my shoes I held doubts as to whether his word was true or not. That case full of his tools looked barely used, but Fookes held good to his word. I left my shoes at his door last thing at night, waiting as my head hit the pillow for the strike and ring of those fine silver-headed hammers and nails, but I heard not a thing. In the morning, like a fairy story, they were more than repaired at my door, they had been fully restored to an even better state than the original shoemaker had made them. The heel had been hammered back into the sole, the leather had been buffed and shined. I took them back into the nursery and slipped them on, and there I saw what he'd done. On the sole of one shoe he'd tooled a flower, an eglantine. On the other shoe he'd tooled the hips. All of me stiffened with anger: what did he expect in return? My mind frothed with what I would say to him, the licence, the indignity, what gave him the right?

Something scratched at my toe. Out on the floor fell his card – *FRANCIS FOOKES SHOEMAKER* – *finest leathers and craftsmanship. May the Manufacturers of the Sons of Crispin be trod upon by all the World* – and it took all the wind out of me. He should have tooled all the thorns, because that is what I was, no petals, no hips, just half-wild and full of prickles.

I went down the stairs and knocked on his door, all ready with my thanks and appreciation, but there was no sound from within the room, so I knocked again. My knuckles on the wood went unanswered. Had he already gone down to breakfast? I listened for sounds in the kitchen, but there was no rise and fall of voices. My curiosity overrode my better judgment and I pushed open the door a little, expecting to see him asleep in the bed, but I saw nothing, the room neat, the bed appeared not to have been slept in. On the threshold I waited, straining to hear any sound of movement in the house, before I let the room swallow me.

Inside, the smell of lavender soap engulfed me; his towel on the nightstand was damp. On the floor a telltale drop of sudsy bubble, a rainbow caught in its white net, a dark whisker from his shaving. Across the dresser he'd made a makeshift workshop, all his tools rolled out on a piece of leather to protect the wood, the old nails of my shoes bent in a pile.

My fingers lingered on the drawer and I pulled it out, my heart skipping a beat; the joints long since beeswaxed made a small scream, wood on wood. There were all his linens, his clothes, his neckcloths, his trousers – all filling one drawer. My fingers slid around the edges of them, testing for the thing I sensed but couldn't see, a sense all their own, so that I was able to slide out the oblong shape I felt beneath Fookes's things without one item of clothing losing its folded edge.

There in my hands was a book, too thin to be a Bible. The red cloth boards were stained and worn. I opened the cover and saw the strange beast and bird on a verdant page and I felt the cold spread down my arms, numbing my fingers. *Views of Australia*. I peered into the image as if it were merely a window, with a childish hope of seeing my father there, a bright dot on the horizon. I flicked through the pages with desperation, almost squinting at the light on each page – a moon pausing through its transit to peer through the clouds at a Romany camp. I blinked again, the people were the natives. Another page, the township glowed against the green, the body of bright water, a little figure in a blue coat made me hesitate, his back towards me.

Downstairs the clock struck the hour and I hurriedly flicked to the end of the book, ready to return it to the drawer, to hide any sign of my trespass, ready to fold all the light and shade of those images into my mind as I would a jewel to wonder at its facets, when I saw the false back to the book. Outside, a magpie clittered and my fingers itched to see what was in the false space. I heard the front bell chime and Makepeace's slow ascent from the kitchen below. I slid off the false endpaper, made of card, just a fingertip width to see what was inside, struck with the ingeniousness of it, when I saw the wedge of notes, a hundred pounds or more.

I'd never seen so much money in one place; I ran my fingers over it. How long would that much keep us going? My father had the ability to fan money and know its count, but that was a skill I hadn't mastered. Here was Fookes's fortune already, the money with which he'd build his shop and his new life, kept safe in the secret of the book. My fingers knew what they were doing before I did; they skimmed the surface of the pile, gentle as a breeze, and slipped what I had taken into my pocket. I slid the false endpaper back into place and concealed the book carefully in amongst the linens where I'd found it, even more disgusted with myself than when I had entered. What stopped me from a new life? My father had worn the convict chains, not I, yet why did I feel their weight? The sins of the father carried on the weight of his child, they were a warning, yet they were not enough to deter me. My father perhaps had been right, what else had my hands been moulded for, but this?

I closed the door to the room and made my way down the stairs. Makepeace stood at the front door.

"Have you seen Mr Fookes?" I said. "I wanted to thank him for mending my shoes." But Makepeace didn't answer me. She remained standing with her back to me. "What is it? Who was at the door?" I said, feeling the uneasiness seep up through my feet and hands, feeling the urge to bolt the door.

Makepeace turned and looked at me and I saw that something had frightened her. An envelope was in her hand.

"Come with me," she said and I gave her my elbow to lean upon, her footsteps uneven. She seemed glad for the steadying weight of my arm. We made our way down to the kitchen, the remains of breakfast long since over. Two cups of old tea. A plate scraped clean. She led me to her room.

"Sit," she said and handed me the envelope. It was addressed to us both. I bristled, the envelope had already been opened, why hadn't we opened it together? Inside the envelope was one small single sheet of paper folded in half with some sort of plant wedged between its fold.

"Careful now," Makepeace said and I took heed, slowly unfolding the paper. There was nothing written on the page, not a word. Inside were only the pressed petals of some sort of golden-flowered plant, the pollen smeared a mirror image on the opposite part of the folded page. I leaned down and smelled it. Sunshine. I picked up the envelope again, there was no return address.

"What is this plant?" I asked.

But Makepeace shook her head and pulled out a book from her bureau, a small Bible, my heart making a racket in my chest.

"Open it," she said and I flicked back through all the Lord's words to the once blank pages, and read the names and dates written with different hands, the light of a small window barely bright enough to read by.

There was Amberline Stark joined to my mother's name Patrin Scamp 1818 with my name and birthdate beneath. And then there was my father's name joined to Ada Fitzroy 1821. These marriages proved what I had always known, that my father had had two wives. I slammed the Bible shut.

Patrin, Patrin – my mother's name. I said it aloud in the stuffy room and my hand reached for the doll in my pocket as was my habit, but she was in the cellar. "Patrin," I said again and my palm burned hot. I said her name a third time and her love for me tore through my chest, a physical thing. I needed her more than ever. At the small windowsill sat Makepeace's little garden pots – the foxgloves bursting through the soil, a pot of straggly rosemary, comfrey. A remedy in each. If only a plant could be pounded by the mortar and pestle to make a simple to fix my situation. But it was I, Eglantine, who was the green thing, pounded by life and circumstance, destined to be turned into something else, but a remedy for what?

Makepeace opened the Bible again and pulled out more envelopes that I hadn't seen, four in all. She laid them out on the coverlet in the order they had arrived and then placed the contents on top of them, a strange posy. A strange blossom pressed and preserved, the petals red and waxy curlicues. A strange sparse daisy-like thing that felt like flannel beneath the fingers. Tubular scarlet blooms tipped with white, strung in a row delicate as a necklace. The most fragile flower was a vibrant purple, each of its petals delicately fringed like something one would find at the haberdasher's rather than something nature would make. I sighed and the yellow pom-poms of pollen, the most recent arrivals, rolled off their paper and onto Makepeace's coverlet.

"I've never seen any of these flowers in my life, if that is what they are," she said, "and I know not the uses of them." She looked at me. "But I know who sent them. One each year."

"But no letter? No words?"

"Sadly, though he tried, he never learned them. He was unable to sit still, always moving."

The thought of my father finding these plants, picking them and finding someone to address them to us filled me with sadness. Who knew what hardships he'd had to endure, what his loss of us had been to him? What sort of life had he carved for himself out of that wilderness? I thought of Fookes's book with its hidden fortune, its strange beasts and birds, its glowing pages of land and water. I had willed that little figure in the blue coat to turn around and speak to me, and now he did, his voice flowers. My mother was as mysterious as a ghost, but my father had raised me, even if it was in his peculiar way, yet now I hardly recalled the details of his face, the texture of his voice. I'd been but a girl when he left, would he even recognise me? Makepeace lifted the blooms and placed them carefully back into their corresponding envelopes, a dust of pollen on her hand.

Fookes was waiting for us in the kitchen when I came out, his coat shoulders damp with mist, a fine net of it weighting the ends of his curls, his eyes falling straight to my feet.

"Are they to your satisfaction, Miss Eglantine?" he said.

He tried to rein in the optimism in his voice, his hope coiling up through him like a vine. I stood and looked at him and I saw it, caught it fleeting yet unguarded, his high regard for me. Blood rushed to the tips of my ears. Why else had he taken his awl and made his pictures for me, except for a show of his handicraft and regard?

"They are fine, Mr Fookes, very fine indeed."

It was Mr Fookes's turn to blush then, his mouth breaking into a grin.

TWENTY-SEVEN

Patrin, 1821

Egg gave a small shout; Amberline had returned, looking finer than ever in his new clothes, flushed almost. A lone white flower hung deprived of water in his buttonhole. Where had he been? Our daughter ran out to him, flying into his arms, and he kissed her scarlet cheeks until she crowed. He placed her back down on the ground gently and looked at me, his hands running down the length of Egg's braids, seemingly thinking they had grown. He pulled out a reed that had caught in her hair and thought nothing of it, just tossed it onto the flames.

"Patrin?" he said, his hand blessedly cold on my face.

"Papa, Papa," Egg sparkled and the weight of my answer hung in the room. Was our secret going to come out of her mouth? Would she give us away?

Little Egg clambered up into his arms. My tongue was as dry as a husk in my mouth.

"Patrin?" He walked over to the bed, pulled back the covers and looked at my arm that felt as if it was writhing, turning into a fish, all my skin shimmering from side to side.

I heard the scrape of the bucket, the slam of the door, the slop of his return as he came back with it filled from the well. He brought in a bowl of water laced with salt and dabbed a cloth drenched with the saltwater onto my arm. It stung but the fever was lapping me in waves. Still I burned. When I woke again strips of bark were pressed up against my arm, tied carefully with rag, a cold flannel on my head. He held a cup of water he was trying to get me to sip, but I barely found the space in my throat to swallow.

When I opened my eyes again Amberline and Little Egg were at the table, their voices low. With a calloused thumb he peeled the thick flesh of an orange.

"Watch this, Eglantine," he said and drew her to him, squeezed the orange skin so a fizz of fragrant oil arced across the room, hitting a beam of sunlight. Egg tried herself, but had not the strength in her fingers to release the golden spray. Amberline popped a segment of orange in her mouth instead and her eyes crinkled and lit up at the taste. The room was bright with the smell of oranges.

From her pinafore pocket Egg pulled a small doll made of wood, dressed in the finest silk, embroidered with delicate red roses across the bodice and sleeves, picked out again at the hem. I'd never seen the doll before; where had she got it? A blue silk sash shimmered around her waist. I tried to sit up in the bed. Around her doll's face were dark little curls, framing inquisitive eyes, a bright curious painted smile and rouged cheeks. From her little ears hung two glass earrings. In the doll's arms was a tiny baby, bonnet edged with the same embroidery as the mama, its minuscule mouth a red dot. The cold wound down my back, but Egg was so absorbed in the dainty sweetness of her new treasure that she thought of nothing else. I recalled the little blonde girl with her dolls in the long grass and their picnic of petals.

"Where did you get it from?" Amberline asked.

"It's mine," Little Egg said, her words sounding true, but I saw through the glass of them to her wanting. By saying it aloud she attempted to make it true. "I took her."

"What a fine creature she is, fit for a queen. You are the apple of your father's eye." He smiled at her, his hand on her hair, praising her.

What had I done? Here she was emptying her pockets like her father did. I was as much a thief as Amberline was, for I had taken Little Egg's chance to have the life she deserved, what else could my Little Egg be but a thief's daughter?

Egg crawled into his lap and began looking in his pockets, and with each brush of her hand against the lining he squashed it flat against his jacket and she laughed. He closed his eyes, waiting for her fingers to dart in and out. The more she tried the more she laughed, until her fingers looped on something. She pulled it out gleefully and marvelled at her catch, a piece of marzipan shaped like an apple. He'd set the bait for her to find, starting to teach her his ways, but where would that lead her? At what cost to herself? Amberline caressed her face and delighted in her relish of it, as she chewed through the painted red flesh and winced at the sweetness. Marzipan was not so sweet after all.

In the night the fever swelled. I kicked the blanket off and drowned back into sleep, but when I managed to pull my eyes open again the world turned to water, our room filled with it quickly as a bucket from the stream. Egg sat on the side of my bed, her hair rippling upwards with the current. Her new little doll and its muslin baby darted in amongst the reeds of her hair. A row of little bubbles leaked out of her mouth like a strand of pearls.

Little Egg, I called and found my mouth and lungs full with water. She looked up and with a kick of her legs floated above the bed, her arms wavering through the water. She bid me follow. My limbs were weightless. Little Egg flung open the door and I reached for her shoe, but it came away in my hand, an oyster shell. Once out of the door the street had vanished.

In its place was a river and it pulled me with its will, the current its fingers. Egg turned and made sure I was behind her, her little hand unfurling to reach mine. The dolls were like cleaner fish, hovering close to her arms, closer than I could get. I kicked against the water, trying desperately to make for the surface, but the river was master and the waters rose higher. The river weed twined around my ankles and pulled me down, my hand reached for Little Egg, but she was further down.

On the riverbed, in the streaming green light, the sound of the water bubbling in my ears, was a large figure reclining on a bed of purple loosestrife, Ragged-Robin and cuckoo flower. Above me the world darkened as the lily pads closed ranks and dimmed the light. I clutched at the roots of the trees with my fingertips, trying to find my way down. Something whipped past my eyes and I reached for it, hoping it was Little Egg's hand but it was just the knobbly flower of the bur-reed. The figure was concealed in the silt, but I knew that eye.

Little Egg's doll now fluttered around me and I saw the ripples of her breath slice through the water. A large barnacled hand rushed through the water in front of me, the coil of our hair that I had thrown in the well ringed around his finger, a dark band, reaching towards Egg. I desperately clutched for her fingers, but she was beyond my grasp. The large barnacled hand caught my fingers as if they were merely fish in a net. All of me longed for breath.

I opened my eyes. Little Egg was holding my hand and I was drenched in sweat. Amberline's mother sat on a chair beside the bed, the sound of rain from the eaves confused me, the music of the water still clinging to me, a fever dream.

"Mama," Egg whispered loudly. I looked at the little wooden doll in her arms, the hem dripping and staining the coverlet.

"Where is her little one?" I croaked, not realising how rasped my voice had become. Little Egg looked down forsakenly, her hand patting the bedclothes, flipping up the blankets. She poked her head under the bed, but there was no baby there.

"She will show up," Amberline's mother said quietly. "Let your mama rest now, Eglantine." I tried to look in the bedclothes myself for the missing doll, but my own arms were strapped with stiff bandages and I had not the strength.

"Rest now," she said.

Little Egg slipped off the bed and was flicking back the covers of her own bed, her footsteps prowling all corners of our home. But I knew, try as she might, she'd never find it. The last thing I'd seen of the great barnacled creature was the contents of his other hand, great reedy bobbins cupped like a cradle. Within his fingers' confines, the tiniest doll, the little ruffle of her bonnet fluttering like a fin, her face like a pearl.

* * *

In the morning the fever had broken and they came. The *shanglo*, the constables. They knocked on the door and let themselves in when it delayed in opening. They pushed past Little Egg and she fell on her bottom and she howled. I tried to raise her up with my arms, weak as they were, to hold her close.

"Where is your father?" I whispered into her dark hair.

Little Egg watched the strangers, in their black muddy boots, making marks all over the floor that I had struggled to keep clean, their rough handling of our few possessions. A cup fell from the table and rolled to the floor. It didn't break, but it spun on its base around and around, like a spinning top. One of them ran his hands around the lip of the table and there on a hidden shelf he pulled out something wrapped in cloth, his face as animated as Little Egg's had been as she'd pulled out the marzipan, the victory of it, and I felt the dread pull down at us. As if it was a gift, he unwrapped it slowly, his fingers taking delight in the unveiling, but I knew what it was, I felt it in my arms, licking across my skin. And there it was, the brightest thing in the whole room, a little gold oblong which had once been the widow's chatelaine, sunshine captured in metal, and we were to be punished for it. That was the fire for them, their hands overturned everything and they were rewarded for their harvest, for on the ground lay things that

Amberline had yet to sell or transform, the floor littered with pieces of silver.

They put their arms on me and I felt my father's strength surge in me, they were the rats not I.

"It will be better if you leave the child with someone, a neighbour," the *shanglo* said, but I'd not leave my child with any of them, I'd not release my grasp of her. I shook my head. They gripped my elbow and went to lead me out.

"For mercy's sake let me change out of my nightgown and dress my child," I said and the *shanglo* holding my elbow looked at me, and I felt the fabric of my nightgown press around me in the draught, worn and thin, sour with the sweat of my fever. The *shanglo* looked to the door and the chimney and the small pane of our window and saw there'd be no escape, so they left just as they'd come, but I knew they waited on the other side of the doorway, their shadows filtering under it.

Quickly I dressed Little Egg and myself in every piece of clothing we had, stuffing the pockets with whatever food we had, feeling under our bed for anything Amberline may have stashed there, but found nothing. Just as we shrugged on our coats the door swung open and the *shanglos* took us away.

TWENTY-EIGHT

Eglantine, 1838

The longer Fookes stayed in the house the more accustomed to him both Makepeace and I became, so that it seemed implausible that he would be hitching his star to a ship and following it to the other side of the world.

It was a morning for washing, the sun already striking under the curtains with the promise of heat. Makepeace asked me to strip all the sheets in the house as she got the copper ready. I knocked on Mr Fookes's door and he bid me enter, the curtain already pulled back, sunshine spilling on the floor. He was sitting on a chair in his shirtsleeves, hammering at a piece of leather between his knees as he fixed a sole to a shoe.

"Miss Eglantine," he said, leaping up and sending the nails he had resting between his lips spinning across the floor like so many compass needles all seeking their north. Immediately I stepped in and bent low to help gather them as Fookes did also, our heads hitting together. His forehead met my cheekbone with a smash.

"Oh dear Lord," Mr Fookes said, rushing towards me on hands and knees, and I leaned back against his bed, my hand to my face, all the world condensed to the brightness of my pain. Fookes pulled my hand away and ran his fingers over my cheek, the pads rough like a cat's tongue, and I sat dumbfounded.

"Are you hurt, Miss Eglantine, does it hurt when I touch

you?" he asked. It did the opposite of hurt. It felt like a spark newly kindled. He looked at me with such concern that I felt a laugh bubble up in me against my will and spill out, but he took my laughter for a cry. "Forgive me, Miss Eglantine, I'll get Mrs Makepeace," he said, his face so earnest and remorseful.

"Please, Mr Fookes, I'll be fine in a moment," I said, feeling the laughter bubble up inside me again, knowing how cruel it would be if I let it free. A tear hung in my eye, fractured with light before it escaped and ran down.

"I'm so sorry," he said, taking a handkerchief from his pocket, clean and unsullied, a plain piece of linen free of initials, free of spoils hidden in the corners, and offered it to me. I took it. Both of us still sitting on the floor, our spines resting, side by side.

"Mr Fookes," I began.

"Francis will do," he said.

"Likewise Eglantine."

I looked at him again but found I didn't know what to say, all my words had been extinguished just by the proximity of him.

"Let me take those," he said and carefully took the nails from my hand. I let him take them when I could have easily just tipped them into his palm. He gently opened my fingers and together we looked at the dents they had made in my skin, phantom pink nails printed in my flesh.

"I'm sorry, I should have looked where I was going," I said. "I'll be all right in a few moments and I'll leave you to get on with your work," I added, the throb beginning in my cheek. "What are you making?"

Fookes leapt up from his place beside me and I felt the draught rush into the space where he had been and was only too glad when he retrieved the half-made shoe and returned to the floor beside me. "It's the latest fashion," he said and handed me the dainty slipper. I slid my hand into it and looked at the shape of it against my skin; the leather was soft but strong.

225

"It's not finished yet, but it will be soon. I've made a dance shoe into a leather shoe, for the changed conditions."

"Fit for the princess, soon to be queen," I said and he broke into a broad grin.

"Let me show you something," he said. He got up again and went to his drawer, his hands locating the corners of the book, and I felt a quick flash of shame. I'd looked through his things and taken his money, I had trespassed on someone who'd shown me only kindness. I thought I was going to be sick. Again he took his place beside me.

"My uncle was a shoemaker, it was him who I was apprenticed to," he said as he laid the book open on our laps, diligent not to knock the corners of the pages; this was his precious thing – a thing of print and paper – what worth would my father find in it? Nothing metal shone. Was Fookes trying to catch me out? Did he know? I kept my eyes on the book and off his face, listening for the catch in his voice.

"One day a fellow came to get his shoes repaired, in poor form they were, and my uncle did his best to breathe new life into the old leather, cutting a new sole. My uncle said he was a rather strange character, scented with gin when he came to collect the shoes; though he had nothing to pay for their retrieval he was most desirous of their return as they'd travelled all the way around the world, he having arrived from the Colony with his daughter. His name was Lycett. In offer for my uncle's services he gave my uncle this fine copy of the book he'd made." Fookes ran his hand over the page with a proud caress. "And my uncle in turn gave it to me, a gift upon my leaving."

"I thought you'd leave our company after you found out about my father," I said bluntly, feeling the weight of the book on my lap, knowing that the pages hummed with light.

Fookes looked me straight in the eye. "Why would I do that? It's not your crime, it's not your punishment," he said and all of me wanted to believe him – we'd taken our succour from my father's thefts, just as much as from mine. My mother had lived a life upon the open road, but all I had was the make-do of the wind in the windows, the sounds of the river, the water that seeped up through the foundations of our house as if trying to carve for me a road made of damp for my feet to walk upon. My pouch in my pocket rolled. Was this why the house kept trying to give itself away to water, was she trying to liberate me in the only way she could?

"After all, if Mr Lycett can return a free and changed man, who's to say your father can't?" Fookes said brightly, trying to cheer me, turning the page for me to see the glowing light, each picture seeming to capture the dawn or dusk of the day, a pink flush. With each page turned, the air stirred and I looked at Fookes's face beside me, lit by its own glow. He didn't know what crime I had committed against him. Makepeace called up the stairs for the sheets.

Makepeace said nothing when I went down with the sheets bundled like folded sails in my arms, but she looked at the bruise forming like a blue pansy on my face, her hands reaching out to touch it, and I stepped away, unsure why.

* * *

That night when the house was still I woke up with all my senses spiked and alert. I sat up in bed, perspiration dripping from me. I knew what I must do. My feet cat-quiet, I tiptoed into Fookes's room and stood listening to his breathing. In the dark I made out his arm flung over his head, his covers kicked to the foot of the bed. The drawer opened with a squeak and I cursed silently as I slid the money back into the secret slot, smoothing down the pages until I was satisfied their disturbance would remain undetected. Fookes turned in the bed and I felt my heart thud, and I froze. Fookes mumbled and then slid back into his dreams. Before I left, I nimbly drew the blankets up over him.

Fookes's door barely closed with a click when I heard something slide through the letter slot in the front door, light as breath, and I was down the stairs, propelled by my fear. There on the floor was an envelope. I swung open the door, not caring that I was in my nightgown, not caring that it was night. All the sounds of the river sang loud – the lapping of high tide, the carousing of voices far in the distance, the cut and sluice of a boat on the water, a cat wailing on a wall. I ran down the front stairs, to the road, but look as I might in both directions, all I could make out was shadow.

Reluctantly I returned to the house and carefully closed the door, not wanting to rouse Makepeace or Fookes. I lit a candle and tried to still my hands, the contents making a shape in the paper, the writing addressed to Makepeace and me as per usual. The paper was damp and made no noise when I tore it open – again, there was nothing written inside, my father knew nothing but his name – but there was a flower there, the petals intact and true, not pressed with time and sea air, not a clock of time's passing but newly plucked, vivid with life, small as it was. A forget-me-not.

* * *

At breakfast the next morning Fookes sat opposite me, his eyes wandering to the bruise that crowned my face. Makepeace had already given me comfrey to take its thundercloud colour away, the blue of forget-me-not, but I said nothing of that either, it remained in my pocket.

"Mrs Makepeace, with your permission, would Eglantine accompany me today? I've some things to buy for my kit and I would like a woman's opinion," Fookes said before finishing his bread and butter.

Makepeace took a long glance at me and at Fookes. "As long as you are back by dark, I don't see why not. But please bring her back, Mr Fookes, with fewer bruises than you find her with." Fookes blushed before he bustled out of the kitchen to ready himself.

"Am I to have no say in it?" I asked as Makepeace wiped her face with her hands and rested them on the table.

"Would you dislike it so much?"

The kitchen seemed too hot, too stifling. The weather was turning, as was I. My mother's pouch bounced in my pocket as I stood up.

"Go on, Eglantine, soak up the sunshine like a sponge."

I took the latest post from my pocket and passed it to her. "Won't you join us?" I said. Makepeace looked pale; when was the last time she had seen the sun?

She peered into the envelope and tucked it into her blouse.

"Next time. Too long we've lived like birds in a cage, my dear, we'll have forgotten how to use our wings."

I looked at Makepeace, she wouldn't meet my eye.

By the time I retrieved my bonnet and coat, Fookes was waiting for me, his hat in his hands, the brim spinning through his fingers, making a circumference of it, a small globe. Together we stepped out into the street. I paused for a moment and I let the sun seep into my skin, beneath my eyelashes, like a river made of gold.

Fookes offered me his arm and I looked at it, unsure of what he meant by his deliberately protruding elbow before I realised what was being offered, his safe escort. I wrapped my arm around it and felt the heat of him through the fabric of his coat sleeve, and was glad to take it for the city as we came closer was all hub, an assault on my ears; each street we moved through overlapped the roar of the next until I felt I was under the water. Makepeace was right, we'd both been cooped up too long – chained to the house as if it was our keeper.

We entered a shop and Fookes ordered all he needed – leathers and nails, a new coat and hat, a few metres of fine silk and velvet – he let me choose the colours – the silk blue, the velvet green. The fabrics to the touch felt like plush; I drew a road with my finger upon the nap. The packages were wrapped in brown paper and string and Fookes offered me his elbow again as we set off.

"When does your ship sail, Mr Fookes, Francis," I said. I had grown so accustomed to the sounds of him in the house that I realised it would soon be very silent without him.

"The day after the Coronation," he replied. That was only a few weeks away, the shops were already starting to brim with things to celebrate Princess Victoria taking the throne – mugs, flags, ribbons and rosettes all printed with her handsome young face on them. Every time I looked at them I thought of my poor doll down in the dank cellar – had I really stolen her or was that just another tale of my father's?

"Do you think she's looking forward to being the queen?" I asked, feeling pity for her. "The gaze of the world trailing her every movement, the attention on her womb, the wondering when she will spring forth a prince?"

Fookes stopped then looked at me and I felt his arm stiffen beneath mine. Had I offended him?

"Would that be so bad? To marry the man of her choosing, for them to make a little family of their own?" he said, the street moving on around us. "Who'd care what the world thought, the world be damned."

An elderly woman walking past with a basket full of turnips, the dirt raining down her skirt, muttered under her breath at his language, but for me his words were a spark. Would that be so bad, to start out anew, have my own family, shake off the ties that bound me to the house by the river, to the actions of my father? Would he have me if he knew? When I said nothing, Fookes and I walked on. His packages wrapped up in brown paper and string occasionally hit my legs, my fingers brushed against the opening of his waistcoat pocket, a fingertip on the lip of the lining, my fingers swimming in and out of the pocket as my father had taught me, but I hit upon something, calloused and warm, Fookes's own fingers met mine through a slit in the lining, the frayed edges tangling our fingers together.

Our fingers were joined like two fishes as we walked along the riverside, the river like a glistening road, two seagulls taking their rest side by side, their orange beaks crossed, bobbing along the water, until the sight of the house made me extract my hand, feeling all the windows were eyes.

Inside Fookes smiled at me, then hauled his packages upstairs.

"Makepeace, I'm back," I called but she didn't reply. In the kitchen the fire had died down, but the smells of bread and meat were still thick in the air. Her bedroom door was ajar, but she wasn't inside. My fingers held air in my pocket. Where would be the harm in retrieving my doll?

The cellar door took some shoving, the wood having swelled in the damp. The stairs wetter and darker than I remembered, my foot slipped with each step. I retraced my steps, retrieved a candle and took it down the stairs with me, my hand shielding the flame as it danced, the pucker and suck. The walls had grown greener. The pillowcase still sat at the bottom of the stairs and, resting the candle on a stair, I lifted it, feeling the moisture on its edges and braced myself for finding my doll turned into something rotten and green like an ear of unripe corn. But as I reached into the pillowcase, my hand found nothing, the whole thing had been emptied, drained. I shook it, turned it inside out, but not even a dust dolly remained. I held the candle aloft and looked throughout the cellar – the low-lying puddle like a mirror at the bottom, the river rising up through the ground, the invisible member of our household. Something floated on the surface, I fished out the item with my shoe. A plain pocket handkerchief made of coarse stuff, old and worn and unfamiliar. Could it have been in the pillowcase and floated down? Had it been there since I brought the pillowcase down to the cellar? But if it had, wouldn't it have sunk by now? I dropped the handkerchief on the stairs, the haste of my movements extinguishing the light.

The kitchen was still bare of life. I walked slowly up the stairs, my shoes slippery with water and slime; I could see the trace of my footsteps behind me. I went past Fookes's room and heard him happily whistling. The sound of it broke my panic, but my toes grew colder, the ice travelling up my spine, shooting down my arms.

Back in my room I flicked off my shoes, the toes of my stockings tinged green, and leaned behind the door, feeling the house shift beneath my feet, my breath ragged. Sitting on my bed, as if the room was inhabited by the ghost of the child I had been, was my little wooden tuck-comb doll, her dress fringed with the same green tint as my stockings, like lace made of purslane, her hands limp. The glass of her earrings still shone. Her painted face still dear and sweet, her little mouth as red as a rosehip. Who had put her here? Makepeace? The ghost of my mother? I picked up my doll and held her, the familiar shape of her in my hands made me feel small and insignificant, as if my hands had been made only to hold her, her wood carved to fit their shape.

TWENTY-NINE

Patrin, 1821

How quickly the wheel turned, our fates caught now in the spokes of it, trampling us beneath. We were taken to a holding cell, dank and crowded, but I kept all my attention on Little Egg in the hope it would keep her from the darkness and desperation that surrounded us. She asked for her papa, her arms hot and sticky around my neck, tears leading her to exhaustion. She slumped in my arms that barely had the strength to hold her up with the throb that emanated from them. Amberline. There wasn't a part of me that wasn't angry at him; for all the sacrifices made for him, he treated us like any other piece of silver to be melted down for his own purpose. We were but shining things that had caught his fancy, not for what we were but for how we all of us could serve. My father, my mother, myself and Little Egg lost to the fire of his ambition.

All the other bodies pressed around us, their smells overwhelming me. I rested my back on the bars, their cold a comfort, slipped down to the ground and slept. My mother came to me in my dreams, her hand brushing the hair from my face, and I longed for her to speak to me, to hear her voice that had comforted me when I was a child, woken from a bad dream in the *vardo*, the footsteps of the magpies on the roof as they rattled at the dawn. I woke hearing my own name with a fierce ache. My mother was gone, the *vardo* was ash and there was no dawn seeping from the horizon.

"Patrin."

I blinked. Amberline's mother was on the other side of the bars. "Patrin," she said and I struggled to understand where I was, disoriented. Little Egg's tight grip around my neck brought me vividly back to my surrounds.

"Patrin," she said, "take this." She thrust a bottle through the bars, but the distance felt too far for me to reach, though she was close enough. My arms felt like anchors. Mrs Stark took the cork out of the bottle and pushed it through the bars again, bidding me drink. This time I managed to reach out my weighted arms and the bitter liquid trickled through my cracked lips, spilling onto my clothes, splashing onto Little Egg's head, though she didn't wake.

"Patrin," she said, but I could barely stay awake. "This is no place for a child. Let me take Eglantine, let me keep her safe," she said, and I felt all of me spring to alertness, all of me not fuel for the fever just yet.

"A child's place is with her mother," I said.

"Patrin, please, think of the child." She reached out to touch a part of Egg's exposed soft arm.

"I am thinking of my child," I said, feeling ears listen amongst the crowded cell, but that didn't deter me. There was one bucket for thirty or so women to relieve themselves in; we had only the privacy of our own hearts.

"I know what your father did to save him, Patrin. Now let me save your daughter as Josiah saved my son," Mrs Stark said and Little Egg stirred in my arms.

"What of Amberline? Too much of a coward to come now, too much of a coward to come forward then," I said, easing my tight grip on Egg's arm. She sighed in her sleep, her breath feathered on my neck. "I'll not give her to you, she's all I have in the world, Amberline's seen to that," I said.

Mrs Stark wiped her face with her hands, took what coins she had in her chatelaine and handed them to me through the bars, along with food wrapped in cloth. She kissed her fingers and reached her hand through the bars to my head. "Saint Sarah keep you safe, Patrin, you are more like your mother than you know."

My tears pricked at my eyes, but I would not let them fall.

* * *

The day came for my sentencing. We were led to the court to face the judges and I pleaded my innocence, but what weight did my words have? They fell through the air like dust. The judges dispensed their verdict, banished for life, without return, banished instead of the noose, and they looked at me as if I should be grateful for their mercy from upon high, but all I thought of was my child. How would I keep her safe?

They came for us in the night-time, chained together, human links in life's necklace, and bid us step up into a boat. Little Egg, scared of the darkness and the sounds of people crying, cowered with terror in my arms, her little hands gripping my neck.

All the city glittered, lamps, candles, lanterns, lights – all the shine for Amberline – spilling out onto the water, a rippling road made of light, though we were headed to the darkness. All this time I had waited for Amberline to come and see us, to come and say the gold was his, that it had nothing to do with us. I had waited in vain for him, he'd no more save us than His Majesty would.

As the boat pulled away from the shore the sound of people wailing increased, the last of England, the last time of walking the ground of their loved ones, no more to see their faces, we were bound for a living death. I wrapped my cloak around Little Egg and prayed to Saint Sarah to deliver us. The boatmen rowed on the river smooth as a conspiracy, aiding our removal from all we knew, cutting through the water and pulling us onwards, out into the darkness, away from the shore. I longed to put my hand in the water and will the spirit of it to keep us safe, to keep us from moving away with the rower's current, to hold us still and guide us, every ripple and slap of water a patrin, to guide us back to the shore.

In the distance I saw a ship loom out of the darkness and my heart darted in my chest like a swift, Saint Sarah had heard my cry. But as the boat sculled towards it, I saw it was no ship, that it wasn't even worthy of the name, it was a ship in shape only. All sails, all masts, all gone. It was only a hull. A lantern was lit and hung off the prow, revealing the red coat of a soldier keeping watch. A cry went up from our boat; I covered Little Egg's ears, she was stiff with fear, mirroring my own. And the prison hulk before us responded, all those already entombed in her sounded a bitter welcome – the striking of wood on wood, calls and cries, snatches of voices, the shout of names, despair meeting despair. A high-pitched whistle rang above it all.

Our boat saddled aside the hull and a series of ropes was sent down and fixed with knots before we were forced to climb a rickety staircase that ran up the side of the boat like a badly stitched wound. Faces stared at us from close range through the portholes, distorted by the lack of light and the glass. Above a soldier shouted and like cattle we were placed on deck, the chains hitting the wood. Little Egg, exhausted, slept on my shoulder; the creep of fever still swirled in my limbs, but I willed it away, the weight of her head the only thing that kept me tethered. I would keep her safe. On an old and rotten rope whipped someone's laundry stretched out between two broken masts. The whip and blow of it the most normal sound in the world, but out here in the middle of the waters it sounded like the lungs of death. I looked up at the night sky and every star was extinguished with cloud. They called our names and counted us then led us below. We were the Empire's slaves.

Down below the deck the smell rushed at us – all the sweaty, sick and crowded were caged together like animals and we to join them. Somewhere someone was singing *too-ra-lai* and Little Egg whimpered in her sleep, all the while my arms burning, the fever licking up me like a flame.

How many days were we kept from the light? How many days did I lie on damp straw, Little Egg in my reach? She held her doll to her chest while she layered it a bed of straw, her glass earrings catching the light. When I woke again, someone was holding a cup of water up to me, but it was not even a raindrop. I could have drunk the whole river if I put my lips to it.

One night I heard our names being called, coming to me across the water, quiet at first, then insistent. The river called my name, I was sure of it. The spirit of the water had come to deliver me. *Patrin*, it cried, *Patrin*. I staggered to my feet and peered through the porthole, where I saw a lantern swaying like a wrecker. Amberline was there, standing at the helm of a boat, the oars still, a veil of rain coming through to drench me.

"Patrin!" Amberline cried.

Amberline's words were like salt when I craved water.

"Hurry, pass Eglantine out to me, Patrin, before the soldiers come," he said and I stood and looked at him. Little Egg was asleep on the straw, her hair crowned with it, wrapped in my own cloak. Could I give her up? Someone cried out in their sleep and it startled me. This was only the start, here on this prison ship; we had the voyage to survive, not to speak of the country they would banish us to.

"Patrin," Amberline called again.

All of me longed to keep her, but gently I lifted Little Egg into my arms, happy to feel that weight of her, the hot warm life of her in my arms, and I began to tremble. How would I be able to give her up? I buried my nose in her neck, her hair, the soft plumpness of her cheek. If only it were possible to place her back in the safety of my body, I'd be able to keep her safe, but what was my body, damp and broken, I could barely hold her weight. I tucked her doll in her pocket, she'd not be without it.

Amberline reached towards her, his hands clutching around her tight. I saw in his face that he loved her, but what of my love? My love was stronger than oceans, stronger than water, stronger than rope. Her little shoe fell off into the dark lap of waters below with a little *plink*.

"For God's sake, Patrin, jump," Amberline shouted. The guards were coming, their shouts echoed out across the water. I squeezed out of the porthole, feeling my clothes tear, the threads holding me, I kicked against the air. Shouting came from behind me. The water rushed up to me as I fell; Amberline's hands reached for me, trying to steady the boat in the water. Little Egg woke, her little voice calling, "Mama!" All of me reached for her, though the river was as cold as I was hot. Behind me a splash, a guard swore as he too entered the water, his scarlet coat turning black as it soaked up the river.

"Hurry, Patrin," Amberline shouted, but the guard was a stronger swimmer than me. The water creased from his pounding stroke, close to reaching for me.

I pulled at the cord around my throat, not daring to break the knot. She and I were both strands meeting, she and I of the same thread, my daughter and I. My love was like an end of the knot, the more you pulled at it, the tighter it became. I threw Amberline the *putsi*. The guard was so close I smelled the rum on his breath.

Little Egg's head rose and fell with the lap of the waters, so close but I couldn't reach her. "Mama," she cried again and somewhere along the riverbank a curlew woke and replied to her.

Amberline's hands hesitated on the oars. "Go!" I screamed. What good would it be for all of us to be taken? "Keep it for her. Tell her that I loved her. Keep her safe," I said and felt the whole river swell beneath me, my hands shaking, all of me already longing for her. The guard's arm was on me then, pulling at me,

I had no strength to struggle against him. The river knew me and I knew it. I owed it as much as I did my father.

"I promise," Amberline said. "God keep you safe, Patrin."

Amberline gathered the oars to himself and began to row, lost in the shadow of the hulk. I watched the clouds part, the stars spitefully revealing nothing, but I heard the movement of the water in their wake, the startled sob of her cry winnowing out in the darkness, until I was washed with a wave.

THIRTY

Eglantine, 1838

In the morning I woke with a start, blood rushing in my ears as I listened to the house: Fookes's familiar steps below as he made his ablutions, the long stream of piss into the chamber-pot, the sound of his yawn winding up through the floorboards. But the house felt different, the echoes somehow denser, thicker, my ears muffled like the sensation of snow covering the street, everything coming to me as if softened by eiderdown. I flung off the bedclothes and stood up. Outside, a hot sheen was already rising off the river, a fug in the making. On the stairs Makepeace's chatelaine jingled and went silent. Today was my birthday and my doll sat on a chair, innocent of her arrival, her smiling eyes looking back at mine. Surely it was Makepeace who'd found her and replaced her upon her throne, a childhood gift recovered.

I dressed and slipped on my shoes, one still damp from the puddle in the cellar, my feet concealing Fookes's posy – the petals and the hip. Makepeace was back on the stairs, swiftly closing Ada's old room behind her, startled to see me.

"Happy birthday, my girl," she said, kissed me on both cheeks and swept me down the stairs with her, my arm caught up in hers. A spicy sweet smell met us halfway down the stairs and I felt my stomach flip-flop with hunger.

In the kitchen Makepeace had baked buns sprinkled with currants, the butter was already soft, yellow peaks from the heat of the kitchen, a thick puddle of sunshine. From the folds of her pockets she extracted a small box wrapped in brown paper. "It's just a little something," she said.

"But I thought the doll was my present," I replied, and Makepeace looked at me strangely. Fookes bustled into the kitchen and looked at the small box in my hands.

"It's your birthday?" he asked and I nodded. "Many happy returns." He grinned and I looked at his open face and found myself smiling in return. "Aren't you going to open your present?"

I looked at the box in my hands, wriggled off the twine. Inside were two gold loops, a pair of earrings, each hanging with a little piece of glass that caught the light, sending a blue streak across the kitchen wall. Where had she got them from?

"They are beautiful, thank you," I said, folding her in my embrace, feeling her smallness, the sharpness of her bones. She was growing frailer.

"See, a lodger makes the difference," she said, reading my mind. "Come, let me make a hole in your ears and you can wear them," she said and sat me down by the fire. Fookes took his seat opposite and flipped and rolled up his shirtsleeves in the growing heat. Makepeace took a needle from her chatelaine to the fire and let the tip glow red, before she brought it over and brushed the hair from my neck.

"Saint Sarah bless you," she said as she ran the tip of the needle through my ear. I smelled the iron of my own blood and it made my stomach swirl. Black spots suddenly painted on everything, including the inside of my eyelids, as she pushed the wire into the hole; the glass dangled against my jawline. Fookes poured the tea, piled a scoop of sugar in and bid me drink. I was barely able to hold the cup, such was the tremor in my hands. Makepeace repeated the needle to the flame to my other earlobe and the threading of the wire into my flesh and I felt a wave of darkness leap up and claim me.

When I came to I was back on my bed, my doll staring at me, my earlobes throbbing, and I wondered in that moment between the dark and the light whether we had swapped places, that she was the living one and I was as heavy as wood, kept in the dark and the damp, the first evidence of a crime.

Makepeace sat on the bed while Fookes stood nearby.

"If it's no trouble, Mr Fookes, your room would be more suitable for the new lodger, but the one across the hall is more than ample for your needs. And it is quieter," Makepeace said.

"No trouble at all, I'll move my things whenever it is convenient," he said.

I sat up and felt the room tilt, my ears heavy as anchors.

"Eglantine?" Fookes said and rushed forward to help me.

"I'll be fine," I said, dismissing the spin of the room.

"You need something to eat is all," Makepeace said, already up and off to gather a tray, leaving Fookes and I alone. He lifted the doll off the chair and placed her in his lap.

"What's this?" he said, plucking the pouch off the floor; it must have fallen from my pocket. I had to control my impulse to snatch it back from him, frightened he would try to open it, the last remnants of my mother's lost life.

"It was my mother's," I said and he smoothed the leather over his leg, the knot holding true.

"The cord – I can fix it for you if you like? So you can wear it around your neck," he said and looked at me. "Let it be my birthday gift for you, humble as it is."

"But leave the knot, the knot ..." I said, my thoughts stumbling over my words. The knot she had tied with her own fingers, with it, her spirit tied to me, I was sure of it.

Fookes handed me the pouch and bounded down the stairs, quickly returning with a piece of leather cord, needle and thread.

"You just show me where you'd like it," he said and he sat beside me, sewing the cord with his nimble hands, pushing the metal through the tough leather, just as the needle had pushed through my flesh, his stitches neat and small. When he finished he looped it over my head and I felt the cord nestle close to the skin of my neck, brushing against it soft like a lip.

* * *

I listened to Fookes as he moved things across the hall, fading to silence when he entered Ada's old room. Makepeace came upstairs with the tea and breakfast buns as if I was an invalid, and with quick fingers I made sure the pouch was concealed completely beneath my blouse.

"Who is the new lodger?" I said.

Makepeace put down the tray, a shake to her hand sending the china cups and saucers chiming against each other.

"A private man of middle age, a widower. I've said we'd afford him his privacy. And Lord knows we need the added income," she said.

"So why does Fookes have to change rooms? Surely my footsteps will bother the new lodger," I said, stamping for effect. I prickled with indignation.

Makepeace looked up at me. "I don't see why it's a concern of yours," she said tartly.

I felt tears smart at my eyes, Makepeace had never spoken harshly to me, not my whole life. Why would she speak to me like that now?

Downstairs there was the sound of something falling, all Fookes's tools scattered on the floor. We both heard Fookes curse and listened to his footsteps as he began to gather them. The colour returned to Makepeace's face.

The sound of the footsteps came up the stairs.

"I've cleared the room, Mrs Makepeace," Fookes said, "not much to clear really."

"Won't be long now, Mr Fookes," Makepeace said.

"Yes, goodbye to old England forever and all that," he said, looking at me. "Are you recovered enough now for some air, Miss Eglantine? With your permission of course, Mrs Makepeace. I thought a walk down by the riverside before the day gets too hot?"

"It's up to Eglantine," Makepeace said and bustled out of the room.

I swung my legs off the bed. Fookes took two buns and filled his pockets with them and followed me down the stairs. Outside in the street, the salt was already heavy in the air, warmth soaked into us like a liquid. He offered me his arm and I took it, glad to twine myself onto him, steady as earth, feeling Makepeace's words run through me. Perhaps she was right, perhaps I had been kept sheltered, kept as my father's prize when I had no shine at all.

The river unspooled in either direction like mercury, rippling and silver, barely distinguishable from the sky. A heron dipped out of the air and barely caused a disturbance in the water, before retrieving a fish, its scales blinding, as if made of metal, before it disappeared down the heron's throat. A lighterman went past in the distance with his pole in the water, the languid glide of his heavy load, the pole disappearing and reappearing with a song in his lungs reaching out across the water.

"So what's in the pouch, if you don't mind me asking? What makes it so special?" Fookes said quizzically, pulling a bun out of his pocket and handing it to me, before pulling out the second one for himself, biting into its crust and flinging a morsel onto the silty rocks below for the seagulls to squabble over. At first I bristled at such a question. I looked at the bun in my hand and though I'd been hungry suddenly lost my appetite; the tide had dragged in a threshing of duckweed, perhaps I would be better supping from that.

"It was my mother's, that is all I know. Inside are a few bits and pieces, lucky charms I suppose," I said, feeling all my words were shaped false. "I'm sad to say it, but I don't remember her at all."

"Nothing at all?" Fookes said, plucking out a currant and putting it in his mouth.

"Nothing except the missing of her." I picked up a stone, hurled it across the water and waited for it to skip, but instead it sunk straight down, swallowed like medicine.

"What happened to her?" Fookes asked gently, his sleeve brushing my own, but I stepped away.

"I don't know," I said. How didn't I know? Why had no one told me? I'd been fed on half-truths and bitter silences and now they soured my stomach, I wanted to retch over the edge of the river.

"Ask Mrs Makepeace? I'm sure she knows everything," he said and laughed nervously, and I smiled at him. She would know, but she wouldn't tell; that tale belonged to my father, but he'd never tell it now.

"So does your ship leave from London, Mr Fookes?" I said, keen to move on, away from all the gall that swirled in my own head.

"No, from Southampton, where I'll stay at the immigrant depot, before being tugged out to sea to meet the ship."

"Depot?"

"A hostel of sorts, where they try and get everyone used to shipboard life, so staying here with you and Mrs Makepeace is luxury."

I turned back to look at the house, the sunlight striking across the windows; the house felt more coop than castle.

"Have you thought of leaving? What is here that holds you?"

I thought of a hundred things in an instant, but none formed itself into a coherent answer.

"There's Makepeace, for one," I replied.

"She come with you, find your father, be reunited. A new start for all of you," Fookes said, and the pictures in Fookes's books opened up in my mind's eye, all the unfolding light upon the water, the strange animals caught in an oval of green, the small figure with his blue coat with his back to me. The thought crept into my mind of all those strange blooms that had arrived, what message did they hold? If he had found someone to write the address, how was it that he didn't get them to write a letter? Five blossoms for five years; were they a message or a sign, but if they were how was I ever to read them? The ocean roared between their message and their meaning; how would we ever be reunited?

"You could come," Fookes blurted, "yourself," and I felt the blood pulse through to my newly pierced ears and felt that if Fookes looked at me long enough he'd see the truth skip through me, like a stone across the water. In the distance along the foreshore a figure bent down and walked like an oyster-catcher, eyes to the ground, scavenging the tide.

"Me, myself? Whatever would I do?" I said. Fookes knew nothing of my uselessness for real life. I'd grown as my father had wanted me, a jewel in the dark of its velvet case, until it had been time for me to show the lightness of my fingers, a harvester of pockets, my eye on the shine.

"Come with me," Fookes said, placing his hand on mine, and I looked at it, floating over mine.

He pulled me towards him, I felt his body firm against mine; the roughness of his coat lapel scraped my cheek, his hand slid around my waist like I was something to catch, but he didn't know what I was, I'd run through his fingers like water.

I was back at the house as fast as my feet allowed me. A door slammed upstairs and I sent the one downstairs swinging in reply, Makepeace appearing at the top of the stairs flustered and surprised to see me, her lace cap sitting slightly askew on her head, the silver starting to run through her dark hair.

"I thought you were on a walk with Mr Fookes," she said breathlessly.

"Not any more," I said, walking up the stairs, bristling at her question, with the touch of Fookes's hand on my hip.

Makepeace moved in front of me, her body blocking my way. "What happened? Was he untoward?" Her questions buzzed in the air and all I wanted to do was smack them between my fingers and be done with them. Makepeace still barred my way, until I stood on the step beneath her. "Eglantine, answer me," she said.

Though I was a full step below her, it was I who looked down on her. She took a step backwards but kept my gaze. She didn't want answers to my questions, she was wanting to delay me. The door to my father's old room was closed. I brushed past her and tried my hand on the door, but it didn't give way to me, it was locked from the inside.

"Eglantine," Makepeace hissed under her breath, "leave it be, our new lodger is resting."

"When did he arrive?" I said. I'd not seen anyone approach the house, but then I'd been caught up with Fookes.

Petulantly, I stamped up the stairs and into my room, swinging the door, a bang to end all bangs, the sound echoing across the house.

Fookes's question skimmed across my mind again and again and again. I strained to listen to the movements of the lodger, but I heard nothing, our new lodger resting like the dead. I kept to my room, listening, the room growing stifling with the heat. I opened the windows and all the brine and salt came waltzing in. There was no sign of Fookes down by the water's edge, no sound at the front door or in his room. Occasionally I heard some faint sound, but it was no more than a pigeon's flap or a rustle, for all I knew it may have been the wind singing down the chimney.

By early evening hunger drove me down to the kitchen. Makepeace sat alone at the table, sewing buttons on a shirt: fine linen, mother-of-pearl buttons.

"Is that for Mr Fookes?" I said, thinking it too grand for the likes of him.

Makepeace didn't look up, her needle looping through the air, the tip of it catching a glint like a dust mote struck with light. "No, it's for the new lodger," she said, snapping the thread off with her teeth before affixing another button.

"Does this lodger have a name?"

Makepeace looked up and eyed me. "Mr Brown to you and me," she said. "It's too hot to cook anything in this weather, help yourself to bread, cheese and pickles."

I looked at the cheese already sweating beneath its cloth. "Have you seen Mr Fookes?" I said, slicing the cheese, flicking off the mould and taking a bite, sharp and creamy.

"Not since you came in like the devil's own," she said and I felt my shame simmer.

"He asked me why I didn't go with him," I said, scoffing the cheese down, drinking a glass of water. I hadn't realised how thirsty I'd become. "To the Colony."

Makepeace lay down the sewing in her lap. "Is that such a bad thing?"

Her words struck me: why would she agree to such a thing, see it as a possibility? "I …"

"Are you too good for a shoemaker with plans to not just make do but make better?" she said.

"It's not that," I said, floundering.

"He's not handsome enough, nor refined? You find him unsuitable?"

"No," I said, I found him handsome enough; the tips of his fingers pressing my own had filled within me a sensation like hot and cold across my skin, his hand on my waist had done the same. "What good would I do him, I who know nothing of life or the world?" All I know is the inside of a stranger's pocket. "He'd expect an honest woman for a wife, and in that I am sorely lacking." Angry tears sprung to my eyes.

Makepeace stood up and came over to me, her hand resting on my cheek, dry amid all this clamminess. "You'll learn," she said, kissing both my cheeks. "You could do worse."

As she came close to embrace me, I felt the familiar dance begin in my fingers, all the joints outstretched and ready, supple like a pianist who already heard the song she was about to play. Why would I fight it when it was all I knew? She didn't even blink as my fingers unlooped the key from her chatelaine and neither did it make a sound as I dropped it into my own pocket. I was as subtle and as secret as the water that seeped from its secret river course to the earth beneath our cellar, wending its way upward through the dark.

THIRTY-ONE

Eglantine, 1838

All night I listened for the sounds of the new lodger moving beneath, but aside from the odd shuffle the room was silent, as if he had slippers made of thistledown. Fookes was in his room, I heard the tap of his footfall, the faint sound of his cough, the sound further away and soon it would be on the other side of the world. How dare Makepeace suggest I could do worse, when I didn't know the parameter of any other human being – no relationships other than those I fostered in this house, not knowing anyone other than my father and my grandmother? I was rudderless in knowing what sort of man Fookes was. He had all the attributes of a kindly gentleman portrayed in the pages of the newspaper – neat and polite, manners learned at his parents' knees, all the old courtesies, but what did that translate to me, thief that I was? All I knew was that when I was near him the air changed, like a window open in my soul, a gulp of breath.

At dawn, before the house stirred, I walked barefoot down the stairs and leaned my ear against the door of my father's old room, the grain of the wood rough against my cheek, hearing nothing except my own heart knocking against my chest, loud as if I was knocking on the wood, my mother's pouch hanging a conduit between flesh and door. The key was in my palm and I was certain that the room was empty. In the distance a cart splashed in the ruts of the road. I held the handle and turned the key to silence the chance of the wind rattling the door.

The room was empty, the bed unslept in. Why would Makepeace lie and say there was a new lodger if there wasn't one? I stood behind the door and made myself look at the room again; something was different, something had shifted. I teased the curtain open a little, the light trickling in, a pigeon rested on the sill, his mottled grey feathers smeared against the glass, before he disappeared into the morning. What was I missing? The drawers were empty, the bed was made but there was an indentation along the length of it as though an invisible guest still lay there; the mirror above the mantle showed me the whole room back in miniature, a porthole of the room. That was when I saw it, feeling sick to my core, frightened as if a spirit stood behind me till I realised it was a coat hanging, the length of a man, on a hook behind the door.

The coat was deeply soiled, the hem had soaked up a great deal of water and had turned the lower half of the coat a different shade. A long tear had been mended in the lining, stitched roughly with some sort of string or twine, the cuffs soiled, the buttonholes made ragged by mismatched buttons, some just a stick stitched on tight and used like a toggle. I ran the fabric through my fingers as if I was a blind person, my eyes closed, the familiarity leaching into my fingertips, and let my fingers swim into the pockets, careful not to touch the sides as if fearing a slap; it had once been such a fine article, the sorrel colour of a fine horse's coat, but now it was worn to threads on the shoulders. All that the pocket contained was a sprig of rosemary, the tiny blue flower still in the bud. The owner of the coat I was in no doubt of, though worn and travelled, distressed and repaired.

The whole house was silent except for the shout of my thoughts. I stepped out of the room, locked the door behind me and palmed the key. Fookes turned the handle of his door, so I made haste back to my bedroom, filled with confusion. I pulled on my stockings and shoes. The red birthmark around my neck began to sting, the leather of my mother's pouch brushing against it; I pulled my blouse away, the skin an accusation. There was a quick rap on my door.

"Come in," I said, thinking it was Makepeace, my mind so dammed with questions I didn't know which one would trickle out first. But it wasn't Makepeace, it was Fookes.

"May I come in?" he said, standing on the threshold. "May I speak with you privately." He didn't wait for me to reply but entered, closed the door quietly behind him and stepped towards me, all of my mind rushing and loud.

"Makepeace won't be happy that we are in here alone," I said, panic spreading all down my neck.

"She's gone out, before dawn, I heard her go," he said, stepping closer. "She might be back at any moment, so please let me speak." He put up his hands, seeing that I was keen to sweep him out of the room, all of me bristle and broom.

"I didn't make myself clear yesterday, and for that I'm sorry, I'm not a man of words." His voice made my skin prickle. He reached and took my hand and I looked at my fingers, foreign as fish, in the net of his. "Eglantine ..." His hand was hot and dry and it pulled me closer.

"What is it that you want, Mr Fookes, Francis?" I said, unable to stop the twist of sarcasm in my voice. "There is nothing I can give you." I pulled my hand away.

"No, it is what I can give you. Yesterday when I spoke of your coming with me, I didn't mean for you to come as some piece of luggage but as my wife, Eglantine. Would you accept my hand?"

I felt twisted with my cruelty, his earnestness stoking my sting. "But I don't know you, Mr Fookes. I know nothing of your plans, your person, you'll be gone in mere weeks," I said, feeling the ugliness of the words as I said them, "and you are, after all, a mere tradesman, a shoemaker." My father's words were in my mouth. I was his puppet even still and I would remain so. I had become what he had wanted of me, regardless of what I felt; even though we were separated by the span of the globe, I still did his bidding.

Fookes's face blanched, each of my words filching any affection and regard he might have, my sleight of hand damaging his estimation of me. I saw myself in his eyes: small, dark, a thorn. But as I said those words I meant the opposite – I didn't care if he was a shoemaker or a chimneysweep, I cared for him however he came. His hands were honest hands that practised an honest trade, unlike mine, and soon he'd be gone, just another person I loved who would leave only a silhouette as a memory of themselves, sharp and black.

"I'm afraid I don't believe you." Fookes stepped forward, his face so close. I willed him to defy my bitter resistance.

Gingerly he reached a fingertip and ran it the length of the raised and angry birthmark that swelled at my throat. His touch made me ashamed of all that I had said. What had I done to deserve him? But instead of pushing him away with the tide of it, I pulled him in closer.

"But I have done things, things that you would not approve of," I made myself say, feeling the burden of all that my father had made me become, of how much I wanted to say yes to Fookes. "I'm a thief," I said, "that is how I provide, it is all I know."

Fookes placed his mouth on mine and kissed me, the fractious knot dissolving into disarray. A tangle of arms. His skin warm as light.

* * *

I never laid eyes on the mysterious Mr Brown. Occasionally I heard a cough or a cry that woke me from sleep, but often I wasn't sure if it was some other sound, a passer-by in the street, the house settling, a sound coming from across the river. His coat sometimes appeared in the corners of my dreams – I was wearing it, a scarecrow flapped in it, a drowned person floated in it – leaving me distracted, unfocused, awake and listening to the house again. Fookes came silently in the night, barefoot, his tread the only thing I listened out for, his mouth the only thing I craved.

The night before the Coronation I hardly slept, the night hot, my skin sticking to the sheets. I got up and pushed open the sash of the bedroom window, hoping for a lick of the breeze, but there was none. The night was still with anticipation. The darkness was filled with carousing song; celebrations had started early, the sun was but a hope on the horizon.

Makepeace had brought up water from the river before dawn split the sky and land. She had twice boiled it for good measure, sending the kitchen thick with steam, until the house was filled with the hot cloud of it. The table was laid with our wedding breakfast, a cake dusted with sugar, a bowl of raspberries, a jug of cream and a bottle of whiskey. While the water cooled, Makepeace dressed my hair in sweetpeas she'd found wind-sown in one of her pots, tenderly threading them through my braids.

"Your mother would have loved to have seen this day," she said, holding me at arm's length and taking me in. "Your father too." Her emotions stuck in her throat. If Makepeace's old ways were true, if all the things of the departed weren't destroyed their spirit would linger, then whatever remained of my mother remained on earth, lingering still, caught in the pouch which hung close to my skin. Was that why my father had never destroyed it, was it his gift to me: if not a living mother, a spirit one? I closed my eyes and tried to imagine her face, but all that came to me was the sound of water.

I heard Fookes's footsteps on the stairs and felt my heart chirr like a magpie as he neared. Fookes gently swept my hair to the side to bare my neck, around which he draped a simple strand of coral, the little click of the clasp; his breath on my neck made me shiver, bedecked as I was, a religious icon, made out of portable property ready to be carried on a procession through the streets. The coral nestled right across the mark the Lord had given me at birth; in the side of the copper pot I saw my reflection bulge, the scar on my skin and the strand of beads intertwining.

"It was my mother's," he said and the gap widened of how much I didn't know about him – his parents, his life. I told myself that we'd fill these in, these pages of the book our lives were yet to write, but the cavernous lack of knowledge yawned up at me, making me wonder if he'd be waiting for me after the months at sea; would the equator act as a magnet did on a watch's mechanism and send his affection for me haywire? While lying in the circumference of his arms all these thoughts were kept at bay, but for how much longer? It had been arranged that I'd follow Fookes a few weeks after his departure, unable to get a berth on his ship, and I pushed the thought of his loss out of my mind, though it was but hours away.

"Now join hands," Makepeace said and we did. "You are promised to each other from this day forward." Fookes looked at me and grinned, a line of perspiration atop his freshly shaven lip. "Now drink from the cup." Makepeace handed it to Fookes and then myself, still hot so that it scalded my tongue, burned my lips. "You ever will drink from nothing but the same cup else," she said, wrapped the cup in a cloth and bid us step upon it; the crunch and grind of the porcelain sounded beneath our heels. Makepeace kissed us both. We drank whiskey, ate cake and made ready to join the throng of people to welcome the new queen.

Fookes held my hand and we went out into the morning. The whole city seemed to buzz, a hive waiting for their new queen bee, but for Fookes and me it felt like a celebration just for us. From the fronts of the buildings hung flags, limply waiting for the wind to turn them to banners. Already people milled in the street, taking up vantage points. Hawkers set up their wares in carts – Coronation pies, mugs, ale. Fookes tried to flag a hansom cab, but no driver would stop, all were occupied, urgently trying to make their way through the growing congestion.

A newspaper boy sang out in a pure voice, "Three thousand and ninety-three gems, the Black Prince's Ruby, St Edward's Sapphire, a cross pattée will crown her." And I had to stop and lean into the gutter, Fookes's hand on my back as I retched the whiskey, the cake and the raspberries into the street, the paperboy's chant like a rhyme, the sort of portable property my father would covet in one spectacular item. Fookes bade me sit and catch my breath, but the excitement of the crowd bobbed me along, and I was keen to see her, the doll a happy little wooden fish rolling in my pocket.

We ploughed on through the streets towards the centre of the city, a shoal of people all waiting, jostling, animated. Fookes kept close to me and we marched onwards through to the thickest part, a human road towards Westminster Abbey, his hand gripping my elbow to prevent us getting separated, our feet barely touching the ground.

By the time we got there, the princess had already entered the abbey and the crowd were in a hush of whispers, as if they too were inside the walls and witness to the miraculous ceremony. All around us people bustled. I smelled a man's cologne, a lady's skirts pushed up against my own, the smell of pickled herrings on someone's breath. The breath squeezed from my body. Fookes looked at me with concern, but I dismissed it, seeing his whole face lit like a child at a fair. "God Save the Queen" started to sing from the front of the crowd, Fookes's voice joining the mass of voices. But there was still no sign of the new queen, we were all subjects waiting, the sun hot on our heads. Around my neck I felt my perspiration pool, and I longed for a glass of water, anything wet, when someone caught my eye. He had his back towards me, tall in his stovepipe hat, the coat familiar and tattered, looking against the crowd, looking for something the rest of us weren't looking to see, our eyes towards the abbey. The man surveyed the people around him, and when he saw me he looked as if he had found what he was looking for.

From inside the abbey there was movement and the people responded to it with a huzzah upon their lips. I stood on my tiptoes to try to catch a glimpse. Fookes put his hands around my hips and lifted me, and for a moment I caught sight of her, a smear of thick satin, a slash of scarlet, a glint of light, the new queen fast as a butterfly, before I landed back on the ground, Fookes's face flushed and smiling down at me.

"Did you see her?" he shouted, but I could barely hear him in the melee, the singing and calling her name, *Victoria*.

I nodded and looked over Fookes's shoulder, but the man had disappeared through the crowd like a salmon, darting against the tide, his hat just one of the many that bobbed like flotsam and jetsam above my eyeline.

The desire to run started in my feet, the urge to escape the mass, but I was wedged into my few inches, a handkerchief-sized piece of the London street, so I was forced to step sideways, shuffling through the crowd, as if trying to find my seat at the theatre. Here and there a pocket presented itself to me, an invitation to my hand to dart quickly inside it, pluck whatever was in there and let the crowd sweep me on, but all I did was hold my doll, encased in my own pocket all that much tighter.

From the swell in front of me I heard a shout and I froze, thinking someone had called thief. Then the sound came upon the sound of thousands and the tide swept me forward towards the front. If I had just dug my elbows into the nearest Londoners, my feet would have left the ground and I would have been carried aloft with them.

The drums pounded in time with my heart, a high throttling beat, followed by the blast of trumpets, the glint of which I could see in the distance, the sunlight striking them gold. Then guns pounded the air, deafeningly close. All around me thousands of hands clapping, a cacophony of flesh on flesh. All their voices a-roar – and I was plunged forward and almost lost my balance in the crush of all those people wanting to glimpse their new sovereign and majesty, a celestial angel of satin, diamond, ermine and red velvet. Red like the birthmark around my neck.

Fookes scooped an arm around me and pulled me upward as I struggled against a wall of people and noise. I shouted but the sound of my voice was muffled by the density of the crowd. My ears pounded with the peal of the city's bells chiming throughout my body, all heralding a new era, a new empire all on the shoulders of a new queen, but I carried a new weight, a new concern. The man who had spied me in the crowd was surely my own father.

THIRTY-TWO

Eglantine, 1838

When we returned to the house it was as quiet as it had ever been; all Fookes's belongings had been neatly packed for the following morning, his room left tidy, waiting for the next lodger, his baggage beside the door. I passed my father's old room and all that came from there was a gust from beneath the door. Makepeace had strewn my room with blossom and Fookes and I were glad to disrobe, to catch the fleeting breezes that the river sent, ripples of goose flesh across our skin.

That night, as Fookes's breath was hot on my neck, sleep deserted me. All of me was strained to what was to come – Fookes's departure – the house a port between the near and far away. The man at the Coronation loomed large in my mind. If my father had returned, he'd broken the terms of his sentence, and the law would be only too willing to wed him again to the clap of iron. Makepeace would have told me, surely? Did she know? I no more believed in her fantastical Mr Brown than I did the man in the moon. I strained to listen to the room below, but I heard nothing, nothing but the sound of our own breathing.

Fookes and I rose before the dawn, dressing reluctantly, our clothes heavy and hot, slowing us down. Our footsteps were quiet on the stairs, Fookes carrying all that he had come with. Makepeace had made him a parcel of food and she'd left it on the bottom step, wrapped in brown paper and string.

I opened the door and interrupted a blackbird mid song, his notes familiar and commonly beautiful, yet struck against the growing glow had the feeling of an elegy, its notes the lilting things of what we wanted to say. Fookes made me promise to come to him otherwise he'd be forced to turn around and come and get me, and I made him promise not to forget me. The river heard our promise and it caught the light like a mirror did the sunshine, sending its glare into our eyes.

"We'll build our own house, just you and me," he said, kissing my face, my eyelids, my cheeks, my hair, my mouth. "Something as fine as in Mr Lycett's book."

And I nodded, not wanting our parting to be tainted with my argument, for there'd be time enough for Fookes to know how it came to be that I'd been raised in this house here, this house that was haunted by the water, time for him yet to know. If my father had returned, he'd not only have the law to answer to, but he'd have me as well. I was a woman now, I'd have my questions answered, I'd know all I wanted to know.

Fookes leaned close to my ear and whispered, "You don't have to steal any more," and folded some of his precious money into my hand. My fingers instinctively clasped it before I tried to hand it back to him.

"I did it only to keep us above water," I said, frightened Fookes was breaking things off, but he twined his arm around me and drew me closer. His mouth was sweet and soft on mine, then I leaned close to his ear and whispered my secret, our secret, and he stopped and looked at me, his whole face lit before he twirled me down off the stair and into the street and back onto the stair again. His love retied me in a new knot that I didn't want to be untangled from.

"I'll see you in Richmond," he said, neither of us wanting to say goodbye. I tucked the coin heart inscribed with my name into his palm and hoped my name would stay in his heart.

As I watched him walk away, the dawn made everything pink, like the petals of my namesake eglantine, concealing the smog and smut, making the world rosy. I watched Fookes until he turned and waved, then rounded a corner and disappeared from my sight. I felt the pouch around my neck throb then, the doll in my pocket turn, two compasses spinning to a false north, directing me to gaze upward towards the house, a slash of light concealing the barb beneath, the face in the window looking back at me.

I was in the front door and up the stairs, pushing at my father's old door with my shoulder, but the door was still locked and would not give way. I hit it with my fists and felt the wood shake my bones.

"Eglantine." My father's voice was familiar and strange, but I would not turn around. I was frightened to turn around in case I'd imagined him. The money Fookes had given me fell to the floor, Makepeace swept it up into her chatelaine.

"Turn around, let me see you, it's been so long," he said. And I did as bid and saw my father, smaller and thinner than I'd catalogued him in my memory, his face concealed in a grizzled beard, his skin darker than I recalled, his eyes crinkled at the corners.

"Dear God, you are no longer a little girl," he said. But I'd not been a little girl when he left, I'd already begun my menses, already concealed in my stays, already stunted in the ways of the world. His arms reached out towards me and I dutifully stepped into them and embraced my father, the bones in his back protruding beneath my fingers, his hair curling around the collar of his jacket, unkempt, his pocket gaping, my fingers in and out of it as he'd taught me, though there was nothing there. Still the same scent of him. He gently pushed me back to look further at me and I felt embarrassed by the scrutiny.

"The spit of your mother," he said admiringly and I went to cover my throat protectively, the coral rope around my neck, the red of my birthmark, the pouch hanging there, exposed to his glare. "You found it," he said, his voice choked, and reached out a finger to touch the pouch, but I stepped backward, fearing he would snap the cord and claim it for his own, the only thing I had to remember her by.

"Oh, daughter," he said, "the things I have seen, the things I have done." He started crying then, but I was unmoved, as river-smoothed as stone. He grew silent as we both heard Makepeace in the kitchen, but still he cried, no handkerchief to catch his tears. I would not offer him one of my own. "Eglantine," he said, "your mother, she'd be so proud of you."

"Proud of what? Becoming your creature?" I replied, the vehemence in my voice surprising me. He glared at me, his eyes glistening and wet.

"She gave it to me to give to you," he said, his voice lost in the constriction of his throat. "She left the knot tied, to bind you to her. Makepeace would have had me burn it, but I kept it, though it may have taken away Patrin's peace. I kept it for you."

His words made the world go white before my eyes. My own tears welled in my eyes, sending facets of light across the room. I swept them away with the back of my hand before I began to walk away, leaving him standing there, a shadow of himself. I'd not give him the consolation of comfort.

There was a loud progressive rap at the front door and we both froze, my father's fingers to his lips as he faded back up the stairs. The pounding began again in earnest and I rushed down the stairs, thinking it was Fookes returned, but Makepeace was already standing in the hallway, hesitant, her eyes flitting to the staircase, to me, suddenly making me complicit in her concealment of my father. She shook her head. The banging continued, but the door's hinges had rusted and the damp had made it swell in its frame.

"Eglantine," he called to me quietly from the top of the stairs, his voice strangely calm, lost in the pounding of the door. The familiarity of it hurt. I'd pushed all that I had missed of him down into myself, concealed and private. I'd banished him as easily as the judges had done, finding it less painful just to close him up in my memory, behind a door without a key. I recalled a particular feeling when I was small, a surprise gift of memory of my mother laughing, of us being three points of a triangle, a family, when I'd been the apple of his eye.

The knocking ceased and we stood there, waiting for it to begin again, my father stepping quietly on the stairs, his feet avoiding the squeaky ones, his feet remembering, until finally Makepeace slid a finger between the curtain and glass and found the doorstep clear.

My father shambled past us down towards the kitchen and all I could do was stare.

THIRTY-THREE

Eglantine, 1838

My father was bent over the fireplace, snapping kindling between his fingers, feeding the flames, though the day was already thick with heat. I heard Makepeace go upstairs, leaving my father and me alone. I slid into a chair and watched him, the familiarity of his movements, the slight whistle as he raised the fire even higher. Why had my father and Makepeace kept silent about his return? I prickled with questions, I was fierce with them, but I sat and waited, I'd get my mark in sight, but he was in the rhythm of his movements, oblivious to me. From under his shirt he pulled a pouch and tipped on the table a silver reticule, a thimble and a watch chain. The gall of it.

From Makepeace's pots and pans he found what he was looking for, a little iron pot and trivet, and he sat them in the flames, letting out a satisfied sigh at the bend of the flame around the base of the pot, sending the black soot of it glowing.

"Yesterday's harvest?" I asked, jolting the table, watching the silver shift and threaten to drop onto the floor. My father turned around and swept the silver into his hand, placing it in the pot.

"Don't think I didn't notice your fingers lace my pockets. I taught you well, my girl," he said, peering into the pot, the smell of the metal beginning to melt sending acid into my mouth, I swallowed it back down.

"As instructed." I frowned and my father stepped back and looked at me, surprised.

"Don't be like that, we'll remedy that, my girl, now I'm back," he smiled, his front tooth broken, and sat beside me, clasping his hands over mine. "We'll fix this house back to the glory that it once was, we'll make it a fine home again."

I looked at the walls, the bricks spoiling with damp, the salt crusting them, sucking up any moisture that had been in the mud; on the floor already were anthills of brick dust. What held the house together was lies, I was not going to add mine to the mortar.

"And how do you expect me to do that?"

"As I taught you, my girl, as I taught you," he laughed, patting my hand before adding more wood to the fire, giving his mercurial stew a little jiggle with a stick. "All the time I was away I thought of the account of my life, of the promise I made at your mother's death to keep you safe, the promise I had failed to keep, the distance that I had to overcome to keep it," he said.

"You came back for me?" I said in disbelief, the melted silver beginning to bubble, to send a rippling reflection on the wall of the hearth like the rain did through the window, my father and me submerged in the kitchen. I felt hot, perspiration bleeding into the fabric beneath my arms. How had his teaching me to be his shadow kept me safe when he'd get me to filch from the devil himself if we needed it? He turned and faced me and I felt as small and as inconsequential as I had when I was a child.

"Of course I did. And I taught you well to provide for yourself and Makepeace," he said. "You still carry your doll in your pocket, I see. Why did you leave her in the cellar, oh so cold and all alone?"

I wrapped my fingers around her in a protective fist; why had he shown such interest in her to take her, my first theft, and return her to my room, unless he was interested in returning me to being his mere apprentice?

"Do you know how you came to get her?"

I looked at him as I would do a mark, trying to see the value of what he was trying to say and why he was saying it now.

"Your mother had tried to run away from me. She packed you up at her first opportunity and took you to try and find her mother, her people, to beg to be let back into their ways with their *vardos* and fires and superstitions, shunning the beginnings of the life I was forging for us." My father's voice increased in volume. "Makepeace told me."

I had to hold firm to myself not to get swept up in his words; he'd been married to Ada all the same while, the life he'd been forging was all for him and for him alone. But I let him unwind his story, just to see my mother float up in it, just to glimpse her name, to feel her close.

"Her father, Josiah Scamp, had been a man above honour, he'd worked as a ratcatcher for all the grand houses and estates which they travelled through. Your mother returned to the grounds of Kensington Palace, all the windows, Eglantine, so many, all like the cuts on a stone; we'd been there once to clear out the rats and it was her hope that she'd find her mother there, but to no avail. All she found was the young queen-to-be and you found your playmate."

What was he talking about? The queen had been my playmate? The first time I'd seen her surely had been at the Coronation, that flash of ermine and satin? My mind raced, my memories all began and ended with the water, the river, the sounds of voices coming across it.

"How do you know I took the doll, that I stole it? I was but a child," I said.

"Because you are my child and your fingers are fine instruments. Why wouldn't you take something that caught your eye, when she already had so many? She'd not have missed it. You could return it to her now, but she has plenty of baubles and playthings by the looks of it."

I turned the doll in my pocket, dancing her through my fingers like a coin. I had no recollection of such a thing, all I recalled was the feeling of her, safe beneath my chin, just as my own head was beneath my mother's. All of us coiled within the other like life within a seed.

"And what of Josiah, why was he a man above honour?" I said, pushing against the sweep of him. Of my mother and her family I'd been told nothing, he'd wanted to keep me all for himself. The thief's daughter.

My father wrapped a rag around his hand and turned his back to me to face his silver. He lifted it from its trivet and poured the silver into a keepsake Fookes had brought back for Makepeace: a Coronation cup with a fine picture of the young queen's likeness staring out from a cartouche. The cup steamed with its metallic brew and my father's face was bathed in the steam. He picked up the mug and sat it in a shallow bowl of water to cool it before it cracked the mug and ran over the table.

"He saved my life," was all he said. "And I owe to him and your mother to make more of what remains of it. Will you help me, Eglantine?"

"But I'm to leave and go join my husband," I said, feeling anything that was mine shift and tilt, give way to the will of him.

My father laughed. "To meet your little shoemaker? Married by the old ways, a bit of water and a shared cup. Makepeace told me. Hardly binding, is it? You'll stay and help me rebuild my empire, my girl; too long it's been allowed to crumble."

Too long I'd been his creature, his proxy, his doll. I'd chosen Fookes as much as he'd chosen me. Neither of us had stolen each other's hearts, what we had we had given freely. I'd have my life as if it were a kingdom and I'd live it as my own queen. I stood from the table and swept all with my hand. Time slowed. The dish of water made a crown of droplets before it splashed onto the cobbles and turned the colour of blood, the dish clattering beneath the table, spinning on its base. The Coronation mug hit the ground and cracked, the silver, half cooled and half cooked, oozed out like a wound that wouldn't be stopped, leaving a silver pool on the floor.

* * *

I opened my drawers and piled everything I owned on the bed; I'd not had time to gather all the things that Fookes had collected, I didn't even have a bag. Makepeace came through the door, her chatelaine silently folded into her skirt.

"What on earth are you doing?" she said, looking at all my linens, my few clothes and my bonnet on the bed.

"Did you know about his plans? To keep me here for himself, to be his hands and eyes and ears and not follow Fookes at all?" I said and Makepeace began to cry. I stood transfixed by it, her tears welling up in her eyes, her face cracked and contorted. She reached into her pockets for a handkerchief, but on finding none swept the lace cap from her head and wiped her face. Makepeace had been my one constant, the house's erstwhile keeper, my guardian, my grandmother, she'd been all the family I'd had to rely upon.

"I kept his return secret, yes," she sobbed, "but I did it for you, to allow you your peace, your chance to follow the road that called you."

"So you encouraged me to marry Fookes to get out of my father's way?" I said, folding my clothes into the smallest parcels that I could make of them.

Makepeace came and put her arm on mine. "I encouraged you to find your way out, to find some life, to have your own fresh start," she said and I looked at her face, washed with tears. "But what am I supposed to do? He is my child, Eglantine, the baby I gave birth to and raised as best I knew how. All these years he was gone from us, but for him to return, is it not a miracle? Isn't it the will of Saint Sarah, to bring him home across the waves? Perhaps one day you'll understand what a mother's love is," she said. She looked at me squarely in the eye until I had to break her gaze.

My father appeared in the doorway and looked at all my belongings spread out, some in piles, some still strewn, and looked from Makepeace to me.

"Amberline, you owe it to her, the truth about Patrin. She has the right to pay her respects," Makepeace said and I watched my father lean on the doorframe, letting the house support him, bear the weight of whatever he'd withheld from me all this time.

"When is your ship due to sail? Though why you'd want to go to that forsaken place, it's beyond bearing, but I see now that you are your own woman, Eglantine, and I've been too hasty. Forgive a poor father who has missed his family for wanting to keep you close, to make up for lost time."

But I knew about time, you never made it up, it was as shimmering as a rainbow in a raindrop and was only allowed its allotted space before dispersing. I could no more make up time than be back in my mother's womb nor alter the creature I'd become at my father's making, but I could surge forward, read my own signs, strike out, my feet were Romany after all, my shoes yet tried as a traveller's.

"A month," I said, looking at him briefly before I continued ordering my clothes. I felt all my hackles rise; would he bar my way through the door, would he turn the key and try to keep me his own little convict?

"Would you stay this month then and not leave early? Let me make it up to you, Eglantine. All the time I was away all I thought of was returning to see you grow, but you've gone and grown into a woman without me." He managed a smile and straightened himself. He walked towards me, a limp in his gait that he tried to disguise by walking slowly.

Makepeace stood, watching, and I tried to catch her eye, but she wouldn't look at me; between the two of them I felt the pull of the third, the tiny swell of a human life.

* * *

What was a month? For one born already it was but a cluster of days in a season, but for an unborn baby it was like my mother's namesake, a patrin, the signs of the leaves, each month a different message telling it to grow, to turn, to unfurl into the baby it would become. For the first week my father took to his bed, the miasma of London air seeping into his lungs with a wild cough rattling through the floorboards. Makepeace gave him teas and broths and concoctions made from the simples she bought, her own herbs neglected by inattention, while she helped me gather all the things the immigrant guide suggested – Fookes's money disappeared into six chemises, six pairs of stockings, two flannel petticoats, two lighter petticoats, two pairs of good shoes, one warm cloak with hood, one hat or bonnet for hot weather; our needles worked in unison in the kitchen listening for my father's call. At the back of my mind was always the thought that he'd prevent me from going, that the knocking would come again. Makepeace and I dared not open the door, we kept the curtains drawn and took extra care in case it was the law. In the night my father called out, his shout into the silence making me wake in a sweat.

As he gained his strength he bade me sit by him and show him my hands, my long fingers and fine wrists, his hands running over their veins and the shape of my nails, and I let him.

"Remember the game we used to play, Eglantine, how light your touch was? Do you think you can still remove the handkerchiefs without the bells ringing?" I drew my hands away. He shuffled over to his chest of drawers, forgetting that Makepeace and I had cleared the lot out to take in lodgers. He opened the drawer and on seeing it bare shut it with a bang.

"Was there anything of mine kept?" he asked, but there was nothing to say that would satisfy him.

"You don't know what you are heading into, Eglantine," he said, sitting on the edge of the bed in his clothes that Makepeace had laundered and mended. I'd not go pluck coins for him as if they were just fruit from an overhanging tree. He licked his thumb and wiped a thread off his jacket. "It's not bloody Eden, not by a long shot, no Elysium, it's at the end of the earth."

"Well what is it like then?" I said, watching him flex his fingers and shift his coat onto his shoulders.

"It's hell, that is what it is. But you can make hell hospitable if you can deal with the devil. The voyage was death, but once we were all chucked off the ship we were assigned masters to work for, but allowed to return to our own huts and have the evenings for ourselves. I'd never felt more like a Romany in my life, living in a lean-to, the weather mild, seeing the stars wheel across a southern sky, woken by the crazed caw of the cockatoos sharpening their beaks on the bark of my hut.

"The first master I had was a kindly man who had me mind his sheep and move them from pasture to pasture, but it is an idle man's job and my mind grew idle until the blacks came and helped themselves to the flock and my master returned me to the depot. My next master was a despot, tight with the food and quick with the punishment, but I'd not be a slave to any man. He was a Methodist minister who avoided the rum and lived closer to the town. He picked me from the depot to care for his horses, though the only thing I knew about horses was from observing how gypsies dealt with them when I lived with your mother's family, but I knew that rum was worth more than gold to some. He kept jugs of it in his stable, not to drink but to use as currency, so I took my chance and filtered off whatever I could, replacing it with water. From my cot next to the horses I woke every morning with the smell of the sea, the air crisp with eucalypt and a possum who used to scratch his way across the roof, furrier than a cat he was and had a louder hiss as well. When I rode my master to the city for his services, I'd wander off down to the harbour to watch the tall ships unload their goods and scavenge any remainders, the sailors all chattering their different languages like a flock of parrots, selling off whatever I'd harvested from my dry Methodist until I was able to buy myself some sailor's clothes and sign on, knowing this house with you in it waited for me."

I looked at him squarely, sensing the thin gossamer threads of a lie. It wasn't his words that gave him away, it was his hands, they grew stiller and stiller as his story went on.

Bang, bang, bang! My father and I started at the mad knocking again; the sound of it made my father shrink into himself, every pore of him listening. Though he'd regained his robustness, his skin browned by the sun, he seemed to blanch and go transparent, his hand to his heart, breathing ragged. The knocking was persistent and determined for the good part of a quarter hour and then at last it went quiet. Makepeace appeared in the doorway, her mortar and still in her hand, the blooms of the foxglove mashed beneath the pestle. She bid my father open his mouth and she dipped the tip of her finger in the mash and wiped it on his tongue, leaving him gasping for a sip of water. I passed some to him and he drank it down.

"The man is still on the doorstep, Amberline," Makepeace said. "He seems most determined to strike camp there. Who is he and what does he want?" My father looked at each of our faces, lay down and turned to the wall. That man was the truth my father was hoping wouldn't speak.

Makepeace and I left him and closed the door, the sound of the knocking started up again and echoed through the house, leaving Makepeace and I stranded on the landing, feeling like the house was being demolished knock by knock around us.

"Come, Makepeace, out with it, who is it at the door?"

But she shook her head. "He's not said a word. His heart has been strained by all he's been through. He makes light of it, tells it like a snippet from the papers, but I've seen his back, turned to rope with the lash," she said, her voice wedging in her throat. The knocking continued.

The banister was slippery beneath my hand as I held on to it for support and took each step as slowly as possible, avoiding the step that creaked, avoiding walking on my heel, I needn't have worried for the knocking concealed any sound that I made. Makepeace's footsteps followed behind me, her chatelaine silenced.

I stood behind the door, watched it rattle in its frame and when the knocking halted again I opened the door an inch, wedging my foot behind it. On the doorstep stood a gentleman of means – his coat collar high around his neck, a snowy cravat tied with a fine knot at his throat. As soon as he saw me he swept his hat from his head and raised it in the air, his hair oiled down, pressed with the circle of the hat, like the puddle of water one made when adding water to yeast.

"Good morrow, miss, I'm here to make an appointment to see Mr Stark, who I believe is at this residence," he said, his vowels so round that I could have stuck my finger in his mouth and popped a bubble.

"And who are you to be asking?" I said bluntly, not liking the cut of him, his fine clothes, his tone.

"A gentleman, that is all. You may call me Mr Royston. And you are?" he said, leaning in, his hand coming around the door like an insect. "Don't tell me – his daughter, he's spoken highly of you, he has, all the way from Sydney to London." He looked me over as if I was a piece of porcelain that had endured the fire only to be found wanting with a hairline crack.

"Whoever you are, sir, please state your business and be gone," I said, standing closer to the gap of the door, ready to throw my weight on it if I needed to. I'd not be intimidated by a dandy.

"Of course he gave me a pretend address, but I caught him in the noose of his own lie now, didn't I? Just tell your father, Miss Stark, that I've come to have his debt settled and to take rightful ownership of all he promised me," he said and laughed, reaching out his hand to touch my cheek. Shocked, I used my shoulder to try and force the door closed, but his hand was already on my neck, his arm barring the door from closing.

"It's Mrs Fookes, I'll have you know, and my father is in New South Wales," I said, extracting his hand from my neck, readying my knee for his groin.

"Is he now?" His eyes smiled. "If he reneges his side of our agreement," he patted his coat pocket, "I'll be forced as any good citizen should to notify the correct authorities as to his whereabouts."

"You do that," I said, "for he's not here, and they'll arrest you for the nuisance you are." With great effort I pushed the door closed. He narrowly avoided having his fingers broken with the force of it.

Makepeace and I stood behind the door, waiting for the blows to rain down on the other side, but they didn't come. I was livid, still feeling the damp suede imprint of Mr Royston's gloved fingers on my neck. I looked to Makepeace, but she wouldn't meet my eye.

My father stood at the top of the stairs, shaking his head.

"What tangle have you made, Amberline?" Makepeace said beneath her breath. "Untangle it."

He beckoned for us to come to him and I railed at being bid to do anything at all at his command, but I saw how unsteady he was on his feet.

He sat back on the bed, his head in his hands. "Forgive me," he said.

"Forgive you for what?" Makepeace said, the anger staining her cheeks red so that she looked painted in rouge like a doll. "What is this 'agreement'?"

"He found out who I was, the marks on my back sign enough that I was no sailor, and I made a bargain that wasn't mine to make, to keep myself safe until I returned," my father said, broken and slumped.

"What did you promise, Amberline?" Makepeace said. My father was silent. But Makepeace had no patience left for him. She slapped him on the face, her hand cracking like doom, and my father, child-surprised, looked up at his mother in shock.

"I promised our home to him, this house," he said so quietly it was a strain to hear him.

"After all we've risked to keep it?" Makepeace said, her voice rising.

My father looked at the floor, avoiding our faces and I recalled the touch of the man's hand on my skin, the lines at my throat prickled hot with panic, frightened of what he was going to say.

My father spoke again, barely able to make the words with his mouth, the ghost of his voice came through his lips. "And I promised him Eglantine."

I was mute with my own fury. I was not some thing to barter for and exchange.

"You'll fix this, Amberline, and you'll do right for once in your life," Makepeace said. "You'll take Eglantine to see where her mother lies and then we'll take whatever is needed to bribe her onto a boat to New South Wales and get her free of this mess, even if you have to go and steal it yourself." Her voice was firm.

"And you'll do it tonight," she said before leaving the room and taking me with her.

THIRTY-FOUR

Eglantine, 1838

In silence we packed all that would fit into a small bag; not all of the recommended list of items would fit, so Makepeace made me dress in as many layers as she thought I could stand, and with each tie of petticoat and shirt I felt the tightness around my waist increase, the heat threading up and down my torso in waves, and I willed the sickness to heal. My hands began to shake at what we were to undertake, at the thought of leaving, of saying goodbye. All the unsaid surged around us, Makepeace and I doing our best to avoid each other's eyes, both of us stewing in our thoughts. Makepeace led me down to the kitchen and made me eat though my stomach rebelled, making me drink a cup of milk and the cream. She filled my pockets with bread for sustenance and protection and sewed whatever remained of the coins to my chemise, so that I was like Saint Sarah, readying for the moment to be carried into the ocean. We sat waiting in the cool of the kitchen for the sun to fall out of the sky and into the river. My father returned at the first sign of darkness, he had made all ready, but neither Makepeace nor I acknowledged him.

"Have you your doll, Eglantine?" my father said and I looked at him, treating me like a child from now until the end of time. I nodded and he sighed.

Under the cover of darkness, we scuttled along the street to the waterman's stairs. My shoes slipped on the mossy steps.

Makepeace led the way, her lace cap grey as moth's wings, catching the last of the light to the wherry waiting at the bottom of the steps. My father stepped in with ease, his sea legs still upon him, and he reached out his hand to guide me in, but cumbersome as I was in my layers, I'd not take it. My skirts dipped to the black dye of water before I took my seat and watched Makepeace hitch up her skirts with one hand and twist them to the side, her stitched and worsted stockings revealing themselves like a stork's bony knees. She sat down beside me and patted my hand as I felt the ripple of her movement into the boat, the river stretching in all directions, black as molasses, crumbs of starlight stuck in it, forever shifting. From out on the water the lamps of various vessels swung like pendulums, but our lantern remained unlit.

My father took an oar, pushed it against the jut of the step and for a moment the rocking ceased as we glided and I felt myself go still at the relief of it, but it was brief. My father started rowing and Makepeace and I sat on our watery pew, her hand curling around mine, and I focused on counting my father's long strokes rather than let tears fall, little traitors from my eyes.

My father kept a cracking pace, panting with his labour. We passed cargo ships and under the shadows of bridges, the black strip of shadow beneath them darker than the inside of an eyelid. The river lulled me and I felt my eyes close watching the dark peaks and swells of the Thames, until I fell asleep and dreamed each of them was a watery hand reaching out of the water, but I didn't know if they were ferrying me onward or trying to pull me down. I woke with a start, my father's command in my ears bidding us to pull our cloaks over our heads, against the light.

Beside us loomed a huge ship, its hull high above us, pouring off it the sound of singing; my father rowed harder then, using the oar to push off from the leviathan and with his steady strokes we cleared it. At some distance I saw the British Naval standards flying and felt my father's need to be quick, for to be seen by them would return him to nothing but a fish in their net. I'd been hasty, harsh, angry. What would I have done to leave a prison, a banishment, a hell?

"Father," I whispered, but he bid me be quiet with a slight click of the tongue.

"The voice can carry across the water," he whispered, his voice disguised by the splash of the oar, and he pulled us further downriver. The clouds raced above us, rushing in their own celestial waters; which star would guide me? My father steered closer to the bank, out of the lanes of further vessels, the buildings petering out and turning to the shapes of trees, willows washing their fronds in the water.

My father paused for a moment and was about to light the lantern when the moon slipped out of a pocket of cloud and looked down on us, an eye, whether benevolent or not, time would tell.

"You were born in the river, did you know that, Eglantine?" my father said, and I felt the surprise of it – how could one be born in a river. "I wasn't supposed to be there, but how could I keep away? I wanted to see my child. My, how your mother laboured, until her own mother led her into the water to ease her pain. She pulled you out of your mother and out of the water and I felt the earth spin beneath my feet with my unworthiness, my unreadiness to be a father."

My father's voice drifted off and I begged for him to continue. Born in a river. How much of my past had he locked up in himself? How I wanted all those stories, the brightest, shiniest things, better than silver or gold, and now the time to pry them was diminishing, no matter how fast and slender my fingers, already melting, disappearing.

"I never was going to let you go," he said, his voice quiet, and I felt the river swell around the wherry. "I'd not have sold you off, nor the house, not if my life depended on it, but I fed him the possibility of it, bait on the line, to reel him in."

It burned that he used me to win his own freedom. "Always your instrument, more than a daughter," I said, and my father went quiet. All of me was conflicted – I'd lose him.

We reached an inlet and he manoeuvred the boat down along the breeze as the night grew darker. I ran my hand in the water and splashed it up onto my face, trying to keep myself awake.

My father stood and removed his coat and stepped out of the boat. The water splashed up to his thighs as he led it to the sandy side of the bank, disturbing the swans who slept in the reeds, ghost galleons silently pushing out from the safety of their cover, their feet spinning beneath the water, their cygnets balls of down on their backs.

"I'd keep my promise, Eglantine, I promised to protect you, to keep you safe. I promised your mother, the day she passed you through the ship porthole into my arms, when she was arrested for the crime I'd committed. I'd promised her father, Josiah, when I'd been too cowardly to speak up and the law broke his neck for it." My father's voice grew rough in his throat, dry as paper. Here was the truth out of his mouth and he expected me to believe it? How could I believe anything that he said? He'd made not only my mother pay for his crimes, but my grandfather also. I stepped backwards and felt my footing falter, Makepeace's hand caught my arm, but I shook it off. His words made the skin at my neck pucker and rise, heat and itch. This was the first I'd heard of it, of my other grandfather, my mother's father. All the love that belonged to me, all the love of a complete family, my father with his dreams of grander things had denied me. He'd stolen enough from me. I retched, but all that came out was bile. I wished he'd never come back at all.

The dawn was approaching through the thick mist, slowly lightening the sky. It clung to our clothes like the finest of lace, made of spider web and water.

My father held out his hand for me to step onto the side of the riverbank but I didn't take it, not knowing why we'd stopped here. All there was were reeds and grass and a lone oak, a bower over my head; last season's acorns crunched underfoot. Makepeace stayed in the boat.

"This is where she lies, Eglantine," my father said, "this oak tree is her mark."

I stepped backwards, my spine hitting the trunk, my breath squeezed out of me, the bark pressing through all the layers of clothes on my back, willing her to me. But the tree was just a tree.

"How is her mark an oak and not a stone in a graveyard? Didn't she deserve better?" I said, bitterness spreading through me.

"Once I reclaimed you from the prison hulk and got to the cover of the shoreline, I kept watch, ready to turn myself in for her. I had you settled and calm, a piece of marzipan gripped in your palm, asleep from exhaustion. All I wanted was to get you safe, get you back to the house, to provide for you. But the uniforms followed not long after and came closer towards us and I took cover in the tree roots, pulling my coat over our heads. They came to shore with their load, with their dead. With your mother. How I wanted to leap on them, pummel their brains at the comments they made, their collars turned up against the cold. They were cursory, barely scraping the topsoil from the riverbank before tossing her into the hole and sprinkling the dirt back over. To them she was nothing more than a doll of rag and flesh. I heard their rum-soaked voices from across the water, slurring the words to a shanty song, and I waited until they disappeared altogether before I crept out and pulled away the soil with my bare hands, wiping the dirt from her face and kissing her lips. I dug deeper into the earth for her resting place, not wanting the first flood of the river to send her out into the waters. Before tucking her under the soil, I placed an acorn in each of her hands as she once told me her mother did for a lost child, so that whoever came past would know their resting place, and so the dead would not be lonely."

I heard all the birdsong then, now the whole tree was singing, alive. In the blue light the twin trunks of the tree swayed, the roots stretching down to the water, shoring up the soil of the riverbank, dipping into the water. The leaves' dark shapes moved, their tips painted gold with the sun's thin light. In the pockets of soil around the tree bloomed foxglove. Petals for her slippers.

"How would you know one tree from another?" I said, my voice pouring out of me, an overfilled bucket from the well. "How many trees line this riverbank, why this one?"

My father ran his hand over the bark and picked up an acorn from the ground. "That is what I was worried about too, hoping that you'd kept your doll. All the time I was away, I hoped you were taking good care of her, hoped that if I didn't return you'd find where to look," he said.

I pulled my doll out of my pocket and held her aloft in the air, the sunlight striking the glass of her earrings and sending diamonds of coloured light across my face. My hands shook or she shook in my hands, impossible to tell which. How many times had I held this doll, how many times had I told her all my secrets, asked her my many questions and waited for the first voice that ever spoke my name to reply? When all the time she'd been made of wood and my fancy.

"She is just a doll," I said. "How could she have told me anything?"

A wind came across the water and started to ruffle the leaves and swirl around Makepeace's cap. I watched as she carefully removed it and slipped it into her pocket, stepped out of the boat and came to stand beside me. All the while the oak leaves murmured in unison, flipping their green sides silver and back again. All whispers. All hums.

"Lift her dress," my father said and I wanted to laugh. I'd lifted her dress many times, helped her in her toilet, but it had never been removed completely. I tipped poor Miss Poppet upside down, her skirts falling around her face like a daisy's petals.

"Turn her around, look," my father said, and I did. Miss Poppet's back was its same usual wooden self, scratched and marked, familiar. "Look again," he said. And I saw. There on Miss Poppet's back was a crudely carved map, the tree marked with a star, the inlet an arrow, the river a road – all these little signs my father had recorded for me so I'd find my way back. I looked at him, bent as he was, unsure in the dawn light whether he held the tree up or the tree held him. Whatever had happened to them along the way, there had been a point as fixed as a patrin, that they loved each other, that they loved me.

I pulled Miss Poppet's skirts down, smoothed her clothes and had a look at her dear familiar painted face, her eyes upturned in a perpetual smile. I dug a hole close to the trunk with my hands, flicking dirt away and leaves and acorns. The hole refilled, but I kept digging. A magpie chirred above me and I looked up, the morning light hitting his plumage all dark iridescence, his eye caught by Miss Poppet's shining face as I laid her in the grave I had made, before sweeping the dirt over her. My mother had turned into a tree, so it seemed only right that I return my doll to the oak she was, a seed of a different kind. I took all the acorns I could find and circled where she lay.

THIRTY-FIVE

Eglantine, 1838

By the time we left my mother's grave the morning was already full upon us, the daylight stippling the water with blinding light. We'd stayed overlong, my father exhausted from his efforts. He pulled the wherry into reeds and obscured it before he urged us to hurry as we headed off past the river's edge over into some farmer's furthest field, a few sheep dotting the distance like wool waiting to be spun, the long grasses damp and slippery underfoot. Makepeace and I moving alongside my father, hindered by the drag of our wet skirts.

It was midmorning by the time we reached some semblance of a village. Makepeace and I approached the local inn and asked for a room in which to bide the time until the sun fell back down into the river, somewhere to wait for night. We were shown to a room, small and soot-blackened, a faint damask furred across the walls. Makepeace asked for refreshment and we were given ale and cheese which we happily drank and ate, putting aside some of the cheese for my father who as a precaution had decided to take refuge in a copse we had passed outside of the village.

Makepeace and I lay down on top of the counterpane, which smelled of oily hair and unwashed bodies, grateful for the ease of weight off our feet. As soon as I closed my eyes I was back on the river, my ears full of the slap and pull of my father's strong

283

back taking us across the waters, my hand trailing in the V of the wherry's wake, a barnacled finger reaching up and circling my wrist, neither pulling me in nor letting me go. I woke, all of me hot. I sat up in the bed and pulled at the top of my blouse and looked at the threads of my own skin, red, raised and bleeding in the mirror. This birthmark had its own tides. I traced each bump and rise of it like the raised ridge that joined a globe. Would I yet cross that line myself? I thought of that rope going around my poor grandfather's neck and my poor mother drowned in saving me. Would it be me who paid the debt for my father's crimes?

Makepeace woke as the village church bell chimed ten o'clock, the day still staining the sky.

Together we made for the copse of trees, sticking close to the buildings, the village quiet. The only sound came from far in the distance, someone playing a fiddle and a blackbird's twisting note drawing a close to the day.

Shadows were long inside the copse and Makepeace took my hand as if I was a child still, afraid of the dark. A chill came out of the earth, dark and damp. Makepeace stood just outside, whistled and waited for a response; an owl replied and my father limped into sight, his coat half torn from his shoulders, a large gash across his shirt.

"Father," I said and ran to him, but he held up his hands to fend me off and I saw the darkness spread on his shirt, his blood a river from the source of him. We eased him to the ground and Makepeace tore at her petticoats, turning the strips of them into wads of bandage to stem the flow.

"What happened, Amberline?" she said, pulling his tattered coat from his shoulders, tearing another strip of bandage to bind him in, no light or time to take a measure of his injury.

"Royston showed up, must have followed us all the way, the devil," he said between breaths, his skin blue with shadow as Makepeace bound the wound tight, the bandage around his ribs.

"But he got the worst of it," my father said and gestured over his shoulder.

I stood up from my father's side, my hands sticky with his blood, and stepped further into the trees, snapping twigs and leaves, unsure of where exactly my father's assailant was. The moon was freshly risen like new baked bread, but its light was not strong enough to penetrate the canopy. My skirts caught on something and I tugged at them to release them, but whatever held them would not let go.

There leaning against a tree was the gentleman my father had taught a lesson, his hand wrapped around the edge of my skirt.

"Come closer," Royston demanded and tried to reel me in by my skirt. I tried to pull it out of his grasp, and slapped at his hand till he released it, the last of his strength he'd used just to hold on.

"Your father will get the noose for this," he said, "and none too soon."

I looked down at him, unable to stand if he tried, and spat on the ground at his feet. I tore my own petticoat and tied his wrists, his hands uselessly trying to fend me off, his eyes white with fear. I ran my hands over his body, to feel if he was bleeding anywhere, but I found nothing damp except his own piss. His leg was at a sharp angle; my father had concussed him and perhaps had broken his leg, but I felt no wound upon him.

"And then you'll be mine to do with as I wish," he said.

I took another strip of petticoat and rammed it into his mouth to shut him up; I'd no more space in my ears to hear his voice, I could barely hear myself think, all my heart pounded, wanting to exact some sort of punishment upon him.

My fingers ran their old course, lightly through his pockets, and I pulled out a watch on a fine chain, a pouch of coin, a mirror concealed in a slip of velvet. I had no want for them except to destroy them. The watch and mirror I dropped and felt the crunch run up my leg as I stamped them into the ground;

the coins I threw into the air and heard them rain down in all different directions. My father had risked me as his snare to catch his own freedom, but no more.

From the gloaming I heard a noise and I stood back, but it was only a plume of breath from the man's horse, come back for his master. I reached for the animal's bridle and he, kindly beast, took pleasure in being led, my voice a whisper.

Makepeace whistled and I followed the sound. Together we helped my father up and onto the horse. Noises floated up from the village, the sound of dogs and crying, and Makepeace hesitated.

"Mother, take her, take her now, before it's too late," my father said. I reached for his hand and cupped it to my cheek.

"Go, Eglantine, go. Don't make the mistakes that I did. Don't be fooled by things that glitter and shine and think they are equal to a life. You were my one jewel, and it's taken me my whole life to know it."

Makepeace slapped the horse's hind and my father urged it on into the darkness, the vibrations of its gallop running up my legs. My father's arms were around the horse's neck, holding on for all he was worth.

"Come, girl, come," Makepeace said. I had no time to think, no time to pause and gather myself.

We saw their fiery torches before they saw us and Makepeace made haste for us to melt into the hedgerow, our clothes getting caught on thorns, branches and brambles as she bid the shadows be our cover. We disturbed a vixen from her den, she up and appeared, her copper little mask in the moonlight, nose a-twitch before disappearing back to her kits. There were probably two score men, their feet falling into march, splashing in puddles and talking low.

"They say he's a violent man and we are to keep our wits about us," an older voice said.

"He's bound to be," said another, "especially where he's been. Keep your eyes to the shadows, watch for him now, unless you want his knife at your throat and your gizzards on the ground."

I knew they were talking about my father, but he was not the father I knew; with their words they were painting him as a monster. When they passed by us the lit torches made a sound like all the world burning, everything made its tinder; the heat of the flames flared on my face, on my neck, a sweat trailing around my birthmark and asking for a scratch. The smell of the fat-soaked cloth used as a wick made my stomach turn, but whatever came back up into my mouth I swallowed rather than make a sound. Beneath us, in the ground, the foxes listened.

We waited until the torches were but a pinprick on the horizon before we broke cover, then we walked as fast as our feet allowed us, keeping close to the hedgerow, away from the road, until we heard the rushing waters and I felt it rush through me, beside me, with me, leading us to the port. All the sails were pulled at by the wind, like a giant's sheet whipping dry on the line.

* * *

Makepeace paid a handsome fee for my immigration papers and graced the palm of a ship's captain to bribe me aboard. She took my face in her hands, smoothed away the hairs that had escaped their bounds and drank me in.

"Holy Sarah be your guiding star, my darling," Makepeace said, her kisses wet on my eyelids, her tears on my cheeks. She pulled out the pouch concealed at my throat, pulled out the wedding ring within it and slipped it on my finger. "You know your mother called you Little Egg? She was determined to give you your own name," she said tenderly, "but I hope that we've done right by you." She reached her hand out and placed it on my belly.

"But what about you? What about Father?" I said, the ocean sending soft spray over us.

"Our fates are already written," she said, leading me to the gangplank, the captain waiting at the top, eager to conceal my arrival in the darkness.

As I walked forward, looking at the waters below, all dark reflections of things I couldn't make out, a huge shout sounded and I turned around.

I heard Makepeace's startled cry. A group of men appeared, a living wall between us; my father, held up between two of the men, his head lolling to one side. Makepeace rushed over to him. She tried to say something, but her voice was stolen by a blow, her cap knocked to the ground. One of the soldiers caught me in his sight and I felt all the terror of it. Makepeace was on the ground, her chatelaine crushed beneath a soldier's boot.

"Leave her alone!" I screamed. "Leave her alone!" All of me wanted to rush back down to the dock, to help them, my father, my grandmother. The soldier raised a hand and struck her again. My voice got lost in all the commotion, rising upward like smoke dispersed by the whipping of the sails, but one soldier heard me and walked towards me, his hands lowering his musket from his shoulder and lifting it to me.

"Stop!" shouted Makepeace. "I don't know who that girl is, hand on the Bible," she said, stumbling to her feet. I looked at her but she wouldn't look back at me.

"Hurry along," the captain said and I felt my helplessness prickle through me. "You don't want to go wasting your family's hard-won money now, do you?" he said and I looked at his face and saw a kindness there. He took my elbow and led me across the deck, where a sailor sat whittling at a piece of wood, his wood shavings spinning through the air like sparks.

The captain then led me to the rear of the ship, down some stairs and knocked on a door. An older woman answered and stepped aside for me to enter. Spread down the centre of the room was a large table and chairs, fanned on either side by hammocks strung from the ceiling and filled with the sleeping. Beneath my feet the ocean swelled, restless, ever moving. The matron showed me my hammock and I crawled into it, like a caterpillar in its cocoon, and slept in the ship's belly.

THIRTY-SIX

Eglantine, 1838

When I next opened my eyes a lantern was lit and sent ghost waterfalls up the walls, light reflected from the porthole as big as a mermaid's mirror. Around me moved other women, their voices felt far away, the ship all sway on the greenish waters. Someone retched, seasick and as helpless as a newborn. All I desired was fresh air, great big gulps of it, but all I could do was breathe the fetid air and make do. The matron came with water and a flannel; sometimes I thought she was Makepeace and I reached for her, but the matron just returned my arm to my side.

Time passed differently on water, the clocks kept time with the tide, though the captain kept his ship run to his own instrument. Early the women rose and breakfasted and were ushered up on deck to help under the strict supervision of the matron until they returned for dinner; the smells of cooking made me bury my face in the calico hammock, feeling my whole body revolt – at food, at sleep, at life itself. All of me was heavy, confined to my hammock; I had no will to move, grown suddenly homeless, rootless, made an orphan by everything my father had created, but even then I loved him. I pushed away the thought of him swinging. He was my father. He'd kept me safe in the only way he knew how, he'd given me whatever love he had, taught me what he knew – none of it perfect, but mine. And what of

Makepeace? Her cry still echoed in my ears. I was a ship lost of all ballast at the mercy of whatever wind blew, spinning into the darkness. I retched in the motion of the ship with my loss.

At some point I woke and the layers of my clothing had been removed; I'd been peeled of layers like a pearl until I was just a speck of dirt. I looked around for them madly, for I'd lost my bag in the fray, but I saw them folded at the foot of my hammock. The matron, seeing me try to sit up, came over and placed a hand on my back.

"All is well, Mrs Fookes, all is well," she said and I looked at her clearly for the first time. She was not like Makepeace at all, she was tall and broad, her grey hair pulled back severely from her face, but she was not unkind in her expression. "It's not uncommon for women in your condition to find the voyage an added chore," she said. "No point sending you to the infirmary and risking you and the baby." She said it, the word hanging in between us like a question, answered.

"But the fresh air would do you good if you found a way to raise yourself," Matron said. I tried to do as I was told.

The brightness was blinding, light reflected on both the wood and the water. The world danced with light. I shielded my eyes with a saluting hand, too dazzled by the open sea, with no green earth to rest my eye upon. A sailor was stitching a tear in a swathe of sail, a toothpick dallying between his lips, though he still managed to sing *too ra, loo ra la, aye*. The matron's hand was on my back.

"Look here, Mrs Smith, over the side, the sailors' friend come to say hello they have," the sailor said, the toothpick never leaving his lips. Together we all peered over the ship's edge and saw dolphins streaming alongside in the spray, sending a shimmering fine mist all over us. Matron Smith moved me away from the edge of the ship, tutting at the ocean for sending such streams of water, but I felt it fall on my skin, salty and wet, breaking whatever fever had settled upon me, breaking the trance of it, the loss of all I'd known. My tears seeped through the knotty wood of me.

A seabird hovered close to the side of the ship, observing us before it took a higher current of the breeze, inspecting the other passengers who appeared blinking against the glitter.

A wave slopped over the side of the vessel in an almighty swell of water and saturated all on deck.

"Below decks, below decks," the captain commanded and quickly the others fled below, the sky pressing us down into the hold as lightning licked across the sky, but I stood transfixed by the water, the green glassy swill of it reaching up onto the deck and soaking through my shoes, before Matron Smith tugged at my arm and I let her lead me down below deck.

* * *

The waters raged with a deafening roar and I retreated to my hammock, trying to surrender myself to the wild ebb and flow. Women were sick everywhere; a wooden bowl was pitched off the table and slid across the floor, back and forth, but none had the balance nor the will to retrieve it. Someone was singing. All the while Matron Smith's voice boomed above the din with, "Save me, O God: for the waters are come into my soul."

It was then I saw the eye.

The eye filled the porthole as it swivelled all over us, searching, seeking, peering, and the more it did, the more I felt like a magnetised compass needle, spinning every which way. When it spied me I wanted to scream for it was so vast and so large and I felt the vertigo of space fall between us and drag me down as a funnel does water. Did anyone else see it? And then the eye was gone and the waves subsided, soothed into submission by a magnificent spume of water that reflected a rainbow into the cabin. And I felt the little seahorse within me flutter for the first time and my body move in time with the ocean, instead of against it.

The next time I made it up on deck, a light rain fell and I opened my mouth to it, like a creature too long kept in the desert. The other passengers filled the deck, with excitement, ready to cross the line.

"All hail Neptunus Rex," the sailors cried out, "and his bride, Queen of the Seas, Amphitrite, Goddess of the Waves." Passengers cheered at the sailors dressed as the King of the Sea and his bride, who stood with buckets in their hands, unshaven, dressed in shells and rope.

"Landlubbers, prepare to be initiated into our solemn mystery, the ancient order of the deep," Neptune said and splashed the contents of their buckets all over us, drenching us. From up through the planks of wood and into my feet I felt a deep sound vibrate, loud and sonorous, the echo of the conch, so low that even the seagulls observed it in silence.

The celebrations continued on deck until the early evening, the first stars casting their shimmering reflection in the water. When the bell was called for dinner, my fellow passengers dispersed below decks, but I was reluctant to follow. I stayed on deck and watched the ocean stream behind the ship as we moved slowly through it. The sails hung slack against their masts, an embrace in repose; above them pooled a strange greenish light around their highest tip and I stood and watched it, like the reflection of a jewel through a loupe. I watched the rippling wonder of the double moon, one in the sky, the other in the water, shedding light like a briar rose does petals across the dark water.

I held my hands over the edge of the deck, hovering above the water, and thought how easily it would be to add one foot, then another; I'd not be alone as I exchanged water for breath. All it would take would be one step. What if I had left all I knew to arrive still at nothing? There was no guarantee that Fookes had even arrived or that he would have me still. All my pain would be gone, just as my mother's had, the water slipping over my head, filling my nose, my lungs, my mouth, a liquid caress.

All the water called to me. My feet itched with wanting to move, to stretch, to leap.

But what of my mother's sacrifice, all she had done to save me? I would not deny the life that grew in me. I would not undo what could not be undone.

I unlooped the *putsi* from around my throat and held it suspended out over the water, weighed in my hand, a dark heart. The ocean beneath was spangled, each wave tipped by starlight, and I felt my mother's presence, her voice in my ear, her breath in the hush of the water. She was the sea in my heart.

I let the *putsi* go. My eyes held it for a moment before it disappeared into the dark, hitting the water with a tiny splash, and was gone. Piece of velvet, river pebble, curl of hair, beans and fragments of petals. Gone was the thin coral like a cut. Across my throat I felt a lightness, the salt air made my skin tingle, and I made my way back to the cabin.

* * *

After crossing the line, the ship hit its stride, the wind in the sails driving us over the water, the days and nights blending together in a parade of sunrises and sunsets, fogs and storms, nights where forks of lightning seemed to erupt from the waters like Neptune's trident. The air grew warmer and birds began to take their rest up amongst the sails at night, their beaks beneath their wings, never lifting their heads as I made my nightly orbit around the deck, my footsteps growing less frantic, more determined, I'd forge a road yet.

When we rounded the headland into Port Jackson I squinted against the light. The cliffs were rosy stone and they flanked us on each side, the sailors' singing filling my ears. From below deck they all came, all the fellow passengers, their faces sunlit and bright, all of us looking in anticipation of arrival but each seeing different things, the future spread before us in shades of gold. But what future would I have? When Makepeace read the seeds, all she saw was a journey where I was not alone, but what then? As we passed through the heads and into the swell of the harbour, the passengers all raised their voices to sing to the captain, "For he's a jolly good fellow" and the captain dipped his hat to the ladies.

The harbour was filled with ships of every size all jostling for space, the sailors called out to each other, the sound of human activity, a roar from the port after the constant sea-song of ship, water and wind. People were as small as dolls on the horizon. As night fell everyone returned to their cabins ready to disembark in the morning. Lights hung off the prows of the ships and on shore, pretty as any jewel strung with ribbons.

The morning brought new birdsong, a strange black and white bird carolling us from the deck. Such music in one bird, I'd never even imagined, the strangeness of its herald.

"It's a magpie-lark," Matron Smith said. "But not to worry, she's not after silver things."

I laughed then; it was welcome to all the silver I had and I'd not care.

Magpie, black and white not a green sheen of feathers in sight, not even a hint. *Kakkaratchi*, I heard my mother's word for it as clearly as I heard the magpie's *wardle-ardle*.

"*Kakkaratchi*," I said aloud. The bird turned and looked at me with her amber eye and swooped to shore.

We were in the first boat that came to land, and I declined a gentleman passenger's hand to help me find my feet. My legs still tipped with the ebb and flow of the water; I didn't care that my petticoats trailed all the way from the ship to the shore, flicking the water, my hand like a salmon against the tide. Once on shore I'd follow the directions the matron had given me to find my way to Richmond, where Fookes had told me I'd find him.

But would he be there? Fookes's face wavered in my memory, pieced together with ripples; I didn't remember the sound of his voice. Did he still think of me or was he in pursuit of his fortune without another thought?

I heard my father's scoff, *my little shoemaker, married by a bit of water and a shared cup.*

I stepped onto new land.

THIRTY-SEVEN

Eglantine, 1838

The whole quay was filled with noise and it struck at me as a physical thing after the sounds of the open sea. A man stood singing just like in the streets of London, "*Fish fish-o*," and I felt the globe shift beneath my feet, the fish scales shimmering with light. I stepped over small wicker cages where black swans were trapped, their scarlet beaks poking through the gaps. A woman with her skirts hitched up to her knees, her bare feet brown with dirt, sat plucking the feathers of a living bird. She plucked at its down, the finer feathers floating in the air around her; the rest of the down she placed in a basket beside her, the animal too exhausted to strike her back.

It was difficult to get my bearings, to follow Matron's directions; the light seemed to seep into my eyes, my brain, addling me with glitter, the water struck golden. The salty lap of it hit the sandy strip of beach and I was afraid.

A riverman was leaning against a tree, enjoying his pipe, the smoke twirling up into the green-grey leaves of the eucalypts. I watched as the smoke vanished, apprehensive. On the ship I'd begun to feel weightless, the vessel lending me its buoyancy, its possibility. But now all I felt was heaviness. What if Fookes wasn't there?

"Can I help you, miss?" the riverman asked, his white clay pipe still hanging from his lip, dangling in the balance, his boots caked in thick river clay. I stepped forward and felt his eyes on the swell of my belly. "Missus," he corrected himself. His stare set off an itching on my belly as if a swarm of ants ran across the surface of my skin, but I was unable to scratch.

"Mrs Fookes," I corrected him and watched his face for recognition of the name, hoping that he'd say something of my Fookes, but he said nothing. His boat was not as large as the boat my father had rowed upon the Thames; it was wedged into the sand, the prow marked *Gypsy Queen*. The name made me shiver.

"Are you headed down Richmond way?" I said, looking at the scrub closer to the shore. I prayed that Fookes had kept his path. A group of natives in their *vardo* made of sticks were gathered around a fire, partially clothed, their voices low. Another man stood smoking a clay pipe, a soldier's jacket covering his chest, but as for his trousers, they were completely missing. I looked away. A large parrot raised its scratchy voice from the nearest tree and it echoed out above us, a yellow crown of feathers arching on top of its head.

"Aye, Richmond by and by," he said. "For a fee."

With effort I pulled the wedding ring off my swollen finger, dropped it in his palm and watched the circle of it spin. He picked it up and bit it between his teeth.

"I'll take you there and back again for that. Ready when you are." The riverman held out his hand to help me in, and this time I gratefully accepted the help.

The riverman pushed the boat into the clear water, and it made a dark tidal stain on his trousers, before he hoisted himself up into the fine boat, made of a beautiful honey-coloured wood. The water was sparkling; greenish blue and wondrous, the light fell through it like star-shine. One of the natives walked down towards us. She was dressed in petticoats and a blanket that she wore tight around her shoulders, a scarf tied firmly under her chin. Around her neck hung a pouch woven in threads of ochre and brown, and a brass crescent etched with words. Her hair and her face were as dark as Saint Sarah's herself.

"Thanks for keeping watch on the cargo and the boat, Cora," the riverman said.

"Come with you up river, sir?" she said and the riverman nodded. She waded through the shallow water towards the boat, but the riverman didn't hold out his hand for her, though she was in need of assistance. I reached out but she declined and lifted herself into the boat, the edge of her blanket starting to steam in the sun.

"This is Mrs Gooseberry. Mrs Gooseberry, this is Mrs Fookes."

I nodded at the native woman, my eyes never leaving the pouch of woven grasses around her neck; I felt a longing run through me like a note of sound ringing my entire wooden body, as hard as a woodsman's axe.

With an oar in each hand the riverman rowed us out across the water, the salt, the eucalyptus, the strange fuzzy blossoms blooming along the bushes and the sunshine making a peppery perfume as we passed.

Cora Gooseberry took a pipe from the folds of her petticoat skirts and looked at the riverman for a light, but he shook his head that he didn't have one. Undeterred, Mrs Gooseberry took the pipe in her teeth and sucked on the unlit stem.

My eyes followed the glittering water to the coastline that turned inlet to riverbank under the oars. What was this hell my father had spoken of? All I saw was strangeness and promise, all of it overlit, not even my bonnet shielded my eyes from the glare of this world.

Downriver a native woman picked her way over the small inlet, a baby strapped to her body with a blanket. Mrs Gooseberry called out to her and waved. She was missing part of her finger. The woman on the shore stood and waved and called back, the language their own.

I watched that missing finger until it curved back around the base of her pipe.

"What happened to your finger, Mrs Gooseberry?" I asked. The riverman never lost the rhythm of his rowing for a moment, the rushing of the water ceased and we glided on across the water that grew darker and deeper as we went down the river.

"Women's business," Mrs Gooseberry said and smiled and nodded.

"They cut a part of the finger off the girl infants when they are a few months old, the second part when they reach puberty," the riverman said and Mrs Gooseberry frowned at him.

"But why?" I said, feeling the nausea rise and fall in me.

"An offering of some sort, to the deep," the riverman said, the sun beating down on the boat, a sheen of sweat beading his face.

A kingfisher, a flashing shot of brilliance, dazzled my eye, golden and blue. It plunged into the water, a fish with jewelled scales flip-flopping between its beak before it flew back to the safety of the trees.

I looked at the brass crescent sitting on Mrs Gooseberry's blouse and Mrs Gooseberry's face lit up.

"I am a queen," she said, tapping her crescent-shaped breastplate. "Governor made me so." She grinned wider then. The queen. Her doll, my faithful constant, now buried with my mother in the embrace of the oak, the river eroding the soil, year by year. The Coronation. My father's return. Attracted by the brightest jewel in the kingdom. I was a thief's daughter, but no matter how agile my fingers, no matter how many times I fished out things from my father's pockets, no matter that I'd taken a doll from a child who'd have more dolls in her life than a hundred children, I'd never be like him. My mother had been stolen from me. The loss of her shaping all that was to come. I leaned over the edge of the boat to splash water on my face, but it rose up to meet me.

The water filled my ears, my nose, my throat.

The boat disappeared above me like a dark cloud on the horizon.

The water turned from light to dark as I fell towards the bottom of the river, fish drawn to the bubbles that strung up above me, a rope to the rescue, but I had not the strength to climb it, my arms and legs not at my command.

The riverbed came closer and in the dim light the tiny minnows swam around and around, opaline flashes, the foreign bracken and the bladderwrack brushing out to touch me like fingers. And then there was a rushing sound as if all the waters of the world were converged in one place. And then I stopped falling. I was on the bottom of the riverbed, the white sand cradling me.

A curious eye peered at me, the eyelid ribbed like a cockleshell, drowsy at half hemisphere.

In the ripples of his beard of bulrushes little seahorses hooked their tails, little twirling fins. His grizzly chest was covered in sea lichen and moss and tiny molluscs whose frilled lips held on with a kiss. His breath made its own tributaries.

Oh, how the thing laughed then, a wide stormy laugh, a little fish darting in and out of his mouth during its duration. The water vibrated around us, a living thing.

"You know me not, little human thing?" he said and his eyes flashed, seaglass. Then he sighed, the sound of water rushing. He sucked deep on an abandoned clay pipe and puckered his lips upon it; a plume of bubbles soared to the surface of the river. With a barnacled hand, he caressed my hair which rippled upwards in the water like black coral.

All the world was refracted light. I blinked and she was there.

My mother. Patrin. In the water, willing me to move, but all I wanted was her and I reached out. Her dark hair had not faded, nor had she aged; all the love she had for me shone from her face. We were the cogs to each other's wheel, orbiting each other, even after death. She'd been with me all along, always the water. She pulled at my arm and I blinked again. The air dispersed from my lungs and all the faceted light of the water turned dark. But then my mother called to me by my secret name; it swelled in my chest like a song, the name she had given me at birth, and something in me snapped open, desperate for breath.

Above me was the shadow of the boat's hull, the reflection of faces peering over the edge, hands breaking the surface.

My mother pulled at me and I felt my body leave the sandy riverbed. I saw the diamonds in the water, all sparkling, shooting stars through the water, my clothes heavy. I hung on to my mother, my heart tied like a rag on a wishing tree, full of her, up towards the light. Together we broke the surface, the water teeming from my face. She was with me in the water, one arm around my waist, the other holding the side of the boat. She had her hand beneath my arm, trying to pull the heavy weight of me, my skirts, dragging over the edge like a fisherman's haul.

On the boat I heaved with air. The riverman leaned over and helped Cora Gooseberry, Queen of Sydney, back into the boat. I blinked river water from my eyes. It was she who had pulled me clear, pulled me back to life.

THIRTY-EIGHT

Eglantine, 1838

We continued along the river, the trees thick with green cover, ghostly spirals of smoke creeping above the canopy. Occasionally a clearing, farmhouse, horse, sheep. The lowing of a cow.

At a point along the river, at a jetty made of raw planks, the riverman tied up the boat and looped the rope around a split post. He helped me and then he helped Cora Gooseberry, who had been the strength of my arms, the fulfilment of my desire, her grip the wish of my fingers. The taste of river water in my mouth, a bubble of it blocking my ears. *Riverling*, it said. All of me had been enveloped in the river's embrace and I'd not been afraid, but now walking on the dry earth and feeling the water shed from me, the fear began to swell at how close I'd come to drowning.

"Just up that way, Cora will show you, Mrs Fookes," the riverman said and I felt the earth firm beneath my unsteady feet. The name *Mrs Fookes* made me want to look over my shoulder, not familiar with the sound of it, my new name.

Coach, carriage, wheelbarrow, cart. Where shall I live? Big house, little house, pig-sty, barn. My mind drowsily circled the old rhyme beneath the beating of the afternoon sun as Cora Gooseberry kept a steady pace, waiting for me a few steps ahead when I lagged.

We kicked up clouds of dust that seemed to turn and spin golden. Ahead of us a creature ran up the rough bark of a tree and watched us. *Rooko-mengro*. Tree fellow, though it was no squirrel I'd seen. A *kakkaratchi*, a new magpie, swooped low in the flickering trees, a black and white streak alongside them, before it stopped and sung for me a carol, a full chortle of joy.

Over the rise a church had been built and a graveyard opposite, but I didn't want to linger there, I'd had enough of graveyards in this life. Sloping away from the church was a hill, canopied in tree branches, framing a small glimmering slick of water, a beautiful lagoon that acted as a mirror to the sky; clouds unfolded above and below like a bolt of fabric, the wind blowing it wide. A black swan cut through the glassy water. Beside the lagoon was a shelter made from branches, a living tent, a blanket folded inside, waiting for the occupant to return. Cora pointed the way I was to go and I kissed her cheeks in thanks. She patted my stomach with a tender hand and ambled away, the silvery trees falling in behind her.

I walked up the hill, past a grand house with a fine garden, to where a marketplace was packing up for the day, and was met by the smell of fruits and vegetables that had turned overripe in the sun. Opposite was a field of scraggly grass, where I stopped. There was Fookes, stripped to the shirtsleeves, his back bent away from me, taking the beating of the sun as he took a brick in one hand and a scoop of mortar in the other.

I stood there for a while, all of me wanting to call out to him, but I hesitated. Our promises back in London were fogged by all that had happened since. I followed his steady, familiar movements – his hat perched on his head, the tilt of his head – until I could stand it no longer.

"Fookes," I called and I watched him stand up and put his hands to his forehead to shield his eyes from the light. "Fookes." I longed to reach out to him, but I stood, still damp from the river and my own sweat, and waited. Uncertain.

"Eglantine?" he said, the mortar slipping from his trowel into the dirt, followed by the trowel itself. He moved fast, the mortar on his hands suddenly on me, wrapped around the growing girth of me, his lips on mine.

"How did you get here?" he said in disbelief. "Your ship is not due." He wiped the sweat from his face into his hair and held me back from him to take me in and I felt changed from the young woman at my father's house. "Eglantine," he said again, my name lost in the press of his kiss. "Why, you all soaked through!" His hands outlined the shape of my face, catching in the wet tendrils of my hair, a rope to reel me in with and kiss me again. His thumb traced the strand of coral he'd given me at our wedding and I saw the silver heart inscribed with my birth on a cord on his chest.

"Do you not see it?" he said, a catch of excitement in his voice.

"See what?"

Fookes led me around the boundary of a ditch, bricks grew up in one, a wooden peg pulling string taut between them, a phantom wall.

"Our home, well the start of it," Fookes said proudly. Fookes was ruddier than he'd been back in England, his skin beneath my fingers hot and unfamiliar, the sun burrowing into him. He'd been remade from sunlight, as would I be. The light was an elixir for us all. I put my hand against the bricks of the chimney breast which stood a sort of tower attached to an inner wall around which the house was being built. I closed my eyes and breathed in all the smells of this new country and couldn't place any of them, warm and dry like a sort of spice. When I opened my eyes the external walls, yet to be built, shimmered in the air.

Together we walked through the invisible rooms of the house that would soon be our home and I felt my mother's blessing in every pore of my skin, in my every breath and beat of my ragged heart. I had been her baby, my mother a gypsy, my father's lady, and now I'd be my own queen.

Fookes cupped my hands in his as he told me of an old tradition, to bless the house, to leave something in the hearth or the threshold, something tucked and secret, something to keep us safe against life's storms. As he spoke I knew what I must do. I carefully eased them off and handed them to Fookes, still sodden and thick with river water, and felt the heat of the earth rise up into my feet. These shoes that had been dipped in all the world's waters. Half rose. Half hip.

Fookes lifted me up and in all my life I'd never felt so light. In a cavity of the flue I tucked my shoes that had travelled so far, and I was reminded of the little baby shoe my father burned with their spotted foxglove petals against the fever. So small.

Back on the ground I looked into Fookes's face and I saw myself in his pupil, a tiny image. My breath quickened, for it seemed my mother looked back at me from his eyes.

"Eglantine?" Fookes said, concern on his face.

"Just then I saw myself in your pupil. I saw myself, yet I saw my mother," I replied but felt what I'd said to be overfanciful and wished I had kept it to myself. A soft breeze came, curled around us, ruffled our hair and flipped the leaves of the gums, their white bark as sinuous as limbs. A strange bird coo-eed out in the breeze-tossed branches.

"Do you know what the word pupil means?" Fookes said. I shook my head. The grass ran like water with the wind. "You've heard the expression 'apple of my eye'?" And the wind seemed to blow beneath my clothes and my skin, and my father's words hushed in my ear, the quick scatter search for the marzipan in his pocket. I shivered.

"It was my father's name for me," I said quietly. Fookes took my hand in his and at his touch my father's voice vanished from my ears.

"Someone once told me that pupil means little doll, when you can see yourself in another's eye." Out of habit I dipped my hand into my pocket for the secure clutch of that little wooden body, as long as a seedpod, as familiar to me as my own skin, but I knew she was entombed now with my mother

Fookes lifted my face and looked right into my eyes, not the little doll's, not his reflection. He looked right at me. And I felt a strange hush fall; the wind dropped and let me be. All the little stars in God's heaven were as numerous as the freckles inside the cup of a foxglove blossom. The cicadas chanted their hallelujahs until they rang in my ears and I felt my own skin stretch and shift in time with them. A moth danced between our faces, drawn to the flame. And I felt my baby unfurl and stretch, growing. Waiting to be born.

Who can say what sparks the idea for a book? For me, it's not just one idea – rather, it's a kind of a weaving of many ideas, many inspirations, until it is hard to find the first thread. One such thread was the memory of Dickens's character Fagin, who "mothers" the young Oliver Twist. Fagin was in fact based on true life, the returned convict Ikey Solomon. I was also taken by the description of Queen Victoria's dolls, small wooden tuck-comb dolls, a type of wooden peg doll, and how she cared and collected 132 of them throughout her childhood, sewing clothes and inventing biographies for them, sometimes based on real people or characters at the theatre. I was also struck by the childhood of Victoria herself, the princess the ultimate doll, captive to the whims of the power brokers around her, and her collection of dolls. I was also fascinated with the idea of dolls being transitional objects, the term coined by D.W. Winnicott in 1951 to describe the special meaning that children attribute to their toys, an extension of attachment to the mother and the promise of her return.

I was also captivated by the Romany tradition of burying dead children by the side of the road with acorns in each hand, resulting in entwined trees so they'd never be lost or forgotten. And ultimately I always knew that somehow I would also use in this novel the house of my convict ancestor William Price, built in Richmond, NSW, circa 1827, and which still stands, now an antique shop, the interior nearly unchanged, the banister burnished by the palms of generations. I was struck by a concertinaing of time. Here was a house, the beginnings of a new empire, a new life, humanistic as Georgian houses can be, built within a whisker of a decade of his transportation. What had William left behind? The sorrow of banishment, the loss of his family, his country and all he'd know and the burden of a singular crime, all the past sealed in the foundations by a hand hopeful for the future.

Victoria as a young princess showed great interest in the "Gipsies", and drew them in her sketchbook. When one of the women gave birth to a son, she sent food and blankets and considered requesting they name the son after her uncle, Leopold. Later at Buckingham Palace, she employed as a rat-catcher a gypsy named Mattie Black. As a young woman and towards the end of her life, she had her palm read by the Rom.

As I was writing the scenes of Josiah Scamp, I came across the story of Joshua Scamp (*The Journal of Gypsy Law Society*, Third Series, Vol. IV, p. 190, published by Liverpool University Press) who, upon taking the platform, to be hung for theft, proclaimed: "You see what you have brought me to, live soberly and take care of your wife and your family." He tied the knot of the noose with his own hand and was hanged. His son-in-law later confessed to the crime. Joshua Scamp's family persuaded the rector to have him buried in St Mary's in Odstock, Wiltshire, 1 April 1801.

Gypsies or the Romany were transported to Australia in great numbers and are usually only discoverable by their occupation listed in court records, such as Basketmaker, Hawker, Horse dealer, Tin-man, or Dealer and are concealed in the records. One of my other convict ancestors shares one of these occupations, a tin-man, but we will never know whether he is romanical or not.

Cora Gooseberry (?1777–1852), wife of King Bungaree (who was the first Australian to circumnavigate Australia with Matthew Flinders), was known as the Queen of Sydney to South Head, and also known as Queen Gooseberry. Her Aboriginal name was Kaaroo, Carra, Caroo, Car-roo or Ba-ran-ga. She was known throughout Sydney, and camped around Pitt and Market streets, Sydney. Macquarie, unaware of Indigenous societal structure, gave out gorgets or breastplates from 1815 in an attempt to create "leaders" whom he could then use as an intermediary between the tribal groups and the government.

For understanding Romany life in the early nineteenth century, I relied on *The Gipsies' Advocate; Or Observations on the Origin, Character, Manners, and Habits, of the English Gipsies*, by James Crabb, London, 1832. Also *Gypsies of Britain*, by Peter Vesey FitzGerald, Readers Union, 1974. To learn about the child Victoria, her relationship to her dolls, and Georgian childhood, I relied upon *Becoming Victoria*, by Lynne Vallone, Yale University Press, 2001. For insight into early colonial and Aboriginal contact and connections, I referred to Grace Karsken's *The Colony: A History of Early Sydney*, Allen & Unwin, 2009; and for understanding early colonial superstitions, I am grateful to Ian Evans for allowing me to read his thesis on concealed shoes and other objects, "Touching Magic: Deliberately Concealed Objects in Old Australian Houses and Buildings".

ACKNOWLEDGMENTS

I would like to thank readers Karen Ferris and Ruth Quibell for their kindness and support in reading the manuscript at a very early stage in a time of chaos.

I would also like to acknowledge the generosity of spirit and keen-eyedness of Lucy Treloar, who read a later draft of the book. Her support and suggestions were invaluable.

I'd also like to thank Melissa Harrison for sharing the story of the entwined trees above and to Hilary Davidson for sharing her vast knowledge on shoes. I'd also like to thank Grace Karskens for taking the time to discuss with me the Indigenous history of the Darug people of Pugh's Lagoon at Richmond, NSW.

I would like to thank James Kellow, Shona Martyn and Pam Dunne and all the team at HarperCollins Australia.

With gratitude to both my editor and publisher, Julia Stiles and Catherine Milne. To Julia Stiles for her sensitive, astute and enlightening work on *The River Sings*; if it sings, it is because of her. And to Catherine Milne for her passion, belief and commitment to this book when it was just a mere unloved sapling. Her insight and care are a treasured gift.

And lastly, I would like to acknowledge The First Nations people of Sydney, the Gadigal of the Eora Nation, the traditional custodians of this land, and pay my respects to the Elders both past and present – on this land, this novel was written.

Sandra Leigh Price's first novel, *The Bird's Child*, was published by Fourth Estate in 2015. She lives in Sydney.

Instagram: sandraleighpricewriter